There were other, more significant pleasures awaiting him. The deaths of Strozzi and Marchesi were still to come.

No doubt they had been to the police. No doubt they had taken steps—especially when the death of Cafferelli left no doubt about the motive or the identity of the killer and his next victims—to track him down and deal with him. But Pistocchi was not worried. They would never find him. It was impossible. Let them try! His cover was perfect. He didn't even exist.

———————— ★ ————————

THE LAST CASTRATO

JOHN SPENCER HILL

WORLDWIDE.

TORONTO • NEW YORK • LONDON
AMSTERDAM • PARIS • SYDNEY • HAMBURG
STOCKHOLM • ATHENS • TOKYO • MILAN
MADRID • WARSAW • BUDAPEST • AUCKLAND

For my son Christopher who planted the germ and sustained its growth

THE LAST CASTRATO

A Worldwide Mystery/February 1997

First published by St. Martin's Press, Incorporated.

ISBN 0-373-26229-9

Copyright © 1995 by John Spencer Hill.
All rights reserved. No part of this book may be reproduced or transmitted in any form or by any means, electronic or mechanical, including photocopying, recording or by any information storage and retrieval system, without permission in writing from the publisher. For information, contact: St. Martin's Press, Incorporated, 175 Fifth Avenue, New York, NY 10010-7848 U.S.A.

All characters in this book are fictitious, and any resemblance to actual persons, living or dead, is purely coincidental.

® and TM are trademarks of Harlequin Enterprises Limited. Trademarks indicated with ® are registered in the United States Patent and Trademark Office, the Canadian Trade Marks Office and in other countries.

Printed in U.S.A.

Special thanks to Cam La Bossière, Irene Makaryk and Paula Greenwood for their interest and encouragement; my wife, Jan, for surrendering me (again) to my word processor and for her invaluable proofreading skills; and Frances Hanna—Italophile, friend and wonderful agent.

"In the balance or reconciliation of opposite or
discordant qualities consist the mystery
and production of art and life."
—Samuel Taylor Coleridge

ONE

PART ONE

The Cardinal

THE CORPSE HUNG from the cross above the altar, its head slumped forward, its arms hooked crudely over the crosspiece like a pinioned fowl. The body was that of a man in his early fifties, slight and balding, with haughty chiselled features: a grotesque icon, a parody of sanctity. In place of thorns he wore the silk skullcap of a cardinal in the Roman Church, twisted askew as if he had dressed hastily, and the scarlet cassock of his office fell in folds to the polished toes of a pair of hand-tooled shoes.

No mark of violence was visible on the body. But that was only because the sagging head concealed the six-inch gash that had severed the carotid artery and let life out in a pulsing stream. He had died quickly, surprised by death, his features as composed as if he had fallen into a restful sleep. But there would be no waking for Umberto Cardinal Cafferelli, Metropolitan of Tuscany—at least no waking in this world.

Outside, early pigeons gathered on the grass plot adjacent to the area where the tourist buses parked, staking their claims for another day of mendicancy. On the eastern horizon the pink fingers of dawn were rolling up the thick blanket of night, and soon the sun rose in a cleft between the hills, scattering radiance over the domes and sleeping towers of Florence.

Inside the chapel the growing light, filtered through leaded panes, drew obscurity aside like a curtain. What was surprising was how little was revealed. There was no sign of a struggle, no sign of a weapon. The cardinal's sapphire ring and Rolex watch had not been touched. The blotches on his cassock, predominantly on the upper torso, were not shadows, as they might in the half-light have first seemed, but gouts of blood; yet there was none on the floor near the corpse or elsewhere in the room. The body itself was the only evidence that a crime had been committed.

Still, it was possible to draw certain conclusions. First, the body had been dead for several hours: so much was clear from the advanced state of rigor mortis and the fact that the blood stains were tacky and nearly dry. Second, it was probable, given the lack of evidence at the scene, that Cardinal Cafferelli had been killed elsewhere and the body transported to the chapel. Third, the location and posture of the corpse made it probable that the murderer was making an announcement of some sort, a deliberate statement, although what it might be was impossible to say.

Slowly, noises from the world outside invaded the silence with the crescendo of commerce as the city came to life. A delivery van rumbled through the piazza, grinding its gears and belching exhaust, followed by a battered pick-up, its rear deck laden with crates of cabbages and tomatoes. The volume of traffic steadily increased: cars, pedestrians, vans, motor scooters, the first orange ATAF buses of the day. Only the body on the cross did not stir. It would be another hour until the custodian of the basilica arrived to make his grisly discovery in the sanctum of the Lady Chapel.

TWO

THE RAPIDO EASED into Santa Maria Novella station and stopped with a jolt. Cordelia Sinclair closed the Atwood novel that lay open on her lap and shoved it into the brocade carry-all at her feet, then sat back and gazed out the window at the utilitarian terminus. It was like a thousand other railway stations in a thousand other cities: functional, gritty, tastelessly commercial. With an elegant name like Santa Maria Novella, she had expected something special...something—how could she put it?—well, something architecturally decorous, something more grand and imposing than this to serve as the introduction to the birthplace of men like Brunelleschi and Michelangelo. It was not surprising, therefore, that, looking out on a grimy concrete wall and a straggling line of peeling orange baggage-carts, she felt cheated. It wasn't at all what her dreams had prepared her for. Besides, for the past twenty minutes they had crawled at a snail's pace through a succession of seedy suburbs, past factories and endless faceless warehouses. The whole approach to the city was a travesty of the heritage of cultural grace and beauty of which Florence was a symbol for the rest of the world. Why was it, she wondered, that railways the world over always presented travellers with the ugliest possible image of the place they were about to visit? Perhaps it was a cynical ploy to keep them moving, to keep people buying tickets and moving on.

The train lurched forward briefly, rolling another hundred yards, then came to rest and the door at the front of the carriage banged open. Outside, smiling faces thronged the platform, pressing forward expectantly, and searched the tinted panes for familiar faces. No one recognized Cordelia, of course. There was no one waiting there for her.

So this is it, she thought. This is Florence. I'm here at last.

It was her chance—planned for over a year now—for a new beginning. Her chance to put Charles and *his* career finally behind her and start over. Her chance to discover who she was, and to experience life for the first time on her own terms.

She tried, at this threshold of her new life, to analyse her feelings. And now that she had actually arrived, she discovered they were more confused, more contradictory than she'd expected them to be. Excitement and expectation were mingled with anxiety and even, in an odd way, with something approaching disappointment. *I'm in Florence!* her mind kept telling her—but the crowd of strangers on the platform and the grimy, non-descript train-station beyond her window made her feel as if she were disembarking at some perfectly ordinary destination like Peoria or Decatur, only a hundred miles or so from home—places she imagined to be dull and unremarkable, although in fact she had never visited either of them. But Florence wasn't Peoria or Decatur—and she was separated now from the world she knew and had grown up in, where she felt safe, by a dark, wide, impassable ocean. The queasiness in her stomach reminded her of that. She was on her own. For the first time in her life, she was completely alone—a stranger in a strange land.

For a panicky moment she wished she hadn't come. She would have given anything to have wakened up in the creaking wicker chair in her bedroom in Evanston and found that it was all a dream. What am I doing here? she asked herself. Her head swam and her heart pounded. Everything seemed suddenly alien and frightening. What had possessed her to trade the known for the unknown, the security of home for the perils and nameless terrors of a far-off land?

Such thoughts were silly, of course. She knew that. The only peril she faced was the risk that she'd find out who she really was, and her only real terror was the dread of being disappointed with the discovery. But those dangers, she told herself, were as real in Illinois as they were in Italy—and it was high time, in any case, that she screwed her courage to the sticking place and made an effort to face herself. It was high time she confronted the hidden self she had spent so much of her life avoiding.

She stood abruptly and straightened her dress, then slung her handbag over her shoulder, caught up the carry-all at her feet, and marched defiantly toward the exit. The train was a miniature Babel. On either side, as she passed along the aisle, voices in half the languages of Europe gabbed at one another. It was, she thought with sudden amusement, as if she had stumbled into an international convention of Berlitz instructors.

Her progress was halted by a knot of baffled Swedes—tall, blond, oppressively Nordic—who clogged the aisle with their baggage and obstructed passage. Uncertain whether or not to disembark, they had paused to seek enlightenment from a family of equally confused Germans. Neither group, it seemed, spoke the other's language and they were reduced to a parodic facsimile of communication by grunts, florid gestures, and the use of over-precisely articulated, though still mutually incomprehensible, phrases in their native tongues. Their puzzlement, Cordelia gathered, centred on the word *Firenze,* which was painted in large letters on a board over the station. The Swedes and Germans had no idea what it meant. *Firenze* was not marked on the maps they had brought with them from home.

Cordelia had no wish to multiply confusion by introducing a third language. She squeezed past with a muttered apology in Italian and made her way to the exit, where a rotund conductor with a cherub's face and broad smile handed passengers down to the platform. She took a deep breath and descended the metal stairs, releasing her carry-all into his waiting hand.

'Have a pleasant stay in Firenze, signorina.'

'Thank you,' she said, mustering a carefree smile and sounding more confident than she felt, 'I intend to.'

But the fact that he had called her 'signorina' made her glow with pleasure. *Miss Cordelia Sinclair.* For the first time in her life, she could make her own decisions and her own mistakes. What lay ahead she had no way of knowing, no way of anticipating. All she knew was that the future was hers to shape as she pleased, without interference from Father—and without (thank heavens!) the suffocating presence of Charles Passmore to whose consuming ego she had sacrificed her own identity through five years of self-abnegating wedded servitude. That thought alone—the realization that she was free of Charles—was enough to banish temporarily the jitters she felt about being alone in a strange country, and it put a lilt in her step as she made her way down the crowded platform toward the glass doors leading into the terminal building.

Once inside, she made arrangements at the ticket counter to have her luggage delivered, then set off on foot to find Signora

Ghilberti's house in Via della Scala and the little flat she would call home for the next four months. Fifteen hours ago she had boarded a direct flight to Rome at O'Hare International in Chicago, then taken the Rapido north to Florence. It was her first trip to Italy and she had planned it for months, poring over maps and photographs of the city with a care that had almost deluded her into believing herself a native fiorentina. She knew the streets and piazzas of Florence as well as she knew those of Evanston, the Chicago suburb where she had grown up. At least she thought she did.

But reality overpowered imagination.

She left the station and stepped into the full effulgence of a May morning. The air was clear, the sky cloudless, and sunlight poured from above like a shower of gold on the unresisting earth. She got her bearings and started off at a brisk pace, taut with excitement, trying outwardly to appear composed. But she did not get far: in the piazza, above the glinting roofs of a rank of blue and yellow cabs, she was suddenly confronted by the Tuscan Gothic façade of the Dominican church of Santa Maria Novella. The sight was overwhelming. She felt dazed and disoriented. It was as if she had emerged from a time-machine and landed in the middle of the fifteenth century. The basilica was familiar yet somehow strange and terribly *foreign,* and its sudden presence startled her, taking her breath away. She knew its outline from a dozen photographs, but nothing she had encountered in books had in any way prepared her for the visceral impact of its squat and sober symbolism on her unsuspecting senses. Crouched before her, it seemed to have shouldered its way by brute force up into the light from somewhere deep in the black belly of the grasping earth, and yet at the same time to have floated down from the empyrean with the celestial lightness of a feather. Contrasting bands of black and white marble rose in alternating rows on its face—like an allegory of good and evil—straining upward together toward the voluptuous curves of two Renaissance volutes that supported a severe classical pediment at the apex. It was at once stark and passionate, comforting and ominously minatory— seeming both to threaten and to promise peace. Its symmetry was a study in paradox, its fearful harmonies an image of the entwined fruits of Paradise and Calvary, frozen together inseparably in stone. It impressed upon her, although she was not herself a believer, a sombre sense of the enduring reality of sin and salvation in human history, of unforgivable evil and the transfiguring mystery of atoning grace.

'Taxi?' a driver inquired, holding open the door of his cab for her.

Cordelia shook her head. 'No—no, thank you,' she managed, unable to wrench her eyes away from the imposing spectacle across the piazza.

When she had disembarked from the train, it had been her intention to walk quickly across Piazza della Stazione, as if she had done so a hundred times before, then to make her way along beside the basilica and across another piazza that led into Via della Scala. Instead, she found herself craning, her gait barely a crawl, and gaping open-mouthed at every structure that seemed likely to have been hallowed by the touch of time. So bedazzled was she by the glories of the past that met her gaze on every side that she did not even notice the blue-domed Fiats stationed outside the church or the two uniformed policemen who stood in the portico turning tourists away. Santa Maria Novella was closed for the day while forensic specialists dusted for prints and combed the interior for clues.

She cut at an angle across Piazza Santa Maria Novella and turned right into Via della Scala, a street lined on either side with three-storey medieval houses, their fronts dotted with shutters and blotched with peeling stucco. Number 57 was on the north side of the street, a hundred yards or so beyond the piazza. A weathered brass plate beside the door said: *Pensione Ghilberti*. The plaque, she knew, was misleading. The landlady did not serve meals and the advertisement Cordelia had answered made it plain that her apartment had its own cooking facilities. Presumably, Signora Ghilberti had run a boarding-house at one time and had simply not bothered to change the sign when she converted the house to apartments.

The street-door opened into a short hall from which a staircase ascended on the left. Filtered light spilled in through lace-curtained sidelights and, when she closed the door behind her, Cordelia found herself in the stuffy womb-like silence of an enclosure whose décor was not Italian but Edwardian English. It declared its origin in every detail: the brocaded wallpaper and deep blue carpet, the gilt-framed reproduction of Constable's *Hay*

Wain, the carved mahogany table and, beside it, a marble urn containing an umbrella and half a dozen ostrich feathers.

On the right was a door that led to the landlady's flat. In the centre of a plaster rosette on the wall beside it was a black button. Cordelia pressed it and heard, far off, the silvery chime of a bell. A moment later the door was opened by a tall, willowy woman in her sixties. Despite her Italian name, her ancestry was obviously English. Her complexion was fair and she wore her hair, grey now but with a hint still of its original auburn, pulled back severely from a high forehead. Her fine-boned, aristocratic features reminded Cordelia of the photograph of Virginia Woolf that hung in her father's study back home in Evanston. There was, she thought, the same wistful sadness in the eyes, the same aura of melancholy detachment that hung, like an invisible veil, protectively around her.

'Signora Ghilberti?'

'*Sì.*'

'I'm Cordelia Sinclair. I wrote that I'd be arriving today.'

The landlady's appraising eyes flickered over her, pronounced themselves satisfied, and the thin bar of her lips curved upwards into a smile.

'Oh, yes. Do come in, dear,' she said in a richly-vowelled voice deeply redolent of her English birth. 'I received your note, of course. It arrived last week. I've been expecting you.'

She stepped aside, ushering Cordelia into a room crowded with overstuffed sofas and heavy mahogany tables of antique design. It was, like the hallway she had entered from the street, an Edwardian period-piece, filled with memories of a lost Empire—and filled as well, Cordelia suspected, with the memories of a girlhood lost in the mists of a long-ago world.

'You'll be tired after your long journey,' Signora Ghilberti said, closing the door. It was a statement, not a question.

Cordelia did not feel tired, but said agreeably, 'Yes, I suppose I am rather.'

The words were out before she could stifle them. Why, she wondered bitterly, do I always have to be so damned accommodating?

It was the story of her life. For the whole of her thirty-two years, she had spent so much time and energy being agreeable to others that she had no idea what *she* liked, what *she* wanted, who *she* was. Her mother had died of cancer when she was a baby, and Cordelia had spent a lonely childhood and youth as an only child, trying to please her father, trying desperately to measure up to what she supposed were his expectations of her. It was only years later that she realized she could never please him, that he held her responsible in some subtle psychological way, beyond even the considerable powers of his own understanding to fathom, for the loss of the only woman he had ever loved and for reminding him by her very presence of the aching void in his life that, try as she might, she was ultimately powerless to remedy or remove. When she married, she had tried, too, to please her husband, until Charles's calculating egotism had alienated her love and given her, finally, the strength to leave him. It was to find out who she was and, if possible, to find a way of making her own mark in the world that she had enrolled in the doctoral program in music at Northwestern and come to Florence to research her dissertation. Yet here she was, once more, meekly surrendering her will to the first person she met on this first day of her new life. It was with something like shame that she followed Signora Ghilberti through the drawing room and into an adjoining room that seemed to be a study.

'Sit down, dear. I'll just fetch your key,' the landlady said, disappearing through an archway that led into the private recesses of the apartment. 'I won't be a moment.'

Cordelia elected to stand.

Looking around, she had the impression that she had somehow fallen asleep and wakened in the animated pages of an Arnold Bennett novel. In this room in which she found herself standing the past had utterly usurped the present, and the year, for all she could tell from her immediate surroundings, might have been 1910. The lamps bore fringed shades and were set out on lace doilies like exhibits in a museum. A starched linen antimacassar graced the back of each chair and there were three of them along the back of the sofa. The papered walls were crowded with reproductions of Stubbs and Turner in heavy, gilt frames. A glass-fronted bookshelf groaned under the weight of leatherbound editions of the British poets, and in one corner, like the silent sentinel of a once and future dream, stood a suit of armour with the red cross of St George blazoned on the breastplate. There was everything, Cordelia thought, but the Union Jack itself. In the kitchen, no doubt, the tea and sugar canisters bore the whiskered visage of Lord Kitchener of Khartoum.

'Your flat is the one on the top floor,' Signora Ghilberti said, returning. 'It's furnished, of course, and you have your own balcony with a lovely view over the city. But you know that already from the advertisement. I think you'll find it pleasant and fully equipped, but if there's anything you need, dear, you'll let me know.' She produced an antique long-shanked key on a yellow ribbon and handed it over. 'I keep a spare here with me,' she added, 'just in case you misplace this one or lock yourself out.'

'I'm sure it won't be necessary,' Cordelia said. 'I'm careful with keys.'

She paid a month's rent in advance and moved toward the door. She was anxious to see her apartment, anxious to settle in and begin her new life.

At the door, Signora Ghilberti paused with her hand on the knob and said:

'This is a quiet and respectable house, signorina. I have values that some might dismiss as old-fashioned, but I expect them nonetheless to be respected. I discourage alcohol and cigarettes and I positively forbid overnight male companions.'

Cordelia smiled. 'I drink very little and don't smoke,' she said, 'and there will be no men.'

'Good,' Signora Ghilberti said, nodding. 'It seems we understand each other perfectly. I have no doubt your stay will be a very pleasant one.' She opened the door and stepped aside to let Cordelia pass. 'Oh,' she said, remembering, 'there is one more thing, Signorina Sinclair. I hope you'll be able to join us in my flat for tea later this afternoon. Signor Farinelli, my other lodger, and some of the neighbours are looking forward to meeting you.'

'Of course,' Cordelia said, 'it will be a pleasure.'

'Four o'clock, then?'

'I look forward to it.'

She started up the stairs, but had taken only a half dozen steps when the door below opened and Signora Ghilberti reappeared:

'I nearly forgot, dear. A letter arrived for you yesterday.'

She passed an envelope up between the balusters and Cordelia stooped to take it. A quick glance showed that it bore a family crest on which was superimposed a conductor's baton. Her heart leapt in her breast. She could hardly believe it. She had written on a whim, expecting to have her letter ignored. But here was a response. It was too much to hope of course, she told herself, that he would actually agree to see her. He was too busy, too famous for that. But at least he'd had the courtesy to reply.

'Thank you,' she said evenly, resuming her ascent. 'I was expecting it.'

'Four o'clock sharp,' the voice fluted from below.

'Four o'clock sharp,' Cordelia echoed from the landing.

On the second floor, a card in a brass holder on the door read *Farinelli*—and, as she passed, she heard the sound of music coming from inside. Was it a Palestrina motet? The tune was familiar, but it was impossible to identify it through the closed door with certainty.

A skylight lit her way to the next landing and her own door. The card said *Sinclair* and she flushed with pride and independence at the sight of the name she had legally resumed after the divorce had gone through. The door opened into a large room, airy and bright, which was kitchen at one end and bed-sitting room at the other. Off the latter was a tiled bathroom containing an antique lion-foot bathtub with overhead shower and a pedestal washstand. The furniture in the living area—mercifully not Edwardian—was plain and serviceable: a steel-frame bed and wooden wardrobe, a bureau with mirror, two comfortable chairs, a round table to eat at with two chairs, a roll-top desk and an empty bookshelf. It was more than adequate. At the kitchen end the room opened, through a pair of French windows, onto a rooftop balcony enclosed by a low wall with potted geraniums spotted around the coping. It was all she had hoped for, and more.

She sat on the bed and tore the envelope open with trembling fingers. The handwritten note inside was clipped and businesslike. It said:

Signorina Sinclair,
I will set aside an hour to answer your questions following rehearsal on Tuesday next. Meet me in my office at the Teatro Comunale at 6 p.m.
Marchesi

She threw herself back on the bed and laughed out loud. It was the chance of a lifetime! She could hardly take it in. Already she loved Florence—and she had only just arrived.

THREE

DETECTIVE INSPECTOR Carlo Arbati paused in the arched portal to light a cigarette, then stepped into the sunlit piazza. Lean and muscular, his dark curly hair and boyish good looks gave the impression of a man ten years younger. He had just passed his thirty-fifth birthday on Sunday—a day spent, like other Sundays, with a maiden aunt, his only living relative, whose perpetual topic was why he hadn't settled down and started a family. The inquisition was always worst on birthdays, which marked the passing of another year without issue. The fact that Carlo had never met a woman he actually *loved* and wanted to marry meant nothing to his aunt; she was interested in an heir, not her nephew's feelings.

But at the moment, Inspector Arbati was not thinking about his aunt in Prato or the improbability of his ever finding a wife. He had other things on his mind. The spectacle he had just witnessed in the Lady Chapel—and 'spectacle' was the only word to describe it—was the work of a pathologically twisted mind. The sight had surprised but not shocked him. Over the years he had seen too much to be shocked any more; yet, even now, the perverse ingenuity of which the human mind was sometimes capable still managed to surprise him.

He launched a thin stream of smoke at the cloudless sky. 'Well, Giorgio,' he said, 'what do you make of it?'

Detective Giorgio Bruni, short and rumpled, furrowed his brow thoughtfully, struggling to gather into one incisive observation the meaning of the hundred impressions that lay in his mind like a pack of scattered cards. In his mind's eye he saw the cardinal's office, which they had visited first, where the murder had taken place sometime the preceding day. Imagination transported him back to the richly appointed room in the Curial suite and he saw again the immense, filigreed walnut desk—worthy, it had struck him, of the CEO of a multinational conglomerate—the rare and expensive artwork on the walls, the cheque book showing large transactions, the leatherbound notebook filled with incomprehensible, coded jottings—and then, of course, the blood-spattered chair and white oriental carpet defiled with blackened gore. Nothing had apparently been taken; nothing, it seemed, was out of place. The victim's blood was the only tangible evidence, the sole physical reminder, of the scene of human suffering that had been acted out some hours earlier—ten or twelve perhaps, but the pathologist would be more precise about the time—in the impassive and neutral vacancy of that silent sanctum. Then the scene changed and Bruni saw again the interior of the chapel from which he and Arbati had just emerged, where the lifeless body of the cardinal hung in blasphemy: the scarlet skullcap twisted askew, the scrawny throat slit from ear to ear, the cardinal's Rolex watch glinting in the holy gloom, the polished tips of his hand-tooled shoes protruding from beneath the hem of his cassock. He tried to make sense of all that he had seen. He tried to pull the facts together, to find some pattern in the chaos of impressions, some hidden thread of meaning on which to string the confused beads of observation. He pursed his lips and squinted at the empty sky; he chewed at his lip and summoned into play his full powers of reason and analysis—and in the end, in spite of the diligence of his labours, he still came up empty.

'It seems,' he said finally, 'that robbery wasn't the motive.'

Arbati winced. 'No, I'd say not,' he agreed.

His partner was gifted with many qualities, Arbati knew, but a synthesizing intelligence—what Agatha Christie's Hercule Poirot called 'using the little grey cells' to reconstruct a puzzle—was not among them. Detective Giorgio Bruni's skills were dogged perseverance and a meticulous eye for detail, for leaving no stone in an investigation unturned. In temperament and appearance, they were as different as it is possible, perhaps, for two men to be—a pair of polar opposites. Arbati, standing over six feet, was ruggedly masculine and well proportioned in body, yet sensitive and imaginative in spirit. He was a man who prided himself on his intuitions, who trusted his hunches because they had so often been instrumental in cutting through background clutter and taking him directly to the heart of the matter, to the real truth that lay behind the deception of plausible appearances. Some, it was true, found him aloof and arrogant, but his detached manner had more to do with shyness and reserve than it did with self-assertion. He was an impeccable and fastidious dresser, a lover of fine cloth and fine tailoring, conscious always of the sartorial image he presented to the world. Giorgio Bruni, on the other hand, was a study in contrast: short and wiry in shape, gregarious in manner, with one of his brown eyes set slightly awry under shaggy brows, he was blunt in speech and methodical in procedure, invariably sceptical about his partner's wild hunches (as he thought of them) and slow to accept them until they were set on the firm foundation of empirical evidence. Yet in spite of his obsession with order, Bruni was painfully careless about his physical appearance. His well-worn suits were baggy and seldom pressed, his hair was in a permanent state of rumpled disrepair, and he had been known on more than one occasion to turn up on the job with unmatched socks whose colours and patterns were at violent war with one another. So different were they, in fact, that their incongruities had earned them the sobriquet of being the odd couple of the Questura.

Yet they made a formidable team of criminal investigators. And, while there was no doubt that Arbati was the head and Bruni the feet in their union, they had grown to be close friends over the five years of their partnership, learning over time to value each other's gifts and to take into charitable account each other's differences. And so it was that Bruni admired Arbati's synthesizing intelligence and sincerely respected—though it was beyond his own modest capacity to comprehend them—his superior's insight into the labyrinthine psychology of the criminal mind and his intuitive grasp of the recondite truths that often, as it had turned out in their investigations, lay below the complex and distorting surface of brute fact. For his part, Arbati liked to bounce his theories off his partner: it helped focus his thoughts and eliminate absurd conclusions, and often Giorgio would draw attention to some anomalous, apparently insignificant detail that would prove to be the catalyst in linking seemingly unrelated facts and breaking open a case. It had happened that way more than once. But today, Arbati thought, didn't look as if it was going to be one of those days.

'A Mafia hit?' Bruni suggested, flicking aside a pebble on the cobbles with the scuffed toe of his duty shoe.

Arbati shook his head. 'Hardly. If the Mafia were involved,

we'd have found the victim stuffed in the trunk of a car with a bullet in the back of his head.'

They watched in silence as two figures emerged from the church bearing a plastic body bag on a stretcher and loaded it into a waiting ambulance, where a small but curious crowd had gathered. The bag contained the mortal remains of Umberto Cardinal Cafferelli, bound for the forensic pathology laboratory at the university.

'The location of the body,' Arbati said, watching the departing ambulance, its dome-light flashing, 'strikes me as being particularly important. We know the murder itself was committed in the Curial office, then the corpse dragged half-way across the city and draped over the cross here in the Lady Chapel. Not any cross, mind you—but this particular cross in this particular church. But why?—that's what I keep asking myself. There are at least a dozen churches between here and the murder scene. So, why did the killer go to the trouble? Why was he willing to run the risk of attracting attention, perhaps even of being caught, by moving his victim so far from the scene of the crime?' The ambulance with its shrouded cargo turned the corner and disappeared from view. Cardinal Cafferelli, he supposed, would have known the answer to that question, but Cardinal Cafferelli was in no position to answer it now. If there was to be an answer, it was up to Arbati to furnish it—or to track down the man who was capable of doing so. 'What's so special,' he wondered aloud, talking more to himself than to Bruni, 'about Santa Maria Novella? What does this church mean to the killer?—and what would it have meant to his victim, if he'd been alive to appreciate its symbolism? You know, Giorgio, I have the distinct feeling that the murderer is trying to tell us something—that he's trying to tell us why it was necessary for him to commit this crime.'

Giorgio Bruni raised his eyes to the empty heavens as if in search of succour. There was no point in arguing. Arbati was off again on one of his crazy flights. There wasn't any evidence— any *hard* evidence, that is—to support theories about the killer's motive at this stage of the investigation. No, not by a long shot.

Bruni shrugged. 'Fine,' he said, 'and just what do you suppose our killer *is* trying to tell us?'

Arbati flicked the stub of his half-smoked cigarette onto the cobbles and crushed it underfoot. 'That, my friend,' he said, 'is precisely what we're being paid to find out.' He looked up at the sun-drenched façade of Santa Maria Novella and said: 'Well, there's nothing more we can do here. See what you can run down on those deposits in the cardinal's cheque book, and maybe the cryptographers at Military Intelligence can give us a hand with the codes in his notebook. They may lead to something. Anyway, see what you can find out. I'll clear up the paperwork and pay a visit to il professore later this afternoon after he's had a chance to look at the body.'

A sudden inspiration struck Bruni. 'You think they're connected, don't you?' he said. 'You think Cafferelli was murdered by the same guy who killed Mora and Rosso?'

'It's possible,' Arbati said noncommittally.

Bruni shook his head. 'Give it up, Carlo. It's a wild goose chase. There's nothing to link them.'

'All three had their throats cut.'

'Florence is a city of knives,' Bruni countered. 'Only the Mob uses guns—and if I remember correctly, you've just ruled the Mafia out of this case.'

They walked toward the blue-domed Fiat beyond the cordon of yellow police tape.

'Let's call it a hunch,' Arbati said.

'You and your bloody hunches,' Bruni grumbled. 'All that matters to the judge, my friend, are facts.'

Arbati smiled to himself. It was typical: Giorgio missing the forest for the trees. 'Tell you what, I'll leave the facts to you and you indulge my hunches. A deal?'

It was the way they always worked and they'd had the same conversation a hundred times in a hundred different ways. To convince Giorgio of anything without solid physical evidence was like a theoretical physicist trying to justify an unorthodox hypothesis to a mechanical engineer. At this early stage in the investigation, it was best that each should get on with the job in his own way. Giorgio would come around in time, Arbati knew—and he knew this because he *knew*, with absolute and irrefragable certainty, that Cardinal Cafferelli was the victim of a serial killer. His third victim, to be precise. All he had to do now was prove it.

Bruni shook his head. 'You're hopeless.'

'A deal?' Arbati persisted.

'Of course it's a deal,' Bruni grunted. 'Just produce some cold, hard facts before you expect to make a believer out of me.'

'I intend to. That's why I want to talk to il professore.'

'You think he'll back you up?'

'I hope so.'

Bruni shook his head. He knew what a stickler the little pathologist was for fact, how he hated speculation in any form. 'You're dreaming in technicolour,' he said.

They separated at the car park, Giorgio taking the car. Arbati watched him depart, squealing away from the kerb and out into traffic like Ricardo Patrese at the wheel of a formula Ferrari. Giorgio had missed his calling—and no doubt, Arbati thought sourly, he'd be hearing again from the watch commander when he got back to the office about the dangerous handling of municipal vehicles. Eager citizens, defending the public safety, were quick to report even minor abuses of privilege by the police. An alert citizenry, Arbati reflected, was a mixed blessing, a two-edged sword.

It was almost noon and time for lunch. Arbati was particular about restaurants. As a matter of course, he avoided the noisy, trendy places in the centre of town that catered primarily to tourists, seeking instead the solitude of establishments further off the beaten path, where the fare was simple and the ambiance relaxed. He decided today on the outdoor tables at Il Cibreo, an upscale trattoria overlooking the Sant'Ambrogio market. It was a longish walk but he was in no hurry and the midday sun was warm but not hot. It was still early in May, a time of year when walking was a pleasant diversion, the searing heat of summer no more than the vague memory of a distant past or the not-quite-imaginable reality of a future yet to be born. He set off with long strides across Piazza dell' Unità heading for the Duomo. It had been many hours since breakfast, and the first gentle stirrings of renewed desire roused and fluttered in his stomach like hatching birds. A brisk walk would sharpen appetite, would make the meal a reward for his exertions.

As he did every lunch time, Arbati purged his mind of police matters and turned his attention to poetry. The hours from twelve to two belonged to him, not the city, and his writing had made him, rather to his own surprise, something of a local literary celebrity. His first slim volume had sold exceptionally well ('un miràcolo maggiore' these days for a book of poetry, according to his delighted publisher), and a second volume, *Tommaso incredulo*, was working its way through the press, scheduled for release in the autumn. In Arbati's view, there was no conflict between the two pursuits. Police work forced him into contact with the seamier side of human character; poetry kept him in touch with its finer tone. Together, they balanced each other and made him something of an idealistic realist—a man who accepted that pain and violence were inevitable facts of existence but who never allowed that perception to obscure the higher truth that the human spirit in the purity of its essence was an earth-bound angel deprived only temporarily of wings. He had described the paradox of the human condition in one of his poems as the journey of a corruptible pilgrim, exiled but undaunted, descending through the dark valley of self toward the light. He still thought that image said it all.

As he made his way along Via Cerretani, with the cupola of the Duomo rising ahead of him like a civic crown, he found himself wrestling with the problem of psychological androgyny, the fusion of male and female attributes that lay, he was convinced, at the heart of human personality. A new poem was gestating, its inspiration the *Venus and Mars* of Botticelli—a painting new to Arbati—on loan from England and on display at a special exhibition in the Uffizi. From the first moment he had seen it, the painting had possessed him with a giant's hand, drawing him back to the gallery again and again to stand before it mesmerized, transported, oblivious of all around him. Somewhere in that narrow panel of two reclining gods a new idea was struggling toward the light. His task was to find it and set it free.

On the far side of the Duomo he turned right into Via del Proconsolo, then left into the Borgo degli Albizi. Tourist congestion thinned as he approached Piazza Salvemini, and by the time he reached Il Cibreo he was almost alone with his fellow fiorentini. It was still early for lunch and the restaurant was not crowded. He took a table under the pergola overlooking the outdoor market and ordered stewed tripes with tomatoes and a quartino of chianti. He ate alone, his mind revolving the problem of his new poem. In some mysterious way that he did not yet understand, the idea of androgyny was central to what made humanity human. Men and women were not so much two distinct sexes as they were unified beings in whom the same opposing characteristics had been differently reconciled. Each individual was, in his own way, a unique blending of masculine and feminine traits.

A scene in the open market below the patio where his table stood attracted his attention: it was an emblem of the very idea he was struggling with. At a fishmonger's stand, while the proprietor sat to one side and dandled a giddy infant on his knee, holding its stubby arms out and swaying like a wind-buffeted tree, his wife, who was serving customers, brought her mallet-like fist down on a crate of ice and fished up an octopus for inspection. A maternalistic male and a masculine woman. But the little scene, Arbati realized, could not easily be dismissed as an instance of role-reversal. That, of course, would have been the simplest explanation. But it was a solution that was too facile, too reductive—because it overlooked the essential facts that husband and wife were being themselves and that both shared the same instincts, the same desires. The father was not *mimicking* maternal behaviour as he played with the child; he was being himself—a loving father. The wife was not butch or mannish; she was decisive and competent. They could have traded places without ceasing to be themselves. They were androgynes.

Arbati returned to the problem of his poem. The general idea of what he wanted to say was clear enough in his mind. What he needed now were images to clothe it, the flesh of human feeling to give it form and substance, to make it live and breathe. *Hoc opus*, he thought wryly, recalling his Virgil, *hic labor est*. But for some reason the task was still beyond him; the words refused to come. He had struggled for days to bring them up into the light, to make at least a tentative start on the poem, but his muse had deserted him, and no words had come. He struggled again with it now, over the tripes and chianti, but got nowhere. A silent waiter removed his plate and brought him his espresso without disturbing his concentration; he focused his mind to a sharpened point and drew on all his powers, but still nothing came. The poem was intractable. He knew then what had to be done. He had to see that Botticelli painting in the Uffizi again. There was something in it that he had missed—some esoteric meaning that, when he finally understood it, would unlock the barred gates of his inspiration and allow him to write. The answer, he knew, lay hidden somewhere in that portrait of the two languid, reclining gods—and he had to hope that this time, or the next, Botticelli's enigmatic canvas would yield up its mystery to him.

He checked his watch: it was only one-fifteen. Good, he thought. There was plenty of time. The Cafferelli case hadn't generated much paperwork, and Professore Mangiello wouldn't be ready with his results until after four o'clock. The pathologist was a fussy man who intensely disliked being hurried, being caught off-guard or unprepared. It was always a wise precaution to be certain he was ready with his results before invading the private fiefdom of his green-tiled and antiseptic sanctum—and today in particular Arbati wanted to find him in an open and generous mood.

He paid his bill and set out for the gallery, gliding with long strides, not noticing the sights around him, his mind on his destination. Twenty minutes later, the colonnaded face of the Uffizi came into view as he turned into Via dei Neri. At the ticket counter, he was briefly delayed by the last of a line of tourists, mostly American, who had emerged from a tour-bus, but he was soon inside the vaulted hall, moved swiftly past Titians, Raphaels and da Vincis toward the Botticelli exhibition. And then he stood again before it, consuming and consumed. The painting seemed to have grown richer since the last time he had seen it—more deliciously sensuous and, it also seemed, somehow more transcendent and sublime. Venus, the goddess of love, reposed on the grass on a crimson cushion, her expression pensively watchful, the soft voluptuousness of her physical form refined by an aura of spirituality, the calm and otherworldly composure of a Madonna, and her auburn hair fell in ringlets to frame a face of transparent amber like flowers blooming in a shade. Mars, the god of war, a languid youth, naked, disarmed, his eyes closed and head of curled black hair dropped back, slept with one elbow resting on his discarded cuirass. The figures were symbolic of grace and strength reconciled—the balanced opposition of male and female—and the impression created by the two overlapping bodies was that of a single, undivided personality: an androgyne. But there was something more; something vague and numinous about the composition of the figures that Arbati could not put his finger on. There was something about the watching Venus and sleeping Mars that vexed him, gnawed at his spirit from within, seeking release. He tilted his head to one side, concentrating hard, willing the silent gods to divulge their secret. What were they trying to tell him? What truth about their relationship had he half perceived but failed to fully apprehend—?

'Excuse me, but *we'd* like to see this picture too.'

The grating, querulous voice shattered his reverie. How long had he stood there gaping? Time had stopped for him. He turned and found himself confronted by a sturdy, middle-aged American matron in a tweed suit. She clenched, in one hand, a glossy exhibition catalogue, in the other a culture-dazed husband. The man's glassy and idiotic look, half apologetic, half submissive, declared the price he was paying for his exposure to High Renaissance art. He would clearly have preferred a billiard table and a smoky pub.

Arbati stepped aside, his cheeks reddening. 'Of course, signora,' he muttered. 'I'm sorry. I was just leaving.'

He left the gallery and walked through almost deserted streets. The sidewalk cafés were full but there were few pedestrians and little traffic. Most businesses closed in the early afternoon, reopening at three, and Arbati had the streets pretty well to himself. As he walked, he revolved in his mind the enigma of the two gods, hoping for insight, but discovering none. When he reached the Questura, there was a message waiting on his desk from Giorgio saying that the cardinal's cheque-book entries looked as if they might hold promising leads. The note jolted him back from Botticelli to more mundane duties. He poured himself a mug of coffee from the glass-globed pot simmering on the eternal hotplate, then set about the task of typing up a preliminary report on the Cafferelli case, pounding with two fingers on an old Olivetti, promising himself with every stroke that one day he'd learn to do it properly. He had been making the same promise for years. Typing was a wonderful and time-saving accomplishment, but he was never able to spare the time to learn it. It was, he thought, an ability we should be born with—a piece of software preloaded into the machine at birth.

When he finished the paperwork, it was still too early to drive out to the university. He wanted to arrive when he was absolutely certain that il professore had finished the autopsy and was ready for him. There was nothing more that needed his attention in the office and he decided to walk to kill time. On the way he could drop in at Le Fonticine and make a reservation for dinner. The idea of bistecca with some of Silvano's grilled porcini mushrooms appealed to him. And the timing, he judged, would be just about perfect.

He left the Questura and headed north, turning over in his mind how best to tackle the problem of the prickly pathologist. Even on good days, Mangiello could be a tough customer, especially if he suspected you wanted something from him. And Arbati did want something. He was convinced now that his instinct about the murders was right. The body that he and Giorgio had examined in Santa Maria Novella basilica that morning had confirmed it for him beyond a reasonable doubt. They were dealing with a serial killer. What he had to do was produce enough evidence to demonstrate it. There were two hurdles to clear before he could do that. The first was Professor Mangiello; the second, as always, was Giorgio Bruni.

The sun was warm and fell on his back like a comfortable shower. He even managed at his lanky gait to work up a mild sweat. He paused briefly at Le Fonticine and made a reservation for eight o'clock, giving himself plenty of time to shower and change after work, then set off north-east toward the university. If he could turn up enough evidence to convince Giorgio, he knew he'd have more than enough to bring the public prosecutor on side when the time came. Giorgio was always his toughest sell— and this time he was counting on help from Professore Mangiello. He was expecting—no, he was hoping against hope, he realized— that the pathologist's examination of the cardinal's corpse would confirm the physical connection he suspected with the murders of Mora and Rosso—the crucial link which he needed to substantiate his theory of a multiple killer. Right now, the fate of that hypothesis rested in il professore's hands—and that was why, as he passed through the gates and into the campus grounds, Arbati offered a silent prayer to any god who chanced to be listening that today would find the moody Mangiello in a pliant and accommodating humour.

It was ten past four when he swung open the glass door of the forensic sciences building and started down the linoleum corridor to the professor's laboratory. He heard the music long before he reached the door. The professor was renowned for performing his dissections to the strains of the classics: always baroque, always upbeat, always loud. Today it was a Vivaldi concerto for massed trumpets and orchestra. Arbati puffed out his cheeks and reached for the handle. *Here we go then,* he muttered under his breath. The door opened and a stereophonic avalanche of brass in close harmony, mixed with the pungent scent of disinfectant, washed out over him and spilled into the reverberating corridor.

A birdlike figure shrouded in a green lab coat with matching cap and surgical mask looked up from the corpse of a young woman, whose chest was peeled back in layers like an open book. Arbati closed the door and found himself in a spartan room with green walls and a green tile floor. It struck his poet's eye with irony that the colour of growth and fecundity should so predominate in this house of death. With quick, angular movements, Professore Mangiello completed the incision he was making, then made a brief notation on the pad at his elbow before laying aside his scalpel and pulling the mask down under his chin.

'You want to know about Cafferelli, I suppose?'

Arbati nodded. 'Yes. Anything interesting?' They were shouting to make themselves heard over the din.

The professore held up a finger and stepped to a bank of sophisticated audio equipment stacked on a stand against the wall. He twisted a knob and the trumpets expired, the breath of life sucked suddenly out of them. The sound rang on unabated in Arbati's ears for several seconds and he wondered how Mangiello could bear the decibel level so high.

'An interesting case,' the professor observed, pulling off his gloves and nodding at the exposed cadaver on the stainless steel table. 'Suicide. A diabetic, she was. Blind most of the time. Almost certainly a case of self-inflicted insulin overdose. Very difficult to prove.' He crossed to the desk and riffled through a stack of filing-folders, peering myopically down his nose through a pair of gold-rimmed half-glasses. Selecting a folder, he handed it to Arbati. 'I expected you sooner, inspector. I finished with him over an hour ago.'

Arbati took the file. 'I was held up in traffic. Anything unusual in your report?'

Mangiello shook his head. 'No, a perfectly straightforward case,' he said. 'Severed carotid artery. He bled to death. A first-year medical student could have told you that. I daresay you might even have worked it out for yourself.'

'Time of death?'

'Between seven and ten last night, I'd say, give or take an hour.'

'Any chance of narrowing it further?'

'I didn't get my hands on him until nearly noon today,' Mangiello said testily. 'There's a limit to the miracles that even modern forensic science can provide us with.'

Arbati ignored the tone. 'What about the weapon?' he asked.

'Something very sharp. Not a kitchen knife, I'd say. A straight razor, perhaps.'

Arbati ran his eye over the typed autopsy report. 'Did you notice anything about the wound that seemed unusual?'

The little pathologist wrinkled his nose like a rabbit scenting danger. Finally, weighing his words, he said, 'There was an attempt—perhaps deliberate—to rupture the thyroid cartilage and sever the vocal cords.'

'That's not in the report,' Arbati observed evenly. No emotion showed on his face but the tempo of his breathing increased marginally. It was the moment he had been waiting for.

'It's an opinion, not a fact.'

'Would you be willing to include it in your report—as an opinion?'

'Certainly not, inspector. I don't speculate in my autopsies. They're official documents.'

Arbati tried a different approach. 'In the past two months,' he said, 'three men have been murdered in the same manner. You have performed post mortems on all the victims—Mora first, then Rosso, and now Cardinal Cafferelli. Would you say, professor, that a severed carotid artery is an unusual manner of death?'

'I suppose so, yes.'

'How unusual? How many cases had you seen before this recent spate of murders?'

Mangiello thought for a moment. 'Not many,' he said. 'Two, perhaps three—the results of industrial and, in one instance, a freak motorway accident. Murderers and suicides usually prefer one of the external jugular veins. They're close to the surface and much easier to locate.'

Arbati's interest rose. It was more than he'd dared hope for. He said: 'You're telling me that you've seen only three cases, all accidental, in a career of what, say, twenty years—?'

'Twenty-seven years.'

'—and then three more, all clearly homicides, in the space of just two months? It seems to me likely to be more than coincidental.' He decided to press his luck. 'You said Cafferelli's murderer, in your opinion, deliberately tried to cut the vocal cords. Thinking back, would you say the same of Mora and Rosso?'

The pathologist shifted uneasily. 'Can I assume we're talking off the record?'

Arbati nodded. 'For the moment, yes.'

Mangiello pursed his narrow lips into something resembling a bird's beak. 'Now that you mention it,' he said, 'the similarity is remarkable. I don't like speculation, inspector, but there's clearly a common thread here. The incisions were all in the same area, all very deep—all aimed in the first instance, it seems, at the thyroid cartilage. Yes, I'd say the vocal cords were probably a target in each case.'

'But you won't say so in your report.'

'No.'

Arbati tried again. 'How much of what you've just told me would you say under oath in the witness box?'

Mangiello gave him a disarming grin. 'All of it, of course,' he said—then added slyly: 'Assuming, naturally, that someone were to ask me the right questions.'

Arbati permitted himself a thin smile. It wasn't enough—not yet—to convince a professional sceptic like Giorgio, but it was a beginning. And it was more than enough to confirm Arbati's gut suspicion that they were hunting a serial killer. He said:

'I'll hold you to that promise, professore. I'll even coach the public prosecutor about how to examine you on the stand.' He turned at the door. 'Thanks for your help—off the record, of course.'

As he closed the door, he heard the professor's voice call out, with what passed in him for humour, 'Oh, inspector, shall I expect you next week with another body?'

Arbati chose not to dignify the quip with a response. The door clicked behind him, and before he had taken two steps along the corridor, the trumpets of Antonio Vivaldi again filled the air with their brassy harmony.

FOUR

AT THE SAME TIME Carlo Arbati left his office at the Questura in Via Zara to walk to the university, Cordelia Sinclair pulled the plug in the antique lion's-foot tub in her flat on the top floor of Pensione Ghilberti and watched the bath water swirl away between her ankles in a gurgling vortex. She felt like a new woman, revitalized and reborn. A long soak in a hot bath had always had that effect on her, ever since she was a child.

Despite the ten-hour flight from O'Hare and only an hour or so of fitful sleep on the plane, she hadn't felt the least bit tired when she had arrived in Florence that morning. She couldn't have slept if she'd tried. Everything was too new, too exciting. Anyway, she told herself, there'd be scads of time later to catch up on sleep. Right now there was too much to see.

She had stood for a time—wondering where to begin, what to do first—on the little geranium-rimmed balcony outside her kitchen window, her senses working at full stretch, drinking in the sights and sounds and smells of the city around her. How strange it all was! How wonderfully unlike anything she had ever known, and yet how oddly familiar at the same time. All the pictures of Florence she had pored over for the past fifteen months, lying on the big brass bed in her room back home trying to imagine what it was going to be like, had finally come to life. But how different reality was from books and photographs! Being here was ten times—no, a hundred times—better than just *thinking about* being here.

At noon her bags still hadn't come. From a call-box in the street she rang the station and was told they'd be delivered sometime in the afternoon, but she was too restless, too anxious to be *doing* something, just to sit around in an empty flat waiting for them. How could she waste her first day hanging about for something as mundane as a luggage-delivery? No, it wouldn't do—it wouldn't do at all. Her watch told her it was time for lunch, but she wasn't hungry; she was too excited to worry about eating.

She needed to be *moving*—her spirit craved action, new sensations, new experiences. And so she had decided on a walk along the Arno, a long and ambling walk to taste at first hand the glories of the place she had spent the last year and a half only dreaming about.

Cordelia loved to walk. It was the best way, especially in a new place, to really see things. Setting out from Pensione Ghilberti, she made her way through streets where ancient buildings slept in the lap of departed centuries. Every church and public building she passed was filled, she knew, with priceless treasures. Florence was a vast museum: the home of Michelangelo and Leonardo, of Botticelli and Petrarch and Dante. Yet what struck her, rather to her surprise, about the architecture was the absence of the grace and beauty she had expected to find. On every side, the buildings presented her with austere and forbidding façades. Their crenellated exteriors gave nothing away, offered no hint of the riches within; they seemed calculated to repel rather than inspire. In spite of the warmth of the day she felt cold, almost like shivering. It was another of the paradoxes of Florence—one of many she had encountered since arriving. The city, she decided (searching for an image), was a kind of oyster bed where the pearls were hidden inside thorny shells.

Her path led her toward the river. She emerged eventually, after half an hour of rambling through claustrophobic medieval lanes, at the foot of Ponte Vespucci where, for the first time, the prospect opened out. Like most European cities, Florence is built around its river. The silver Arno, Dante had called it. She turned left into the Lungarno, a cobbled street bounded on the water side by a waist-high wall, and her pace slowed. The sudden expansion of the scene as she turned the corner had overwhelmed her senses and she walked as if mesmerized, as if she had stepped through the looking-glass and found herself, inexplicably and unawares, in some weird world of fantasy on the other side. If there were people on the streets, she didn't notice them. Ahead, the river stretched away in a broad sheet like an unfurling of aluminium foil. Above its crowded banks, the venerable spires of Santa Maria del Carmine and Santo Spirito struggled out of the surrounding tumble of terracotta roofs, and in the middle distance the Pitti Palace—once the home of Medici princes—crouched on its hillside lost in sepia memories of long-vanished power. But it was

Ponte Vecchio that riveted her attention. She could barely believe that it was real. Two storeys high, the ancient bridge spanned the water ahead, its shops overhanging the river and supported at the rear by angled wooden brackets. It looked for all the world like a fairy castle suspended by some miracle of rare device in mid-air above the Arno's surface. She found herself holding her breath and expecting it to disappear in a puff of smoke like a conjuror's illusion.

But it didn't disappear. It grew more solid and substantial as she approached. And then, finally, she was standing on it, moving across it, taking it for granted, almost as if it were just another ordinary street of shops. She spent an hour window-gazing in the exclusive jeweller's shops that lined it on either side as they had since the sixteenth century. The cases in Gherardi's displayed jade and turquoise and specimens of exotic coral. In the window of Piccini's was an emerald tiara and matching necklace that took her breath away. Certainly there was nothing to match it, she thought wryly to herself, at the jewellery counter of Marshall Fields' department store back in Chicago. The idea made her stifle a giggle behind her hand and she wondered if hunger and fatigue were finally catching up with her. To bring herself back down to earth, she bought a croissant and a Coke from a vendor's stand and stood under the arches in the centre of the bridge, looking out over the ancient city and tranquil river. Is it possible, she wondered, even now, standing here on this fairy-tale bridge, that this is all just make-believe—?

The drain made a sucking sound that brought her back to the present. Swirling, eddying, the soapy bathwater fell away into the dark hole of the drain pipe and disappeared. She had been day-dreaming, she realized. For the first time in many days she had relaxed completely and let her mind wander. And best of all, she'd awakened to find that it wasn't a dream. She really was in Florence—really was here in this antique tub, really had stood on Ponte Vecchio sipping a Coke, really was making a new beginning.

The idea of taking a bath struck her suddenly as a symbolic gesture: a ritual cleansing away of the past at the start of a new life. The thought was not without its irony. She had fled the New World to discover herself in the Old. She was Columbus in reverse, her lion's-foot tub a sort of porcelain *Santa Maria*. It was an absurd notion and the thought of it made her smile. But still, in a way, too, the image was also perfectly accurate, perfectly apposite—and *that* thought made her smile too.

She stepped from the bath and towelled herself dry. Soft patches of sunlight, filtered through the lacy curtains that covered the window, fell in mottled patterns on the wall and floor. For an instant she caught sight of herself in the full-length mirror on the back of the door and looked away. It was an instinctive reaction. It was also, she knew, an evasion: a fear of seeing herself that was born of a fear of what she might see. Ever since she was a child, she had avoided mirrors. They were cold and impersonal, and they revealed too much. They distorted the reality she chose to perceive.

She forced herself by an act of will to confront the image.

The figure in the glass was tall and slender. Its auburn hair fell below the shoulder, framing an oval face. The body was smooth and, it seemed to her critical eye, also younger than its thirty-two years. In the dappled light the skin glowed amber: burnished like living bronze, yet restrained and graceful in the curving line of breast and thigh, giving the impression of something between an Aphrodite and a Madonna. Her eyes met the reflected eyes. She saw herself seeing herself and wanted to tear away before she saw too much. No, she decided—*no*, this time she wouldn't look away: she would face herself. She steadied her gaze. She made herself keep looking. The eyes: mirrors of the soul, the ancients had called them. She tried to penetrate their blue opacity, but it was like staring into a fathomless sea. The liquid surface flittered with a fierce desire, but the abyss beneath remained silent and dark—unknown, unplumbed. Who was she really—? Under the physical mask of skin and muscle and bone, what was the inner being of Cordelia Sinclair—that secret self she had never faced and had come to Florence to discover and set free—really like? Was it strong and self-possessed, or timorous and vulnerable? severe and aloof, or warm and trusting? independent and self-reliant, or defenceless, exposed, and malleable? She stood before the reflected image and demanded an answer, an epiphany. She stood without moving—confronting herself—obstinately awaiting an insight. But nothing happened and the moment passed. Only the image of her physical form, reduced to the light of common day, stared back at her from the silvered surface.

A blouse and pleated skirt lay on the bed. She had spent longer in the bath then she intended and would have to hurry now. Signora Ghilberti had said four o'clock—and from what she had seen of her landlady, four o'clock meant four o'clock sharp. She dressed quickly, pulling her hair back at the sides into a barrette behind. She wore little makeup, only lipstick and a hint of eyeshadow, and a pair of gold hoop earrings was her only jewellery. She hadn't been quite sure what to wear but had decided in the end that the occasion called for something in the casual-dressy line. Presumably even Signora Ghilberti, for all her funny, old-fashioned ways, wouldn't expect her dressed to the nines just to meet the neighbours.

It was odd, she thought, digging in the top drawer of the bureau for her brown belt, how quickly she had come to feel at home in this little corner of a strange land. When she had come back from her stroll around the city, feeling lonely and far from home, her luggage was there waiting for her on the polished parquet of the landing outside her door, like an affable and slightly scuffed-about gathering of old friends. Within minutes, the apartment was transformed by familiar books and clothes and toiletries, so that before long it felt like home. Well, almost like home anyway. How peculiar, yet at the same time how oddly ordinary it was to look out past the Laurel and Hardy poster she had bought at J. C. Penney's in the South Evanston mall and see, beyond the low, geranium-lined wall of her balcony, a sea of medieval roofs spiked with television antennas. In the distance, like a picture in a book, was the cupola of the Duomo and the slender marble finger of Giotto's *trecento* campanile, whose delicate veining seemed almost to give it life in the brilliant sunshine.

She slipped into a pair of comfortable slingbacks, then checked her appearance quickly in the mirror. She was ready to face the world.

On the way out of the door, she glanced around the apartment—*her* apartment—and a lump rose in her throat. She was on her own at last, and she was happy—happier than she had ever been in her life. The past and her failed marriage were behind her, almost (it seemed) forgotten, and the future lay before her like an open road. On the rolltop desk was the note she had received from Maestro Marchesi. It was propped against her copy of Palisca's *Florentine Camerata* in such a way that it was visible from everywhere in the room, and the sight of it sent a thrill of anticipation through her like an electric current. She could hardly believe, even now, that he had actually agreed to see her. Guessing that he would be at home in Florence after the opera seasons in Paris and Munich were over, she had written on a whim, expecting nothing for her trouble. How wrong she had been! On Tuesday—five days from now—she would meet the man himself, a conductor the equal of Solti and von Karajan, whose face she knew from a dozen record jackets. It was like having an audience with the pope, she thought, only better. She had already drafted a list of questions to ask him about the Camerata and she carried it in her purse like a talisman. She wasn't really superstitious, of course; the list was merely a precautionary amulet against his suddenly changing his mind or having to cancel because of another appointment. The opportunity to meet him in person, to sit down and talk with a musician of his stature about her thesis and what she hoped to do after finishing it, was the most important thing that had happened to her in her whole life. She simply couldn't run the risk of some chance quirk of fate coming along to spoil it.

She locked her door and descended the two flights of steps to the ostrich-plumed vestibule below. It was only a minute or so past four o'clock. She breathed a sigh of relief: she was right on time. In the centre of the plaster rosette beside Signora Ghilberti's door she pressed the button and stepped back to wait.

Inside, the others had assembled before her. When the silvery chime of the doorbell tinkled in the stuffy silence, Signora Ghilberti cast a reproving glance at the pendulum clock and rose from her seat. It was nearly three minutes past four. The trio of figures on the sofas stood in unison, awaiting the introductions. Signor Farinelli, whose flat was the one below Cordelia's, was a tall, well-built man in his early forties with large, luminous eyes and a warm smile. The di Bancos were a middle-aged couple, he tanned and overbearing, she mousey and retiring. They lived in a *pensione* further along the street and Lydia di Banco was a member of Signora Ghilberti's bridge group. The two women had known each other for many years, since the time when Lydia had come as a teenager to visit her father—now dead—who had been one of the boarders in the days when Signora Ghilberti and her husband (also now dead) ran the house as a pensione. It was

Signora Ghilberti's opinion that, like her poor father, Lydia had made a bad match. Choosing incompatible mates, it seemed, was something genetic that ran in the family.

'Come in, dear,' Signora Ghilberti said, holding open the door. Her eyes flickered in tacit rebuke to the pendulum clock, then back to Cordelia; but the smile of a gracious hostess remained firmly fixed in its place. 'Everyone is waiting to meet you.'

The introductions followed. It was apparent from the body language that Signora Ghilberti didn't much care for Signor di Banco and that the antipathy was, from his point of view, fully reciprocated. Cordelia wondered why he had been invited and why, if in fact he had, he had bothered to come. Perhaps he was one of those possessive husbands who refused to let their wives out of their sight. For her part, poor Signora di Banco, staring nervously down at her shoes, looked as if she'd sooner die than have to make a decision on her own. They struck Cordelia as a sad and miserable—not to mention boring—pair, and their presence in the room seemed to give off an air of the bitterness and despair that characterized their lives. Signor Farinelli, on the other hand, the man who lived upstairs, was another matter entirely. Cordelia liked him instantly. He had a pleasant face lit by frank, intelligent eyes that seemed to weigh all they met with a slightly bemused detachment and that also seemed to miss nothing. He was a big man, well-proportioned and (she thought) probably very strong, who had perhaps once been an athlete, although it was difficult to judge the physique that lay under the folds of his jacket and loose, open-necked cotton shirt. But what attracted her to him in particular was his voice. It had a wistful, melancholy quality that made her think of a wind sighing in pine trees. It was a sound she knew all too well from nights lying alone, until finally sleep came, in the loft of the cottage on Lake Michigan where her father escaped to write his books in the summer. In her mind it was a sound indelibly associated with loneliness and isolation. She wondered if Signor Farinelli had endured, like her, a lonely childhood deprived of love and motherly tenderness.

'Well, sit down everyone,' Signora Ghilberti said in her nasal, fluting voice, sweeping the starched napkin from a plate of cucumber sandwiches. 'Now that Signora Sinclair is here, I can pour us our tea.'

The room was one Cordelia had passed briefly through earlier

in the day when the landlady had fetched her key for her. Like
everything else (or so it seemed) in Signora Ghilberti's world, the
inflection was Edwardian. Two heavy sofas and a pair of antique
wing-backed chairs were grouped around the oval periphery of a
large, low mahogany table in the centre of the room. The walls
beyond were lined with filigreed, glass-faced cabinets whose
shelves displayed china plates and Doulton figurines. The windows overlooking the street were covered by thick velvet curtains
that successfully excluded every vestige of natural light, such il-
lumination as there was in the room coming from a strategically-
positioned pair of shaded floor lamps. It struck Cordelia with the
force of a revelation that the dated decor and the atmosphere of
stiff cordiality probably replicated pretty accurately what the tone
of life would have been like in the prim and whiskered silence
of an English country vicarage between the two world wars. She
had no difficulty at all imagining a youthful Signora Ghilberti
dutifully tending her pater's dovecote or taking the morning air
in a lilac-scented garden under a frilled parasol.

On their hostess's instructions, the guests resumed their places.
Inquiring first by a look if it were taken, Cordelia sat in one of
the wing-backed chairs. She had already made one gaffe by arriving three minutes late. She had no intention of making another.

'You're from Chicago, I hear,' Signor di Banco said, stretching
for one of the sandwiches and wolfing it back as if he hadn't seen
food for a month.

'Evanston, actually,' Cordelia said. 'A suburb of Chicago.'

Di Banco helped himself to another sandwich. 'I've often
thought of visiting Chicago,' he said importantly, ignoring the
qualification.

'Really?'

'Yes, my firm does business there.' He settled smugly back
into the yielding cushion. 'On the Exchange, as a matter of fact,'
he added significantly. His wife, tucked beside him, stared at her
knees as if her neck had locked on her.

Signora Ghilberti poured from a flowered pot into delicate
china cups. The opening di Banco had offered was a temptation
too great to resist. 'Signor di Banco,' she said drily, passing Cordelia the first cup, 'is a teller at the Banco di Firenze. I hope the
tea isn't too strong, dear.'

'Chief teller,' he corrected, reddening, trying to salvage what he could.

'Quite,' she replied, her point taken.

'He comes by his name honestly, at any rate,' Signor Farinelli interjected, heading off the *impasse*. He caught Cordelia's eye and winked knowingly. Di Banco, his look said, was a pompous bore.

'Cream and sugar, dear?' Signora Ghilberti inquired. 'Or do you prefer lemon?'

'I take it plain, thanks,' Cordelia said, wishing it were coffee.

Signor di Banco, deflated, lapsed into moody silence. He sat stolidly in a corner of the sofa, scowling, his arms crossed, nursing his punctured dignity. Beside him, mutely sharing his pain, his wife's eyes never left her lap. The sight of them irritated Cordelia. She had decided the first moment, before he had even spoken a word, that she disliked Signor di Banco. He was too full of himself to have any feeling left for others. As for his wife, she was that sorry paradigm of marital conditioning—the eunuch helpmate, sapless appendage of her mate. Cordelia felt her presence in the company as an embarrassment and an affront—an all-too-acute reminder of what women were content to endure from men, of what she herself had suffered in her five-year union with Charles Passmore. In a way, of course, she pitied Lydia, but she blamed her too—blamed her for placidly accepting her lot, for acquiescing so willingly in her own disempowerment. Lydia di Banco was the image of everything Cordelia had come to Florence to erase forever from her own life and memory.

It was left to Signor Farinelli to keep the conversational ball in play. After a moment of awkward silence, he said:

'Your father is a professor, I understand.'

The statement took Cordelia, her mind still on the di Bancos, by surprise. 'Oh, yes—' she said, catching herself, 'yes, he is. He teaches English literature at Northwestern. He's a specialist in Shakespeare.'

Farinelli smiled. 'Then it's no accident, I imagine, that your name is Shakespearean.'

'*King Lear* is one of his favourites.'

Farinelli nodded. 'Cordelia. The true daughter, the only one who loves him.'

The recognition pleased her. But a pang reminded her that for her father the name probably implied obedience rather than love. Lost in his books, Professor Sinclair suffered something of Lear's blindness.

'Actually,' she said, 'he was hoping for a son. He wanted to call him Horatio. My mother died before they could have another child.'

'I'm sorry,' Farinelli said. 'All the same,' he added graciously, 'he's better off in the long run with a daughter named Cordelia. A loyal daughter is preferable to a philosophic son.'

The interlude eased them over di Banco's humiliation and the talk turned to Cordelia's trip and her first impressions of Florence. Her TWA flight had been ten hours, she explained, nonstop from O'Hare. She had taken the FS express train from Fiumicino to Rome, then caught the Rapido on to Florence.

'Goodness me,' exclaimed Signora Ghilberti, who considered commercial aviation a dangerous innovation still in its infancy, 'all the way from the middle of North America without stopping for petrol. Fancy that!'

'Have you been to Italy before?' Farinelli asked.

Cordelia shook her head. 'No, this is my first time. I spent a semester on exchange in England as an undergraduate and managed to get as far as Paris one weekend, but this is my first visit to your country.'

'I hope your bags arrived safely,' Signora di Banco said, lifting her eyes fractionally and speaking for the first time. 'I know how I'd hate to be away from home without things I knew around me.'

'They came this afternoon,' Cordelia said. 'The airline didn't even manage to lose anything, which I imagine is something of a record for them.' Poor Lydia, she thought. Why don't you just walk out on him? But she knew what prevented that: fear. Like women everywhere, Lydia di Banco had been conditioned to fear trusting herself to her own abilities. To this day, Cordelia had no idea how she had summoned the strength to leave Charles. But that first step had been the hardest. After that, it was downhill all the way and a matter of taking it day by day.

'Your Italian is very polished,' Farinelli observed, steering onto a more promising topic. 'Is it something you learned in school?'

'I started there,' Cordelia said. 'I took a couple of optional courses in Italian literature as an undergraduate. When I found out for certain I was coming to Florence, I enrolled in an immersion course in conversation. I've been working at it for almost a year now.'

'You've learned well, signorina.'

Cordelia felt a glow in her cheeks. 'You're being kind, Signor Farinelli—probably far too kind. Tell me, how many times have you seen my grammar showing in the past few minutes? Be honest with me now!'

Farinelli laughed. 'Once or twice,' he said. 'I admit it. But you have such a pretty accent that I hardly noticed.'

'Flattery will get you everywhere,' Cordelia said. 'Now, what about you? Do you read your Shakespeare in Italian or English?'

It was Farinelli's turn to be embarrassed. 'In English,' he said. 'I read a great deal, as a matter of fact,' he went on with a self-deprecatory shrug. 'I'm something of a library cormorant, I suppose. I feed on almost anything.'

'He's being modest,' Signora Ghilberti interjected in her brusque Oxbridge fashion. 'Our Signor Farinelli is a very accomplished gentleman. He speaks three languages and reads many more. His English, by the way, is perfectly flawless.'

Farinelli's cheeks burned.

'Well, I'm impressed,' Cordelia said, amused at his discomfiture now that the shoe was on the other foot.

'He even reads ancient Greek,' the landlady added.

'Then I'm doubly impressed.' She grinned sweetly at his confusion.

Farinelli waved them off. 'Come, come ladies,' he said with mock severity, 'we're not here to talk about me.' His large, luminous eyes settled on Cordelia. He liked this American girl. She was witty and her intelligence had a cutting edge. He parried her serve and backhanded the ball adroitly back into her court. 'So tell us, Signorina Sinclair, what do you think of our city? You've been here almost a day now. Long enough, surely, to have formed an initial impression. So give us your first thoughts.'

The sudden change in direction caught her off-guard. A hundred images, ideas, impressions from her walk earlier in the day tumbled through her mind. 'Oh,' she stumbled, 'well, frankly, it's all a little overwhelming. I hardly know where to begin—'

'The first stage of Stendhal's disease,' Signor di Banco grunted, forcing an entry into the conversation. He was apparently finished sulking for the moment.

Cordelia gave him a quizzical look. 'Stendhal's disease—?'

'Art poisoning,' Signora Ghilberti said tartly, shooting di Banco a withering look.

Farinelli explained:

'Visitors are sometimes so awed by the sheer volume of culture in Florence that it makes them ill. Unconsciously, they treat it as a kind of art examination. It's not really a laughing matter though. The symptoms can be quite severe: angst, disorientation, clinical depression, persecution complex, a loss of the sense of identity. Local psychiatrists have coined the phrase "Stendhal's syndrome" for it. The French novelist, it seems, suffered many of its symptoms when he was here in the nineteenth century.'

'A sensible girl like you, of course,' Signora Ghilberti added hastily, 'is perfectly safe.'

Farinelli passed his cup across for more tea. 'Coming back to my question,' he said, 'I *would* be interested in knowing your first impressions. I assume they were positive?'

'Oh, yes, very much so!'

'More tea, dear?'

'Yes, thanks.'

While Signora Ghilberti replenished the cups, Farinelli settled back, his head cocked to one side, his eyes fixed on Cordelia with bemused expectation. He was a complex man, Cordelia sensed. And she felt instinctively that there was something sad at the bottom of those large grey eyes, some deep and hidden sorrow in his life, but she couldn't imagine what it might be. She dismissed the thought. It was only a vague intuition, after all, and perhaps she was mistaken.

How could she find words to describe her impressions of Florence? Her feelings were so complex and contradictory! Certainly, it was not as she had imagined it would be, lying on her bed in Evanston flipping through brochures. Then, it had seemed a remote and romantic kingdom, a sort of Disney World designed hundreds of years ago by Brunelleschi and Giotto. The reality, when she had finally emerged through the doors of Santa Maria Novella station into the sunlit piazza, was something altogether different—something more powerful, more sobering, more disturbing than anything she was prepared for. She remembered the

impact of being suddenly, unexpectedly confronted by the fifteenth-century façade of the basilica. It had taken her breath away
and sent a cold shiver down her spine. Although familiar in its
geometry from a dozen photographs, nothing had prepared her
for its psychological power. Its symmetry had seemed, rising suddenly in her path, obstructing her passage, to possess the terrible
beauty of a scowling angel. It had seemed a living thing—a minatory spirit whose rows of black and white marble symbolized the
inextricable intertwining of good and evil in a world where life
and death are separated by a heartbeat, where joy and sorrow are
masks on opposite side of the same face, where even the sweetest
nectar turns to poison as the bee's mouth sips it from the honeyed
bole. There was nothing of fantasy or Disney about it. It confronted reality with a hard, unsentimental eye; it provided no easy,
comfortable escape from the ambiguity of existence. It was sublime and darkly threatening—elevating and terrifying—at the
same time. And then, to make the whole thing still more bizarre,
she had heard on the radio that the body of a Roman Catholic
cardinal had been found hanging from a cross in that very church.
She must have passed it on her way from the station. The thought
made her shiver.

How, she wondered, could she put such feelings into words?
How could she express the power of emotions so confused and
dimly apprehended that she herself did not understand them?

'The architecture isn't what I expected,' she said at last. 'It's
stunning, of course, but I have to confess that I find it rather
forbidding.' She paused, then went on, recalling the image that
had suggested itself to her on her walk. 'In a way the buildings,
especially the churches, reminded me of oysters. The pearls are
inside, protected on the outside by tough shells.' Even as she
spoke the words, she realized how inadequate they were and
wished them unsaid.

Farinelli flashed a smile. 'It's a colourful image,' he said, 'but
one where the intention is easily reversed. After all, although the
pearl needs the oyster, the oyster doesn't seem to need the pearl—
which might, I suppose, if we're talking about churches, be taken
as an argument in favour of puritanism and getting rid of pearls
altogether. But then,' he added slyly, 'I don't suppose any metaphor ever runs on all fours, does it?' He sipped his tea, as if
giving her a moment to catch up, then went on: 'But I think I

know what you're trying to say. There's a curious coincidence of opposites in austere beauty that somehow seems to reflect a more general experience of life. Every sorrow somehow contains a promise of joy; and every joy, no matter how powerful, has a melancholy tinge. Beautiful music makes us cry; a beautiful painting makes us feel sad. Nothing we experience is pure—not even love, the most selfless of our emotions. In some mysterious way, pain always coexists with pleasure in our lives, evil with good, loss with gain. Even life itself is in constant tension with death. With our first breath we begin dying, cell by cell, until decay finally overwhelms regeneration and we perish utterly.'

Signor di Banco stifled a yawn, then heaved himself forward on the sofa, snatching up another sandwich. Farinelli ignored him. He went on:

'On a first acquaintance, many people find Florence a contradiction; and I suppose it is so. During the Renaissance, it was the centre of religious art and European finance. God and Mammon glorified together. Michelangelo carving the *Pietà* while the Medici princes counted their florins in the Uffizi. Now, the Medici are gone and the Uffizi is a shrine for art, but a shrine that turns a profit. Strange perhaps—a contradiction—but, really, just a microcosm of the paradox of the human condition. If you want the truth, I think that's the function of architecture, perhaps of all art: to impress on the beholder a sense of the paradox of man—neither angel nor beast, but some strange creation in between them. That's why the best architecture attracts and repels. It abuses and flatters the viewer at the same time, making him feel puny and insignificant beside its grandeur, yet also powerful and magnificent because it was made by human minds and hands. It magnifies our predicament and presents it in such a way that we can't help facing ourselves when we're in its presence. No wonder we find it so unsettling.'

Cordelia was speechless, transfixed. How effortlessly he had opened her homely metaphor and discovered the pearl inside of it! How easily he had put into words her deepest inarticulate feelings! It was as if those frank, penetrating eyes had plumbed the bottom of her soul—as if somehow, after less than an hour's acquaintance, he knew more about her than she did about herself. She was used to being in the company of intelligent people. She had grown up in a university town and her father was an international authority in his field. But she had never encountered an intelligence like this. Farinelli's mind was faster and more agile than any she had met—and also, she sensed, infinitely more complex. She remembered the sadness she had earlier noticed in his eyes. He was a man who had known both good and evil. She was sure of it now. His mind was a dark labyrinth, intricate and convoluted, with a Minotaur of some kind crouching at the core. There was something frightening as well as fascinating about him.

Signora Ghilberti broke the spell.

'I remember how harsh and implacable I found the buildings when I first arrived,' she said, reminiscing. 'It was just after the war and I was newly married. Guido—my late husband, God rest his soul—had grown up here and positively insisted on coming back to see what the Germans had done to the place. We won't stay, he said. But we never left. He cried when he saw the buildings and bridges they'd blown up. It was a kind of pilgrimage for him, I suppose, when I think about it now.'

'Is that when you bought this house?' Lydia di Banco asked.

Signora Ghilberti nodded. 'Yes, Guido was a civil engineer and there was plenty of work for him here, cleaning up after the Hun. The Arno bridges had to be rebuilt. The German commander had ordered them destroyed to slow down the Allied advance—all except Ponte Vecchio. That, I suppose, would have been too great a desecration even for a Nazi. Anyway, we bought the house in the summer of 1945. We'd only been married a few months and we had no money, so we let out the upstairs rooms and took in boarders.' Her tone became sentimental. 'Oh, they were happy years—! We used to sit around a big table in the dining room after dinner and talk and laugh and tell stories until long after the sun went down. Sometimes in the evenings, when the others had gone up to their rooms, Guido and I curled up on an old sofa in the lounge—it's gone now—and he'd recite Petrarch and Dante by heart with the tears running down his cheeks.' Her voice grew husky with memory. 'He was a wonderful man, kind and cultivated. I miss him terribly. We never wanted children, only each other. The boarders were all the family we needed. They were well-behaved and there were never any nappies to wash.'

Cordelia strained to share the memories, but there was nothing in her experience to connect them with. Her marriage to Charles had been devoid of poetry, empty of romance. Charles was a man who never cried, who was perhaps incapable of tears—though he had often enough reduced her to them. Looking back, it was hard to see what had brought them together, unless it was the despairing hope she harboured that somehow his strength would compensate for her fear of achievement. Like Cinderella, she had been waiting for something external to come along and transform her life. But Charles, though he was charming, was no prince; and he had his own career to think about. It was, in fact, all he ever did think about. Passmore Investments Inc. was the centre and circumference of his universe, and Cordelia merely an appendage, a satellite. For five years they had shared a surname and a bed but little else.

'When Guido died,' Signora Ghilberti continued, 'I stayed on. It wasn't easy. I thought of leaving—I even went back to England and rented a cottage in Devon for a while. But too much had changed there, so I came back. My happiest years had been here. I missed the England of my girlhood but I missed Guido more. So I came back and made my little piece of England here where I could still be close to him.'

As she had that morning when she first arrived, Cordelia sensed again, below the imperious exterior, the melancholy presence of Virginia Woolf.

'I'm glad you did,' Farinelli said. 'Your piece of England has become rather dear to me.'

'How gracious of you,' their hostess said. 'If I'm not mistaken, Signor Farinelli, you were the first tenant I let a flat to after converting the pensione over to apartments.'

'Yes,' he said, nodding, 'back in September of 1979, when I was at *La Nazione*.'

'Fourteen years,' she mused sadly. 'Has it been so long?' She turned to Cordelia and said by way of explanation: 'I couldn't bear the thought of boarders without Guido—I would always have seen an empty chair at the table—but the thought of living alone was equally intolerable. I should have taken down the brass plaque outside, I suppose, but I needed to have something to remind me of those happy days.' She added softly, 'I still do.'

For a long minute the four guests sat in respectful silence, unwilling to break the mood, like visitors gathered at a cenotaph. Finally Farinelli, steering tactfully toward neutral waters, turned to Cordelia and said:

'You've come to Florence to write a thesis, I understand.'

'Something to do with music,' di Banco chipped in a fraction of a second too quickly.

Cordelia nodded. 'Yes, I'm doing some research on the Camerata,' she said, expecting the polite indifference that usually greeted her from strangers when the subject of her thesis came up. Either they had never heard of the Camerata or, if they had, their eyes seemed always to be wondering what had possessed her to choose such an obscure and tedious topic. She added by way of explanation: 'They were a group of composers at the Medici court in the 1580s and their idea of setting themes from classical mythology to music was the beginning of modern opera. Before them, as far as we know, no one except the ancient Greeks had ever tried to use music dramatically.'

The pendulum clock in its recessed niche announced the hour in five stately bongs and the sound had nearly died away before she realized that Signor Farinelli was speaking, his face and voice animated with feeling:

'A fascinating group. They met, if I remember correctly, at Count Bardi's house in the Oltrarno near Piazza del Carmine. It was an age of discovery and they were an important part of it. Peri, Cavalieri, Caccini, Galilei—'

'The astronomer,' di Banco hazarded, determined to be involved.

'His father, in fact. Vincenzo Galilei,' Farinelli corrected.

'Quite,' Signora Ghilberti interjected decisively with the air of a tennis umpire calling a fault.

Struck down a second time, di Banco relapsed into bleak and moody silence. His wife laid a consoling hand on his knee but he brushed it peremptorily aside.

Cordelia did not notice. She stared at the man across from her with frank admiration. 'Have you studied music, Signor Farinelli?'

'Not formally.'

'You learned it on your own?'

's, yes.'

, Cordelia sensed, she had unintentionally touched ps he felt his lack of formal training made him ior to those who, like herself, had had the benefit aining. She flushed and looked away. 'I'm sorry,' she said. 'I didn't mean to pry.' When she raised her eyes, she found that he was still looking at her. Not with reproach but with sympathy. In her sudden embarrassment, he had recognized a kindred spirit. Intuitively, he understood her pain, her confusion.

'It doesn't matter,' he said. 'I've made out well enough in my own way. Degrees and diplomas aren't the answer to everything.'

'They're not even a secure meal-ticket any more,' she agreed, feeling mercifully let off the hook. Seeking safer ground, she said, 'What is it that you do for a living, if you don't mind my asking? I assume it's something to do with the arts.'

'He writes,' Signora Ghilberti chimed in. 'His reviews of cultural events around town in the *Firenze Spettacolo* are very well known and often reprinted. You must read them sometime, dear. I find them very elegant, very judicious.'

Di Banco flexed his wrist and looked ostentatiously at his watch. Cordelia's heart hardened another notch against him. He was a boor as well as a bore, and his philistian manners reminded her forcibly of her five years with Charles Passmore. It was exactly how her ex-husband had responded to any topic of conversation not directly connected to himself or his narrow interests in money and the stock indexes. Talk of culture always prompted him to stifle a yawn and caused his eyes to glaze over.

'Have you ever written about the early opera?' she asked, pointedly ignoring di Banco.

'Yes, one or two little pieces. They're not much, I'm afraid, but I'd be happy to pass copies along, if you'd like to see them.'

'Oh, yes, very much,' she said, hardly able to believe her ears. What an incredible coincidence it was. Someone living right downstairs who had actually *published* in the same area where she was doing her research! 'And perhaps,' she said, venturing further, 'you could make time one day for coffee and a chat, some time when you can spare me an hour or so. I'd like to pick your brains. And besides, for an American,' she added with a bright smile, 'I make a mean cup of cappuccino.'

'I'd consider it an honour, Signorina Sinclair.'

Cordelia smiled brightly. 'Then I'll consider it a date,' she said.

The di Bancos rose and made their excuses, and the company disbanded. Cordelia and Farinelli ascended the stairs together. When they reached the landing outside his door, she said:

'Tell me a little more about your writing.'

'What would you like to know?'

'Well,' she said, 'what sort of things exactly do you write?'

'Music reviews mostly. Sometimes historical pieces on architecture or painting. Occasionally, if I'm asked, a review on an exhibition at the Uffizi. But mainly I stick to music reviews. I know more about music than I do about painting or architecture.'

'I wouldn't have guessed that from your analysis of architecture a few minutes ago.'

Farinelli smiled but said nothing.

'Well,' Cordelia went on, 'so tell me then, do you work for a particular paper?'

'For whoever is willing to pay me, in fact. I work freelance.' He shrugged. 'It pays the rent.'

'I think you're being modest.'

'Perhaps I am,' he said with a sudden grin. 'They keep offering me salaried jobs and an office, but I prefer to be my own man. I like working alone.'

'Will you be covering the Monteverdi festival next week in Teatro Comunale?' she asked, remembering the note from Maestro Marchesi that lay on her desk upstairs. She was dying to share her secret with someone who would appreciate what it meant to her.

'Of course, yes,' Farinelli said. 'After all, it's a rare event when a native son who's become so famous in the world agrees to make music for those of us he has left behind.'

Was it her imagination or was there a hint of bitterness in his voice? She hesitated fractionally, then said:

'I wrote to Maestro Marchesi from the States and asked him for an interview. He's agreed to see me on Tuesday after the rehearsal. Isn't that wonderful?'

She felt, rather than saw, Farinelli's frame stiffen. For a moment he said nothing, searching for the right words. Finally he said:

'I'm very pleased for you, Signorina Sinclair, but be careful. Marchesi is not a nice man. You're an attractive woman and there are many stories about him.'

FIVE

THE OPENING BARS of Mozart's *Nozze di Figaro* filled the air like a scent of waking flowers. Maestro Antonio Marchesi detested the cacophony of the world—the sound of telephones and automobile horns, the yapping of dogs, the puling cries of children—and he had done everything in his power to insulate himself against its intrusion into the imperial tenor of his existence. In the foreign hotel suites where he stayed when he was on tour, the telephone never rang: messages were delivered by uniformed minions on soundless feet. At home, the jangle of the devil's instrument had been permanently silenced. Telephone calls were routed through the sophisticated computer system that controlled the environment of his villa in the hills beyond Fiesole. Marchesi was a man wealthy enough to employ technology to neuter technology. When a call was received at the villa, Mozart was electronically summoned—a performance conducted by Marchesi himself with the Vienna Philharmonic. He was especially fond of it because the recording, lavishly praised by critics when it first appeared, had launched his international career.

Marchesi closed the biography of Gluck he was perusing and pressed a button on the inset electronics panel in the table at his side carved from a single piece of Pietrasanta marble. Mozart abruptly ceased and the line was opened.

'Pronto,' he said.

'Tony?'

'Who is that?' Marchesi demanded.

'It's Nikki,' a lugubrious voice announced through the miniaturized Bang and Olufsen speakers built into the chair's headrest.

'What do *you* want?'

'What the hell do you think I want!' the voice snapped back waspishly. 'The bastard has killed Umberto! First Mora, then Rosso—now Cafferelli.'

'I read the papers,' Marchesi said, without interest.

'You're not worried?'

'No.'

There was a pause, then the voice, taking on a querulous edge, said:

'We have to talk, Tony. Now. But not on the phone.'

'I'll be in all evening,' Marchesi said without enthusiasm. 'You can come over if you insist on it.' His tapered finger, hovering like a hawk over the bank of buttons, descended, breaking the connection.

'Damn,' he muttered.

He marked his spot in the Gluck biography and laid it aside, then crossed the room decorated with furniture inspired by Moorish design to the built-in bar and splashed two fingers of bourbon into a crystal tumbler. He had acquired a taste for American whisky on tours of the United States. Now, he imported the stuff by the case.

The prospect of seeing Strozzi again filled him with irritation. He hadn't seen or thought about Nikki Strozzi for years and he had no desire to see or think about him now. Strozzi belonged to the forgotten past—a past Marchesi had no desire to revisit.

He walked to the window and pressed a tile in the floor with the toe of his Armani loafer. The curtains before him parted, revealing on the other side of eight-foot panes a panoramic view of the Arno valley. It was growing dark and the orbed cross on the lantern of Brunelleschi's masterpiece, seven kilometres away in the Piazza del Duomo, caught the last stray rays of the dying sun. The vast and ugly suburbia that surrounded the city was invisible now, its presence transformed into a coronal of light encircling the darker core of the old historical centre like a milky-way of winking stars. The curtains were seldom open in daylight. The distant desecration of factories and petrol stations, apartment blocks and squalid suburban housing, offended the maestro's sensitive and discriminating eye. At night, when the offensive landscape was obliterated by darkness, the view was at last tolerable.

The formal garden of cypress and sculptured yew that stretched below him was lost in gloom. As an additional precaution, given the circumstances, the grounds were now patrolled by guards armed with machine guns and accompanied by dogs. They were out there somewhere in the shadows. Marchesi resented their necessity, the restriction of freedom their presence implied. Perhaps the infra red motion-detectors that ringed the villa would have sufficed, but Marchesi was not about to take that chance. Not with all that was happening.

'Damn it all anyway!' he muttered again.

He drained his glass with a jerk and stalked back to the pool of light cast by the halogen floor lamp behind his leather chair. Every movement bespoke vexation. He sat down and turned a dial on the console at his elbow. The room brightened as if by magic, lit by fluorescent tubes set behind valances near the ceiling. He punched another button and moments later a voice said:

'Gate Security. Bruno speaking.'

Marchesi said:

'I'm expecting a Signor Nicòlo Strozzi. Clear him through when he arrives.'

The house was a sixteenth-century villa, designed by Buontalenti and set on a pine- and olive-covered hillside outside Fiesole, with Florence in the distance. Marchesi had bought it with the hefty royalties he received from his Columbia and Deutsche Grammophon recording contracts. Money had never been an obstacle. Leaving the Renaissance exterior largely untouched, he had modernized the spacious interior with contemporary furnishings and all of the most modern conveniences, including climate control. The renovations had taken two years and cost a fortune. Marble had come from quarries in Carrara and Pietrasanta, exquisite granite from Peru, handloomed carpets from Iran, black walnut panelling from Canada, handtooled leather for the furniture from Morocco. And every inch of the structure, from the central *torre* housing his sound-proofed study to the courtyard loggia where speakers delivered digitalized versions of his performances, was crammed with the latest marvels of electronic wizardry. From his study chair or from his Victorian brass bed he could check that doors were locked, open or close skylights, raise or lower the temperature and humidity of the purified air, run his morning bath at precisely 39 degrees celsius, or warn the kitchen staff to expect him for breakfast—all with the twist of a dial or press of a button. There was no comfort or luxury that he had overlooked.

Once the guards at the front gate had been alerted, there was nothing to do but wait. Marchesi was not accustomed to waiting and he was not good at it. He was used to being waited on. He tried to pick up the thread in the Gluck biography but found he couldn't concentrate and tossed the book aside. He riffled irritably through a picture magazine with no better success, flipping its leaves with convulsive impatience. Time dragged its weary length along and it was nearly an hour later when an obese figure in a white silk suit was shown into the glass-fronted study by the maid. Although the evening was cool, Strozzi was sweating profusely and clutched in his hand a rumpled cambric handkerchief with which he continually mopped at his ample brow. Except for a horseshoe fringe of lank hair prematurely aged to a sickly yellowish white, he was as bald as a billiard ball. The beady ratlike eyes, deeply sunken in the folds of his fleshy face, held a look of perpetual surprise, as if he'd been caught—or expected to be caught—with his hand in the till. He was the same age as Marchesi, but his porcine features and dishevelled appearance—although his clothes were expensive—clashed sharply with his host's deceptively youthful look and elegantly fitted smoking-jacket. Both men were fifty-three.

Marchesi rose and crossed to the bar. 'It's been a long time, Nicòlo,' he said. 'You'll have a drink, I suppose?'

Strozzi lowered himself gingerly into a camel-saddle chair, half-expecting it to collapse under the stress.

'Glenfiddich, if you have any,' he grunted.

Marchesi returned with the drinks. 'So, what's on your mind?'

'Pistocchi, of course. We have to do something.'

'Like what?'

'Like *find* the bastard, for chrissake!' Strozzi's face was suddenly beet red.

Marchesi crossed his legs, smoothing a crease in the fabric. 'Take it easy, Nikki. You'll bring on a seizure,' he said drily. 'Did you try the telephone directory?'

'You always were a patronizing bastard, Tony. Even at school.'

'Some things never change, do they?'

Strozzi sipped at his drink and worked at suppressing his rage. 'In fact,' he said, 'I've put a private detective on the case.'

'With what result?'

'Nothing so far. Not a sign.'

Marchesi shrugged. 'Maybe he changed his name. Or moved out of town.'

'Possibly.' Strozzi shifted his bulk and the chair beneath him creaked ominously. 'You don't seem to give a damn where he is.

Why is that, Tony, I wonder? Is it because you spend so much time in France and Germany that you think he can't get at you?' He added with a leer: 'What's to stop him getting on a train?'

Marchesi shrugged. 'I've taken precautions. I'd advise you to do the same.'

God knew, Nicòlo Strozzi could afford the expense of hiring protection. He was chairman of the Banco di Firenze and sat on the boards of a dozen corporations. He lived like a Medici prince. Yes, life had treated him extremely well, considering where he had started.

'Damn it all, Tony,' Strozzi exploded, 'he's killed three of us! Slit their bloody throats! And he *crucified* Cafferelli, for God's sake! What does it take to put the wind up you?'

He wiped his forehead, then dabbed convulsively at his neck with the dank cloth.

Marchesi said evenly:

'Symbolic gestures. Puerile attempts motivated by revenge and envy. And besides, you're dramatizing, Nicòlo—you always were prone to histrionics. Cafferelli wasn't crucified; he was hooked over a cross. There's a difference.'

'He's dead all the same. They're all *dead*,' Strozzi said savagely.

'They were careless,' Marchesi said with a shrug, 'especially Cafferelli. He should have known better. When the others turned up dead, he must have known he might be next. He should have been prepared. Cafferelli was a fool.'

'You really do think you're invulnerable, don't you, you arrogant swine?'

Marchesi smiled thinly. 'Swine is not a seemly word in your mouth, Nikki.'

Strozzi's mouth opened and closed soundlessly several times as if he were hyperventilating. When he gained control of his voice once more, he said darkly:

'He's down to only two of us now, Tony. Eenie, meenie, miney, mo— One of us is next.'

'Us—' Marchesi threw his head back and gave a harsh laugh. 'I Camerati dell'arte! The Companions of Art! What a bloody farce!'

'We were young and idealistic,' Strozzi said defensively

'We were young fools, Nikki,' boomed Marchesi. '*Raving, bloody fools*— Let me pour you another drink, my friend!'

He rose with a flourish, snatched up Strozzi's glass, and strode to the bar, his shoulders shaking with mirth at the absurd memory of the Camerati dell'arte.

Strozzi said quietly: 'I intend to go to the police.'

Marchesi wheeled, his black eyes flashing fury.

'If you do,' he said in a low, guttural growl, 'I'll cut your bloody throat myself!'

'I have as much to lose as you do,' Strozzi protested, taken aback.

Marchesi's lip curled into a dangerous sneer. 'No—no, you do not,' he said, spitting the words like bullets between clenched teeth. 'Not by a long shot, my fat friend. I *earned* everything I have, everything you see around you—earned it with sweat and genius.' He pressed the glass into Strozzi's hand with a warning squeeze. 'You clawed and cheated your way to the top with cunning and deceit.'

Strozzi said weakly:

'The point remains: we both have a great deal to protect.'

'I have more, Nikki,' Marchesi hissed. 'Much more. I have a *reputation.*'

SIX

By ALL RIGHTS, Cordelia knew, she should be dead on her feet. She had been awake now for how long? Twenty-six hours was it? Twenty-seven? Something like that. Yesterday at this time she was boarding a plane in Chicago. She was tired all right—she had to be—but her body refused to accept the urgent messages being sent to it by her brain. Her body was still operating on American Central time and wanted action, not sleep. And in the end, like appeasing a colicky child, there was no choice but to give it its way. She decided to go out and see what night life in Florence was like. It was just after ten-thirty and the discos would be moving into high gear. Maybe a couple of drinks in a smoky room watching people gyrate on a dance floor would make her feel like sleeping. It was worth a try anyway.

L'Esperimento was a club near Palazzo Corsini. It was recommended highly in the guide book she consulted and it wasn't far away. She found it easily. It was on the top floor of a commercial building, over a row of shuttered businesses that included a dental clinic and a travel agency. She was alerted to its presence more than a block away by the pulsing rhythm of a bass beat which reached her ear along the quiet street like the crump of distant mortar rounds. There was a neon sign over the door and she took the elevator to the fourth floor. At a table outside the entrance to the disco, a diminutive creature in a black tube-dress and coral lipstick admitted patrons. She was flanked by a behemoth in sunglasses, obviously the bouncer, whose muscular torso was severely testing the seams of his mauve silk shirt. There was, the girl said, a cover charge for men but not women. Gender, it seemed, still had its advantages—and Cordelia didn't quite know how she should feel about that. Could she be truly independent if, at the same time, she accepted special privileges based merely on the accident of her sex? She brushed the problem aside. This was hardly the time or place to wrestle with the paradoxes of gender equity.

When she pushed open the frosted glass doors and entered the club, it was immediately apparent why it was called L'Esperimento. The style was art deco and reminded her of a film set from the Poirot mysteries that were popular on PBS television back home. Shiny chromium railings separated a sunken dance floor from the elevated area surrounding it, where patrons drank and chatted between musical sets at little marble-topped tables scattered among potted palms. But Poirot's ordered, genteel world stopped abruptly with the potted palms. Overhead, a star-burst strobe fired pulses of white light on dancers twisted into surreal postures and frozen briefly in stark relief like images in a jerky film. The walls all around the room were covered with eerily enlarged photographs of the human eye. At the far end on a small stage a band was playing—two electric guitars, a keyboard synth, and drums—dwarfed by a black mountain of Marshall Stack amplifiers, and to one side, in a recessed shell of illuminated glass-bricks, was the bar. At the moment, the band was giving its own rather peculiar rendition of *Zooropa,* a spooky song by U2. It was the sort of place, Cordelia thought, where a hip Mr Spock might think of taking someone like a funky Miss Marple for a night out on the town.

She found an empty table overlooking the dance floor, and in the twinkling of an eye a young man wearing a black T-shirt and canvas change-apron materialized at her side.

'What'll it be then?' he shouted over the din, placing a napkin and clean ashtray on the table before her with a flourish.

Cordelia ordered a dry vermouth with an olive.

It was quite a change in scene from the afternoon tea in Signora Ghilberti's stuffy apartment. A sudden thought struck her and she wondered if Signora Ghilberti—or even someone, for that matter like Signor Farinelli—had any idea that such places as L'Esperimento even existed. Some perverse sense of comedy presented her imagination with the ludicrous image of Signora Ghilberti seated across from her at the table, stiff and stricken under the flashing strobe, wincing at the driving beat of U2 and sipping convulsively at her cup of Earl Grey. She found herself laughing out loud. Not that anyone around her noticed, of course, the decibel level in the room being what it was. It would, she thought, taking the idea a step further, be like trying to drag off her old Aunt Hattie, who went to the supermarket in a mink stole, to sit through an evening at a demolition derby or a hog-calling competition. Trapped in the little hermetically-sealed jars of their lives, people like that had a narrow, parochial view of the world. It would do them all good to get out for a change and see something on the other side of the glass. If I had the nerve, Cordelia told herself, I'd bring Signora Ghilberti here some time—yes, I really would. But in real life, of course, she could never have summoned up that much courage. Only in imagination.

The waiter brought her drink and she sat for a time nursing it, watching the dancers twist and jerk on the parquet below. She hadn't been in a place like this for years. Not since her undergraduate days so long ago, when Motown was still 'in' and Diana Ross and the Supremes were hot items on the pop charts. The world had changed since then—had, in a sense, passed her by. The breezy crowd around her, she couldn't help but notice, were loose and carefree in the arrogant way of insouciant youth. They dressed differently, danced differently, thought differently about themselves and the world than she did. They were free and independent spirits. They had no past to regret and did not feel the future as a burden; the only reality that mattered to them was the present moment—this instant, this disco, this current dance. They were travellers without baggage in the continuum of space and time, and their noisy, turbulent presence around her made every one of her thirty-two years weigh like a millstone. She felt conspicuous and out of her element. It seemed suddenly a foolish delusion to pretend that she could somehow turn the clock back and start her life over—

I'm getting maudlin, she thought. I always get stupid and insecure when I'm overtired.

But the monster, once roused, was not so easily subdued. A gnawing paranoia swept over her before she could intercept it. She felt alone and naked in that gathering of sunny youth. She felt certain she was an object of their pity and ridicule, giggled at behind her back like an old maiden aunt chaperoning at a slumber party. She wanted to melt through the floor, to—

Stop it! her mind shouted. Stop being so damned silly! No one is staring. No one has even noticed you. Look around. They're all into their own thing, their own private space.

Reason gained the upper hand and the monster crept sulking back into its lair.

'Like a refill?' a voice asked.

The T-shirted waiter stood beside her. With a start Cordelia realized she was clutching an empty glass. She didn't remember having finished it.

'Yes,' she said, 'the same again.'

She decided to splash some water on her face. The band finished off a hit by The Clue with a thunderous chord and started on a piece she recognized as being by a group back home called Big Audio Dynamite. She owned the tape and occasionally played it on her Sony Walkman when she went jogging.

She rose and wove her way among the crowded, smoky tables and arching palm fronds to the door marked *Gabinetti* over the stylized logos of male and female figures. When the door closed behind her, the sound of the band receded to a muted pounding, like the roar of a distant surf. The tiled washroom was empty—or so it seemed at first—but one of the cubicles was closed and the tart bitter-sweet tang of marijuana hung heavily in the air. Cordelia smiled to herself. Some things, it seemed, never changed.

She checked her appearance in the mirror over a row of scallop-shaped basins. The eyes were tired but otherwise, she thought, everything was pretty much as it should be. She wasn't twenty-two any more, it was perfectly true, but she was a pretty good looking thirty-two. She pursed her lips and squinted narrowly at the image in the glass. No, she thought—no, I'm really *not* out of place at a disco—even if I'm not poured into a size four satin sheath and tricked out like a trollop. She ran a comb through her hair and freshened her lipstick. Good, she thought—yes, good enough. She gave her reflected image a curt nod and turned on her heel. She was going back out there. She was going to have that second drink and soak up the atmosphere of the place, and then—since it was almost midnight—she was going to go back home and fall into bed and sleep like a baby.

When she emerged from the washroom, the band had stopped playing. They were taking a break and in their absence the sound system was playing recorded music at half the decibels. The reduction in volume was almost like silence. When she reached her table, she found a fresh drink waiting for her—and so was something else.

He looked up and grinned, but did not rise, as she approached.

Her first thought was that the place was full and she would have to share her table. But then she noticed an empty table nearby. Had he not realized, then, that this table was taken? She took her seat and gave him a quizzical look.

'I was watching you,' he said, 'before you went out. You're here by yourself. I'm alone. It seemed natural to be friendly.' He raised his glass in a salute. 'My name's Gino.'

He was twenty-one, she guessed, possibly twenty-two. A stripling. Dark and curly-haired, he was angular in frame and feature and was probably quite tall. It was impossible to be certain about height, however, with him slouching in the chair as he was. He wore a loose-fitting shirt of bright blue silk, open at the neck, with a floppy, over-sized collar. Around his throat on a heavy gold chain hung a garish medallion, also in gold, in the shape of an astrological symbol. It might have been Taurus but Cordelia wasn't up on her zodiac well enough to be sure. Taurus though, it struck her, would have been singularly appropriate. On his left forearm, just above the wrist, was a tattoo of what seemed to be a cherry with an arrow through it. His whole being, as he sat awaiting her response, exuded a smug air of insolent self-confidence and raw animal vitality.

Cordelia folded her hands in front of her. 'Well, Gino,' she said, meeting his eyes, 'my name is Cordelia—and, as it just so happens, I'm alone by choice.'

Gino was unfazed. He had apparently met this sort of objection before. His strategy was blunt and direct, verging on brutality. He said:

'I find you very attractive.'

Cordelia sipped her drink and looked over the deserted dance floor. There was no sign that the band was in any hurry to return.

'I'm not in the market,' she said, 'but thanks all the same for the compliment.'

Gino changed his tactics. 'You're English,' he said. 'I can hear it in your accent.'

'American,' she corrected.

'Even better,' he said. 'I like Americans. From New York?'

'Chicago.'

A wide grin split his face. 'Ah—Chicago,' he said. 'Al Capone. *Ra-ta-ta-tat! Ra-ta-ta-tat!*'

Gino had a lot to learn.

Cordelia fished the olive out of her drink and sucked on it meditatively, ignoring his presence. Maybe he'd take the hint and buzz off.

But Gino was nothing if not persistent.

'How long have you been in Firenze?' he inquired, fingering his medallion for strength.

Cordelia stared in fascination at the empty dance floor and ignored him.

'My uncle owns a taxi,' he pressed on, bloodied but unbowed. 'A big Buick Roadmaster. It's the only one in the city. I could pick you up some afternoon and drive you around to see the sights. The San Lorenzo market...the Visarno Hippodrome...with a bit of luck I might be able to pick us up a couple of tickets for the football finals on Sunday at the Stadio. I can't promise anything, mind you. They've been sold out for weeks. But my uncle knows a guy who—'

Apparently Gino's truncated sense of Florentine culture didn't extend to the paintings in the Uffizi or the world-famous collection of Michelangelo statues in the Galleria dell' Accademia.

'Look,' Cordelia interrupted, turning to face him. 'I'm not the least bit interested in football, I'm afraid. And to tell you the truth, Gino, I'm not the least bit interested in you either.'

He said lamely, as if the meaning of her words needed time to sink in:

'Well, if you wanted then, we could take some wine and pizza up to the camp grounds at Fiesole. The view from the top is very beautiful, very panoramic. Especially in the evening when the sun is setting.'

Cordelia stared at him hard. 'No.'

'Perhaps in a day or two you will change your mind, yes?'

'It's not in the cards, Gino. Not tomorrow, not the next day, not ever.'

Could this creature not understand a plain message, even when it was delivered by mallet? Perhaps he and his uncle's Roadmaster had never been turned down before. Well, there was a first time for everything.

'Let me at least buy you a drink,' he proposed.

'I don't think that would be a good idea,' Cordelia said coldly. 'I think it would be a better idea if you took your drink and went back to your own table. I really would prefer to be alone.'

When he had finally shuffled off, Cordelia heaved a sigh of amused relief. It had turned into a more eventful evening than she had anticipated.

Well, well, well—she thought to herself—how about that! My first gigolo and I've only been in Italy a day. It looks like you've still got what it takes, old girl. It was a silly thought, but she didn't even try to suppress the smile of flattered pleasure she felt forming on her lips.

The members of the band were moving back toward the stage for the next set. Cordelia looked at her watch. It was nearly twelve thirty. She would listen to a song or two while she finished up her drink, she decided, and then start for home. Home. It was odd to think of the little flat where she had never yet spent even a single night as being 'home,' but there was no doubt a lot of strange things that she was going to have to get used to in the days to come.

Suddenly, she felt very tired. Whether it was an effect of the vermouth or a result of the effort expended in fending off Gino's doggedly puerile advances, she didn't know. Perhaps it was a little of both. In any case, the long day seemed to overtake her in a single stride and an overpowering desire for sleep fell like a down-filled blanket over the idling engine of her restless spirit. A line of poetry—she couldn't remember where it was from— flashed through her mind: *Tomorrow to fresh woods and pastures new.* The poet had put it well. Tomorrow was a new beginning and she was ready to meet it.

She drained the last swallow in her glass and picked up her bag. The band were on stage tuning their instruments as she headed for the exit. In the half-light near the door she caught a fleeting glimpse of a blue silk shirt and gold medallion. He was leaning cavalierly against the wall locked in earnest conversation with a dark-haired girl in a red dress. Good luck to you, Gino, she thought, shaking her head. And in her heart she felt only the tiniest twinge of what might have been, if she hadn't known better, a pang of irrational jealousy.

SEVEN

FRANCESCO PISTOCCHI was an angry man, a man consumed by a burning and implacable hatred for those who had wronged him. He was also a simple man—in many ways, even a childish man. His emotions were blunt and visceral desires: not much more, in fact, than savage instincts. There were no grey tones in the palette of his emotional life. His response to events was confined to the primal imperatives of white and black—love and hate—and love was a feeling he had not experienced for many, many years. What he understood best was hatred—and in particular the deep psychological satisfaction of revenge. The wonderful reality about revenge, as he knew from experience, was that it worked. Unlike most other solutions, it actually did make you feel better.

He was in an olive grove on an isolated slope outside Fiesole. He was sitting on the ground with his knees drawn up to support his elbows and he was staring across the valley through a pair of powerful binoculars at a villa on the far side. The curtains were open and the lights were on in the central tower of the big house. Inside the lavishly-appointed room into which he stared, two men were talking—and Francesco Pistocchi, although he could not hear their words, knew what they were talking about. They were talking about him.

A breeze fanned the leaves in the trees around him and picked at the lapels of his light jacket. Overhead, a three-quarter moon sailed through a sea of scudding cloud and her beams threw moving, fantastic shadows over the retreat where he sat silently watching.

He increased the magnification and brought one of the figures into sharp focus. The man was seated and had a drink in his hand. He was grotesquely obese with a fringe of yellowish-white hair and he was dressed in an expensive white suit. So powerful were the binoculars that even from a distance of several hundred yards Pistocchi could see the sweat beaded on the man's brow and the frightened eyes shifting from side to side like those of a hunted animal.

A wolfish grin split his lips. It was what he wanted; it was the effect he had worked toward producing. He wanted them to feel the terror of death stalking them. He wanted them to know that out there somewhere he was waiting for them—that he had first taken care of Mora and Rosso and Cafferelli—and that he was coming next for them. It gave him pleasure to see their fear. He had saved them until last precisely for this purpose: to watch them squirm. He had saved them until last because they had been the ring-leaders, because in that chapel long ago, when they had destroyed his life, it had been the two of them—Strozzi and Marchesi—who had been the ones in charge. And now the time had come for them to pay. Sometime when they least expected it he would suddenly appear—and in the terror of that instant they would know that, for the wrongs they had done to him, the angel of death had come for them. His coming would be a shock, but it would not be a surprise: they would, of course, be expecting him. He had prepared the moment for them. He had led them step by step through the deaths of the others to the moment of their own death. It had been a nice touch, he thought, to think of hanging Cafferelli's body in the chapel where it all had taken place so long ago. He was glad he had gone to the trouble. It was a gesture that had the pleasing effect of turning the terror up another notch.

Pistocchi lowered the magnification and swept the binoculars over the dark and spacious grounds of Marchesi's estate. The grounds were surrounded by a three-metre wall fitted with infra-red motion detectors and the gate opening onto the public road was manned by a pair of armed guards. More guards, he knew, accompanied by dogs, patrolled the lawns and gardens around the villa. He could not see them at night but he knew they were out there. Neither the wall nor the sensors presented a significant problem. Pistocchi was a powerful and agile, as well as a cautious and clever, man who was capable of scaling physical obstacles and foiling or simply avoiding electronic ones. The roving guards and dogs, however, were quite another matter. They introduced the element of chance, of an unexpected encounter on the other side of a dark bush or shadowed hedge. But then there were a variety of ways, when the time came, of dealing with those problems too.

Like Marchesi's villa, Nicòlo Strozzi's palatial retreat in the hills south of the city was an armed fortress. Pistocchi had watched the security precautions increase marginally after Mora's murder, then again—this time dramatically—after Rosso's body was found abandoned in his red Alfa Romeo in Piazza della Signoria. By that time, the three survivors of the Camerati dell'arte had begun to suspect that the murders were not entirely coincidental. Oddly, Cardinal Cafferelli, perhaps foolishly believing himself protected by a higher power, had taken no additional precautions. That had made Pistocchi's job an easy one.

He smiled at the memory. The cardinal had come back to his office late in the evening, as he invariably did before retiring, to check that the wall-safe was locked and to look over the list of appointments his secretary had made for him the next day. Pistocchi had been waiting with his razor behind the heavy velvet curtains. When the cardinal was seated at the desk, he had stepped silently up behind him. Cafferelli had struggled, but met death with a blind and thrashing terror unbecoming his profession, but there was no one in the empty building to hear his strangled cry and, being a man much smaller than his assailant, he had not struggled long. It had been a satisfying death. The only awkward part had been moving the body across the city from the Curial offices to the chapel at Santa Maria Novella. But Pistocchi had come prepared. Wearing an old coat and battered cap, he had loaded the corpse into a wheeled trash-can and pulled it through the quiet streets like a municipal employee on his nightly rounds. He was too insignificant for anyone to question or to remember. At the basilica, he had slipped in through a little-used side door whose bolt he had rigged earlier in the day with a length of nearly invisible fishing-line. It had been a flawless and masterfully executed plan, and the memory of it gave him considerable pleasure.

But there were other, even more significant pleasures awaiting him. The deaths of Strozzi and Marchesi were still to come.

No doubt they had been to the police. No doubt they had taken steps, especially when the death of Cafferelli left no doubt about the motive or the identity of the killer and his next victims, to track him down and deal with him. But Pistocchi was not worried.

They would never find him. It was impossible. Let them try! His cover was perfect. He didn't even exist.

With that thought, Francesco Pistocchi packed away his binoculars and slipped silently into the shadows of the concealing night. They would hear from him again soon enough.

ONE

PART TWO

The Maestro

THE TELEPHONE was answered on the first ring by a cop who looked unnervingly like Woody Allen after a prolonged course of steroids and weight-training. Head and body seemed unrelated, the composite result of some bizarre and tragic experiment in transplant surgery, and his nickname, Thal, was thought—though no one actually *knew*—to refer to the drug his mother was assumed to have swallowed in mega-doses over the nine months or more of his gestation. The scene around him was a beehive of activity. On other desks other telephones sounded and were swiftly silenced, and the air crackled with commands, questions, clacking typewriters, rustling papers, and occasionally the petulant whistle of the fax machine. The operations room on the second floor of the Questura was in full cry after the confederacy of crime. A losing battle, but one being gamely contested despite the odds.

'It's for you,' Thal announced, extending the receiver in one of his great paws.

At the adjoining desk, where photocopies of bank records blanketed the surface like leaves in the aftermath of an autumn storm, Detective Giorgio Bruni looked up with a scowl. His jacket was slung over the chair-back, his tie hung loose around his neck, and there were dark circles under his eyes. The cast in his left eye made it impossible to tell if the grimace he shot was aimed at the proffered instrument or the man who held it. It had been a long day and it was only ten a.m.

'Who is it?'

'Your wife.'

'Tell her I'm dead.'

'He says he's dead,' Thal said into the mouthpiece, then grinned and extended the receiver again:

'She says you will be if you don't take the phone. It's important.'

'It always is,' Bruni sighed and stretched for the receiver. 'What is it, Tessie?'

'I had to take Kiki to the hospital.'

'What for this time.'

His son, age three-and-a-half, was an out-patient regular. He was accident prone. The nurses and doctors knew him on sight. Kamikaze Kiki, they called him.

'He stuffed the cat in the washing machine.'

Bruni bowed his head and shut his eyes. 'Tell me what happened,' he said in a martyred voice.

'There isn't that much to tell. He's okay. I just thought you should know, that's all.'

'I'm listening. What happened?'

'Well, he moved a chair while I was on the phone with your mother—she's coming over for dinner Thursday, by the way—and climbed onto the machine. He had the cat in my canvas shopping bag. Don't ask me how he managed it, I don't know. Anyway, he stuffed them both through the hatch. When the cat twigged to what was going on, she bolted and knocked Kiki backwards into the sink. He could have drowned. The sink was full of water.'

Bruni massaged his temples with thumb and forefinger, his head bowed, his eyes still closed. 'So the machine was running at the time?'

'Rinse cycle. Second load of coloureds. Blood and suds everywhere.'

'Christ. Go on.'

'He split his head open on the taps. It took twelve stitches to close. He's also covered with scratches.'

'Any permanent damage?'

'No. Just stitches and scratches. He was lucky.'

'How's the cat?'

'Clean.'

'Poor little mite,' Bruni said. Kiki's head had so many scrapes and stitches it looked like an old World Cup soccer ball. Twelve more stitches wouldn't matter much in the long run.

'Which little mite?' she asked suspiciously.

'Kiki, of course.'

'Just checking.' Satisfied, she changed the subject: 'So, have you caught our murderer yet?'

'Which one?'

'The one who killed Cardinal Cafferelli.'

'I'm working on it.'

'What does that mean?'

'It means, not yet. I'm working on it. Soon.'

At the dinner table over the pasta and in bed after love-making they made a habit of talking over cases he was working on. Tessie was a good sleuth. She'd read every mystery novel in the local library—many of them more than once—and had waded, too, through at least half a dozen leatherbound tomes (without pictures) on criminal psychology. He admired her for that. She was full-bottle on motives and methods. There was nothing she didn't know about guns and poisons. She also understood in depth the intricate, twisted workings of the homicidal mind. Over the years, most of his best ideas had really been hers, though of course he'd never been able to admit it out loud. She was a lateral thinker, like Carlo Arbati. Giorgio's mind worked in straight, unswerving lines; he was a plodder. Tessie should have been the detective and made him stay home with Kiki. And the cat.

'You sound testy,' she said.

'I'm not testy,' he snapped. 'I'm busy. Up to my ears.'

Lately, there hadn't been much talk or much love-making, for the simple reason that they hadn't seen much of one another. Three unsolved murders in as many months, all of them prominent figures. There was a ton of pressure from upstairs for a solution. The politicians and the press were crying for an arrest. Giorgio spent long days at the office, and when he finally staggered home at night, often not before ten, he was too tired for anything but sleep. Tessie complained she was the only widow on the street with a living husband. She had a point. She missed the long talks, he knew—along with everything else. They both did.

'So, what else is new? You're always busy,' she said. 'Tell me about the case. I'm bored, Giorgio. My life is going to hell in a hand-basket. I'm dying to talk to somebody who can manage words over two syllables.'

'Where's Kiki? Remember what happened to him while you were gassing with my mother.'

'He's sleeping. The doctor gave him a sedative. Talk to me, Giorgio.'

Bruni shot a poisoned look at Thal who was listening in on them while pretending to work. He cupped his hand around the mouthpiece and said:

'I can't talk on the phone, Tessie, you know that. Not about police business.'

'Speak to me, lover,' she said seductively. 'Blow in my ear.'

'Just a minute,' he said. He thrust a sheaf of documents across at Thal. 'Take these down to reprography. Three copies. Wait for them. Oh—and pick me up a coffee from the canteen on your way back. Black, one sugar. Take your time.'

Thal scooped the papers up and loped off, beaten, his knuckles inches from the floor.

'Who was that?' she asked.

'Thal. He was eavesdropping. I sent him off on an errand.'

'He gives me the creeps. A rocket scientist's head on a gorilla's body. It's not natural.'

'He gives everybody the creeps. That's why we keep him off the streets.'

She said: 'So, tell me about the case. What did you find out about those big deposits in the cardinal's cheque book?'

'Very interesting,' he said. 'As a matter of fact, I've got the evidence spread out right in front of me. We subpoenaed the bank records. Fifteen cheques in the past twelve months, all over ten million lire. And guess what? They all lead back, in one way or another, to organizations fronting for the Mob.'

She whistled.

'And you know what that means,' he said.

'Motive,' she said. 'It means somebody—namely, the Mob— had a motive to bump him off. And motive is everything. As far as the Mob is concerned, as we all know, means and opportunity are never allowed to stand in the way when there's murder to be done; the only thing those boys need is something they can con- strue as a plausible motive and the deed is as good as done.'

'Bingo,' he said, grinning from ear to ear. 'And that's not all.

It means Carlo's crazy hunch about a serial killer is a long way off the mark. We've turned up nothing so far in Mora's or Rosso's background to connect either of them with the Mob. Which means there's no link between the victims except the fact they all had their throats cut. No link, no case—and therefore no serial killer. For once, my love, I'm right and Carlo's wrong.'

'Let's hope you're right,' she said. She changed the subject—Arbati's hunches were too often spot on—and she didn't want Giorgio getting paranoid. She wanted him in a good mood. 'So, our friend Cardinal Cafferelli doesn't sound like a very nice man.'

'A truly nasty piece of work,' Bruni agreed. 'Not the sort you'd want to be doing business with, my love, I can tell you that. He had a grubby finger in just about every dirty pie there is. You name it—extortion, fraud, money laundering, even prostitution—and our boy Cafferelli was right in there. The records we took from his wall safe have turned out to be very revealing. You remember all that artwork I told you we found in his office?'

'A Gentileschi and a couple of Ghirlandaios.'

'Among other things,' Bruni nodded. 'Well, it turns out they were fenced from a heist at a little museum in Milan in 1976. Cafferelli probably picked them up for a song as a job lot.'

'Bastard.'

'But that's not the best of it. Wait till you hear the rest. The museum had originally bought the pieces at auction in 1968 from an anonymous owner working through an intermediary. So—who do you suppose that mystery seller turned out to be?'

'Not really! Cafferelli—?'

'Spot on, sweetheart. Bishop Umberto Cafferelli, acting on behalf of a private trust. It seems some wealthy parishioners from his parish-priest days named him sole executor of their estate and guardian of their twelve-year-old daughter. When the parents died in a plane crash, Cafferelli started selling off the assets before the bodies were even decently cold and diverting twenty per cent of the profits into his own accounts. He probably thought of it as a management fee for services rendered.'

'Benefit of clergy, I suppose,' Tessie said sarcastically. 'So, in other words, he ended up with the twenty per cent he skimmed from the original sale and, a few years later, the paintings he had sold off as well. Nice work if you can get it. He probably engineered the Milan job himself.'

'The thought had crossed my mind.'

'So he's been playing these little games for years then.'

'As far back as the records go,' Bruni said. 'The paper trail gets more complex and the sums involved get bigger as time goes on, but the pattern is the same. And then about a year ago he got mixed up with the Mafia. Before that, he seems to have been pretty much a loner.'

'And you figure, I take it, that he double-crossed his buddies in the Cosa Nostra, so they took they revenge by slicing open his neck.'

'Something like that. Most likely he was holding out on them— skimming off some of the profits on the way up to head office. It fits his *modus operandi*.'

'What about that notebook with the coded scribblings you found in his office? Anything there?'

Bruni shook his head. 'Nothing yet, but the boys in M.I. are working on it. I'd be willing to bet a month's pay though that those entries, once we crack them, will lead us straight to numbered accounts in Switzerland or the Cayman Islands. The cardinal was a very devious man with a taste for anonymous money.'

'I'm lonely, Giorgio,' she said suddenly. 'Come home early tonight for a change, why don't you,' she purred salaciously, 'and we can discuss the cardinal's crimes in a more comfortable place.'

A proleptic tremor rippled through Bruni's groin like the foretaste of a major event on the Richter scale. It had been a long time since they'd made the earth move. Too long. *Far* too long.

'I accept your offer, ma'am.'

'You know what I'm wearing right now?' she asked provocatively.

Bruni closed his eyes. 'Tell me.'

'You remember that black nightie set you bought for our first anniversary.'

'The one with the see-through lace across the front? The one you said you were too embarrassed to wear with the lights on?' Memory flooded back like a bursting dam. His breathing was low and shallow.

'That's the one. The top still fits.'

'What about the bottoms?'

'It's too hot for bottoms, my love.'

'Jesus!' Bruni groaned. When he caught his breath, he said: 'I could make it home for a quick lunch.'

'Save it, lover boy,' she said throatily. 'Just plan to be here for dinner for a change and to linger on afterwards over the dessert.'

Bruni swallowed hard. 'Why don't you take Kiki over to my mother's and leave him for the night. Maybe forever. He wakes up at the damnedest times.'

'Impossible. Tonight's your mother's canasta night and the place will be full of old biddies. Besides, you remember what happened the last time we left him there, right? How could you forget? Kiki thought her cork coasters were cookies and took bites out of three of them. She made it quite plain, as I recall, that she doesn't want him around the place unless he's muzzled and on a leash.'

'Damn.'

'Don't worry, everything's taken care of,' she said, and he could feel the wink come at him through the earpiece. 'The doctor gave me another sedative, just in case Kiki happens to need it during the night. He will.'

A sudden blood-curdling yowl shattered the background. It sounded as if a multiple crucifixion were getting under way.

'Gotta go,' she said hurriedly. 'He's found the cat. I'll keep the pots warm, lover,' she whispered. 'Don't be late.'

She rang off.

When Thal returned ten minutes later with the photocopies and juggling two styrofoam cups of coffee, Bruni was still in a state of anastomotic shock thinking about the bottomless black lace nightie. His eyes were glassy and his breathing laboured.

'Everything okay at home?' Thal asked. There was a worried look on his face.

Bruni look up blindly. 'Couldn't be better,' he managed. 'Kiki fell off the washing machine and split his head.'

Thal put the desk between them. 'Glad to hear it,' he said, wondering whether to take his chances with a lunatic or call at once for the men in the white coats.

TWO

CORDELIA SPENT the morning reading Jacopo Peri's *Musiche sopra l'Euridice* in the rare-book room at the university library. It was, she found, an agreeable spot to work in: spacious, quiet, slightly musty-smelling perhaps but in a pleasant, historical way. All in all, she thought, a place that was definitely conducive to study and the thinking of deep thoughts. Under a high and dust-streaked dome, light filtered down onto oak reading desks, shiny with age and human use rather than as a result of anything so mundane as furniture polish. The desks were circular, each partitioned into four sections, each section furnished with its own hooded lamp that threw out a little gloaming circle of light much like a shade. The floor was deeply carpeted to soak up sound and around the walls rose tall bookshelves whose upper reaches were accessed by rolling stepladders of carved mahogany that ran around the perimeter of the room on oiled rails. Like Sir Robert Cotton's famous library at Ashburnham House, the volumes were classified, not by the Dewey Decimal or Library of Congress systems, but in accordance with their proximity to the marble busts of the Roman emperors set in recessed niches around the walls. None of the books were permitted out on loan and not all of the holdings were on open display. The incunabula and other treasures were stored in fireproof, climate-controlled vaults underground, accessible only by the librarians, who delivered the required volumes, one by one and for a specified time, to the reading desks of those with special passes. Cordelia had arranged for her pass months in advance, her request to the chief librarian accompanied by an official letter from her university back home certifying that she was engaged in legitimate research and that her work required the resources of the rare-book room in Florence. The ticket had been waiting for her at the informatio... ...k when she had presented herself sharp at eight o'clock tha... ...ing, the hour when the library opened.

At ten-thirty, her morning's work finished, she retu...

little treatise to the circulation desk and left the library. It was a warm and balmy Mediterranean spring day. She walked across the campus, enjoying the sun, heading for the new glass-and-marble building that housed the music department. Her appointment with Professor Ecco was at eleven. The meeting had been arranged by her thesis supervisor at Northwestern who had once been a student of Professor Ecco. It was partly a courtesy call and partly also a way of giving her a friendly contact in case she needed help cutting through bureaucratic red tape. University administrations—as Julian Wain, her supervisor, had explained to her in painful detail—were like the government bureaucracies on which they were modelled: nobody you talked to ever knew anything, or where to find anything, or what to do about anything (especially your particular problem), or even cared for that matter whether you lived or died. The one thing you needed in order to survive in a modern university, he maintained, was a friend with clout in high places. And Ecco was the man to know in Florence. Although he hadn't seen him for twenty years, Wain remembered Ecco as a slicer of Gordian knots, a ruthless, seasoned champion in the battle against bureaucratic twiddling and incompetence. He would make sure she was well looked after, well treated by the functionaries and administrative assistants. As she climbed the steps to the main entrance of the music building, Cordelia hardly knew what to expect when she met the man himself. His reputation had preceded him. She was prepared, in fact, for virtually every personality type except the one she was actually about to encounter.

It was still early—only a quarter to eleven—and she killed time by wandering the halls, reading the nameplates on office doors. Many of the names, some quite eminent, she recognized. They made her think about the future. One day, she told herself, *her* name would be on such a door, and some dreaming graduate student would recognize it, and stop, and tell herself that one day *her* name, too, would appear on such a door. The idea made her smile. The hungry generations treading fast on one another's heels: a Darwinian vision of academe.

It was eleven o'clock precisely when she entered the outer office of Professor Ecco's suite. The room was a surprise. It wasn't at all what experience had taught her to expect the anteroom of an eminent professor's office to look like. She had imagined something intimate and homey—maybe not exactly a pipe-and-slippers setting but something at least warm and welcoming, with perhaps a battered, overstuffed easychair in red leather in a corner. What she met, however, was something reminiscent of the foyer of a public building. The room was large but contained little furniture: a utilitarian desk, a filing cabinet, and a potted hibiscus plant (rigorously trimmed) were dispersed over an otherwise unbroken acre of marble tile. The uniformity of the stark white walls was relieved briefly at one point by an abstract canvas—two brown lines and a fuchsia blob—that looked as if it had been dispatched under time pressure with a paint roller. It was as spartan and antiseptic a room as Cordelia had ever been in and it reminded her of those pictures in architecture magazines of empty spaces with two metal chairs and a halogen floor lamp that Danish designers take to be the apogee of elegance. Seated at the desk, a greying middle-aged gorgon wearing a silk blouse and a pair of dangling metal earrings that might (and probably did) belong to her daughter guarded the approach to the inner sanctum. Under a helmet of salt-and-pepper hair set in concrete, she sat rigidly in front of an IBM Selectric typewriter, her fingers skimming the surface of the keys at the speed of light. There was not a stray scrap of paper on the desk, not an article out of place anywhere, not a speck of dust in the room. Even the shiny leaves of the hibiscus appeared to have been recently polished.

Cordelia advanced to the desk and said:

'I'm Cordelia Sinclair, from the United States. Professor Ecco is expecting me, I believe.'

The woman's fingers froze in mid-arpeggio and she looked up, raking Cordelia with a sharp, sinister glance. 'He is, yes,' she said waspishly, as if she were a concert pianist and the sudden intrusion had thwarted her in the execution of a particularly arduous cadenza. 'He won't remember, though. I reminded him when he came in, of course. I go over his appointments with him every morning when he arrives. But that was well over an hour ago. I'm afraid you'll just have to go through it with him again.' She turned back to her work. The brachial synapses refired, the fingers sprang to life, and the typewriter ball whirred over the surface of the paper in a blur. 'Just go right in,' she said without looking up.

Cordelia tapped gently and pushed the door open, hardly knowing what to expect. The room was the antithesis of the one she had just left. It had apparently been the epicentre of a recent earthquake. Books, journals, papers overflowed the shelves, spilling onto the floor, the table, the chairs, the window sill. The desk was buried under two hundred pounds of paper, from which the head of a goose-necked lamp protruded, struggling valiantly up toward the light. The air in the room was dense, almost palpable, with the rich fumes of cavendish tobacco. A small, rotund figure in a three-piece suit, a curved Sherlock Homes pipe locked resolutely in his jaw, was down on both knees on the floor digging in a mountain of files. Hearing the door, he turned and lifted toward Cordelia a cherubic face, pink and genial, framed on either side by two magnificent tufts of white hair that sprouted, like hawthorn bushes in full bloom, from the smooth dome of his otherwise bald head.

'Professor Ecco?' Cordelia inquired.

'Yes,' replied the kneeling figure.

'I'm Cordelia Sinclair.'

His brow furrowed. 'Cordelia Sinclair,' he repeated slowly. Then, light dawning, he said: 'Yes, yes. I'm terribly sorry. The position has been filled.'

'From the United States,' she said helpfully.

He struggled to his feet, tugging his waistcoat down over a protruding midriff, and shook his head sadly. 'Dear, dear,' he said, 'such a long way for nothing. Goodness me.'

She tried again. 'Professor Julian Wain asked me to drop by. He sent you a letter to say that I was coming, I think.'

'Julian Wain,' Professor Ecco said, screwing his eyes in an effort to remember.

'He was a student of yours. About twenty years ago.'

'Twenty years. Dear, dear.'

'He was working on the early operas. His thesis was on Cavalli and Scarlatti.'

'Cavalli and Scarlatti, yes—'

'Their debt to Venetian church music.'

The penny dropped and the round face brightened. 'Julian Wain. Yes—yes, of course. Julian Wain. Wrote a wonderful dissertation—published by Möseler Verlag in Zurich, I believe. I've read most of what he's published since then too. A brilliant musicologist. I received a letter from him not long ago. He's somewhere in the States now, I think.' He riffled hopefully through some loose pages at the periphery of the slaughtered forest that lay heaped on his desk. 'I have it here someplace. You know Julian, do you?'

Cordelia suppressed a grin. 'Yes. He's supervising my thesis. I'm here for a semester doing research. He asked me to stop by and remember him to you. He has fond memories of his time in Florence. They were palmy days, he said.'

'Tall chap with exophthalmic eyes, prominent nose. Walks with a stoop,' Ecco said out of the blue, remembering.

Cordelia blushed. The bluntness of the description—which was deadly accurate—took her by surprise. Among undergraduates back home, Wain was known affectionately behind his back as Ichabod.

'Yes,' she said, feeling like a traitor. 'He still looks the same.'

'And he's well, you say?'

'Very well.'

'Married?'

'No.'

'And teaching where? Perhaps you said.'

'At Northwestern, outside Chicago.'

'Ah—'

They stood facing each other, like two actors on a Greek stage working awkwardly through a passage of stichomythia.

Suddenly, Ecco seemed to remember himself. 'Please,' he said, bustling to clear a chair for her. 'Dear, dear. How terribly thoughtless of me.' He looked around for a vacant place to deposit the armload of books he had gathered up from the chair, then conceded defeat and stacked them on an unoccupied patch of floor. Clearing a second chair for himself, he sat down and they peered at each other over a cluttered table. 'Now,' he said, 'you were saying you have come to Florence to research a thesis.'

Cordelia nodded. 'On the Camerata.'

'The Camerata, yes. Fascinating group. Undervalued.' He fished a Bic lighter from his waistcoat pocket and puffed vigorously on his briar, his round face and hawthorn-bush shocks of white hair swallowed briefly in a fog of blue smoke. Between puffs, he said: 'They should be—more studied—than they are. Pity really. Tell me—what sparked—your interest in them?'

Cordelia jumped at the chance to talk about her favourite topic.

'I think the fact that they *are* so undervalued,' she said eagerly, taking up the line of argument he had offered. 'There's a tendency to dismiss them too lightly as being no more than minor innovators of no real importance in the history of music—but really, you know, they were extremely important pioneers. Their contribution to the development of opera is absolutely seminal. Monteverdi and the composers who came later depend much more than people are prepared to admit on the theoretical groundwork they laid. I'm hoping my research will throw new light on their achievement and put it in a proper perspective.'

The smoke cleared and Ecco's cherubic physiognomy reappeared.

'A laudable aim,' he said, nodding. 'And Julian Wain is directing you, is he?'

'Yes.'

'Then you're in good hands.'

They chatted for an hour about her thesis and the book Ecco was writing on Renaissance madrigals, about Northwestern and Professor Wain, about Cordelia's impressions of Florence and the university library. Although it had begun badly, the visit was a great success. Professor Ecco was a delightful character, warm and witty, interested in her work, full of anecdotes of academic life—a kind of professorial Parson Adams. The hour positively flew by. When Cordelia finally thought to look at her watch, it was already past twelve.

'Oh, dear,' she said, standing, 'look at the time! I'm afraid I've taken up most of your morning.' She added with a smile, 'But it was delightful, professore, and thank you for making me feel so welcome.'

'After a shaky beginning, I'm afraid,' he said, a little sheepishly. 'I'm sorry about the confusion when you arrived. My memory for everyday things isn't what it used to be—and it was never very good. Oh, by the way,' he added with an impish grin, 'if I did have a job to offer, you'd have it. You interview extremely well.'

He walked her to the door. They made an odd couple: he, short, slightly rumpled, inclined to corpulence; she, tall, slender, elegant. Einstein and Aphrodite.

'You'll let me know, of course, if I can be of help in any way,'

he said. 'Sometimes the library can be obstinate about their incunabula. I could have a word with the chief librarian.'

'I will.'

He opened the door and extended his hand. 'I hope we'll meet
again, Signorina Sinclair. Your thesis is fascinating and I'd like
to know how you get on with it. You'll keep me posted, will
you?'

'Of course.'

In the outer office, the automaton of the keyboard had ceased
her labours and spread out her lunch. It consisted of an assortment
of plastic containers stuffed with celery, diced mushrooms, bean
sprouts, and tofu symmetrically arranged, like model structures in
a project in urban planning, around the periphery of a large paper
napkin placed exactly in the centre of the empty desk. To Cordelia's traditional eye, none of the offerings looked even remotely
appetizing. The woman, it was clear, was engaged in a game fight
against the ravaging encroachment of middle-age through the dra-
conian manipulation of diet. Her fountain of youth, it seemed,
depended entirely on watery vegetables and select chemical sub-
stitutes for the common condiments. It was a mystery to Cordelia
how anyone could survive on such meagre, tasteless fare. But
then, perhaps she supplemented it with chocolates and a secret
cache of French pastries on the side. It's what Cordelia would
have done.

'Ah—' the woman said, looking up when Cordelia appeared,
'so he's free at last, is he? Good. He has a luncheon meeting, you
know, with the dean in twenty minutes. He won't remember it of
course. I was afraid I was going to have to come in and pull him
out. He has no memory for these things. I simply don't know
what he'd do without me around to get him off to his appointments.' She dipped a forkful of bean sprouts into a container of
thin white sauce, then asked, 'How did you find him by the way?'

'Very engaging,' Cordelia replied, surprised by the question.

'Lucid?'

'Very.'

'Good,' the secretary said, uncorking a thermos of herbal tea
with a pop. 'Then everything should be fine. He's having one of
his good days. I'll phone ahead and tell the dean.'

Cordelia recognized the signs. The poor woman, doting and
pragmatic, had appointed herself guardian of the great man's af-

fairs, deeming him incompetent to tend them himself. He needed, she had decided, someone brisk and efficient to organize the administrivial minutiae of his life, leaving him free to think great thoughts. She was also, Cordelia sensed, deeply possessive and jealous. No doubt she was secretly in love with her employer, although she had not perhaps admitted the passion even to herself, and it was clear from her manner that she resented his receiving visits from attractive young women. But it was, Cordelia knew, a doomed infatuation. From what she had seen of him, she knew Professor Ecco was the sort of man who could get on perfectly well by himself. His absent-mindedness was a carefully tended trait. Since routine detail bored him, he had contrived to forget what others were always anxious to remind him of. But he was a man, too, who, in spite of appearances, had an extremely clear notion of how he intended his life to run, and there could be no presence (Cordelia knew) more detestable and more likely to foul the placid waters of his existence than that of an Efficient Female. She remembered the story her father liked to tell of the Classics professor in Australia whose secretary, while her boss was away on an archaeological dig in Greece, had rearranged all the books in his vast library according to their size and colour. She had grouped the small green ones together, then the small red ones, blue ones, and yellow ones—all the way up, through a rainbow of octavos and quartos, to a daunting row of anonymous black folios. On his return, for this grotesque invasion of his private world, the poor woman had, to her speechless surprise, been summarily dismissed. The thought made Cordelia, as she closed the door behind her, feel almost sorry for the sad creature whom she last saw reaching for the telephone to alert the dean of Professor Ecco's imminent arrival and his state (as she judged it) of temporary lucidity. One day, inevitably, the poor woman would overstep the bounds and, like the Australian professor's secretary, pay a terrible price. And who knows, Cordelia thought a little melodramatically, today might be that very day—

With that thought she turned and walked quickly away down the corridor, relieved to be heading out of harm's way. At the end of the hall she turned left and descended the main staircase whose curving inner side was dominated by a colourful mock-medieval mural of men and maidens playing various arcane musical instruments and passed out into the sunshine through a pair

of swinging glass doors. Once outside, she stood for a moment
contemplating what to do next, then started off back to the library.
She had taken only a dozen steps when her stomach growled and
she realized with a start that she'd hadn't eaten for hours. She
had been waiting, in fact, anxious to begin, on the library steps
when it had opened at eight o'clock that morning. Since then, she
hadn't given so much as a thought to food. Well, she told herself,
the body demands its due as much as the mind and it's time to
cater now to its needs. It had, after all, been nearly six hours since
she had eaten breakfast.

On an angled board under a parasol pine she found a map of
the campus and located the student cafeteria. It offered the simplest and most economical solution, but it wouldn't be elegant.
Campus eating-places were the same the world over and were, it
seemed, owned and run by the same mercenary crew of misan-
thropes. The staples were invariable: formica-topped tables, uncomfortable but indestructible plastic chairs, aluminium-foil ashtrays no one would bother to steal, flimsy plastic plates and
utensils, and unidentifiable culinary offerings ladled parsimoni-
ously out of stainless-steel tubs. It was no different, she discovered, in Florence. The cafeteria was a large, anonymous room
with an attached courtyard on the ground floor of the Student
Activities' building. Windows ran along one side and the walls
were painted with oblique bars of lime green and bright orange
in a geometrical pattern designed (it seemed) to stimulate peri-
stalsis in one way or the other. The plastic stack-chairs were
crowded with undergraduates in cut-away shorts and thongs, talking, smoking, chewing, gesturing, guffawing. Here and there, ignoring the mêlée around them, a studious loner had buried his
head in a book and was trying to read. The din reminded Cordelia
of a construction site, and over it all hung the sweet greasy smell
of what she eventually identified as sausages sizzling on an open
grill. The atmosphere of noisy production-line efficiency reminded her forcibly of why it was that she had so seldom patronized the student cafeteria back home.

She stopped at the door, having second thoughts, and nearly
turned away, then changed her mind and pressed resolutely forward. It wasn't, she decided, worth the time and hassle of leaving
the campus and searching out a quiet trattoria. All she wanted
was a quick bite and then to get back to the library. There was

an afternoon of stiff reading still ahead of her. She took a tray
from a metal rack and passed along a counter stacked with plastic-
wrapped sandwiches, croissants, apples and bananas, cubes of
cheese, and pieces of ubiquitous institutional pie. Nothing she saw
appealed to her, but nature demanded that she eat something.
Finally, she opted for an innocuous-looking cheese sandwich and
a bowl of what claimed to be minestrone soup served up by a
figure of indeterminate age and gender in a stained smock and
cap. She paid at the till, then found an empty table near the window. The scene around her was more than enough to annihilate
appetite. She had forgotten what undergraduates were like. The
image that rose unbidden in her mind—too quickly for her to
head it off—was that of John Belushi in *Animal House* slurping
up a quivering mound of jello with his lips directly off the plate.
The memory made her shudder.

With the heavy heart of a candidate for martyrdom, she un-
loaded her tray and lowered herself onto the moulded plastic seat
of a chair whose shade of lime-green matched the colour of the
walls. The pangs of hunger, if she had ever really felt them, had
long since disappeared. In spite of herself, her eyes were drawn
to the scene of universal mastication around her. How was it that
Joyce, she tried to remember, had described the dreadful customers in that restaurant in Dublin that he made Bloom stumble into
looking for lunch. *Swilling, wolfing, chewchewchewing gobfuls of
food, their eyes bulging, wiping treacly mouths.* Yes, that was
it—or something very close to it. Joyce's imagination had transformed them into Lestrygonians—guzzling, slavering cannibals.
She averted her eyes from the activity at the tables around her.
Maybe she *should* have taken the time to hunt out an off-campus
trattoria, someplace civilized, but it was too late now. She looked
down and made herself concentrate on the food in front of her.
Stoically, she swallowed the soup and nibbled mechanically
around the edges of her tasteless sandwich.

When she had finished, she emptied her tray into one of the
plastic refuse bins and quickly left the cafeteria, vowing never to
return. The sun and fresh air outside soothed her turbulent senses
like the first streaks of dawn after an escape from a nightmare.
She decided to take a circuitous route through the campus back
to the library, giving her stomach time to settle before she tried

to plunge into scholarship again. Fortunately, she remembered, there was a roll of Tums in her bag if she needed them.

The cobbled campus walks were almost empty—a few pedestrians, an occasional cyclist. The sun was hot and relaxing on her shoulders. Everything in Florence, she had noticed, closed down for a time in the early afternoon. She wandered slowly, aimlessly, her mind purring quietly. At an information kiosk she stopped and read the pasted notices. There were announcements for upcoming events and advertisements for people willing to type termpapers. The rape crisis centre was looking for volunteers. Three or four sheets with tear-away telephone numbers offered used course-texts for sale at reduced prices. It was all very much like home. A glossy poster announced the *Maggio Musicale Fiorentino* beginning at the end of the week with a Monteverdi festival in the Teatro Comunale. In the centre of the poster was a photograph of Maestro Marchesi, hair flying, baton flung up, eyes flaring, looking like a young Toscanini. The image sent a thrill down her spine. What was he like, she wondered, this legend she would soon be meeting in the flesh? Signor Farinelli, her downstairs neighbour, had warned her against him, suggesting he was a womanizer. But she'd dealt with that sort before! All she had to do was think of Gino and his uncle's Buick Roadmaster.

She let her mind go and, drifting, eddying, it circled back by some mysterious pathway of subconscious intent to the people she'd met in Signora Ghilberti's flat. In retrospect, they seemed, as their images rose again before her, an odd and unaccountable group. A coincidence of opposites. First, there was Signora Ghilberti, the landlady—an unrepentant imperialist clinging to a lost English girlhood and a dead Italian husband. Her past was her future, and Cordelia couldn't think of her without seeing in her mind's eye the proud, melancholy profile of Virginia Woolf: aloof and sensitive, haughty and yet at the same time infinitely sad, infinitely alone. The world around her had moved on, had grown older and changed, but Signora Ghilberti, locked in the inviolate citadel of dreams of days gone by, had not moved with it. She was too proud and too obstinate to change. She was a crusty anachronism of course, but there was also, Cordelia sensed, the heart of a warm and sensitive human spirit under the horny carapace of disdain that she chose to affect. The di Bancos were a much simpler matter. There was no ambiguity in her response to them: she had thoroughly disliked them both. Signor di Banco was an arrogant chauvinist and a boor; his wife, mousey and repressed, was halfway herself responsible for her own sorry state. She should have left him years ago. Poor Lydia: she was unhappy—that was obvious. So, why then did she stay with him? There was no possible reason, Cordelia thought with a pity bordering on contempt, except for Lydia's own weakness of will. It was her own damned fault that she was unhappy.

Signor Farinelli was a different matter entirely. The most complex of the four strangers who had gathered in that stuffy drawingroom to welcome her, he alone had seriously piqued her interest, her curiosity. He was intelligent, caring, witty, sagacious, abundant of spirit. He was irresistible. Yet he was also, she had sensed, detached, shrewd, introverted—an observer. Under the sparkle lay a shadow, the scar of some secret pain. She was intrigued. She'd never met anyone like him, and she tried, as she threaded her way down a path that twisted through a maze of flowering oleander and cypress spires, to analyse her impressions of that first meeting, to put her thoughts about him, her intuitions, into perspective. She was attracted to him, yes—though not in any physical way—but attracted, somehow, to his mind and personality. His physical appearance, except for those luminous eyes shimmering like moons on water, she scarcely remembered. But those eyes—mirrors of the soul—haunted her still. They had seemed in some curious way to emit rather than receive light; and she had been ineluctably drawn by their power, compelled, fascinated, fluttering like a moth around a flame. But drawn to what? She remembered how he had seemed—where she herself had always drawn back—to plumb the bottom of her soul, to understand her better than she understood herself—and a shiver ran down her spine. What did it mean? Had he somehow seen into the life of things? attained to some Olympian height from which he could survey, impassively, the unfolded mystery of existence? No— there had been the greeting of a kindred spirit: a moment of recognition—almost (she thought) of reciprocation. He had known instinctively that she, like him, had suffered; and he had reached out to commiserate, to welcome, to console. What then—? How could she make sense of the apprehension that mingled with the admiration she felt for him? What did it signify, this tacit recognition of the similarity between them? Was he friend or foe?

A benevolent spirit smiling on those weaknesses that were his own as well? Or was there something else: was he, somehow, daring her—a stranger in a strange land—to risk all by leaping, yearning for a miracle, from the pinnacle of a tower into the empty air?

When she looked up, she found that she had unawares reached the front of the library. At that moment it seemed to her a refuge, a sanctuary. She hurried up the steps and through the heavy doors. At the wicket, she showed her pass to a uniformed custodian and almost ran into the vaulted, oak-desked reading-room. The familiar scene and silent presence of the ever-living dead lining the shelves in their leather jackets, restored her to calm. She was among friends. She was safe.

Her heartbeat slowed, her breathing returned to normal. Why had she fled? She was not afraid of Signor Farinelli. There was no reason to be. He was kind, avuncular, wise. No, she feared what the penetration of his gaze had seemed to demand. It had invited her to tear away the mask and face, as he had done, the naked image of human insecurity. It had warned that there was no safety in the world, no shelter, no final knowing—all was mystery and miracle. It had invited her to embrace the sad wisdom of man's unknowing, to confront reality, and it had promised, if she did so, peace. But she was not ready yet for such a confrontation, for such peace.

Her place was in an alcove under the bust of Marcus Aurelius. Waiting for her on the desk was a 1581 quarto of Vincenzo Galilei's *Dialogo della musica antica et della moderna,* unopened perhaps for centuries. She had requested it before leaving for her talk with Professor Ecco and it had been delivered in her absence. For a time, she sat and stared at it, wondering, awed. Was it perhaps, she wondered, Vincenzo Galilei's own personal copy? Or had his son, the famous astronomer, once held it lovingly, turning it in his hands and remembering a departed father?

Slowly, reverently, she opened the leatherbound boards scented with age and human history and began to read...

THREE

THE WHITE stretch limousine purred to a stop in the deserted alley beside a commercial pasta factory, long out of business, whose walls were defaced with graffiti and broken window panes. It was a strange area of the city for such a vehicle to venture into. Such showy wealth was a rare sight in the bassifondi that bordered the railway tracks—a district of dilapidated warehouses and cheap rooming houses—and the big car's arrival attracted attention. The locals were sharp-eyed. Appearing to see nothing, they knew everything that happened on their streets; but if the police happened to arrive later and start asking questions, their memories became mysteriously blank. Things happened in their neighbourhood that it was better not to know about. The only wise course was not to get involved. In the experience of those who lived in the bassifondi, getting involved too often meant turning up three days later in a ditch with your throat cut or a bullet in your head. A lifetime of hard experience had impressed upon them the wisdom of cultivating ignorance. And so it was with unobtrusive vigilance that they watched the big car pull to a stop in the shadow of the pasta factory and watched its two occupants emerge.

The men—one grotesquely fat wearing an expensive white suit, the other bulging with muscle and dressed in a dark suit and chauffeur's cap—stood for a moment and looked around to see who might have noticed them. The fat man dabbed at his brow with a crumpled white handkerchief. Seeing no one, they set off down the rutted alley that ran toward the railway tracks between the empty factory and the rusted iron railing that encircled the grounds of an old monastery. The Dominican fathers who had built the place had long since fled and their once-prosperous house was now no more than a leaking roof over the heads of homeless derelicts and opium addicts. The men from the limousine left their car unlocked, unguarded—a tempting target. But no one would touch it. The locals understood only too well that money and ruthlessness went hand in hand, and they also knew—

by an innate instinct of self-preservation—that the heavy-set man in the chauffeur's cap was carrying a concealed gun. The white limousine was as safe as if it had been parked in a police compound and surrounded with uniformed officers.

The alley led down behind the abandoned monastery to a row of houses, three in number, that overlooked a patch of untended open ground overgrown with docks and nettles. Perhaps once, in palmier days, it had been a little park with flower beds and a swing for children. But those days had long vanished. Now it was just an empty lot littered with refuse and choked with weeds. Fifty yards beyond the houses, the rutted lane ended at a wooden barricade and drooping chain-link fence, beyond which were a fetid drainage ditch and the railway tracks. The whole area had the look of desperate decay bred out of apathy and despair.

'Slow down!' the fat man ordered.

The day was humid and Nicòlo Strozzi, drenched in perspiration and out of breath from his exertions, had fallen behind his companion. The man in the chauffeur's cap obediently slowed his pace. Strozzi hated humidity, hated being away from air-conditioning, hated physical exertion of any kind. Even more, he hated being surrounded by the sights and smells of poverty in the squalid bassifondi. They reminded him too forcibly of what his life would have been like if he hadn't been gifted at blackmail, embezzlement and extortion. His pig-like eyes surveyed the squalor around him with loathing and contempt. The sooner their business with Barberini was completed and they were out of the area the better. He wiped beads of sweat from his face with the crumpled cloth that was a permanent fixture in his right hand. Beside him, dark and menacing, always present but never obtrusive, trudged Franco—his taciturn factotum, driver, and bodyguard. The symbol both of his success in the world and of his fear of losing it.

The house they wanted was the one in the middle of the row. They mounted the steps to a small verandah and opened the front door without knocking. Inside, they found themselves in a dingy hall, bare of furniture and carpeted with dirty broadloom that was worn through to the bare floor in several places. Daylight barely penetrated the sidelights and soot-caked fanlight over the door and a sour, musty odour hung in the air like a distant memory of cat urine. Outside, a freight train rumbled past, gathering speed, its vibration rattling windows in their frames and shaking the floor under their feet. Three doors led off the hallway. The centre one, at the back, bore a professionally painted sign that said: AGENZIA INVESTIGATRICE ACME.

Strozzi rapped peremptorily and pushed through the door, followed silently by Franco. The room they entered was a remarkable contrast to the grungy hallway they had just left. It was clean and bright, sumptuously carpeted, with modern, comfortable furniture. An air-conditioner hummed in the window. Along one wall ran a bank of filing cabinets, along another a leather-topped credenza loaded with sophisticated electronic equipment: a television monitor and VCR, a Minolta camera with a telephoto lens, various listening devices, a short-wave radio for monitoring police broadcasts. In one corner, near a potted rhododendron, a large birdcage was suspended from the ceiling. Its occupant, a red-and-yellow parrot, cocked its head and squawked 'Come in, please!' as the door swung open to admit Strozzi and his mute companion.

The man who awaited them behind a large enclosed walnut desk was in his middle thirties, dark skinned and powerfully built. He sat with his hands resting out of sight on his knees. A buzzer, tripped when the front door had opened, had warned him to expect visitors. He was expecting no one. Clipped to the underside of the desk only a few inches from his right hand was a .357 magnum revolver in a leather holster. When the door opened to reveal Strozzi, Barberini's shoulders relaxed and he raised a quizzical eyebrow. His hands remained in his lap.

Officially, he didn't know who Strozzi was. Their arrangement was: no names, no telephone numbers, no paper trail. His reports were delivered to the client orally and in person; all their transactions were in cash on the barrel-head, paid in advance. But Mario Barberini was a private investigator who liked to know who his clients were. For that reason, he had paid an associate he sometimes employed on minor errands to jot down the licence-plate of the white limo, then paid another contact at the Department of Vehicle Registrations downtown to run the number through their computer. It was an elementary precaution—and the ᵕᵕᵕtion might prove to be useful. In Barberini's business, ᵕᵕᵕon was everything. It might mean the difference between ᵕᵕᵕath. And that was an important consideration for Barberini—especially when the life in question just happened to be his own.

Strozzi was to receive a report every other Thursday on the progress of the investigation. That was the arrangement. Today was only Monday.

'You're early,' Barberini said.

Strozzi lowered his bulk into one of the padded armchairs in front of the desk. Behind him, Franco closed the door and took up his post in front of it, his arms crossed. His eyes were empty, indifferent; he was the kind of unfeeling automaton, Barberini knew, who could kill without a flicker of conscience. Carefully, he eased the holster around on its swivel so that the oiled barrel of the Smith & Wesson .357 was pointed directly at the chauffeur's groin. If there was going to be trouble, Barberini had no doubt about where it would come from.

Strozzi dabbed at the perspiration on the nape of his neck. 'What about Pistocchi?' he said, ignoring Barberini's tacit rebuke. 'Have you found him yet?'

'Pistocchi!' the parrot shouted out, and then gave a piercing whistle.

Barberini shook his head. 'No—not yet.'

'Why not? I don't need to remind you, surely, that it's what I'm paying you for.'

Barberini shrugged. 'I need more information. All you've given me is a vague description—thirty years out of date. It's not a lot to go on.'

'Everyone leaves a trail,' Strozzi said.

'This one is cold.'

Strozzi tried a different tack. 'I was told you were the best,' he said, needling him.

'I am,' Barberini said simply, refusing to take the bait. 'But I'm not a magician, signore. If you want better results, you're going to have to give me more to go on, some hard information about this Pistocchi character.'

'Pistocchi!' the parrot sang out gleefully.

Strozzi shot the bird an ovicidal look. 'Like what?' he asked.

Barberini leaned back in his chair and gave the man across from him an appraising look. For the first time, his hands appeared above the desk. 'Like an old photograph,' he said. 'Like

the name of somebody he once worked for. Like an old address—
a girlfriend—a friend of any kind.'

Was it imagination, Barberini wondered, or was there fear at
the bottom of those pig-like eyes? The surface sparkled with hatred and contempt, but underneath there was something else. Yes,
he was sure of it now. Underneath, there was terror—gut-
wrenching, bowel-twisting terror. He smiled to himself. Whoever
this Pistocchi was, he scared the living shit out of Strozzi. And
that, Barberini knew, was a useful thing to know in a business
where information was everything.

Strozzi said: 'What about his parents? I told you we found him
in a village in the hills.'

'The parents are both dead. More than ten years ago.' Barberini
waved a dismissive hand. 'I traced them to Velletri, a village
north of here, and personally talked to everyone in the village. A
few of the old timers vaguely remembered Pistocchi as a boy, but
no one has seen or heard of him for years. He didn't even turn
up, as far as anybody could recall, for his parents' funerals. No—
we can forget about Velletri. It's a dead end.'

'I want the bastard found,' Strozzi growled.

'That's what you're paying me for,' Barberini agreed. 'But I
can't work miracles. If you want more action, put more bait on
the hook.'

'Bait on the hook!' the parrot whistled.

'You want more money, is that it?' Strozzi said.

Barberini shrugged. 'That, too,' he said with a little grin, 'but
mainly what I want is more facts.' He decided to risk a trump
card. 'You know much more about this Pistocchi than you're
telling me.'

Strozzi fished a wad of bills from an inner pocket. He peeled
off half a dozen million-lire notes and tossed them onto the blotter
between them.

'Will that do?'

'For starters,' Barberini said, pocketing the cash. 'Now, let's
talk about Francesco Pistocchi. What does he mean to you? Why
do you want him found?'

Strozzi said nothing.

'What's he done to you?' Barberini pressed.

Strozzi gave a wintry smile. 'The question, I'm afraid, is what

I did to him, Signor Barberini. But that's my business, not yours. Your business is to find him before he *can* do anything to me.'

'We have to trust each other,' Barberini said reasonably.

'I pay you,' Strozzi grunted. 'I don't have to trust you.'

Barberini wondered whether the same line of argument applied to the scowling chauffeur parked like a Centurion tank in front of the door. Probably not, he decided. Franco was too bovine to be anything but blindly loyal to his master, and Strozzi no doubt had complete faith in him. Barberini smiled to himself. He had already won a little victory. In spite of Strozzi's intention of divulging nothing, he *had* told Barberini more than he had known before: he'd told him that Pistocchi wanted to kill him and that his motive was revenge for something Strozzi had done over thirty years ago. What Barberini needed now was to flesh out the generalities with some hard details—something he could use to start earning the salary he was being paid by a man (he knew) who could afford, if it were worth his while, to pay a great deal more. He tried a different approach. He said briskly:

'You last saw Pistocchi when?'

'About 1960.'

'And he was ten or eleven years old at the time.'

'Yes.'

'Since then, you've neither seen nor heard from him?'

Strozzi shook his head. 'No.' He added: 'He might have tried to blackmail me, I suppose, but he never did. I never heard from him. Frankly, I assumed he was dead.'

'Until something happened that changed your mind—?'

'Yes.'

'And what was that?'

Strozzi gave another of his wintry smiles. 'That,' he said, 'is where you step out of your concerns and start trespassing on mine.'

'He tried to kill you?' Barberini guessed.

'No.'

Barberini pushed on. 'He tried to kill someone else—someone you know?'

'He succeeded, actually.'

Well now, Barberini thought, *this* was interesting. Now he was getting somewhere. He flipped through the card-index of his mind, making a mental list of recent homicides. His brow creased in thought. Who had Pistocchi killed? Probably not Cafferelli: Strozzi had engaged the services of Acme Investigations before the cardinal was murdered. It was a pity though—that really *would* have been worth sinking his teeth into. Worth it, no doubt, in a number of ways. The Cafferelli case was sensational. All right then, before Cafferelli, who? He did a quick computation and came up with three names—Minelli, Rosso, Mora. Not likely Minelli, he thought: a truck driver's wife, she was caught *in flagrante* by her husband and dispatched with a meat axe along with her lover. Crime of passion—hard to imagine a connection with somebody like Strozzi. Rosso and Mora were more promising: a rising star in local politics and a prominent industrialist. But which one? Their deaths were a month apart. Barberini needed to know more, needed to fix the approximate date of the murder—

'And when exactly was this?' he asked smoothly.

'I think we've exhausted this line of questioning, Signor Barberini,' Strozzi said tightly.

Barberini's motto was Keep 'em talking. The more they talked, the more they told. He said quickly:

'But you think you're next—that he's after you now?'

'Perhaps not next, but he's after me, yes.'

'Then you're not the only one? There are others—?'

The dark cloud that crossed Strozzi's face made it clear that this, too, was an exhausted line of questioning. Barberini tried a new angle:

'Try to help me understand,' he said suavely. 'Try to help me find something I *can* use to dig the man out for you.' Taking his time, he removed an imported Turkish cigarette from a silver box on the desk. He tapped the end thoughtfully on the crystal face of his wristwatch, then placed the black oval tube between his lips and the flint-wheel of his lighter grated briefly in the silence between them. 'Thinking back to the beginning,' he said slowly, deliberately, launching a thoughtful cloud of smoke at the ceiling, 'thinking back over the thirty-odd years to when it all began, what exactly was your connection with Pistocchi?'

'Pistocchi!' squawked the parrot, who had drifted off into a private avian dream-world but was recalled to the present by the familiar name. 'Pistocchi want a cracker—whoo-ee!'

Barberini grimaced, wishing he'd thought to put the sheet over the damned cage. It wasn't the moment for the bloody parrot to get on Strozzi's nerves. Not when he was just on the point of extracting the information he needed.

Ignoring the bird, he went on, without missing a beat.

'I don't suppose, for example, that you were business partners who had a falling out. The boy after all was only ten years old and you'd have been, what, in your early twenties? So, what's the connection? What brought the two of you together? Did you live in the same rooming-house? go to the same church? work in the same butcher shop—?'

Strozzi grew suddenly impatient. 'What's your *point*, Barberini?' he demanded with some asperity. 'What exactly are you driving at?'

Barberini stood up abruptly. The time had come for a theatrical gesture. He stalked to the window and stood, hands on his hips, gazing at nothing for a long minute. Then he turned, stomped back, and leaned over the desk at Strozzi, his weight resting on two closed fists.

'My point,' he hissed softly, 'is that I need to have more than a name—a name that isn't even in the telephone book. Not in this year's, not in last year's, not in any year's. Believe me, signore, I know! I've checked every goddamned directory issued in the city of Florence and surrounding regions from 1955 to the present day. Francesco Pistocchi isn't in any of them. Even odder is the fact that he doesn't own a car—or subscribe to a newspaper—or even pay municipal taxes. Again—I know: I've been through the records. As far as the privacy-hating bureaucracy that runs all the rest of our lives is concerned, Francesco Pistocchi is thin air. He simply doesn't exist!' The effect was nicely gauged, Barberini thought, and from Strozzi's eyes he could see that his outburst was having the desired effect. He went on, his voice growing sad, sympathetic, almost pleading: 'I respect your right to privacy— your right to keep your secrets secret—but I can't find a man without a face or a past. A man who has no address, no friends, no occupation, no family. I need *something* to go on. I can't find a phantom for you, signore. Nobody can.' Now, he thought, for the *coup de grâce*. He removed from his pocket the bills Strozzi had given him and tossed them on the desk between them. It was a painful gesture, but he managed it. 'If you won't give me some solid facts to work with, signore,' he said in final exasperation, 'if you insist that I keep trying to accomplish the impossible, then there's no point in our trying to do business together.'

Strozzi looked at the bills, then up at the set of Barberini's jaw. The man, it seemed, meant what he said.

'The boy was a singer,' he said finally in a low voice, 'a male soprano.'

'And you think he might still be singing?'

Strozzi nodded. 'It's possible, yes. He was very good.'

'Then leave it with me,' Barberini said. 'I'll do a thorough search. If he's in Florence, I'll find him.' He let his shoulders relax. 'Is there anything more you can tell me?'

'No.' Strozzi heaved himself to his feet and lumbered toward the door that Franco held open for him. 'I've told you too much already.'

'There is one more thing,' Barberini said to the retreating back. 'What do you want me to do with this Pistocchi when I do find him?'

Strozzi turned and smiled thinly. 'I want you to kill him, Signor Barberini. That's why I chose you instead of going to a reputable agency. I want Pistocchi dead.'

'*Pistocchi dead!*' screamed the parrot. '*Pistocchi dead—whoo-ee!*'

'There'll be an additional fee,' Barberini said. 'A hefty one.'

'Naturally—and we'll discuss the amount when you've actually located him. The sooner you find him, the higher the fee. Let's call it an incentive bonus. Now, good day to you, sir.'

The door closed and a moment later the buzzer sounded, indicating that his visitors had reached the front door. Barberini walked slowly to the parrot cage and raised a warning finger.

'One day, my mouthy friend,' he said, 'one seed will be cyanide.'

FOUR

CARLO ARBATI tipped himself back in the swivel chair in his office and put his feet on the desk. His fingers were laced behind his neck and his eyes stared vacantly into space, his mind idling, ticking over quietly, making a toy of thought. From outside his open window on the second floor of the Questura, sounds and scents floated up unnoticed from the street below. The ashtray at his elbow overflowed with twisted cigarette butts: a mute testimony to his mental effort over the past two hours to trace out the intricate geometry of homicidal intention that lay behind, and also somehow linked together, the recent deaths of Mora, Rosso, and Cafferelli. For the three murders were connected. Arbati was absolutely sure of it; he could feel it. Seldom had one of his hunches been so strong, so persistent. But in spite of his certainty, he couldn't find the key he needed—that one elusive but essential piece of hard physical evidence—to unlock the door barring him from the secret passageway that linked the adjoining rooms of their separate deaths. At least he hadn't found it yet. And so finally, since logic and analysis were getting him nowhere, he had decided to try a different approach. He turned his mind loose and let it drift. He surrendered the reins of reason to the creative indolence of the subconscious, knowing that sometimes, when he willed himself to relax his conscious will, patterns would mysteriously begin to emerge and unconnected fragments would start to shape themselves into meaningful wholes.

But today it was not to be.

Freed from conscious supervision, his mind turned truant, leaving the beaten path and wandering off into pleasant, more distant fields. By a circuitous vicus of recirculation, his thoughts returned to the haunts of his youth—to earlier, simpler, happier days. The policeman in him yielded place to the poet—recorder and remembrancer of times past. Pushing aside the cluttered con
the present, memory led him, unresisting, up the A11
to Prato on a tributary of the Arno. His maiden aunt,

eighty, his only surviving relative, still lived there in the same house where he had been born and had grown up. It was there, in Prato, that the poet in him had been born. The streets and lanes of dreaming Prato were the criss-crossing warp and woof of the loom on which his imagination had woven its first childish visions from the multicoloured threads of his existence. Under the railway arches by the river he had battled Red Indians and had turned the tide, alone and outnumbered more than a hundred to one, against an army of six-armed aliens from the planet Pluto. In the over-grown lot behind the cloth-factory he had hunted rhinoceros and polar bear and once, on a warm summer night when he was ten, he had distinctly heard, at the same instant that the moon suddenly disappeared behind a cloud, the voice of God Almighty warn him that he was trespassing on private property. It was only years later that he had realized the disembodied admonition had had its or-igin in the grouchy voice of the night-watchman shouting at him from an upper window of the faceless, coal-black factory.

The house and street where he had grown up were the same. They had hardly changed, in fact, since the fifteenth century. Aunt Angela, frail and birdlike, who seemed herself in his imagination also to be a survivor from the fifteenth-century, was frailer now and more fragile, though she was still lively and full of spirit. He made a point of driving up to visit on Sundays, and always she was there waiting for him—a small thin figure in a black dress framed like an engraving in the trellised doorway. One day he would arrive and find the doorway empty, and from that day he would be alone with the history of their past, with the memory of a decade of Sunday visits. From that day he would be the sole custodian of all Arbati memory—an orphan, a mere metonymy of a family. He wondered if, after she died, he would ever go back to Prato again.

They ate spaghetti—it was always spaghetti she prepared for him—at the carved mahogany table that had been his father's wedding gift to his mother, and they traded stories about the fam-ily from happy, far-off days before the icy fist of Death had in-tervened to break up the original set. There had been four of them then—his parents, his father's sister Angela (who never married), and himself—and they had been inseparable. They had lived a life that seemed to him, in retrospect, an idyll of the life in Eden when the world was still an innocent garden. But the serpent of

change had battered down the gate and torn apart their bower—
and now the survivors were left alone to meet on Sundays, to eat
spaghetti, and to reminisce. He listened to Aunt Angela's stories
and endured her taunts about his 'celibacy' (as she called it, for-
getful of her own), and when the meal was over, he would escape
for an hour to revisit childhood haunts or slip unnoticed into the
Romanesque Duomo, where he had been christened, to study the
frescoes of Fra Filippo Lippi, Prato's most famous son. The old
monk, a notorious libertine in life, had possessed a gift for de-
picting ethereal spirituality. He painted his madonnas from the
inside. Their flesh bloomed with an angelic sensuality born in the
hidden places of the soul; their homesick eyes radiated the lost
light of heaven. And Arbati wondered as he gazed at them in
silent awe if there was something missing in himself, some lust
for flesh-and-blood that Brother Lippi possessed—and even wal-
lowed in—that conferred a secret power on him when he picked
up his brush. Perhaps Aunt Angela was right when she grumbled
that he was afraid of women, that he would never marry because
he feared giving himself fully to another human being. He was
thirty-five and still single. A policeman and poet. Was it possible
that his Muse had become his mistress...a bloodless, sapless sur-
rogate for the real thing—?

The sound of the office door opening brought him back to
reality. Giorgio Bruni bustled in with a satisfied grin spread on
his troll-like features and dropped onto one of the wooden chairs
in front of the desk. Under his arm was a thick file which he
plunked down in front of Arbati with an air of definitive finality.

'Wool-gathering again?' he asked with a smirk.

'In a way.'

Arbati put his feet down and swivelled to face him. From the
silly look on Bruni's face, he knew immediately that the previous
night with Tessie had been a productive one—no doubt in a number of senses. 'You don't have to tell me,' he said with a groan.
'It's written all over your face. The two of you have solved the
Cafferelli case.'

Bruni shrugged. 'Of course,' he said. 'It's obvious as soon as
you look at the facts.' He folded his arms across his chest and
gave Arbati a smug smile. 'It was a Mafia hit.' He added: 'As I
thought it was from the very beginning, if you remember.'

'I thought we ruled the Mafia out?'

'*You* did,' Bruni said pointedly. 'I never did.'

Arbati sighed. 'Okay then, show me what you've got,' he said leaning back, prepared to be unconvinced. Poor Giorgio invariably missed the forest for the trees—and this time it would be no different. He placed too much faith in superficial appearances ever to see the truth that lay hidden behind them. Too easily blinded by raw facts, he missed the secret patterns below the surface that drew simple facts together and made sense of them. That was especially true in the Cafferelli case. Whatever 'facts' Giorgio had dug up about a Mafia connection were irrelevant. No doubt his facts were accurate enough in their own way—Giorgio was an excellent digger-up of detail. It's just that they had nothing to do with the reasons why Cardinal Cafferelli had been murdered. Arbati knew that because he *knew,* although he couldn't prove it yet, that Cafferelli had been killed for the same reason and by the same person or persons unknown who had murdered Alberto Mora and Roberto Rosso. Each had had his throat slit and in each case a deliberate attempt had been made to sever the vocal cords. Yet in the cases of Mora and Rosso not even Giorgio's indefatigable industry had turned up any connection to the Mafia.

Bruni leaned forward. 'Let's start with the bank books,' he said. He flipped open the file and fanned documents out over the desk like a croupier. 'I've traced every transaction back as far as 1965 when he was promoted to bishop. Before that, he was a parish priest in Rome. The records for the years before '65 are spotty and don't reveal much, probably because there isn't much to reveal. Anyway, that changed in a hurry when he made bishop. I won't bore you with the sordid details, but for twenty years Bishop—then Cardinal—Cafferelli built up a thriving little trade in fraud, bribery and extortion. Everything under the counter but using legitimate fronts. It was his source of pocket money for Rolex watches, expensive wine and loose women. He wasn't a nice man, Carlo—and him a prince of the Church too.'

Arbati suppressed a smile. Giorgio Bruni hadn't set foot in a church since the day he was married—and God only knew when he had darkened a church-door before that. He wasn't likely to have much stake in the hypocrisy of the Curia.

'Go on,' he said.

'Well, about a year ago, the sums suddenly get bigger—much bigger. Not a few million lire any more but hundreds of millions.

Our boy had gone big time. He must have figured he'd exploited
the growth potential of his small business enterprises and decided
to move on up to bigger and better things. Look at this,' Bruni
jabbed a knuckly finger at a series of figures highlighted in yellow
marker. 'Every one of these represents money either coming from,
or leading to, well-known front-organizations for the Mob.'

Arbati followed the pointing finger. 'All in the name of God
and profit,' he said.

'Sounds like a quotation.'

Arbati nodded. 'Francesco di Marco Datini. Ever heard of
him?'

'Nope, can't say I have.' Sensing a history lesson coming,
Bruni rose and poured himself a mug of coffee from the pot that
simmered perpetually, winter and summer, on a hotplate beside
the desk. 'You want some?'

Arbati shook his head. 'Datini was a medieval cloth-merchant.
In the name of God and profit was the motto he built his fortune
on. He made money, in fact, the measure of his faith: the greater
his profits, the harder (he assumed) he had worked at praising
God and employing in His service the talents he'd been given. It
was the beginning of Christian capitalism: praising God from
whom all blessings commensurately flow. No doubt it was a comforting enough creed for someone as rich as Datini, but I dare
say the poor who are always with us would find it all rather cold
comfort. Still, he was an interesting character. Iris Origo wrote a
book about him a few years ago. It's called *The Merchant of
Prato*.'

'Really,' Bruni said without interest.

Arbati wondered why he bothered. Giorgio was—and always
would be—bored by anything but what lay directly under his
nose. The variety of human experience over the fifty centuries of
man's sojourn on the planet was as nothing in his eyes. As far as
Giorgio was concerned, time had begun, for all practical purposes,
shortly before his own birth and it extended (with any degree of
real certainty) not far beyond the end of the current week. That
narrow band was reality—all that it was useful to know, all, indeed, that could be meaningfully known; and the rest was merely
fume and fustian. If he'd been willing to give the past a chance,
Arbati knew, willing to learn occasionally from its dusty pages,
he would eventually have wakened up to the discovery that the

present he cherished could make more sense than he'd ever been able to make out of it before. But there was no point in telling him so. Giorgio Bruni was one of those prisoners of the present condemned to relive the past because he chose wilfully to ignore its existence.

Bruni set his mug on the desk and resumed his seat. Taking a ballpoint pen from his pocket, he stirred two packets of saccharine into the dark, steaming brew, then crumpled the empty sleeves and tossed them into the waste basket.

'The way I figure it,' he said, picking up the thread of his argument as if the interlude about Datini had never occurred, 'is that Cafferelli was caught with his fingers in the till. It fits the way he likes to do business. For the past twenty years he's made a virtue of skimming a healthy percentage off the top of every deal for himself. Not an intelligent move, I would have thought, when you're dealing with the Mob. Anyway, if they caught him at it—and I'm betting they did—he was bloody lucky to get away with nothing more than a slice on the neck.'

'It's possible the figures indicate that he was skimming,' Arbati conceded, running his eye over the highlighted numbers on one of the computer print-outs. 'Unless of course he was simply deducting an agreed-upon fee—which is equally possible, I suppose, isn't it? But any way you look at it, he hardly seems to have been lucky, I'd say.' He lit a cigarette and launched a plume of smoke at the ceiling. 'Have you turned up anything on those coded entries in his notebook?'

Bruni shook his head. 'No—not yet. The boys at M.I. are still working on it, but I think we'll find it contains the details of the cardinal's foreign accounts. Switzerland, probably—perhaps Ireland or the Cayman Islands as well.'

Again Arbati nodded. 'And when you were ferreting through the records did you happen to turn up anything more to link him with Mora or Rosso?'

Bruni heaved a weary sigh. 'Give it up, Carlo. It's a blind alley. There's nothing there.'

They had been through it before. Three prominent citizens murdered in the space of two months, all with their throats cut; but not a shred of evidence apart from the manner of death to connect them. Alberto Mora, age 55, founder and sole-owner of Mora Industries, suppliers of textiles to Gucci, Yves St Laurent, Armani, Ralph Lauren, and most of the other fashionable design-houses of Europe—found stuffed in a cleaner's closet in his own factory. Roberto Rosso, age 54, flamboyant politician, philanderer and *bon vivant*, touted as the next mayor of Florence—found early one morning in Piazza della Signoria in the passenger's seat of his Porsche Targa, the hazard lights left flashing apparently to attract attention. Umberto Cafferelli, age 54, Roman cardinal and resident Metropolitan of Tuscany—killed in his office and transported across the city to Santa Maria Novella cathedral, where he was hung on a cross.

'There *is* a connection, Giorgio. We haven't found it yet, but there is one.'

'Then convince me.' Bruni said, throwing up his hands. 'Look at the facts. Agreed: the victims were about the same age. Agreed: they had their throats cut. Agreed: they all turned out, when we started digging around, to be remarkably nasty customers: graft, blackmail, corruption—even, in Rosso's case, probable cause for indictment on a charge of homicide. But there it ends. We know of a dozen possible motives for killing each of them and a dozen suspects willing to do it themselves or willing to pay to have it done. But they're never the *same* motives, Carlo, or the *same* suspects. In short, there is no link. And where there's no link, there's no case.' He slurped at his coffee, then added: 'Rosso and Cafferelli was probably copy-cat murders. Somebody—and in Cafferelli's case I'll put my money on the Mafia—saw an opportunity to get rid of a liability and at the same time send the cops off on a wild-goose chase by making the killings look like the work of a serial killer. It's just as reasonable as your theory,' he added, seeing Arbati about to object. 'So why not?'

Arbati shook his head. 'It won't wash, Giorgio. The *modus operandi* is unique: in each of the three cases the carotid artery was severed and there was a deliberate attempt to hack the vocal cords. Only *we* know that. Those details weren't released to the press, which rules out copy-cat murders. All the media know is that the victims' throat were cut; they don't know *how*. No, Giorgio, this is a single murderer and he's telling us something—at least he's trying to. There's method in his madness. And what's more, he's getting downright cocky about it. He's almost daring us to find him.'

'Wait a minute,' Bruni interjected. 'Not so fast. We don't

know—not for certain—that the murderer was, in fact, after the vocal cords. We only suspect it. Doc Mangiello may think it's what happened—but he's not willing to stake his reputation on it in any of the autopsy reports. Face it, my friend, it won't stand up in court.'

'We're not in court yet,' Arbati said simply. 'We're trying to put together enough evidence to get us there.' He stood up and crossed to the window, looking down abstractedly on the life milling below in Piazza della Libertà. 'Let's assume a connection we can't see at present,' he said without turning, 'and try some lateral thinking for a change. Instead of looking for the similarities, let's consider the *differences* that link the three cases.'

Bruni gave a weary grimace behind his back, and Arbati went on:

'Victim number one, Alberto Mora, was killed in his office, the body stuffed in a handy closet nearby. As homicides go, an ordinary murder with a rudimentary attempt to conceal the corpse. Roberto Rosso, victim number two, was killed in an unknown location, then driven in his own car to a public place—the Piazza della Signoria or, more precisely, the area of the piazza directly in front of Palazzo Vecchio, which happens to be the seat of civic government. An appropriate place, if we assume the killer was trying to make a point, to dump a politician who might well have been the next mayor of Florence.'

'Or a simple coincidence,' Bruni muttered, not seeing where all this was leading.

'Few coincidences are simple,' Arbati observed. 'They only seem coincidental because we can't manage to find a suitable cause in the effect. It's a matter of perspective, and the issue, often, is that we overlook relevant facts, rather than that those facts don't actually exist.' He turned and ground out the butt of his cigarette in the heaped ashtray on the desk. 'Victim number three, Cardinal Cafferelli,' he went on, 'died in his office and was deposited, fittingly, since he was a cleric, in a church. The question is, Why that particular church? There were at least a dozen others on the way. And why the blasphemy of a mock crucifixion? But, leaving aside for the moment questions we can't answer, is there a pattern in all of this, a thread that we can follow?'

Bruni shrugged. 'Beats me, boss,' he said irreverently.

'It strikes me that there is,' Arbati said, ignoring him. 'I don't know what it means yet, but I'm convinced there is. The bodies have been left in progressively more symbolic places and the murderer has escalated the dramatic value of each successive crime. He's making a point. Either he's taunting us or he's losing his grip on sanity—or maybe it's a little of both.'

'Assuming you're right, what's the motive?' Bruni asked sceptically.

Arbati smiled. 'I have a hunch it's the oldest one in the book. Cain's sin: revenge. And if I'm right,' he went on, 'there's something in the background we've overlooked. Something too obvious to seem important. Maybe, Giorgio—just maybe, we've been asking ourselves the wrong question.' He was thinking on his feet now, starting a hare and seeing where it led. 'We've been asking ourselves *who* the link between the victims might be. Maybe the question we should be asking is *when* and *where* a link is even possible—'

Bruni had no idea what he was talking about.

But Arbati was on a roll. 'Get back to your friend in cryptography,' he said. 'That notebook of Cafferelli's may be important. Meanwhile, I'm going to take another look at what we've got so far—but with a new pair of eyes.'

When Bruni had gone, Arbati set out the three files and arranged them in a line on his desk. He poured himself a mug of coffee and tried to wash all the preconceptions he had about the cases out of his mind. Then he sat down, opened the files and began to compare them—this time starting from the *very* beginning and paying attention to every even apparently insignificant detail: name, parents, place and date of birth, place and date of christening, schooling—*And there, by God, it was!* Staring him right in the face! Collègio San Stefano. All three victims had attended the same school in the mid-1950s, a private boys' academy in the suburbs run by the Basilian Fathers. It was a link all right, but was it the link he was looking for? Time would tell. With luck, it would lead him to Lo Squartatore—'The Slasher'— or at least to the identity of his next target in time to prevent murder. For Arbati was convinced that, unless he could get there first, there *would* be another killing. He couldn't say why. He just had a hunch about it.

FIVE

THE ORANGE CAT was back. He sat outside the French windows, staring in, silent, watchful, patiently and immovably expectant. He appeared always at mealtimes and seemed to have come with the apartment, although Cordelia had no idea who he belonged to.

She got up from the table and unlatched the door. With a curt meow in her direction he strode to the kitchen, tail erect, waited while she poured milk into a saucer and set it down, then hunched over it, his eyes closed, and lapped contentedly at the creamy puddle. It was, his lordly mien implied, no more than his just due.

Cordelia finished her own supper and cleared away the dishes. Outside, a yellow sun was rolling down the cambered sky toward the hills. In an hour it would be pitch dark, night coming on suddenly in a single stride, or so at least it seemed to one born and bred under the lingering twilights of the northern hemisphere. The suddenness of Mediterranean sunsets had been a surprise to her—unsettling at first, as if Nature had extinguished the light of day with the flick of a switch. There was a remarkable, almost an apocalyptic sense of ending to an Italian day. But she was used to it now, and tonight especially she felt a warm sense of peace, of well-earned contentment. It had been a particularly productive day. The resources of the rare book room at the university were rich beyond belief. Her reading plan was laid out for the next month, and she was beginning to see how the structure of the various chapters in the thesis should fall into place. She had also braved the jealousy of the gorgon at the gate and paid a second visit to Professor Ecco. He was a delightful character, a useful ally, and would be helpful to her in a thousand ways. He had taken her out to lunch at the Faculty Club and introduced her to some of his colleagues, then spent an hour with her back in his office talking over the progress of her thesis. Without her asking, he had graciously stepped into Julian Wain's shoes and become her academic mentor. Florence didn't seem a strange and foreign city to her any longer. She didn't feel alone, as she had at first. She was, in fact, getting on very nicely with the work of starting her life over, of forgetting her father and Charles Passmore and making her own way in the world. All in all, things were falling, she thought, very tidily into place.

She washed and dried the few dishes from supper, then sat at the desk where she kept her books and papers—she had dubbed the big old rolltop desk that came with the flat 'Thesis Central'—and opened her copy of the letters of Girolamo Mei. Before she could even find her place, however, the orange cat, purring loudly, had jumped up onto her lap and was rubbing his bony head under her chin, demanding attention.

There was no choice but to lay Girolamo Mei aside for the time being. She put the book down and turned her attention to the cat. Experience had taught her it was pointless trying to resist his advances. He was not easily put off when he wanted something.

'What's your name, big fellow?' she asked, running a hand down his silky back. 'Do you live around here? Somebody must wonder where you disappear to every night at suppertime.'

He looked at her with wide inscrutable yellow eyes, then rolled lazily over, stretching out full length to have his stomach scratched. He knew how to exact obeisance from those who had fallen under his spell.

'How on God's green earth can I get any work done with you here?' she said. 'You're worse than a baby.'

But she wasn't really complaining. The companionship he offered was welcome, and there was something homey and congenial in his presumption of familiarity. She stroked the furry tummy and he rumbled appreciatively under her touch like the sound of a distant outboard engine. His purring made her think of the lonely cottage on Lake Michigan. She remembered the long days she had spent daydreaming on its wide verandah, motherless, ignored by a scholarly father closeted inside the cottage with his books. Her only companions then had been the unsociable gulls, the black waves lapping anonymously at the lichen-crusted rocks, and the little breezes that gossiped at a distance among the firs and stands of shivering aspen. Oh, how she wished there had been a cat around then to comfort her! Some warm and companionable presence to fill the lonely hours, to salve the slow corrosive burning of tedium and isolation that ate away her soul during the long days of those eternal summers.

'Miou, gattino! Miou, miou—'

The voice came from below her window.

'Is that for you, my friend?' she asked. The lolling brute deflected her question and, stretching himself like an irrepressible yawn, invited her to continue.

Cordelia thought otherwise.

'I think we'd better see if it is,' she said. 'Somebody might be worried about you.'

She folded him in her arms and carried him out onto the balcony. Late sunlight bathed the cupola of the Duomo, illuminating its gilt cross and throwing long shadows over the terracotta roofs that tumbled at her feet. The evening air spilled fresh and sharp from a cloudless sky and it was growing cool. Soon she would need a sweater. She peered over the geranium-potted coping and spied Signor Farinelli leaning on the railing of the balcony below.

'Is he yours?' she asked. 'Were you calling him just now?'

He looked up and saw her standing above him with the cat in her arms. 'Ah—Signorina Sinclair. Yes, he's mine. Is he bothering you?'

'Not at all. He comes every evening for his saucer of milk. I'm spoiling him, I'm afraid, but he's such a lovely big fellow. What do you call him?'

'His name is Fra Angelico.'

The improbable name struck Cordelia with amusement. 'Really? What an unusual name.' Then she asked, because it seemed an inevitable question: 'Does he paint?'

'He wishes to paint,' Farinelli said with a little grin. 'He has the soul of a great painter. If you look carefully, you can see it in his eyes—a sort of inarticulate platonic longing for the ideal.'

Cordelia lifted the furry head and stared for a moment into the yellow orbs. They conveyed no sense of visionary longing or occult desire. They revealed no hint of transcendence trapped in the dark depths of a feline soul. They were blank and vacuous, as empty of emotion as a pair of glass marbles.

'I see what you mean,' she said, returning his ironic smile.

Looking up, Farinelli's grin broadened, implying approval. 'I trust the work on your thesis is going well?' he said, changing the subject.

'Extremely well—yes,' she said. Signor Farinelli, she couldn't help thinking, was a complex and fascinating man. She had seen it that afternoon in Signora Ghilberti's flat and she saw it again now. His quip about the cat having a painter's soul had been, she sensed, a test to see what her response would be. It had nothing really to do with the cat. He had been gauging her reaction, sounding the depth of *her* soul. She went on, as if she had noticed nothing: 'I've spent almost every day since I arrived in the rare book room at the university. I wish I could just box it up and take it home with me. It's an impressive collection—a real gold mine. Do you know it?'

Farinelli nodded. 'Yes,' he said, 'it's very good. I've used it occasionally myself.'

Weary of confinement and unhappy at being ignored, Fra Angelico stirred restlessly in her arms. He demanded her full attention or else his freedom—nothing in-between was acceptable.

'Shall I bring him down?' she offered. 'He's getting fidgety.'

Farinelli shook his head. 'Please don't trouble yourself. He likes the night and I leave a window open for him. I gave up years ago trying to bend him to my will. He has a mind of his own, as you've no doubt noticed, and he comes and goes pretty much as he pleases. He'll make his way home when he's ready.'

She set him down and the big cat bounded on to the coping of the balcony, then sat between the flowering pots licking a casual paw. He was his own master, the captain of his own enigmatic soul. Cordelia turned back to Farinelli.

'I hope we still have our date to talk about the early opera sometime?'

'Of course, Signorina Sinclair. Whenever you wish.'

She said: 'And I'm still looking forward to reading those articles of yours in *Firenze Spettacolo*. You haven't forgotten, I hope, that you promised to show them to me.'

'I haven't forgotten—no,' he said, looking a little embarrassed. 'But they're not much, you know. You wouldn't be wise to get your hopes up too high.'

'That's not what Signora Ghilberti seemed to suggest, if I recall correctly. She thought they were something quite special.'

'Olivia Ghilberti is an old friend. She's prejudiced.'

Cordelia flashed him a warm smile. 'Who knows?' she said. 'Perhaps I will be too.'

The air was growing nippy as night came on, and without the furry cat to keep her warm, she began to feel the dewy coolness of the evening on her bare arms and shoulders. She made a mental note to get a second blanket for her bed out of the linen closet.

'Well, I'd better be getting in,' she said, rubbing her arms where gooseflesh was forming. 'I'll drop by your flat in the next day or two and we can set up a time to meet for our talk, if that's okay.'

'I shall look forward to it with immense pleasure, signorina.'

There was a formal, old-world quality about his speech that she found civilized and attractive. It was as if, she thought, his vocabulary never ventured out into public unless dressed in a newly-pressed frock coat and top hat, carrying an ivory-headed cane, like a nineteenth-century aristocrat.

'Good night then,' she said, turning away.

'Good night, Signorina Sinclair.'

She went inside and latched the glass-paned doors behind her. For some reason she couldn't explain, she found that she was humming 'Mr Mistoffolees' to herself, a bouncy show-tune from Andrew Lloyd Webber's *Cats*. She had seen a production of it at the Schubert Theatre in Chicago with Charles—the last time, in fact, they had gone out together as man and wife. But why should the tune have popped into her head tonight—? The evening she associated it with had been a total and unmitigated disaster. Charles had been in one of his miserable carping, cavilling moods, finding fault with everything: their seats, the costumes, the orchestra, the singers, the songs. He had especially loathed 'Mr Mistoffolees', because (she suspected) it had been her favourite song in the show. He had mimicked it mercilessly in the car all the way home. In the house, they had fought—and in bed, when she wanted nothing to do with him, he had forced himself on her and she had been forced to submit against her will, her fists clenched at her side, while impotent, futile tears brimmed in her eyes. It had been the last straw. For the first time in their disastrous marriage, rage and humiliation made her finally angry enough to act. The next morning, after a sleepless night, she had packed her things and left. But through it all, magical 'Mr Mistoffolees' had been a sparkle of light—a scintillation of frivolous joy in the dark night of a failed marriage. The song in fact had come to symbolize for her that heroic act of will by which she had gained her freedom and found the nerve to cut, once and for all, the rope of sand that her own sad fear of achievement had used to bind her, for five terrible years, to a life of suppression and wifely servility.

She switched on the reading lamp over the desk and closed the curtains on the French windows. Fra Angelico was no longer on the coping of the balcony. He had slipped away like a phantom into the surrounding night. She sat down at the desk and picked up the letters of Girolamo Mei. Ahead, there still lay an hour's serious reading before she turned to the murder mystery she kept by the bedside to help her unwind before she slept. Quite by accident she had stumbled on an English bookshop in Via Tornabuoni stacked with Agatha Christie and P.D. James and had chosen *An Unsuitable Job for a Woman*. She had bought it for the simple reason that the heroine's name was Cordelia Gray. She liked the idea of a female sleuth, especially one who happened to be a namesake.

She set the wind-up timer for an hour and set it at her elbow. It was something she had brought with her from Evanston. It was too easy, she had found, to get lost in books and forget the time—and tomorrow was a busy day. In the morning, there was work to be done at the library; in the afternoon, shopping for a pair of gold earrings in the elegant little boutiques on Ponte Vecchio; then, at six o'clock, her interview with Maestro Marchesi. She had spent the afternoon polishing the questions she was going to ask him. They were on an index card in her bag and she intended to memorize them on the way to the theatre. She refused to think about it now. If she did, she'd never get to sleep. She found her place in her copy of Palisca's *Girolamo Mei, Letters on Ancient and Modern Music to Vincenzo Galileo and Giovanni Bardi* and began to read—

The tentative tap on the door, sometime later, made her jump in her seat.

She looked up, frowning. Fifteen minutes remained on the timer. Who could possibly be at her door? It was nearly ten o'clock and she was expecting no one. Indeed, she knew almost no one to expect. With a puzzled look, she marked her place in Palisca and went to the door.

On the other side stood Lydia di Banco.

'Can I come in for a few minutes?' she asked hesitantly. There was a tremor in her voice. She wore a long dress and was holding a maroon cardigan clutched against her chest with tightly-folded arms. 'Signor Farinelli let me in. I met him at the front door as he was going out,' she said by way of explanation. 'I tried Signora Ghilberti's door but there was no answer. She must already be in bed and I hate to disturb her.'

'Of course,' Cordelia said, opening the door wide. 'Is something wrong?'

'I have nowhere else to go,' Lydia said, fighting back tears.

She looked pitiful: small, frightened, dishevelled, dowdy. Cordelia led her to the sofa, then went to the sink and filled the kettle for tea. From the corner of her eye, as the water heated over the hissing gas-ring, she watched Lydia wring her hands and cast worried, fearful glances at the door. Cordelia knew then what had happened. She had seen it all before. She knew the signs.

The kettle whistled and she poured water over the tablespoon of dried leaves in the bottom of the pot. The aversion—it had almost been contempt—that she had initially felt for Lydia di Banco on that first and only other occasion when they had met in Signora Ghilberti's drawing-room melted away like summer ice. All she felt now was a profound sadness and compassion—and a deep, visceral sense of sororal outrage. She poured two mugs, adding to one an ounce or so of rum. It wasn't much but it might help. Then she crossed to the grieving figure on the couch and put an arm around her, drawing her close, looking hard into the tearful, evasive eyes.

'He beat you, didn't he?' she said quietly.

The eyes filled with sudden terror.

'Show me where,' Cordelia said. Gently, she pulled aside the resisting arms and slid the cardigan off the narrow, bony shoulders. Black and purple bruises bloomed along the upper arm and on her neck. There would be others under the dress. Charles had never struck her—his methods were more subtle—but Cordelia knew the feelings: confusion, helplessness, a crushing sense of alienation and inadequacy. The physical symptoms were never the worst part. What struck deepest, what hurt most, was the betrayal of love—the horrible, soul-withering recognition that loy-
a'   nd trust had been rewarded with blows. And always, she
      the victims blamed themselves. Always they transferred the
      m the violent male to his innocent mate and then learned

to cover their wounds and smile at the blood and bruises they saw in the mirror. Always they believed that what was required of them was enduring patience and forgiveness. Always they managed to convince themselves that things would get better if only they remained loyal and loving, if only they kept smiling through their tears. And always they were wrong.

'Has he done it before?' Cordelia asked quietly, running a hand over the dark, ruffled hair. 'Is this the first time or has he beaten you before—?'

Lydia di Banco's lip quivered uncontrollably. There was nothing to say; there were no words she knew to speak. She buried her head in Cordelia's shoulder and cried like an inconsolable child, the sobs coming in spasms that wrenched her frame like the gusting of a line of sharp and violent squalls. An uncomprehending victim, she was the child of storm—lost, buffeted, tortured—praying in eloquent tears for absolution from unknown sins, praying in the only way she knew how for release from the thrall of a god whose fists were the only basis of his empowerment. Cordelia knew what she was suffering. She understood her pain and her confusion. For a long time she held her, rocking gently back and forth, letting her cry the poison out of her system. When the sobs subsided, she whispered softly into the tangle of black hair against her cheek:

'You must leave him.'

The look in Lydia di Banco's eyes when she looked up was one of inarticulate horror—a mixture of dread and disbelief and mute supplication.

'He'll do it again,' Cordelia said warningly. 'He'll only do it again, I promise you. He'll swear it won't ever happen again, but it will. It always does. Leave him, Lydia, while you can. He's not worthy of your love. He's proved that much.'

They both heard the door in the foyer two floors below bang closed, then the pounding on Signora Ghilberti's door.

Lydia composed her tear-stained face as best she could and swept the strands of dark hair back from her forehead. Her lip quivered. She took a deep breath. She tried to compose herself.

'I'd better go now,' she said. 'I don't want to cause trouble. You were very kind to let me in, but I'd better go now.'

Cordelia laid a hand firmly on her arm. 'I want you to stay,' she said. 'For your own sake, Lydia, I want you to stay. For mine, too. Men can't get away with treating us this way.'

There were harsh voices from below. Angry voices. He had wakened Signora Ghilberti.

'He'll come here next,' Lydia said, her voice tremulous. 'I know he will. I said I was going to visit you sometime. He knows I have nowhere else to go.'

'Stay,' Cordelia pleaded. 'If you won't stay, then let me call the police. You can't go back to him as if nothing has happened. Please.'

Lydia pulled away from her. 'No, no—I must go.'

There were heavy footsteps on the stairs, then a rap on the door. Lydia sat immobile, transfixed, as if awaiting the angel of death. Cordelia rose and went to the door, stepping into the hall and pulling the door to behind her, blocking the view inside. Signor di Banco's face was drained and white, except where two red patches burned on his cheeks. His eyes were dark and menacing, his shallow breathing barely controlled.

'Is my wife here?' he demanded with strained civility.

'Yes.'

'She's wanted at home,' he rasped hoarsely.

'At the moment, she's visiting me,' Cordelia said icily.

He reached past her and pushed the door wide, without making any effort to cross the threshold. His wife sat on the sofa looking at him with pleading, dog-like eyes.

'Come with me, Lydia,' he ordered.

Cordelia stepped in front of him. 'She's welcome to stay here as long as she wants,' she countered. 'If you don't leave quietly, I'll telephone for the police.'

'Now!' di Banco spat at his wife between clenched teeth, ignoring Cordelia as if she had been a wall in his way and he was forced to speak over her.

For a few long moments the battle of their contesting wills hung suspended in precarious balance. No one moved, no one spoke. It was like the breathless moment of crisis in a Greek tragedy. And then slowly, obediently, Lydia di Banco rose from her seat and began moving toward the door.

'You *don't* have to go,' Cordelia said softly, urgently—but it was too late. Their steps were already retreating down the gloomy stairwell.

Cordelia closed the door and dropped numbly onto the edge of the bed.

O God in heaven, she thought miserably, and her stomach felt like the yawning mouth of some black and bottomless abyss.

SIX

IN THE POOL of yellow light spilling from under the fringed shade of a floor lamp, Farinelli slipped the record from its cardboard sleeve and examined it for dust and scratches. It was an old 78 rpm recording made of bakelite, brittle and irreplaceable. He opened the top of the Motorola Hi-Fi and set the disk on the centre-post, swinging the bar across to hold it in place, then pressed the lever to engage the changer and drop the recording onto the spinning mat.

Somewhere far in the distance, a campanile tolled out the hour—twelve lingering peals—over the roof tops and deserted streets of the sleeping city.

Farinelli took his place again in the armchair by the window. The light from the hooded lamp fell like an aureole around his head and shoulders; the rest of the apartment was in darkness. Inside the ancient Motorola, the armature lifted and swung, paused briefly, then lowered the stylus with a crackle onto the revolving disk.

There was an organ chord, and then the voice of Orpheus, sad and sweet, filled the still air like the perfume of musk-roses blooming in a midnight grotto: *Tu se' morta, mia vita, ed io respiro?* In tones of lambent sorrow—lost, despairing, overwhelmed—the Thracian bard lamented the death of his beloved Eurydice. Then, gaining strength and resolution, the mellifluous voice rose, full and confident, bidding the earth farewell, promising to rescue her or else to join her in the house of death forever.

A dio terra, a dio cielo, e sole, a Dio!

Farinelli listened in embalmed darkness, his face expressionless, his eyes unseeing, and the silent tears streamed down his cheeks.

SEVEN

NICÒLO STROZZI heaved himself forward in his chair like a sumo wrestler executing a clumsy lunge and slapped down the switch on the intercom box that sat on his cherry wood desk. His face was crimson, nearly as deep as the colour of the wood, and he was in a mood to eat anyone who crossed his path alive.

'Where's my damned car?' he bellowed.

'Franco is bringing it around now, sir,' replied the conciliatory female voice at the other end.

'What the hell's keeping him? Damn it all anyway! Let me know the minute he gets here.'

'Yes, sir. Immediately.'

Strozzi subsided into the leather chair with a grunt and wiped away the beds of perspiration that sprouted on his forehead like transparent mushrooms. It was not yet ten o'clock in the morning and the day cool, but already he was dripping like a water buffalo in a sauna. He had showered and dressed only two hours ago but his white suit was damp and already uncomfortable. His clammy shirt was stuck to his skin like wet toilet paper, and the pungent scent of the oils oozing from his pores was beginning to over-power the industrial-strength cologne he had splashed on with a liberal hand after his shower. It was all part of the price he had to pay—willingly enough, in the final analysis—for his excesses with food and drink. Certainly, in spite of the inconveniences, he had no plans to moderate his pleasures of the flesh. He was, in fact, always on the look-out for new ones. A true votary of surfeit, Nicòlo Strozzi made even the professional epicures of history, like Nero and Henry VIII, seem no more than beardless neo-phytes—mere striplings and milksops in the arts of gormandizing and sensual indulgence.

He swivelled in his chair and gazed out at Ponte Vecchio and the brown waters of the Arno flowing sluggishly beneath the full-length panes that covered one wall of his office. He would miss that view. He would miss, too, the joys of caprice and power that

came from sitting in the plush and studded leather chair reserved
for the chairman of the Banco di Firenze. But there was simply
no alternative in the circumstances. He was prepared to take no
unreasonable risk with the thing he valued most in the world—
his life. And besides, he reflected, it wasn't forever—a few days,
a week or two at most. Still, he hated hotels and strange cities.
He detested foreigners with their damned cheek and impertinence,
and he quickly grew restless when he was away from familiar
surroundings and the homage he received in his native city. He
couldn't buy a gelato anywhere in Florence without attracting the
obsequious attention of a dozen of his fellow fiorentini passing
along the street. Florence was home—Florence was the sun that
lit his universe—Florence was milk and honey, prestige and
power, a paradise he prayed never to be alienated from, even for
a single day. As a result, he was a bad traveller, an execrable
tourist. He regarded any trip away from Florence—however short
the stay, however compelling the reason—as a form of exile, of
exclusion and, indeed, of emasculation.

But now, given what had just happened, there was absolutely
no choice in the matter.

Lying open on the desk, the letter that had arrived in the morning mail caught his eye and his frame convulsed as if a seismic
tremor had rippled through his entrails. He stared at the black
script with fascinated fear and loathing. It was a handwritten message on a single sheet of unlined paper: simple, terse, callous,
chilling. Sweat beaded along his upper lip. He had found it on
the desk when he had arrived at nine o'clock. The envelope was
addressed to him and marked PERSONAL AND CONFIDENTIAL. He
had ripped it open, thinking it no more than a request from someone hoping for special terms on a loan, and had then read the
contents—when he realized *who* it was from—with his heart in
his mouth. To his credit, he had reacted instantly, decisively.
Hardly, in fact, had he finished reading before he was on the
telephone to the Hyatt-Regency Hotel in Monaco. He had stayed
with them once or twice before. They were unusually accommodating, given the urgency of his tone, and promised to have
one of the penthouse suites facing the harbour ready for him by
noon. Next, he had telephoned Alitalia and booked an early flight
out of Leonardo da Vinci, then contacted Franco on the car phone,

told him to pack a bag for him at the villa, and then to get his ass back to the bank with the limo as fast as he bloody well could.

He glared malevolently at the signature on the bottom of the page: *Francesco Pistocchi*.

While the letter had been a shock, an appalling and unexpected surprise, Strozzi had never doubted for an instant that Pistocchi was out there someplace—waiting, watching, biding his time, picking off the remaining Camerati at his leisure one at a time. That much he had figured out for himself as he read in the evening papers successive accounts of the murders of Mora, then Rosso, then Cafferelli. Managing to stay reasonably calm, he had taken the necessary precautions in self-defence. He had beefed up security at the bank and at his villa outside town, he had hired on extra guards and dogs, and he made damn sure he went no-where—not even out for a quick gelato—without Franco and his .9 mm Beretta as company. But the letter from Pistocchi was the last straw, the sinister twist in the plot that had finally and irrev-ocably unhinged Strozzi's nerve. It was a macabre and gratuitous tactic—as if the Grim Reaper had taken to sending out advance notices to future victims in order to firm up the grisly last-minute details of their impending departures. The letter, Strozzi knew, was intended to instil terror—and it had succeeded admirably in its purpose. He wondered if Marchesi had received one like it.

He forced his attention away from the note and back to the river. Who would ever have believed that their silly prank, over thirty years ago, would eventually come to this—?

At first he hadn't been sure that it was Pistocchi who was even responsible for the murders. When Alberto Mora was found stuffed in a cleaner's closet in his own factory, his death had meant little to Strozzi. He hadn't seen Mora for years. People were being murdered somewhere every day, and Mora was one of those sleazy bastards who was bound to have his throat cut by somebody sooner or later. He'd shafted so many people and made so many enemies in the process of building up Mora Industries there was probably a line-up of white-lipped customers at the knife counter clamouring for their chance to get a blade on him. But the murders hadn't stopped with Mora; and when Roberto Rosso—another deserving victim in many ways—had turned up in Piazza della Signoria slashed from ear to ear in his Porsche Targa, Strozzi had begun to worry. It didn't look like a matter of simple coincidence. At least it didn't look that way to somebody who, like Strozzi, knew that Mora and Rosso shared a dirty little secret from the dim and distant past. Being a naturally cautious type, Strozzi had taken steps after Rosso's death to improve the security at his country villa as well as his offices in the city. He had also gone on the offensive, hiring a private investigator to track Pistocchi down. If the murders of Mora and Rosso did happen to go back to the Camerati dell'arte and the summer of 1960, Nicòlo Strozzi had no intention of being the next victim.

Any lingering doubt about a link between the murders of Mora and Rosso disappeared, however, when Umberto Cafferelli was found with his throat cut like the others, his body slung on the altar-cross in the Lady Chapel of Santa Maria Novella. The method, the motive, and the message were too plain for Strozzi to miss. If the body had been left anywhere else, there might have been room for a modicum of doubt—but not when it was deposited in that particular church and in that particular chapel. The choice of locale was a warning and a taunt—a deliberate threat to the surviving members of the Camerati who had been there, in that very chapel, on that fateful night over thirty years before.

It was then, when he had learned about Cafferelli's death, that Strozzi had come closest to panic. Mora, Rosso and Cafferelli were dead. Only he and Marchesi were left—and one of them, it surely followed, would be next.

At first, Strozzi didn't know what to do. His initial instinct had been to run—to jump on a plane and go...any place. But how could he do that? How could he leave Florence and the life of ease and power that he had worked so hard to build up? No—there had to be another way. His next thought was to go to the police and demand protection: he was a wealthy man, a prominent citizen. But there would be awkward questions and the police would start digging. How could he explain that he knew who the murderer was and that he, Strozzi, might well be his next target? He lay awake sleepless nights bathed in a cold sweat thinking about it; he had heart palpitations. He imagined Pistocchi behind every bush, in every closet, in every crowd. He put pressure on Barberini, the private detective he'd hired, to pull out all the stops; but Barberini was getting nowhere fast. And all the time, Strozzi knew, Pistocchi was out there, waiting and watching. He decided, finally, that he had no choice but to go to the police. He'd find a way to lie his way around the real truth. He was good at that, he told himself, a born liar. He'd had a lot of practice.

But first he had gone to see Marchesi. He didn't know why. They hadn't met for years. Maybe, stupidly, he expected consolation or fellow-feeling from the only other of Pistocchi's targets to still be walking around. He didn't know now and it didn't matter any more. Anyway, he had driven out to Marchesi's villa to talk with him, to plan a common strategy. Marchesi had looked the same. He hadn't grown fat or bald over the years; he was trim, as handsome as ever—still polished, still arrogant, still patronizing. And Strozzi had hated him—hated him because Marchesi had made him feel like a coward for being afraid for his life. All Marchesi had been able to think about was his bloody reputation. He'd even threatened to cut Strozzi's throat himself if Strozzi dared going to the police and implicating him. And Strozzi believed him. Tony Marchesi was a man who was capable of anything—absolutely anything at all. He always had been.

The whole disastrous plan, of course, had been Marchesi's in the first place. It was he who had founded the Camerati dell'arte and set its agenda, he who had bound its members to fealty and secrecy with a blood-oath, he who had discovered Pistocchi, he who had made all the arrangements for getting the job done. But after those early days at the university when they had been inseparable, the five Camarati, having little in common except a will to wealth and power, had drifted apart, gone their separate ways, meeting only occasionally, like strangers, at parties or in theatre lobbies. They had become rich and famous and none of them had given a thought to Pistocchi for years—though Pistocchi, it seemed, had certainly been thinking about them. Yet what was odd, Strozzi thought, was why, if he'd wanted revenge, he had taken so damned long going after it? More than thirty years. Who waited thirty years to get even? Strozzi couldn't have restrained himself for more than half a day. The only possible explanation was that something in Pistocchi's mind had finally snapped. After bottling up the black poison of his hatred for three decades, he must have been crazier than a shithouse rat and then one day, boom! all the fuses in his brain had blown at once.

Strozzi shuddered and mopped convulsively at his forehead with a crumpled handkerchief.

God, what idiots they had been! *What fools!—what silly bloody fools!*

He looked around the panelled office at the expensive furniture, the engravings and paintings, the exquisite view—all of them the tasteful and splendid symbols of his success. He owed none of it to anyone. He had amassed it with his own talents: not honestly, but what did that matter? It belonged to him. It was all his.

And now he was also in danger of losing it all. And why—? Because he had once been foolish enough to listen to Tony Marchesi. Because he'd allowed Marchesi to talk him into creating a monster—a time-bomb fused to blow up in their faces thirty years later.

He pulled the letter toward him over the polished surface and read it again, his eyes bright with loathing—and with dread:

Strozzi, you are a dead man. The others died quickly, but I have reserved a special fate for you—a fitting death, a slow death. Are you curious? Shall I tell you—? I intend to cut the balls from your living body and stuff them down your throat. You will choke on your own semen. For what you did to me—because it was you, Strozzi, who held the knife— it is a fitting end. Sweet dreams. Until we meet again,
Francesco Pistocchi

For a long moment he held the letter in his sweating hand, staring blindly, helplessly at the black, threatening words. Had Marchesi received a similar note? Probably—but it didn't matter any more. It was every man for himself now. He had no intention of talking to Marchesi again. Marchesi was a glib twit who thought he was invulnerable. Let him look after his own balls.

The intercom hummed and the female voice said: 'Your car just arrived, sir. It's waiting for you downstairs.'

Strozzi heaved himself upright. He crumpled Pistocchi's note into a tight ball and flung it into the wastepaper basket, then crossed the Persian carpet to the door. In two hours he would be in Rome; in four, Monaco. What did he care about Marchesi— or, for that matter, even about Pistocchi? For the next few days he would be safely out of reach. Somewhere where he could plan his next move in luxurious comfort without having to look over his shoulder every waking minute afraid of finding a hand behind him with a knife in it.

In the outer office, his secretary was bent over a green computer screen. Ahead were the brass and walnut doors of Strozzi's private elevator. The fifth floor of the Banco di Firenze, where the chairman's office was located, was accessible by appointment only.

'Is there a number where I can reach you, sir?' the secretary enquired, turning when she heard the latch click.

'No, I'm going to be moving around,' Strozzi lied. 'I'll check in by telephone when I can. Pass along any important mail through Franco. He'll know where to find me.'

'Very good, sir. And when shall I expect you back?'

'I don't know. It depends how things go.'

The elevator doors parted and he stepped inside.

If Pistocchi was going to kill anybody in the next week, it would have to be Marchesi. Strozzi would be in the Hyatt-Regency where the casino had once been kind to him. If Barberini and his goddamn parrot got lucky, the message would come to him through Franco. If, on the other hand, Barberini failed and Pistocchi managed somehow to get to Marchesi, then Strozzi would come back and take his chances with the police. But whatever was going to happen, he expected it to happen soon. For some strange reason, after having waited more than thirty years for his revenge, Pistocchi was all of a sudden a man in a terrible hurry.

The brass-and-walnut doors came together like a theatre curtain closing on an act. A motor whined deep in the bowels of the darkened shaft. The elevator jerked slightly and then began its oiled descent to the lobby of the bank five floors below.

EIGHT

MARCHESI STEPPED FROM the shower and wrapped a thick towel around his loins. His tanned flesh glistened like oiled kid-skin in the shaft of sunlight that fell like a spotlight beam from the skylight overhead. He gazed with satisfaction at the image of the hard, lean body reflected at him from the mirror. He looked forty-three, not fifty-three. Time and a careful diet had treated him kindly. There was not an ounce of fat on his wiry frame and his pampered skin glowed with the rosy sheen of health and youth. The two patches of silver hair over his temples merely accentuated the nobility of his chiselled features and imparted a certain venerability to a face carved from the granite of many generations of Tuscan aristocracy.

He was shaving when Mozart's *Nozze di Figaro,* replacing the shrill sound of the telephone bell, supplanted the Bach sonata playing on the villa's sound system. The straight razor he still used was one of the few concessions he had refused the march of technology. Electric razors gave him a rash and safety razors he deemed timid and plebian. Loftily, as if disdaining an unpleasant odour, he pinched the wings of his nose firmly between thumb and forefinger and made a deft backhand stroke with the blade along his upper lip, then reached for the electronics panel built into the pink-veined Pietrasanta marble of his vanity. The touch of a button opened the line. It was not, he hoped sourly, one of the soloists calling at the eleventh hour with laryngitis.

'Pronto,' he said.

'Oh, Tony, is that you—?'

The nasal female voice resonated with superb clarity of tone through four recessed Bang and Olufsen speakers. So clear, indeed, was her voice that a stranger ignorant of the high-tech marvels of Marchesi's villa might have supposed she was standing behind him somewhere in the same room. But it was not a pleasant voice. Juliana di Marco's tone was brittle and whiny, one of those cut-glass voices of the cosseted *haut monde* who suffer from the delusion that life, in spite of all that it has given them, has somehow never seen fit to recognize fully their inestimable worth.

'Of course it's me,' he said tartly.

'Are you angry with me, Tony? You sound angry.'

Ignoring her, he concentrated on a finely calculated cut along the line of his left jaw. 'Not yet, cara,' he said, rinsing the soap and stubble from the blade. 'But don't try my patience, my darling. What do you want?'

'Will I see you today? I'm lonely, Tony.'

'I have a rehearsal,' he said shortly, then added, remembering: 'And afterwards an interview with an American student. It's going to be a long day. I'll be tired.'

Juliana was beginning to get on his nerves. He wondered if it wasn't time to think about finding himself a new mistress. Somebody less selfish, less demanding—and perhaps, because he was tiring of Juliana's more obvious charms, someone more intelligent.

'I never see you any more,' she whined.

'I'm a busy man, my darling.'

He ran the bone-handled razor under the tap, then flicked the water off and made several expert passes with the honed blade on a leather strop.

Juliana's voice grew suddenly petulant:

'We never go out any more, Tony. When was the last time you took me out?'

'Last week, cara. I remember the evening quite distinctly. We had dinner at Pinchiorri's. The arrosto di coniglio made you nauseous, as I recall, and you complained about the wine.' He made no effort to disguise the contempt in his tone.

Unwisely, she elected to reciprocate in kind:

'You don't care about *me* any more. You don't care about anything except your old fuddy-duddy music. It's all you ever think about.'

He said sweetly, irritatingly: 'How can that possibly surprise you, cara? I'm a musician. Fuddy-duddy music is my life.'

Her petulance flashed like tinder into anger. 'I insist you make time to see me, Tony. *I positively insist.*'

He snapped the razor closed and laid it carefully, lovingly, in its velvet-lined case.

'Unlike you, cara mia,' he said acidly, 'I have a job. I work. I don't have the luxury of waking up at noon and spending the rest of the day wondering which soirée to grace with my presence in the evening.'

'Does that mean No?' she spat. 'Does that mean you won't take me out?'

He reached for the console. 'Yes, cara, that means No.'

He cut the connection abruptly. Tranquillity and the intricate harmonies of the Bach sonata returned. He rinsed and dried his face, then patted on some Polo cologne that made his skin tingle. It was at some point between the face-drying and the eau de toilette that he decided not to see Juliana again. She was a tedious, snivelling bitch and he was sick to death of her carping and whining. An evening with Juliana was an evening wasted on a spoiled and moody child. His first thought had been the right one. It was time to find himself a new mistress.

In the richly appointed bedroom he selected a pair of fawn Armani slacks from a rack of trousers and decided on an open-necked navy pullover to complement them, then set the ensemble off with a Moroccan gold-link chain at his throat. He checked his appearance in the cheval mirror and smiled, satisfied with the image the oval glass reflected back at him. The pudgy softness of middle age and the crow's-foot wrinkles around the eyes that etched the faces of other men his age were as foreign to him as manual labour. He pulled a brush through his long, full head of hair—still staring appreciatively at himself in the mirror—and then at last he was ready to face the world. Feeling lean and smug, he spent the remainder of the morning in the air-conditioned *torre* that housed his library. He began preliminary work on the scores he intended to use for a guest appearance in July at the Concert-gebouw in Amsterdam, then turned to the arrangement of Broadway tunes he had signed a contract to do with Columbia Records. At noon he stopped for a lingering lunch of mushroom canapés and a tart, chilled Moselle in the sunlit courtyard overlooking the Tuscan hills, then relaxed for half an hour listening to Gershwin's F-major piano concerto. At two o'clock precisely he left the villa in his black Ferrari for the twenty minute drive to the theatre.

His route led through the steep, narrow streets of Fiesole. He drove down through the winding and cobbled streets of the town, past the thirteenth-century monastery of San Francesco, then struck out across an open countryside of vineyards and olive groves. The sun was bright and a light south-west wind dragged a few torn rags of cloud across the sky. When he reached the outskirts of the metropolis, Marchesi closed his mind and focused on the pavement ahead to avoid having his sensibilities brutalized by the sight of the slums and commercialized suburbia through which he was obliged to pass. The old city, when he finally reached it, was a sudden relief, like emerging into sunshine after passing through a dark tunnel.

He parked the Ferrari outside the theatre in the place reserved for him and went immediately to his office, a spacious retreat of thick carpet and leather upholstery located under the stage. Although the room was sound-proofed, he could hear above him, like the din of a distant factory, the members of the orchestra tuning their instruments and practising *arpeggi*. The digital clock on the wall read 14:27. The session was due to begin in three minutes. He pressed a button under the edge of the desk, activating a flashing light on the podium in the auditorium that signalled his imminent arrival, and the cacophony overhead subsided. Then, gathering up his baton and the annotated score of Monteverdi's *Orfeo*, he mounted the private stairwell that led from his office into the wings behind the stage.

When he reached the auditorium, the players were waiting in their seats. The only sound in the vast, empty hall was the rustle of sheet-music as musicians located their places in the score. With quick steps Marchesi crossed the apron of the stage and, giving a curt nod to the concert master, mounted the podium. The air was charged with anticipation. Behind the orchestra, the chorus sat in an arc of tiered bleachers. On the maestro's right, four soloists occupied padded chairs in front of the cello section.

Marchesi flipped open his score, gave the performers a warning glance, and raised the baton.

'From the beginning, if you please, ladies and gentlemen,' he announced.

Then the baton descended—and magically, like an inspired response to the sweep of a magician's wand, the obbligato swell of strings and woodwinds perfumed the breathless air with the scent of their tremulous, ethereal harmonies—

IT WAS TEN MINUTES to five when Cordelia, walking from Ponte Vecchio along the crowded Lungarno, reached the theatre. Her appointment with Marchesi was at six but she had arrived early, hoping to catch some of the rehearsal. Excitement had built in her through the day like an electric charge. What a privilege it would be to watch a great conductor put the orchestra and chorus through their paces—to hear him correct the phrasing here, exhort more *sostenuto* there, to hear him mould the individual sounds and voices of chorus and orchestra into a single whole that reproduced the vision of the score that echoed in his mind's ear.

The auditorium was dark and empty, a contrast with the crowded, well-lit stage. Only a few scattered heads, perhaps a dozen, occupied the silent rows of velvet-covered seats. Unexpectedly, one of them belonged to Signor Farinelli. Cordelia moved down the aisle and felt her way along the row toward him.

He turned as she joined him and gave her a surprised look.

'My interview with the maestro,' she whispered. 'It's today.'

He nodded and his eyes darkened warningly, but he said nothing. There was a break in the music while the maestro explained the phrasing of a passage to the French horns.

'What brings *you* here?' she asked.

'I like rehearsals,' he said. 'I find them extremely useful. They tell me what a conductor is after, what effects he's aiming for. It's helpful watching the pieces come together. Then I know what to look for, what to expect on the night of the actual performance. It's a trick I learned when I first started in journalism and it makes my reviews easier to write.'

Marchesi tapped his baton on the podium and raised his arm, ready to continue. The orchestra lifted their instruments in unison. They were in the middle of act two. The messenger, his voice grave and full of feeling, sang: *In un fiorito prato*— It was the point in the opera where the news was broken to Orpheus that Eurydice, gathering flowers to make a garland for her hair, had been bitten by a poisonous snake hidden in the grass. Nothing, alas, could save her: *Ma nulla valse, ahi lassa!*

The words made Cordelia think of Lydia di Banco. *Nothing, alas, could save her.* And why was that? Because Lydia refused to face the truth. The viper who had bitten her was her own husband. Poor Lydia—poor benighted, self-deluded Lydia! How could there be any hope for her when she refused to help herself? Twice, Cordelia had stopped to visit the di Banco pensione at times when she knew Signor di Banco was away at work. They had been frustrating, depressing experiences. Lydia was evasive and refused to talk about the incident, refused even to acknowledge that it had happened. She had banished it from her memory and retreated into a make-believe world of strained and artificial normality. Everything was fine now, she insisted. Her husband, who never found it easy to admit a mistake, had apologized to her in his own way. He had never really meant to strike her; it was an aberration, the result of a momentary fit of anger. It wouldn't happen again. He had promised her.

But Cordelia knew better. She knew bout the secret lives of her friends with abusive husbands back home; she knew about the evasion, the false hopes, the self-protecting lies. She had read much of the available literature on the subject. A wife-beater was a dog who had tasted blood: he always came back for more. After the first time, he could never be trusted again. In vain she had tried to get Lydia to see reason. In vain she had urged her to break free and live her own life. But Lydia's response had merely been a pained and horrified look that had only served to confirm, it seemed to Cordelia, the hopelessness of her own complicity in her disempowerment and vassalage. Why, she wondered, did they always make excuses? Why did they think things would get better when they never did? Was there no way to save Lydia from her fate? *Ma nulla valse, ahi lassa!* Was she, like poor Eurydice, inevitably doomed?

The orchestra and singers had moved on and now it was Orpheus who sang, struggling to come to terms with an ungraspable sorrow, an irreparable loss: *Tu se' morta, mia vita, ed io respiro*— How could he go on living when the light of his universe and of his soul had gone out? How could he understand a reality as numbing and terrible as Eurydice's death?

The words flowed over Cordelia in a soulful, melancholy tide. Even a fictional grief has power to melt the hearts of those willing to suspend their disbelief. By chance, she glanced over at Signor Farinelli and saw that his eyes were brimming with tears. She was not used to seeing a man cry. Not once that she could remember had tears ever filled the eyes of Charles or of her father. Baffled and embarrassed—not knowing how to react—she looked away. Her heart was lodged like a lump in her throat. Should she say something or pretend she had noticed nothing? Had he seen that she had seen him? She was flustered and discomposed, as if she had stumbled unintentionally into the darkened room of some private grief. What did it mean? Was he merely moved by the power of the music—or was there something more to it? She had seen a haunting sadness in his eyes that first time they had met in Signora Ghilberti's apartment. What lay behind it, she wondered? Had he perhaps, like Orpheus, once loved a beautiful wife whose life was tragically taken from him? Cordelia's heart went out in anguish for his unknown pain—longing to help, but powerless to assist because she was afraid to interfere, afraid to pry.

When the aria finished, Farinelli wiped the corners of his eyes, then leaned toward her and whispered:

'It is very beautiful. The most beautiful aria, I think, in all of Monteverdi.'

'Yes,' she agreed, 'it's very beautiful.'

She longed to say more. With all her heart she wanted to beg him to open his heart to her, to let out the secret grief—whatever it was—that he had kept bottled up inside of him until the sorcery of music had raised it to consciousness from the buried catacombs of memory. But what could she say to soothe a sorrow she knew nothing of? What comfort could she possibly give? There was nothing she could do, no solace she could give—and the impotence of her empathy made her feel like crying herself.

For the rest of the rehearsal they sat in silence, side by side, each communing with his own thoughts. As she contemplated Farinelli, a warmth of admiration for him flowed into Cordelia's veins like the surge of a spring tide. How different he was from other men she knew—from Charles and his boorish friends, from the male students she knew at Northwestern, even from her father. How gentle and sensitive he was, how full of compassion and feeling. If only, she thought suddenly, she could distil some of his essence—some of his humanity—and inject it into a man like Vittorio di Banco, then the story for Lydia at least might still have a happy ending. But that eventuality, she knew, was a miracle beyond even the power of her wildest dreams to realize.

The rehearsal came to an end but it was some time before the fact registered on Cordelia's brain. When at last she looked up, the orchestra were packing away their instruments and the members of the chorus were standing in little knots chatting to one another under the bright lights that flooded the stage. The four soloists had disappeared and Maestro Marchesi was nowhere to be seen.

Cordelia looked at her watch in a sudden panic. 'Goodness,' she said with a start, grabbing up her bag. 'I have to be going. He's expecting me at six. I don't even know where to find his office.'

Beside her, Farinelli rose and said, 'I can show you the way. It's downstairs, just below the stage.' He started ahead of her down the row, pausing to wait when he reached the carpeted main aisle. 'And if you're asking yourself how I know that,' he added with a wry grin, 'it's because I once had a job as a janitor in this place. Maybe I'll tell you about it sometime.'

'Then you weren't always a writer of celebrated reviews?' Cordelia said in mock surprise.

'No—' he said, 'no, I'm afraid my origins are rather more humble than that.'

There was a touch of amused irony in his tone, as if he were recalling some private joke about the past. It made Cordelia glad to see that his witty urbanity, his sense of the comic in life, had returned. She found it easier to deal with than his tears.

They descended a flight of stairs through an arched portico that led to a narrow corridor on the floor below. It was crowded with musicians jostling with double basses and bassoons like the participants in some kabuki battle. On the left was a room with long dressing-tables over which hung mirrors ringed with naked bulbs—a make-up room during the theatrical season—which was stacked now with instrument cases on every available surface. It would make an interesting exam question, Cordelia thought, to show pictures of the cases and ask the students to identify which instruments they contained. How many could distinguish a viola from a violin or an oboe from an English horn? It might make an interesting experiment.

'Marchesi's office is halfway along, on the right,' Farinelli said. The ghost of a warning look appeared in his eye, but again he said nothing. 'It's clearly marked,' he said—and then, as if sensing her nervousness now that the actual moment of meeting Marchesi was upon her, he added with a grin, 'And break a leg for luck!'

'Thanks,' she said, the tension broken. 'It does feel a little bit like going on the stage.'

He gave her a thumbs-up and she wove her way through the congestion. She found the door easily. There was an engraved plate in the middle at eye-level marked *Maestro*. She took a deep breath and knocked lightly.

'Passate!'

She turned the knob and stepped, her heart pounding like an Ojibway tomtom, into the room—an intimate sanctum of leather and libretti. The man who sat behind the desk rose and advanced toward her, his hand extended, his lips curved into a welcoming smile.

'Maestro Marchesi—?' she said.

Why had she said that? Obviously, it was Marchesi. She'd been watching him upstairs for the past hour. She knew his face from a dozen record jackets. *Oh God*, she groaned to herself, *I step on the stage and muff my very first line*— She could cheerfully have crawled under a rock but there wasn't one handy.

Marchesi affected not to notice her discomfort. No doubt he was used to tongue-tied admirers. His dark eyes took her in with a glance that made her feel naked, as if there were no point in hiding anything—assuming that was her intention—from their penetrating gaze. He said:

'You're Cordelia Sinclair, I assume, from Chicago. Please, come in. I've been expecting you.'

He showed her to a chair, then crossed to an antique mahogany escritoire that served as a bar.

'It's a great honour,' she said, and her tongue felt like a lump of lead. *Oh God*, she thought, *don't let me say anything else stupid!* She went on: 'To tell you the truth, I can still hardly believe I'm really here—that all of this is really happening.'

He said from the bar:

'I was just about to pour myself a drink when you arrived. Can I tempt you?'

'Yes,' she said. 'A dry vermouth would be nice.'

He poured her drink, then splashed two fingers of bourbon into a tumbler for himself, adding ice from a mini-fridge beside the bar.

Cordelia opened her bag on her lap. 'Would you mind if I taperecord our talk?' she asked. 'I'm probably too excited to try trusting anything to memory.'

'Not at all,' he said, returning with the drinks and a twinkle in his eye. 'Not as long as I get credit, where credit is due, in the footnotes. And royalties, of course,' he added, 'when the work becomes a bestseller on the *New York Times* list.'

That was all it took to break the ice.

'I'll send you my first cheque,' Cordelia promised with a grin.

'Ah—! Now, that's a commitment you may live to regret, my dear,' he said, taking his place behind the desk. 'But I intend to hold you to it all the same, because I'm an extremely greedy man.' He raised his glass. 'Cheers!'

'Cheers! And thanks for the vote of confidence. I guess I was wound up pretty tight when I first came in.'

'Not at all,' he said graciously. 'On the contrary, you were perfectly charming.' He leaned back and fingered the gold chain at his throat. 'Now, if I remember correctly,' he went on in his rich baritone, 'you said in the letter you sent me from the States that you were doing your work on the Camerata. I'd like to hear about your thesis—and especially about what sparked your interest in a group of minor composers like the Camerata. It's not surprising, I suppose, that someone like me should have a special place for them in his heart. They were, after all, all Florentines. But how, I'm asking myself, am I to account for *your* interest in them? It does seem rather strange. Are American doctoral candidates so starved for topics nowadays, Signorina Sinclair, that they're forced to seek out the arcana of minor pioneers in the history of opera to write about?'

He was relaxed and smiling, inquisitively ironic, leaning back with slender fingers linked behind a mane of long, dark hair, his black eyes still weighing her up, seeming to pierce to her core. She was surprised at how good-looking and well preserved he was for his age. It struck her that the posed and glossy photographs on his record jackets did him much less than justice. He was really a very attractive man.

'I met them first in an introductory course on early opera,' Cordelia said, trying to read the temper of the black eyes. 'The professor who taught us the course said everything he had to say about them in twenty minutes and then moved on with a huge sigh of relief to Monteverdi and the big names. Frankly, I was intrigued. I had a hunch there was more to them than we'd been told. It's a mistake to dismiss first explorers too lightly—they always seem to have seen much more than they ever actually get credit for. Anyway, I went off to the library and started digging around on my own—and the more I read, the more I began to appreciate the nature of the debt later composers owed to the theoretical ground rules laid out by the Camerata. Musicologically speaking, they're a fascinating group—and I'm convinced their influence is seminal for everything that follows.' She flashed Marchesi an abashed smiled. 'So naturally I decided to write a thesis on the topic and set the rest of the world straight. And besides,' she added, 'not a great deal has been written about them—which is always a useful fact for a Ph.D. student to bear in mind.'

The answer, it seemed, was satisfactory. Marchesi nodded and said:

'Quite so, I agree. They deserve a better fate than they've so far received. I hope you succeed in giving it to them.'

Cordelia felt as if she had passed some unannounced quiz. The lines in Marchesi's face seemed to soften and the eyes lost their look of bemused, ironic objectivity. But the look that took its place was not what she anticipated. Beneath the mask that she had correctly judged to be no more than a slightly sardonic façade to shield him from the impertinences of the world there lay the enigmatic, sphinx-like image of the man himself. She had expected to see passion in those dark eyes—a depth of fire and feeling. But that is not what met her. Marchesi's eyes were not those of a visionary; they were the eyes of a lawyer: acute, incisive, impartial, calculating. What on earth, she wondered, was he thinking? It was a face—a cryptic and delphian face—that gave absolutely nothing away. To look into it was like staring down into a well.

He said:

'Well now, so how can I help you? What do you want to know about the Camerata that you can't get from books?'

Cordelia sipped her vermouth and said: 'Well, what interests me in particular are the sorts of problems a conductor might encounter in playing their works today. I remember reading some place that you once directed Jacopo Peri's *Dafne*.'

He nodded. 'Some years ago, in Milan,' he said, 'as an experiment.'

'A successful one?'

'He gave a thin smile. 'From my point of view or the audi-'s?'

'Both.'

He pursed his lips, thoughtfully. 'From my point of view, yes, eminently successful,' he said. 'From the audience's probably not. The reviewers found the production slow and rather ponderous, but in my judgement that was because they lacked the historical imagination they needed to sweep their minds clear of inappropriate romantic expectations and appreciate the classical gravity of expression that Peri was after. Modern audiences, you mustn't forget, are brought up on Verdi and Puccini and feel cheated if they don't get plenty of action and a few grand theatrical gestures from doomed heroes. There's nothing in their experience to prepare them for the static severity of the Camerata.'

'Is it something you'd try again?—directing Peri, I mean.'

'Oh, but of course,' he said with a wry grin. 'It's a conductor's job to expand the repertoire of his audiences by tweaking them in the comfortable citadel of their prejudices wherever he can. It wouldn't do just to keep serving up the same few tired pieces they've always felt at home with. No, where's the challenge in that—or the fun?'

For the next half-hour, Marchesi talked fluently and volubly about Peri and Giulio Caccini, about the technical difficulties involved in staging their works with modern orchestral instruments, about his theory of the origin of the Camerata's *stile recitativo* in Greek music. Did she know, for example, that the tragedians of ancient Athens had composed musical scores to accompany their plays? He had, he said, actually seen in Vienna the papyrus fragment, perhaps by Euripides himself, of a stasimon chorus from the *Oresteia*—

Cordelia listened with awestruck, fascinated delight. Though the dark eyes he settled on her never lost their inscrutable, appraising quality, Marchesi was knowledgeable, witty, completely unaffected. Until she had stepped through the door into his room, she'd had no idea there was so much to know—so much that was truly *exciting*—about her chosen speciality. Oh, how glad she was that she'd thought to bring her tape recorder along with her! Without it, how could she possibly have remembered even a fraction of the wealth that he poured out like a river of jewels from a lifetime of musical experience?

He talked about Girolamo Mei and Vincenzo Galilei and what the members of the Camerata were trying to accomplish with melody, how their theories intersected with their music—and all of a sudden the reading she had been doing for the past week under the bust of Marcus Aurelius in the studious silence of the rare-book room came miraculously to life. It was as if the old Florentines themselves—Peri and Bardi and Galilei—had materialized from the mists of time and stood before her, arguing and debating their revolutionary ideas for a new form of musical drama. And in a way, she thought, perhaps they *were* there somewhere in the shadows, listening and nodding their heads in silent approval.

The allotted hour flew by at the speed of light.

Then suddenly the time was up. The interview was over and she found herself standing to go—her tape recorder packed away, her bag clutched under her arm, her head whirling with impressions, information, ideas. She felt completely overwhelmed, swamped by the experience; she felt as if she had lost her bearings in the world of quotidian reality.

She thanked Marchesi without remembering the words she spoke. Graciously, he thanked *her* for giving him an excuse to talk about something long of interest to him. He expressed the hope that their meeting would be useful to her and, as they parted at the door, he raised her hand to his lips in a genteel, old-world way—

And then suddenly, not knowing quite how it happened—wondering if, in fact, she was not merely waking from a dream—she found herself in the corridor outside, walking away.

As she climbed the steps toward the empty auditorium, she remembered Signor Farinelli's warning glances about Marchesi and she wondered what on earth had possessed him to be concerned for her safety. Maestro Marchesi had shown himself to be not only a musical genius but a perfect gentleman as well.

NINE

COLLÈGIO SAN STEFANO was a nineteenth-century structure outside the walls of the old city, the brick façade of its buildings severe and utilitarian. At one time, it had been an exclusive academy, educating the sons of the rich and, mingled with them, the orphans whom the Basilian Fathers, who ran the place, had taken in as charity cases. The mixed clientele was part of a conscious strategy to integrate the sons of the wealthiest and most powerful families in the city with the disempowered offspring of an underclass in the social and economic hierarchy. There were valuable lessons, the good Basilian Fathers believed, to be learned on both sides. In practice, of course, the rich boys patronized and dominated the poor boys, exploiting them and reducing them to vassalage. Occasionally, one of the orphans, envying such sovereignty, managed to elevate himself with fists or guile into a petty tyrant among his peers. In other words, in spite of the best efforts of a dedicated cadre of instructors armed with faith and a visionary theory, the political and social reality that existed inside the college walls was pretty much a faithful microcosm of the wealth-and-power pragmatism that governed the world outside. Yet for all its *naïveté*, the egalitarian theory and the priestly effort to implement it were still laudable.

But Collègio San Stefano's days of eminence were long past. Since the halcyon decades of the 1950s and 1960s, when Rolls Royces and Mercedes had swept up the circular drive to discharge their uniformed cargoes at the beginning of term, the academy had fallen on hard times. There were still plenty of orphans, but the wealthy now sent their heirs elsewhere and Collègio San Stefano had become, like other Utopian dreams in the history of educational reform, a forgotten backwater sustained by little more than its memories of an illustrious past. There were no Rolls Royces any more and the evidence of decline was everywhere apparent in the untended grounds and crumbling college buildings. Weeds had usurped the once-lush surface of the playing field and the rows of weathered bleachers along the sidelines had shed their coats of faded yellow paint in flakes, like fallen petals, into the undergrowth of docks and nettles that flourished below their warping boards.

Arbati steered the black Fiat in through the wrought-iron gates and parked in a gravelled parking area beside what seemed to be the main administration building. Beside him, Giorgio Bruni surveyed the forlorn façade, where strands of ivy, sparse and straggling, clung to the brown brick like abandoned scaling-ladders thrown against the front of an old fortress. The images of decay and desolation were all around them.

'It's not what it used to be,' Bruni said sadly, eyeing the netless frame of the soccer goal on the overgrown playing field. 'We played against these guys, you know, when I was a student at Pius XII back in the '70s. It was getting a little seedy even then, I suppose, but nothing like this. They still cared enough to keep up appearances. I haven't seen the place for nearly twenty years.'

Arbati shut off the ignition and pocketed the key. 'How did you do?'

'Huh?'

'When you played San Stefano, how'd your team do?'

Bruni gave him a crooked smile. 'They whipped our ass, brother. These guys were the city champions three years running. We hated their guts. Every time we bothered to show up, it was a bloody massacre.'

'Cheer up,' Arbati said. 'From the look of the place now, you've got your revenge.'

Bruni looked out at the ravaged scene. 'I thought revenge was supposed to be sweet,' he said.

They left the car and followed a concrete walk, where crab grass sprouted in the cracks, that led to a recessed porch. In the centre was an oak door with a knocker in the shape of a leaping dolphin. It belonged to happier days. Arbati let it fall twice, the sound reverberating like a hammer striking an empty barrel.

After a short interval, the door was opened by an elderly priest, gaunt and unsmiling, in a black soutane. His pinched features radiated an aura of ascetic sanctity and his narrow eyes looked out on the world with that expression of permanent disbelief that is born of listening to too many lies from too many boys over too many years. Even the most dedicated idealist, Arbati supposed, was bound to be affected by an environment like that to which Collègio San Stefano had been reduced. After its years of glory, it had become a final haven for emotionally disturbed boys—a last chance for them to learn to conform their behaviour to the expectations of society before their dossiers were handed over, for final judgement, to the justice and penal systems.

'Inspector Arbati and Detective Bruni,' Arbati said, flashing his identity card, 'to see Father Monticelli.'

The priest nodded and stepped aside. 'Father Rector is expecting you,' he said, closing the door and starting ahead of them without further preamble down a long, poorly-lit hall. 'If you will follow me please, gentlemen.'

The corridor was high-roofed and musty smelling, its oak-panelled walls lined with framed photographs—dated and curling—of sports teams and class years of the past. As they passed, their footsteps echoed like cannon shot along the stone flags. On either side of the hall, from open doors where rows of scowling boys bent over wooden desks and dog-eared notebooks, there issued the drone of mathematics and grammar. It seemed more a prison than a place where fragile minds were being supplied with the tools they needed to meet the challenges of civilized life.

'The place is a bit of a museum,' Bruni muttered, staring around him at the yellowing rows of old photographs.

More like a mausoleum, Arbati thought.

The cassocked figure walking ahead of them glided to a stop, tapped softly at the door and disappeared inside, then reappeared almost immediately.

'You may go in,' he announced.

The man who rose to greet them from behind a cluttered desk was large and florid, perhaps fifty, with huge hands the size of leather bucklers and the broad, muscular shoulders of a bar-room bouncer. He looked more like a retired pugilist than a priest, and even the understated anonymity of his clerical garb did little to dispel the aura of raw physical power rippling in sinewy bulges under the folds of his cassock. The responsibilities at the new San Stefano, Arbati supposed, occasionally required skills that traditional teaching methods failed to supply and it was not hard to imagine that the boys at the school, however untamed and rebellious in spirit, would be prepared to suffer almost any fate before being required to visit the Father Rector's office to answer for their sins.

The office, though cluttered, was spartan. Two wooden chairs with slatted backs stood before an inquisitorial desk. The walls—not surprisingly, given the college's desire to honour its past—were coved with portraits of clerical predecessors. Over the desk hung a large colour photograph of the current pope. Along one wall, glass-fronted bookshelves held leather-bound volumes, perhaps unopened for years, that belonged to another, more genteel age in the history of the school.

Father Monticelli shook hands briskly, then took his place behind the desk. Arbati explained as much as he could about the purpose of their visit.

'I don't suppose I can know why you want this information?' the burly priest said brusquely.

Arbati shook his head. 'Sorry,' he said. 'At this stage the investigation is confidential. Police procedure, I'm afraid. You'll have to wait and read about it in the papers.'

The priest's eyes narrowed. 'I hope you're not dredging up things that will tarnish the reputation of the school,' he said warningly. 'We're proud of our alumni here, inspector. A number of them, as you know, have become quite prominent figures in the community.'

And three of them, Arbati thought, have turned up recently quite brutally dead. Side-stepping the issue, he said:

'As I mentioned when we spoke on the phone, I'm interested particularly in the years from 1954 to 1957. Detective Bruni and I would like to interview anyone who might have taught at San Stefano in those four years.'

The Slasher's victims had so far all been students at the school during the period, and it was possible—even probable—that the link which connected them lay in their belonging to a particular social or sports group: a dormitory wing, a clique of close friends, a sports team, a school club. That kind of information, which an old teacher might well remember, might not lead him directly to Lo Squartatore himself (who was perhaps an envious outsider), but it would narrow the search for his next victim—for Arbati was convinced this killer wasn't finished yet. It was just a hunch, of course, but over the years he'd learned to trust his hunches, especially when he felt them as strongly as he felt this one. If he could narrow the search to a particular group of boys, then it would be possible to make contact with potential victims and convince them to reveal Lo Squartatore's identity. After that, the rest would be easy. The great mystery in the whole affair, he thought, was why those potential victims hadn't come forward on their own instead of waiting for the police to hunt them out. After three murders, they must have had a pretty clear idea of what was going on and of the danger they were in.

Father Monticelli leaned forward and his expression softened fractionally.

'Monsignor Aprile was headmaster here during that time,' he said. 'A fine man. That's his portrait over there, the second from the left. He's been dead for years, I'm afraid.' He folded his massive hands before him on the desk. 'After your call, inspector, I made enquiries about former staff. Those who taught here in the 1950s were, it seems, all of an age—all in their forties and early fifties. Most of them, of course, are dead now; it was a long time ago. But there is one survivor from the period—Father Ucello. Gregorio Ucello. He's over ninety and his mind, I'm told, dwells mostly on childhood. He's unlikely to be of much help, but if you want, you can find him at the Basilian retreat in Rapallo.'

Bruni took the information down in his notebook.

'What about student records?' Arbati asked.

Father Monticelli smiled. 'There I *can* be more useful,' he said, opening a drawer and taking out a manilla envelope which he handed across. 'The college accounts are very complete, going back as far as the 1920s. I've included the record of every boy who was here in the period in question.' He added: 'I expect them back, of course.'

'Naturally,' Arbati said. He started to rise, then said: 'There is one more thing, father. I noticed the photographs outside in the corridor. Is it possible you have yearbooks—or lists of the boys belonging to various clubs and sporting teams?'

Father Monticelli's face lit up as if a bulb had been switched on behind his eyes.

'As a matter of fact,' he said proudly, 'we have an extensive archive. A sort of museum, you know. It contains several thousand old photographs, many of them with the boys' names written on the back. Perhaps you'd care to see it?'

'Later, perhaps,' Arbati said with a conciliatory smile. What he wanted most now was a cigarette and a peek at the contents of the envelope under his arm. 'I suspect you've given us quite enough here,' he said, patting the thick brown envelope, 'to keep us going for a day or two. I'll take a rain-check on the archive, if you don't mind.'

'As you wish, inspector,' Father Monticelli said, disguising his disappointment. But the light behind his eyes had gone out. He rose and extended his hand. 'I'm always here.'

TEN

GOING IN THROUGH the front door of Pensione Ghilberti Cordelia
nearly bumped into Signor di Banco who was on his way out.
What's *he* doing here? she wondered acidly. They glared briefly
at one another with mutual antipathy but neither spoke and the
heavy leaded-glass door closed between them. She saw his profile,
gaunt and sour, pass in the lace-curtained sidelight. Poor Lydia,
she thought. Poor naive, forgiving, long-suffering Lydia. Knowing what a miserable bastard he was and always would be, how
could she blithely go on sharing her life with him? Well, Cordelia
thought, it's not my problem. I did what I could to help, but Lydia
as much as told me to mind my own business. There's nothing
more I can do. She had no plans to visit Lydia di Banco in the
future.

There was no mail set out for her on the mahogany table in
the ostrich-plumed hall and she started wearily up the stairs. It
had been a long day at the library, her head was spinning, and
all she wanted to do was drop into a hot tub and then crawl into
bed with her P.D. James whodunit. There were still the leftovers
of last night's chicken pasta in the fridge for supper. All she had
to do was somehow find the energy to get up two flights of stairs
and heat them up.

She had reached the first-floor landing when Signora Ghilberti's door suddenly opened and the landlady bustled out into
the hall and fluted up after her:

'Ou-ee! Miss Sinclair!'

Cordelia leaned over the railing. 'Yes?'

'There's a parcel that came for you this afternoon by messenger, dear. I have it down here.'

A parcel? By messenger—? Cordelia had no idea what it
meant. Who would have sent her a parcel?

She turned, frowning, and started back down the stairs.

'Flowers,' Signora Ghilberti announced, handing over the long,
narrow box with a colourful florist's label.

Still frowning, Cordelia took it and lifted the lid. Inside, swaddled in tissue paper, lay a dozen long-stemmed red roses and a note in a white envelope. She hadn't the remotest idea what the occasion might be or who on earth they could possibly be from.

'Oh, how lovely!' Signora Ghilberti sighed, clasping her hands to her breast. She added slyly, fishing for more. 'They're from a gentleman admirer, I expect.' Signora Ghilberti's days were long and lonely and she spent her time speculating about other people's lives. She was English, too, and a gift of flowers (no matter who the recipient) always brought out the wistful romanticism that simmered just below the surface of her soul.

Cordelia closed the lid on the box, leaving flowers and note untouched.

'Oh no, nothing like that,' she said casually: 'It's just a little thank you from someone at the university I helped with a little job.'

'How very thoughtful of them,' Signora Ghilberti said curtly, her romantic vision of the floral tribute irreparably dashed.

Cordelia thanked her for taking the parcel in and started back up the stairs.

'Don't you worry, dear,' Signora Ghilberti, quickly recovering her equanimity and her optimism, called out after her, 'the right young man will come along for you one day. Mark my words. You just wait and see.'

Cordelia wasn't at all sure she wanted any young man coming along, either now or ever. She'd had quite enough trouble with the one young man who had managed to ride on his white charger into her life—and Charles Passmore, she thought grimly, was more than enough matrimonial experience for any woman in a single lifetime. She certainly wasn't ready to repeat the experiment in a hurry.

'I'm sure he will,' she replied sweetly, to be civil.

At the top of the stairs she unlocked her door and laid the flowers, still unboxed, on the kitchen table. The orange cat was waiting on the balcony, staring in through the French windows. Seeing her inside, he meowed imperiously—patience was not his long suit—and she let him in and poured his saucer of milk.

'How are you tonight, my fine furry friend?' she said, squatting beside him and running a hand down the silky, arching back. He lapped at the milky pool with closed eyes and purred out his contentment.

'Now,' Cordelia said, standing, 'let's see who these are from, shall we?'

She set the flowers out on the table and opened the envelope. It contained a ticket for the opening-night concert of the Monteverdi festival at Teatro Comunale on Friday. The ticket, she noticed, was for a private box. Accompanying it was a laconic note which read:

Signorina,
You will honour me by accepting the enclosed and being my guest at a soirée at my villa following the performance.
Marchesi

There was an R.S.V.P. with a telephone number at the bottom. For some strange reason, she remembered that for most of her childhood she had thought R.S.V.P meant Refreshments Served Very Promptly. It was odd the things that popped into one's mind. She couldn't remember when it was that she had learned the disappointing truth.

For a long time she stared at the note as if it were written in a foreign language. Then, with an effort, she focused her mind and read it again, slowly—and then again—to convince herself that her eyes weren't somehow deceiving her. The invitation was so totally unexpected, so wildly out-of-the-blue that she hardly knew what to think of it. Oddly, the first thing that came to mind were Farinelli's words to her on her first day in Florence: 'Marchesi is not a pleasant person. You're an attractive woman and there are many stories about him.' Well, she thought, comparing Marchesi with her ex-husband, if he is a wolf, he's at least a cultivated one. And yet, he hadn't given the impression of being unpleasant—to use Farinelli's euphemism—when she'd spent an hour alone with him in an empty theatre. All the same, accepting his offer—so sudden, so generous—might be taken, at least in some quarters, to entail…well, a certain obligation. And really, when it came right down to it, she knew next to nothing about him. He was really almost a complete stranger. And then, too, she remembered how impossible it had been to read the thoughts he was thinking behind those enigmatic, lawyerlike eyes…

She arranged the flowers in a vase—all she could find was a large wine carafe—and set them in the middle of the table. They were beautiful, quite exquisite really, and the fragrance of their perfume hung on the air like dust scattered from a passing angel's wing.

What should she do?

She ran a bath and stretched out in the warm water, letting a thousand liquid fingers massage her skin as she weighed up the pros and cons of the offer. The concert was tomorrow night. Whatever she decided, it would have to be soon. She had less than a day to make up her mind.

Refreshed, glowing, but still undecided, she stepped from the tub and met her image in the full-length mirror on the bathroom door. She remembered how she had stood there once before, her body naked but her soul concealed, and demanded an epiphany, an insight into who and what she was. Cordelia Erin Sinclair: divorced and insecure, alone and desperately seeking, the motherless daughter of a Shakespeare professor from Evanston, Illinois. Oh yes, she knew very clearly what she wanted to *forget* in her life, what she wanted to leave behind; but did she have any idea of what she expected to find—? She stared at the strange and familiar figure who stared out at her from the silvered glass and the old questions returned: Who am I? Who do I want to be? What do I want out of life?

You came to Florence to discover yourself, she told the reflected image, but what have you discovered? Do you know anything more about yourself than when you first arrived—?

In her heart of hearts, she knew the answer to that question. And she knew, too, the instant she recognized that she knew the answer, that in that same instant she had made up her mind about Marchesi's invitation. She knew now exactly what she was going to do.

She towelled herself dry and threw on her fluffy terrycloth robe. Then she walked to the telephone and dialled the number at the bottom of Marchesi's note, tapping her foot impatiently while the call clicked its tortuous way through the relays of the Italian telephone network.

'Pronto.'

It was not Marchesi's voice.

'Is Signor Marchesi in?' she asked.

'May I ask who is calling?'

'My name is Sinclair. Cordelia Sinclair.'

'Ah, Signorina Sinclair, yes,' the voice said, warming. 'My name is Bruno. I'm Signor Marchesi's secretary. I regret that the maestro is at a meeting in the city and does not expect to return until after eleven. He told me you might call. Perhaps you'd care to leave a message?'

Cordelia hesitated. Had Marchesi arrogantly *presumed* that she would accept his offer? But no, it was reasonable for him to expect an answer of some kind from her. The concert, after all, was tomorrow night and time was short. That, surely, was all that was meant.

She said: 'I'd be grateful if you'd tell Signor Marchesi that I accept his invitation with pleasure.'

'I'll be certain he gets the message the instant he comes in, signorina. Is there anything else?'

'Yes, as a matter of fact, there is,' she said, grabbing at a sudden inspiration. 'You can tell him the roses are lovely—and that his invitation absolutely blew my mind.'

She rang off.

Fra Angelico was rubbing against her leg and she picked him up, holding him out so that they were face to face.

'Well there,' she told him, 'it's done—and damn the torpedoes! It's not every day a girl from Evanston, Illinois gets asked out on a date by a world-famous conductor.'

She had come to Florence to discover herself, and whatever Marchesi's intentions toward her might be, she wouldn't succeed in finding the identity she was longing to find by running away from him—or anybody else for that matter. She'd simply have to handle whatever situation she happened to run into when it arose. If she had said no to Marchesi, she would—in the final analysis— have only been saying no to herself. Saying no to the self she wanted more than anything else to set free. She was thirty-two years old and it was time to face the music.

'Besides, big fellow,' she told Fra Angelica, 'if my five years with Charles Passmore taught me anything at all, it was the womanly art of self-defence.'

ELEVEN

CARLO ARBATI poured himself a fresh mug of coffee from the eternal pot simmering on the hotplate and lit another cigarette. It was his sixth cup of the day and the ashtray on the desk was heaped with the broken torsos of a dozen discarded butts. He was getting nowhere with the Slasher investigation and his nerves were beginning to fray. He stood at the open window cradling the hot mug in his hands and glared down for a moment at traffic on Via Zara, then went back to the desk and slumped into his chair. A stack of curled and yellowing forms—the official records of the hundred and thirteen boys enrolled at Collègio San Stefano in the years 1954 to 1957—stared up at him defiantly, thumbing their collective nose at him, daring him to find the key that unlocked their secret. He had been through them a dozen times, combing their pages for hints, clues, intimations, inklings—and had found nothing. Not a single damned thing. The clue he needed to break open the Slasher case was somewhere in that bloody pile. He knew it. He could *feel* it; he just couldn't find it—yet.

Maybe Giorgio, he thought, would get lucky and turn something up in Rapallo. But Arbati wasn't hopeful. Giorgio didn't have much faith in what he called Arbati's 'San Stefano hunch' and, in any event, it was unlikely that Father Ucello, now a very old man, would remember much that was useful.

His real problem, Arbati knew, was to bring Giorgio on side. And to do that he needed some solid evidence. Giorgio Bruni wasn't convinced, even yet, that the three murders were the work of a single killer. And even if—and it was a big if in Bruni's mind—they did turn out to be connected, he still had his money on the Mafia as the guilty party. Giorgio's argument, Arbati reflected, did have a certain plausibility. The three victims had all been affluent and powerful men, prominent figures in Florentine life—and all of them, too, had been involved, in one way or another, with shady dealings on the far side of the law. In Cafferelli's case, the record showed definite links to the Mob; in the cases of Mora and Rosso—both corrupt, both unscrupulous—such links were probable, although no firm evidence had turned up so far to tie them directly to the Mafia. The fact that the victims had attended the same school at the same time was an interesting piece of information—but, in fact, it proved nothing. It was purely circumstantial. While it showed that the three men must have known each other, there was nothing in the school records—or anywhere else, for that matter—to suggest that they had been particularly chummy during their time at San Stefano, or that they had become friends after leaving the school, or that their business dealings or their social lives in later years had ever intersected. And there was certainly nothing in the records—Bruni argued—to lead the police in the direction of a single killer, somehow connected with Collègio San Stefano, who had a single motive for murdering all three of them. And so, Giorgio Bruni remained unconvinced. As far as he was concerned, the serial-killer theory was just another one of Arbati's crazy hunches. But then, he'd seen those hunches pay off more than once before in the past and—who knew?—maybe this one would too.

That morning, Bruni had taken the Rapido to Genoa, then borrowed a car from the local Carabinieri and driven out to the Basilian retreat at Rapallo to talk with Father Ucello, the only member of the 1950s teaching corps at Collègio San Stefano who was still living. The old man was over ninety and, according to Father Monticelli, he was also pretty well ga-ga. But police work was a matter of meticulous method, a matter of doggedly chasing down leads, no matter how improbable they seemed. And if most of them ended up leading to dead ends, there was no way of knowing that until you finally got to the end of the road and found a brick wall across your path.

Arbati looked at his watch and drummed his fingers irritably on the desk. Giorgio would be back from Rapallo in a couple of hours. What Arbati needed in the meantime was something concrete, some definite link dating from the San Stefano years that connected all three victims. Something he could shove under Bruni's sceptical nose when he returned; something that would make a believer out of him. He glared at the stack of forms piled in front of him and they glared back at him. It was a stand-off. Somewhere in that bloody pile was the link he wanted, the elusive clue that connected Lo Squartatore's past victims and pointed forward to his next one. But where was it—where? The cigarette between his lips tasted stale and he ground it out with impatience. He was smoking too much, he knew, but it relieved his frustration—or so he chose to believe. One day, though, he'd quit—one day.

There was a rap on the glass-paned door that separated his office from the squad room beyond. A sergeant carrying an arm-load of computer track-paper pushed the door open and bustled in.

'What have you got, Tommo?' Arbati asked.

The sergeant set the papers on the desk. 'It's those background checks you ordered on the San Stefano boys,' he said. 'They just came out of the printer downstairs. I knew you'd be waiting for them, so I ran them right up.' His red cheeks and harsh breathing suggested the statement should be taken literally.

'Good man,' Arbati said, snatching them up. 'Is this the whole lot?'

The sergeant nodded. 'Yes, sir. Addresses, bank accounts, business dealings, and everything else the data-bank could serve up. It looks like a busy afternoon ahead of you, sir.' The stack of paper was at least two inches high. At the door he turned and said with a grin, 'Well, happy hunting, sir. I hope you find what you're looking for.'

'So do I, Tommo,' Arbati said. 'So do I.'

The printout contained up-to-the-minute information on every boy who had been enrolled at Collègio San Stefano in the period 1954-7. Arbati leafed quickly through the sheets to see if anything caught his eye. Nothing did—so he went back to the beginning and began methodically collating the new information with the facts he already had. When he had finished, the forms Father Monticelli had given him lay stacked in four neat piles in front of him. Of the hundred and thirteen boys at the college during the years in question, twenty-nine had died (all of accidental or natural causes—except, of course, Mora, Rosso, and Cafferelli), forty-three had moved out of Tuscany and were no longer in Arbati's jurisdiction, and six had disappeared altogether. The remaining thirty-five boys—now men—were still living in Florence.

That narrowed the hunt. It was a beginning.

Arbati sipped his coffee and contemplated the last pile, the one containing the records of the thirty-five still living in Florence. The list read like a *Who's Who* of the city's business, civic, and artistic communities: Bernacci, Conti, Manzuoli, Marchesi, Strozzi, Velluti. Only one—Nicòlo Strozzi, chairman of the Banco di Firenze—had originally been an orphan taken in by the good fathers at San Stefano; the rest had come from privileged, indeed very privileged, backgrounds. But there was no reason to exclude Strozzi merely because he had been one of San Stefano's orphans. The first of Lo Squartatore's victims—Alberto Mora, the textile magnate—had been a war orphan raised and educated by the fathers at Collègio San Stefano. It followed, therefore, that all thirty-five names in that pile were potential victims.

Arbati lit another cigarette and launched a thoughtful cloud of smoke toward the ceiling. So far, each of the three corpses left behind by Lo Squartatore had belonged to a wealthy, well-known figure, still living in Florence, who had been a student at Collègio San Stefano in the years 1954-1957. If that pattern held—and there was no reason to suppose that it wouldn't—then at least one (and probably more than one) of those thirty-five gentlemen knew exactly *who* that somebody was. It was also possible, of course, that one of the thirty-five was himself Lo Squartatore.

It was now that the real dog-work began.

Each of the thirty-five had to be questioned. In addition, the six boys who had disappeared from the municipal data-bank had to be accounted for, and cursory checks had to be run on the forty-three who had moved out of Tuscany. Only the twenty-nine who were dead were exempt from further scrutiny. Police work was seldom a glamorous business. A lot of tough leg-work lay ahead—and a hell of a lot of superfluous paperwork, Arbati thought with a grimace. But at least now there was a solid platform from which to launch the investigation. When Giorgio got back from Rapallo—with or without anything they could use to narrow the search—he'd find that his work was cut out for him.

Arbati picked up the telephone and dialled the number of the first name on the list. The opening move in the game was to make the initial contacts, set up the necessary interviews, then sit back and watch what happened.

How much time, he wondered, did they have until Lo Squartatore struck again?

TWELVE

THE PRIVATE BOX directly overlooked the stage. From her seat, Cordelia could almost have reached down and plucked a violin from one of the player's hands if she had been inclined to larceny. It was the most stunning seat she'd ever had in a theatre. Settling back into the plush velvet upholstery, she surveyed the ornate, frescoed images of nymphs and frisking satyrs on the gilded ceiling overhead. *Oh yes indeed,* she thought to herself, suppressing a Cheshire-cat grin, *I could* definitely *get used to living like this.* Fully lit and filled with bejewelled patrons, the theatre was more lavish and imposing than it had seemed on that afternoon a few days earlier when she had sat beside Signor Farinelli in this same hall, then dark and empty, listening to the rehearsal. Gazing around her, she felt suddenly extremely pleased with herself for having had the foresight and good sense to accept Marchesi's invitation. She'd have been a fool to turn him down and miss such a terrific opportunity.

She shared the box with a middle-aged man named Gasparini, the husband of one of the soloists. He and his wife, she discovered, were also invited to the soirée at Marchesi's villa after the concert. Signor Gasparini was a large and florid man, courtly in mien and gesture, who, in spite of the fact that he weighed well over two hundred pounds, did not seem particularly fat. As Cordelia quickly discovered, he had an uncanny gift for striking up instant acquaintanceships and he had kept her amused since her arrival with an endless stream of chit-chat that ran the gamut from the banal to the mischievously malicious. Gasparini was a veteran of the cocktail circuit—indeed, from all Cordelia could gather, he'd made a career out of trailing his wife from one singing engagement to the next—and he obviously relished his role as insouciant social butterfly. It was the part in life's theatre he believed he had been born to play. Everything about him, from his fleshy hands where no callus had ever formed to the lassitude in his hazel eyes, made it plain that he was content—perfectly and

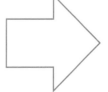

NO COST! NO OBLIGATION TO BUY! NO PURCHASE NECESSARY!

PLAY "LUCKY 7"
AND GET FOUR FREE GIFTS...

HOW TO PLAY:

1. With a coin, carefully scratch off the silver area at the right. Then check the claim chart to see what we have for you—FREE BOOKS and a gift—ALL YOURS! ALL FREE!

2. Send back this card and you'll get brand-new, first-time-in-paperback Mystery Library™ novels. These books have a cover price of $4.99 each. But THEY ARE TOTALLY FREE; even the shipping will be at our expense!

3. There's no catch. You're under no obligation to buy anything. We charge nothing—ZERO—for your first shipment. And you don't have to make any minimum number of purchases—not even one!

4. The fact is thousands of readers enjoy receiving books by mail from the Mystery Library Reader Service™. They like the convenience of home delivery and they love our great prices!

5. We hope that after receiving your free books you'll want to remain a subscriber. But the choice is yours—to continue or cancel, anytime at all! So why not take us up on our invitation, with no risk of any kind. You'll be glad you did!

*SURPRISE MYSTERY GIFT
IT COULD BE YOURS <u>FREE</u> WHEN
YOU PLAY "LUCKY 7".*

PLAY "LUCKY 7"

**Just scratch off the silver box with a coin.
Then check below to see the gifts you get.**

YES! I have scratched off the silver area above. Please send me all the gifts for which I qualify. I understand I am under no obligation to purchase any books, as explained on the back and on the opposite page.

415 CIY A3FJ
(U-M-L-01/97)

NAME

ADDRESS   APT.

CITY   STATE   ZIP

7 7 7	**WORTH THREE FREE BOOKS AND A FREE SURPRISE GIFT**
🍒🍒🍒	**WORTH THREE FREE BOOKS**
● ● ●	**WORTH TWO FREE BOOKS**
🔔🔔🍒	**WORTH ONE FREE BOOK**

Offer limited to one per household and not valid to present subscribers. All orders subject to approval.

blissfully content—to measure out his allotted days shuttling from opera house to opera house and soirée to soirée, sharing his wife's kudos vicariously and never being asked to do anything more arduous than divert a beautiful stranger with his jocoserious conversation. It certainly, as he declared to her with feeling, beat the hell out of working for a living.

He leaned toward her now and whispered behind his hand, 'Good Lord, look at that!'

Cordelia followed his gaze across the auditorium to a box on the far side where an elderly man, dressed in an outrageous electric-blue dinner jacket and ruffled shirt, was fondling a girl in a cerise gown who looked young enough to be his granddaughter. He appeared to be nibbling her ear as she affected a flustered moue and stifled a titter of delight.

'Dirty old toad,' Gasparini hissed.

'Who is he?' Cordelia asked, mesmerized by the spectacle.

Gasparini rolled his eyes. 'Antonio Gandolfo. You've probably heard of him. He's a perennial candidate for the Communist Party—always getting his name into the news one way or another. He makes his money publishing one of those trendy leftist magazines that mix Marxist doctrine into an unholy brew with environmental issues, gay and lesbian awareness, and animal rights. You know the sort of thing I mean. Omnivorous socialism. I imagine old Karl would be fairly spinning in his mouldy crypt if he had any notion what was going on up here in his name. God, look at him nuzzling her, the old lizard!' He made a clucking sound with his tongue. 'Imagine, bringing his tart to the theatre like that!'

'The men of culture are the true apostles of equality,' Cordelia observed, quoting Matthew Arnold.

'Ah, yes!—St Gandolfo,' Gasparini said, improvising on what he mistook to be the introduction of a religious theme, 'separated by the word of Marx and Lenin unto the gospel of promiscuity and the salvation of bimbos.' His voice trembled with wicked fun. He was on a roll; he was in a groove. 'St Antonio Gandolfo, the true saint of socialism. A lover of women—as long as they're young and beautiful. A lover of common man—as long as he has the good sense to remain common. He's the type of bogus tartuffe who chews out waiters in five-star restaurants for not crumbing his table, then runs home and hatches strategies for the workers' revolution. I see him now—yes—in a silk paisley dressing-robe, a bottle of Glenfiddich at his elbow, chewing his Biro and firing up the rhetoric in another squib on the vices of Capitalism.' He gave Cordelia a crooked grin. 'What *do* you suppose these caviar socialists would ever do, Signorina Sinclair, if the workers of the world actually *did* rise up and try to take over?'

Cordelia shrugged. 'They have a vested interest in making sure they never get that chance.'

'Ha! Well now, that's the truth, isn't it,' Gasparini snorted. 'Keep the masses busy chewing on the pap of propaganda—and in the meantime, for their leaders, let the good times roll!'

'I hope *he's* not invited to the party after the concert,' Cordelia said, looking away.

Gasparini grimaced. 'Well, don't count on it. There's a good chance he has been, you know. The Maestro has a fatal attraction for cranks like Gandolfo.' He added with an impish smile, 'I don't suppose you're angling for an introduction, are you?'

Cordelia returned the grin. 'No,' she said, deftly backhanding his serve, 'I was hoping I'd have a chance to see the two of you spar.'

Gasparini laughed—a wheezing cachinnation that sounded as if a salmon bone had lodged in his trachea. 'Oh—I can assure you there's no chance of that!' he said, recovering. 'What you don't seem to understand, my dear, is that I'm a perfect lamb at these parties. Wittily ironic, yes, and maybe just a *teensy* bit saucy on occasion—but never, never tendentious. I have to behave myself, you see, because if I didn't my wife would make damn sure I never got an invitation to one of these affairs again. She's quite an old-fashioned girl, my Birgit, in some ways—and of course she has her career to think of. And just ask yourself, if I *were* banished from the circuit, what would I do then? Well, I'd be in a pretty pickle, wouldn't I? I'd have no option, I suppose, except to go and look for gainful employment or something equally disgraceful.' He feigned a horrified shiver. 'Fortunately for me,' he added with a shrug, 'I'm qualified for very little. Being a bar steward or a cat-burglar pretty well exhaust the possibilities.'

Cordelia said with a smile: 'You make it sound as if you're as much of a poseur, in your own way, as old Signor Gandolfo over there.'

'Oh, but I *am*,' Gasparini said expansively. 'That's the point.

The only difference between us is that I'm more subtle, amusing and cultivated in the way I handle it. And of course it helps,' he added with a straight face, 'that I hold the right opinions in politics.'

Cordelia was spared the necessity of finding a suitable reply by the appearance of a uniformed usher, who materialized through the curtain at the back of their box and enquired deferentially:

'Signorina Sinclair?'

Cordelia turned in her seat. 'Yes.'

'A note for you, signorina, from Maestro Marchesi.'

He held out a silver salver bearing an envelope, across which lay a single red rosebud on a long prickly stem. Cordelia did her best to conceal the blush she felt rising in her cheek and thought she managed it pretty well. The message was brief and said simply: 'Please come to my office after the performance. Marchesi.' The maestro was not one to waste his words. This was the third note she'd received from him and they had all been equally abrupt. Only that afternoon in his office when he had talked for a straight hour about the Camerata had he opened up and become voluble. He was an odd man. Arrogant and, in many ways, aloof and mysterious. But that, of course, was part of the fascination. She had a feeling that it was going to be a most interesting evening.

'A gallant and romantic man,' Signor Gasparini observed when the usher had gone—and then he added, giving her a sly, sidelong glance, 'And a man, too, with exceptionally fine taste, Signorina Sinclair, if I may be permitted to say so.'

Cordelia was not about to be swept off her feet by innuendo and Italian charm.

'And an exceptionally jealous temper,' she countered, smiling sweetly. 'Or so I'm told.'

'That too,' Gasparini conceded, falling silent.

The orchestra and chorus were in their places on the stage. The auditorium had filled quickly and the murmur of voices hummed around her like a sea. Cordelia looked to see if she could find Signor Farinelli—he was out there somewhere, she supposed— but she didn't manage to spot him.

At two minutes to eight, the bulb under the podium flashed, signalling the maestro's imminent arrival. The lead oboe sounded a concert B-flat and, section by section, the other instruments

joined in a crescendo of tuning. The theatre lights dimmed and
the auditorium beyond the footlights grew still, and then the orchestra itself fell silent, like a spent wave that has exhausted its
surge on the shore. Hushed and expectant, the auditorium waited.
After a few dramatic seconds, the four soloists emerged from the
wings and crossed to their chairs. Once they were seated, Marchesi himself—superb in tails and white bow tie, majestic, leo-
nine—made his appearance. He swept onto the stage, nodded to
the concert master, then mounted the podium and bowed to the
audience. He turned back to the orchestra. His baton rose—paused
for the fraction of an instant—then fell, and suddenly the silver
tongues of a flourish of baroque trumpets split the air...

Cordelia sat enthralled, entranced, letting the music spill over
her, letting it fill and caress her senses. The twentieth century
disappeared and she was carried back to an age of gavottes and
stately minuets, of lace ruffs and swirling, bone-hooped skirts.
Her spirit rose and sank, obedient to the sound—joyful as Orpheus called on hill and valley to rejoice, grave as he wept the
fate that had bereft him of Eurydice. Blending and then separat-
ing, instruments and voices wove a magic tapestry as the maestro's baton cajoled, exhorted, threatened, pined, lamented—

And then, quite suddenly, it was the intermission.

During the interval, Cordelia wandered in the foyer to stretch
her legs. She felt elegant and in vogue in the black silk sheath
she'd found at a shop in Via Tornabuoni, set off with a string of
pearls and matching earrings from Gheradi's on Ponte Vecchio.
She wore her hair braided at the back and curled into shoulder-
length ringlets at the side, giving her something of the appearance
of a Botticelli Venus. There was more than one admiring eye that
followed her progress as she wove her way among the groups of
chatting, smiling opera-goers.

The lobby lights dimmed, then brightened, indicating the performance was about to recommence, and she made her way back
to the box. Signor Gasparini, managing to extricate himself from
the bar where she had seen him drinking, only just made it back
to his seat as the house lights fell.

'I ran into an old friend,' he said by way of explanation.

'Dom Pérignon?' she asked innocently.

'Touché,' he said, settling back.

There was brief applause when Marchesi and the soloists returned and then again there was music—a short *sinfonia*, then Orpheus in Hades: *Lasciate ogni speranza o voi ch'entrate*. With his lyre he melts the hearts of the infernal powers and they agree to relinquish their power over Eurydice. He starts back with her for the upper world but, alas, looks back, breaking the gods' command—and Eurydice is reclaimed by the gathering shadows. Alone, Orpheus awakens on a cold hillside and sings *Questi i campi di Tracia*, his lament perfuming the air with the sweet desolation of his loss—*e mai sempre darrommi*—and the maestro's baton pleads, beseeches, draws each quivering tone to the airy fineness of spun gold. Then, like a renascent spring, the strains of a bright *sinfonia*. The golden-haired Apollo descends, granting Orpheus both immortality and Eurydice, and god and bard rise together into heaven, their voices blended, in a final apotheosis: *Saliam cantand' al cielo*—

As the strains of the concluding Moorish dance faded away, applause erupted like thunder, rolling in waves, and Cordelia was on her feet with the rest, clapping, cheering, crying *Bravo!* Three times they brought Marchesi and the soloists back—smiling, bowing, waving—and then the house lights went up and it was over. Cordelia sank into her seat feeling drained, enervated, utterly consumed, as if she had performed one of the roles herself. On the viewless wings of music, Marchesi's artistry had lifted her out of herself, beyond the reach of mundane reality into a higher, purer realm…and then, miraculously, set her safely back again on earth, exhausted, transformed, wondering, almost indeed reborn—

FROM THE SHADOWS of his vantage point on the elevated catwalk, Francesco Pistocchi had a clear view of the conductor's podium and the aisle through the orchestra that led to the deserted stagewing sixty feet below him. He knew the theatre as well as he knew the inside of his own home. He had studied it as a draughtsman pores over blueprints, and its complex architecture held no secrets for him. He knew every nook and remote cranny, every clandestine passage, every possible point of entry and exit.

During the intermission, he had slipped unnoticed into a cleaner's closet. At the back of the closet, behind drums of cleaning solvent, was a door opening into a little known passage that led under the stage to the area where the trap doors were located. From there, climbing into the flies on a series of steel-rung ladders, he reached the catwalk where he now crouched like a leopard. The opera was drawing to a close. Pistocchi's feral gaze fixed itself unblinkingly on a single individual—the gesticulating figure of the maestro. A smile curled his lip. The moment of his revenge was near—very near now—and he found it a sweet and profoundly satisfying prospect. From his throat came a low guttural sound, almost a growl, that had its origin in some atavistic instinct that lay deep in the tangled skein of his being. He did not notice the sound, his attention was riveted firmly on Marchesi. He was aware of nothing else.

Apollo and Orpheus rose into the air on a wooden platform camouflaged as a papier-mâcheé cloud, winched heavenward on invisible wires. The chords of the final *moresca* faded and there was a burst of applause and cheering. With cautious haste Orpheus and Apollo picked their way through the wires and spot lamps on the fly-deck and descended into the wings to receive their accolades. Not once did they pause—nor did they notice the solitary figure crouched above them in the shadows on the catwalk. Their minds were on curtain calls.

The instant they were out of sight, Pistocchi made his move. Time was of the essence now. He had less than five minutes to get himself into position. With the fluid grace of a cat, he crossed the trembling length of his observatory and swung onto a ladder that was bolted to the wall behind a bank of silent, hanging valances. He made his descent swiftly, his crêpe-soled shoes silent on the metal rungs.

There were, he knew, only two doors that led to the maestro's office, and both were guarded. One led down from an alcove in the wings, by way of an interior stairwell; the other led off the corridor that was the main thoroughfare between the stage door and the make-up rooms where the musicians stored their instrument cases. Marchesi was well aware of the danger that threatened him and he had taken those precautions he judged adequate to protect himself. Outside both doors armed guards had been posted, alert for suspicious activity, prepared to deal quickly and efficiently with any attempt at unauthorized entry.

Pistocchi thought of the guards and smiled.

Marchesi had been prescient, but not prescient enough. His sense of security was a false surmise, a fatal illusion. No doubt he thought himself perfectly safe—but a theatre is a labyrinth of obscure veining and secret passages. He had not studied the mazy layout of Teatro Comunale with sufficient care. He had not—like Pistocchi—lived and breathed for many days the myriad intersecting capillaries of its hidden places.

For there was a third way into the maestro's subterranean retreat.

In the half-light of a narrow space next to the building's foundation, Pistocchi removed a section of ventilation ducting. He lifted away a metal screen and opened a hole in the ceiling of the maestro's office. Earlier, he had removed the screws securing the screen and used a bent coathanger to secure it temporarily in place. For a moment he held his breath and listened. There was no sound from within. With feline agility, he swung himself through the aperture and dropped the eight feet to the carpeted floor, landing in a soft crouch on the balls of his feet. He took up his position behind the padded door leading to an inner stairway that connected the office to the stage-wing above—the door he knew from hours of patient watching that his victim would use—then opened the glinting blade of the straight razor that he carried in his pocket. Any moment now he would hear descending footsteps—the door would open—and Antonio Marchesi would step through it to his death. There would be no interruption, no cry that succeeded in bringing help. The office was heavily soundproofed.

Pistocchi's eyes burned with a cold, gem-like fire. As he waited, a tiny smile played at the corners of his mouth. He had waited a long time for this precious moment.

FOR A TIME Cordelia sat overwhelmed, as though she had been stricken by paralysis. The music, the spectacle, the emotional experience of the evening were more than she could assimilate all at once. Not stirring from her seat, she watched the players gather up their things and the audience stream like water through the exits. Signor Gasparini had long since disappeared. Slowly, she found the strength to rise and navigate her way out of the box and down the stairs into the lobby. Scattered groups still chatted in little circles but most of the audience had gone and the ushers were emptying ashtrays and picking up discarded programmes. She entered the empty, silent auditorium, filled so recently with heavenly harmony, and made her way down the steps to the hallway where Marchesi's office was located. In the arid warmth of the theatre, the rose he had sent her before the performance was already past its prime and had begun to show the first unmistakable signs of a deathly wilt. The basement corridor was full of jabbering musicians and they seemed to her, still walking in a dream, like creatures from another planet. She melted through them and, reaching the door of Marchesi's office, put her hand out to knock.

'Can I help you, miss?'

The voice came from a man behind her. She turned and saw that he wore the uniform of a security guard. He also carried, she saw, a pistol in a brown hip holster. She had not noticed him until then.

'The maestro asked me to meet him here,' she said, showing him Marchesi's note.

The door was not locked. The guard rapped sharply, then preceded her inside and announced her arrival. Marchesi did not answer. He sat in a high-backed leather chair behind the desk with his back to them. For a moment they supposed he was on the telephone. They waited—but when, after a minute had elapsed, there was still no sound, the guard spoke again. Still there was no reply—and he moved cautiously around the desk, swivelling the chair. Marchesi's corpse slumped sideways with his head back and mouth open, the eyes spread wide and vacant in death, the shirtfront stained crimson from a gaping slash in the throat. From the centre of the grisly wound protruded the slender shaft of his conductor's baton. It looked like an arrow sticking out of his throat.

'You stay here with him, miss,' the guard said hoarsely. 'I'll ring for the police. Make sure nobody touches the body or anything else in the room.'

He hurried out. Why he didn't use the telephone on Marchesi's desk, Cordelia, herself in shock, never thought to ask. Either he was concerned about fingerprints or he was simply too unnerved by the spectacle to summon up the resources of rational thought.

Alone, she stood in the centre of the room staring at the scene before her as if she had been struck into immobility by a sight of Medusa's locks. Gradually, her senses returned and she began to notice things. He was dead of course—she was quite certain of that. There was no colour in the face, no sign of motion or

breathing. She had never seen death before, but she had no difficulty recognizing its pallid visage when it confronted her. Yes,
he was quite dead. But how was it possible? Only minutes ago,
he had been breathing and alive. Now all that remained of the
living man who had swept her away with the power of music was
a silent, distorted mask emptied of personality that barely even
resembled the face she remembered. The contradiction was too
great for her to fathom. Her reeling mind could not make sense
of opposites of such polarity.

She had no idea how long she had been standing there when
the room seemed suddenly to fill with people and the strange
sound of voices. She felt as though she had wandered unawares
into someone else's dream. The voices spoke around her but not
to her.

'Who's she?' someone asked.

'The one who found the body.'

'Hey, look at this, sarge. Here's how he broke in.'

'Check around for a weapon. Try the wastepaper basket.'

'Right.'

'Any sign of it?'

'No.'

'Keep looking. Vanni, get up through that hole and have a peek
around; see what you can find. Tell her to stick around, Giorgio—
the detectives will want a statement. Did somebody remember to
call the pathologist?'

'On his way, sarge.'

Firm hands guided her to a chair by the wall. Out of the way.
A voice asked if she'd mind waiting, said it shouldn't be long.
Aware from her I.D. that she was an American the man spoke in
carefully exaggerated Italian, as if he were addressing a child.
Did she need a doctor?

She shook her head. 'No, no—' She sat down heavily, her
senses perplexed and retarding, her dulled brain unresponsive to
the commotion around her. Flashbulbs popped, figures came and
went, the telephone jangled, the pathologist arrived and examined
the body, the baton was removed from Marchesi's throat, then
the corpse was loaded onto a wheeled trolley, covered hastily with
a blanket and rolled away.

Eventually, figures approached her.

'This is Detective Inspector Arbati, signorina. He's in charge of the investigation. He'd like to ask a few questions, if you feel able.'

Cordelia nodded dumbly.

It was a dream, she kept telling herself. It must be just a dream.

The police inspector, a man about her own age, pulled over a chair and leaned forward, his hands on his knees. His face was serious, she noticed, but it was not sad. It seemed odd to her, somehow impertinent even, that his expression betrayed no emotion. She could not accept the idea that this police inspector was no more than a man doing the job he was paid to do. Maestro Marchesi was too great a loss to the world to be reduced to an incidental part of someone's employment.

'You speak Italian, I understand,' he said.

'Yes.'

'You found the body?'

'Yes.'

'I see.' He took his time formulating his next question. 'May I ask what brought you to the maestro's office?' he asked finally.

'He invited me.' She fumbled in her bag for Marchesi's note—produced it.

'Did you know him well, Signorina Sinclair?'

'No. Not well. We met once.'

'Yet he invited you to his office?'

'It's nothing sinister,' she snapped, the burst of asperity surprising even herself. In a calmer tone, she explained: 'He invited me to the concert tonight. I was to be his guest at a party afterwards, at his villa.' Her head was spinning. 'We had a date, I guess you could say.'

'Had you been out with him before?'

'No. I told you. We only met once before—here in this room.' She shivered, remembering. 'We talked about music.'

'Are you a musician?'

'No, I'm writing a thesis. He was being helpful.'

'I see.'

Irritation overcame her again. 'Look, are all these questions absolutely necessary? I hardly knew the man. I talked to him once and he invited me to go out with him, okay? When I came into the room with the guard, he was dead.' Her voice dropped. 'I admired him. He was a great conductor—a genius.'

'Only one or two more questions,' Inspector Arbati said quietly. 'We can leave anything else for another time.' His tone became harder, carried an edge. 'Now, I'd like you to think carefully before you answer. What you remember may be important to us. Do you remember if the door to the stage-wing stairwell was open or closed when you entered the room?'

'It was closed.'

'You're quite certain of that?'

'Yes.'

'And the room was empty—except for the body?'

'Yes, it was empty.'

'Did you notice anyone in the corridor outside?'

'It was full of musicians.'

'You're certain they were all musicians?'

'How would I know?' she said sharply. 'They *looked* like musicians.' The questions were no doubt necessary, but the inspector's clinical detachment from the terrible human tragedy that had taken place in the room angered her. A great man had died violently, in that very room. Didn't that affect him at all?

'Did you notice anyone who looked strange, out of place? Someone in a hurry, perhaps?'

She tried to remember. Her recollections of the hallway were a blur. She had been riding on a cloud when she passed through it.

'No,' she said. 'Not that I recall.'

'Did anyone come in or go out of the room between the time you entered it with the security guard and the time the police arrived?'

'No.'

'You're quite certain of that?'

'Yes.'

'In the room itself, was there anything odd? Did you notice anything that seemed out of place?'

'I was only here once before, inspector—' she said tartly.

'Please try to think.'

She said sarcastically:

'Just give me the facts, ma'am. The facts and nothing but the facts.'

'Scusi?' Arbati's eyebrows arched into a question mark.

'I'm sorry, inspector. That was uncalled for. It's a line from an old American television show. A detective show.'

Arbati nodded and stood.

'You've been very helpful,' he said. 'It's a difficult time, I know. I'll have one of my men drive you home. If you have a telephone, please leave your number with him. It may be necessary for me to contact you again.'

And then, with a barely perceptible nod to one of the uniformed officers, he turned on his heel and was gone.

Cordelia stood and looked around the room. So much that was horrible had happened there in the past couple of hours. She hardly knew what to make of it all. One thing she did know, however, was that she didn't much care for this Detective Inspector Arbasso—or whatever it was he called himself. He was too bloodless and calculating, too much like a machine.

And then there was a policeman at her side, guiding her toward the door.

ONE

PART THREE

The Banker

THE DEATH OF Marchesi was the thing that finally tipped the scales and convinced Giorgio Bruni that they had a serial killer on their hands. Although Lo Squartatore's existence was still necessarily based on circumstantial evidence (Bruni trusted only *facts*), his Olympian scepticism had finally disintegrated in the face of a pattern of events too bizarre and compelling—even *without* suspects or a probable motive—to be satisfactorily dismissed as purely coincidental. In a period of little more than two months, four prominent figures—all approximately the same age, all known to one another, all at one time, in the mid-1950s, students at the same private boys' academy—had been murdered in exactly the same fashion. With Marchesi's death, matters reached the point where, for Bruni, it became a more rational act to posit the hypothetical existence of Lo Squartatore than to keep pigheadedly insisting the 'the San Stefano hunch' (as he had once called it) was entirely chimerical. And like many religious converts, Bruni, once he had taken the plunge, became more doctrinaire and inflexible on the subject than those originally born into the faith.

They were in Arbati's glass-fronted office on the second floor of the Questura. Arbati was at the desk, tipped back in his chair, his feet up, a forgotten cigarette sending up a lacy filigree of smoke from the knuckles of his left hand. Across from him, Bruni stood before a chalkboard on an easel, on which he had roughed out a diagram of Marchesi's basement office in Teatro Comunale. He had just finished conducting a thorough investigation of the physical evidence at the scene of crime and was making his report.

'He must have been waiting behind the door for him,' Bruni explained, tapping the board with a piece of yellow chalk. 'When the maestro came through, Lo Squartatore stepped behind him—and *fut!* clean as a whistle.' He drew a stubby forefinger across his throat. 'There are no signs of a struggle. It was all very quick, very professional. The blood starts here,' he went on, indicating the bottom of the stairway that led to the backstage wings, 'and ends in the middle of the room, here, in a pool. We can assume the maestro staggered—or was pushed—forward, then went down on his face.'

'So there's not much chance the killer was splattered with blood.'

'Highly unlikely,' Bruni said, shaking his head, 'and he was careful not to step in what was lying around and make tracks.' He resumed the narrative of his report: 'The evidence suggests he wrenched the maestro's head back by the hair with his left hand and sliced across the neck with his right—all in one motion—then either stepped back or gave his victim a push forward. Anyway, our boy knows how to handle a blade. But then, he's had enough practice, hasn't he? I talked with Doc Mangiello this morning about the autopsy. Death was the result of a severed carotid artery. There was also a probable attempt to cut the vocal cords, but the Doc still won't put that in his report. It's speculative, he says.' Bruni shrugged and ended: 'Basically, the same *modus operandi* as the three previous killings.'

Arbati gave an ironic smile. A week ago, Bruni was convinced the murders were a series of unrelated Mafia hits. Now he was talking as if there had never been a doubt in his mind, right from the beginning, that they were dealing with a serial killer.

Bruni went on as if he hadn't noticed:

'According to the Doc, the killer is right-handed—not that knowing that helps us very much—and the weapon was probably an old-fashioned straight razor. Oddly, Marchesi himself used one to shave with.' He returned Arbati's ironic smile. 'But that's probably just a coincidence.'

Arbati remembered his own words: *coincidences seem coincidental only because we treat facts out of context and miss seeing the links that bind them together.*

'Touché,' he said.

'After the maestro was dead,' Bruni went on, 'the murderer dragged him to the leather chair behind the desk, then propped him up and stuck the baton into his neck. Very graphic, I'd say. Very theatrical. For what it's worth, by the way, the body was dead before the baton went in. Doc Mangiello was certain of that. He also said it had been rammed home with considerable force, as if the murderer was taking another shot at his victim. Killing him a second time, as it were.'

Arbati leaned forward and crushed out his cigarette. 'The baton is an interesting detail,' he said thoughtfully. 'It's consistent, of course, with the escalating drama of butchery in the last two murders. But I think it points, too, to something even more revealing.'

'That our killer is crazy?' Bruni suggested.

'Oh, I think there's no doubt that he's rapidly losing his grip on sanity.' Arbati paused to light another cigarette, then added: 'Hooking a corpse over a cross is grotesque. Stabbing a conductor's baton into a dead man's throat is not just vindictive; it's pathologically insane.'

'No dispute there,' Bruni said. 'He's right round the twist, I'd say.'

'But that's not quite what I had in mind,' Arbati went on. 'I think our slasher is—or once was—a singer. The evidence points consistently in that direction. First, the attempts in the earlier murders to cut the vocal cords, and now a pointed baton stabbed into Marchesi's larynx to underscore the same point. Out killer is taking revenge for something that happened a long time ago and that has something to do with the human voice box. My bet is that that something is singing.'

Bruni nodded. 'It's possible, I suppose,' he said without much conviction. 'Especially since Marchesi was in the music business. But what does singing have to do with his first three victims—a textile manufacturer, a politician, and a priest? Couldn't our killer just as easily have been a public speaker of some kind? A politician, say, or a teacher—or even a priest?'

Arbati said: 'Let's just say I have a hunch he was a singer.'

'Ah,' Bruni said, 'a hunch. Yes—well, that puts a solid foundation under us, doesn't it?'

Arbati went on, ignoring him: 'And what does singing, I wonder, have to do with the Lady Chapel in Santa Maria Novella cathedral where we found Cardinal Cafferelli? When we have the answer to *that* question, my friend, I think we'll discover we've also found our killer.' He took a long drag on his cigarette. 'Incidentally, have we established for certain how he got into the maestro's office?'

'In and out again through the ventilation grate. A slick piece of work. Our boy knew the architecture of that building inside out. Nobody we've interviewed remembers seeing anybody strange in the corridor outside the maestro's office or in the stage-wings after the performance.'

'If he was a singer,' Arbati pointed out, 'he wouldn't necessarily seem strange. Orchestra members might well have recognized him and simply taken his presence for granted.'

'True enough, but I'll bet nobody ever saw him,' Bruni countered. 'That theatre is a rabbit warren backstage and he probably knew every inch of it. There are a thousand places he could hide until the coast was clear.' He poured himself a mug of steaming coffee from the hotplate beside the desk and tested it gingerly with a quivering lip. 'What have you turned up on the San Stefano angle? Anything new and exciting there?'

'As a matter of fact there is,' Arbati said. 'I've got Martini and Thal running checks on former students from the relevant years who've moved out of town. They're also trying to track down the names of the six boys who just disappeared. But, frankly, I'm not hopeful they'll find much.'

'So what's new then?'

'I'm coming to that,' Arbati said. Following Bruni's example, he rose and poured himself a cup of coffee, then said: 'So far, Lo Squartatore has targeted all his victims from among the thirty-five alumni of 1954 to 1957 who still live in Florence. That pattern continues with Marchesi. In the past few days, I've talked to thirty-three of them—all of them, that is, except Marchesi and Strozzi, the bank director. I'd arranged to meet Marchesi the morning after the opening of the Monteverdi festival. He was too busy to see me until then, he said. That decision may well have cost him his life. Anyway—and this is where things start getting interesting—two of the men I talked to remembered that Marchesi, Strozzi, and Lo Squartatore's other three victims were thick as thieves during their last couple of years at Collègio San Stefano. Sort of a private club, they thought. Neither one could tell me what it was about. It was very exclusive, very hush-hush. Whether it survived schooldays or not, they couldn't say.'

'Any other members?'

Arbati shook his head. 'Not that they recalled.'

Bruni pursed his lips. 'Which sort of points to Strozzi as the logical next target.'

'That's how I read it,' Arbati agreed, then went on: 'The problem is, our friend Strozzi has dropped out of sight. His office hasn't seen him for over a week, although he apparently checks in occasionally by phone. I pressed his staff pretty hard, but nobody at the bank could give me any clue as to where he is. The only titbit I managed to extract was that Strozzi's chauffeur—a thug with an attitude named Franco—drops by once a day to look through the mail. My guess is that he forwards anything he thinks might be important to his boss. They're probably in regular communication. On Friday, I had a long talk with this Franco and he swears he has no idea where Strozzi is. He's lying, of course, and we need to have another go at him.' Arbati smiled. 'And that, my friend, is where you come in.'

'You mean,' Bruni said with mock delight, 'I get to spend my afternoon chatting up a thug with an attitude? Lucky me!' He gave a sour grimace. 'And how, may I ask, while I'm off questioning this troglodyte, will *you* be spending the local taxpayers' money?'

Arbati fished a blue address book from his pocket. 'There are still one or two questions I want to ask the American girl who found Marchesi's body.'

'Like whether she'd consider marrying a nice Italian boy?' Bruni asked slyly.

Arbati said wearily. 'God! don't you start on me, Giorgio. I listened to Aunt Angela all day yesterday. It's the only thing she ever talks about. Why are you all so determined to marry me off? I'm a very contented bachelor.'

'It's our considered judgement that you need a stabilizing influence in your life. And besides, she's very pretty—and she wasn't wearing a ring. I notice these things. Tessie and I were talking about it last night. You'd make a nice couple.'

'Get out of here and go talk to your bloody troglodyte.'

'I'm going! I'm going!' Bruni protested, heading for the door. 'But think about it, Carlo. You could do worse.'

'I thought about it years ago,' Arbati said. 'I'm past thinking about it any more.'

But when Bruni had gone, he realized, with something of a shock, that the girl *had* been in the back of his mind most of the day. She had infiltrated his subconscious, and he found, when he thought about it, that he was quite looking forward to seeing her again. He wasn't so sure, however, that she would share his enthusiasm. She had seemed to dislike policemen for not being sensitive enough. But then, she didn't know that he was a poet either.

He reached for the telephone and dialled the numbers quickly.

'Signorina Sinclair?' he said. 'This is Inspector Arbati, of the Carabinieri. I wonder if you could spare me an hour sometime this afternoon. There are one or two little points I need to follow up in the Marchesi investigation...'

CORDELIA DROPPED the receiver back into its cradle and slumped back in her chair. It wasn't what she needed just at the moment. She'd spent three sleepless nights reliving the horror of her discovery in the theatre and most of the morning fighting off the *tyrannosaurus rex* of migraines. She wasn't in a fit state of mind or body to endure Inspector Arbati and more of his cold-blooded questions.

Damn it all! she thought, why did I agree to see him? I probably could have put him off for a day or two at least.

She looked dolefully around the darkened apartment. The drapes were drawn and she was still in her nightdress.

About an hour, he had said.

She forced herself upright.

'Well, let's get on with it,' she said to no one in particular. 'I don't want to look like the Wreck of the Hesperus when he gets here.'

TWO

SIGNOR VITTORIO DI BANCO twisted in his seat with a start. The woman stood above him, looking down through large, horn-rimmed glasses. He took care, although his heart was racing, to let no emotion show on his gaunt, chiselled features.

'Yes,' he said brusquely, 'what is it?'

The woman held out a slip of paper. 'I need authorization for this withdrawal,' she said without flinching. She was, after twelve years, used to his asperity.

The chief teller of the Banco di Firenze scrutinized the chit, then initialled and returned it.

'Is there anything else?'

'No,' she said, turning.

He wanted to say: Don't *ever* come sneaking up on me like that again! But he said nothing. To say anything would merely incite her curiosity.

When she had gone, he turned back to the green computer-screen. Had she noticed what he was doing? There was perspiration on his upper lip and he wiped it away. No, he thought, surely not. I'm being paranoid. But he wanted to confront her and demand to know what she had seen.

He made himself be calm.

He'd been too tense lately, too jumpy. It was the pressure. The not-knowing who might have noticed something. He had to get hold of himself. Lydia didn't help either. Always kind, always concerned, always trying to be helpful. All she ever did any more was get on his nerves—so much so that he'd lost his temper more than once and struck her. It was her own fault. Couldn't she see he was under pressure and wanted to be left alone? And then there was that damned Sinclair woman coming around with tea and sympathy. They were all the same, those Yanks—bleeding-heart liberals and left-wing radicals—over-educated and under-sexed—most of them Jews. He knew *her* type all right.

He brought up the records of another company the bank dealt

with. He increased the service charge on their monthly statement, then sent the difference by electronic magic to the account he had opened for himself in the name of Vittorio Moroni. He had kept the increases modest; but multiplied by several hundred accounts they amounted now to a tidy sum.

They've never appreciated me here, he thought bitterly. I deserve every lira.

In another month it would all be over. Vittorio di Banco, chief teller, would mysteriously disappear. Vittorio Moroni, retired banking executive, wealthy and single, would suddenly emerge like a butterfly from its confining cocoon—in the Caribbean. For a moment, he let his mind wander over the travel brochures he kept hidden from Lydia's prying eyes behind the loose panel at the back of the closet: white sands, elegant hotels, native waiters padding silently on bare soles bearing silvery trays of frosted drinks, tanned girls with long legs and skimpy bikinis. He stayed up nights, after Lydia had gone to bed, leafing through the brochures and dreaming. So well did he know the glossy photographs in those brochures that he could close his eyes and feel the sand between his toes on their palm-fringed beaches, savour *fruits de mer* and Scotch whisky in their high-class restaurants, stretch himself out—oh, never alone—on their firm, king-size beds and hear the green surf rolling in the recesses of his brain like an intoxication…

He had planned it all for years. The scheme was foolproof. He had started right after the last audit, knowing he had five months at least before the auditors returned. Once a week, he moved money out by computer to accounts opened in other banks around the city in various names, never his own. Once a month, he emptied those accounts in person and wired the funds, consolidated into a central account at another bank, to a numbered account at the Royal Bank of Canada in the Cayman Islands, where regulatory officials didn't much bother themselves about where large and mysterious sums came from. It would be easy enough to get at it and spend it once he was settled on Martinique or Guadeloupe or one of the other exotic-sounding paradises in the brochures.

He anticipated with relish the fury of his employer when he found the funds missing. With any luck at all, Signor Strozzi, the fat chairman, who had swept past him for years with never so much as a nod to acknowledge his services and his position in the bank, would have a heart attack and die. It would serve him right.

The prospect of that happy eventuality buoyed him in his task.

Methodically, cheerfully, Vittorio di Banco accessed file after file, steering his own little 'fee-for-services-rendered' (as he liked to think of it) into the account of Signor Vittorio Moroni, swelling his burgeoning total.

THREE

CORDELIA STOOD AT the French windows in her apartment staring out over the rooftops. The police inspector—she had already erased the memory of his visit from her mind—had long since come and gone, leaving her alone with her ghosts and the remnants of her headache. She stared at the scene beyond the glass with a strange detachment. Everything that met her gaze seemed alien, foreign—more foreign even than the day she had arrived and stood in this same place, at this very window, staring out in enchanted disbelief at the ochre tiles flowing away in all directions, at the ancient brick and peeling stucco, at the snout of the Duomo thrusting into the sky like some huge leviathan coming up for air. Since finding Marchesi's body, something in her life—something fundamental in her view of reality—had changed. It was not Florence alone that seemed strange to her; it was *earth* itself. It was as if she had been dropped from another planet and was seeing the world, somehow, for the very first time. She couldn't explain exactly how she felt. She didn't know what it meant. All she knew for certain was that something important had changed. There was a misty, insubstantial quality now about everything she looked upon—like a landscape seen through a rain-streaked window.

And worst of all she was alone. A stranger in a strange land. Never in her life had she felt so completely alone. Some lines from a poem she had once memorized at school came back to her, the words drumming in her mind like an incantation:

Alone, alone, all, all alone,
Alone on a wide wide sea!
And never a saint took pity on
My soul in agony.

Over and over they repeated themselves—and for the first time in her life she had some inkling of what they meant because, for the first time, she actually *felt* their truth. Since Marchesi's death, she had known the terrible emptiness of isolation; and she had come to know, too, like the old navigator in the poem, the blood-chilling reality of life as a waking nightmare. It was not the brutal image in the theatre that haunted her, the memory of Marchesi himself whom she had barely known; it was, rather, the knowledge about herself released by that image—the sudden, unbearable wisdom she had gained that men live as they die, alone. The terrible knowledge that we are somehow all sojourners in a strange land—and that we are strangers not only to others, but strangers even to our most intimate and hidden selves. The nameless terrors of childhood, known vividly once as she had lain in the night-shrouded, spectre-haunted loft of the cottage on Lake Michigan listening to the wind moan like a soul in torment through the black forests that surrounded her for a hundred miles—those childhood fears, repressed by the mind in later years, yet ever circling unnoticed (she now realized) at the periphery of her adult consciousness—became real again and made her suddenly aware of the infinite sorrow and futility of human life that is born and strives and dies and knows not why.

What is life? she kept asking herself. What was *she*—? A speck, an infinitesimal speck abandoned in a forgotten corner of the cosmos? an atom of intelligence shipwrecked in the finite void? an ephemeral, insubstantial shadow in a universe of shadows? No more than that—no more? The prospect was intolerable.

From the profoundest depths of her being, she cried out for some saving truth to make sense of it all, to give meaning and a purpose to her existence. If there had been a God, she would have thrown herself into his encircling arms and wept like a lost child found. But no God spoke to her or called out her name. She was ALONE. And in her solitude she was driven to the sad wisdom that is the inevitable end of all self-circling rationalism: if we are alone and finite in an infinite void, then the everlasting universe through which we roll inexorably toward nothingness mocks us with its cold, imperial majesty. The starry and eternal sky affronts our puny and transient dignity; the glories of the rainbow offer no relief, no promise of transcendent love; the exiguous revolving of the seasons speaks to us, not of renewal, but only of the hasting passage of our days toward the grave. We are fragile sparks in an eternal night—brief flashes of self-consciousness released, and then an instant later reabsorbed, by the mechanism of a point-lessly-revolving universal All.

She turned from the window and, seeking some relief, prowled the purgatory of her apartment. The walls...the desk...the books that once had been her friends—all, all were mute. 'I pass, like night, from land to land,' her mind chanted; 'I have strange power of speech—'

Without quite knowing how, she found herself outside her apartment on the landing, and slowly, as if in a trance, she descended the stairs. At the door on the next landing she paused, as if uncertain what to do, then gathered up her resolve and knocked. A moment later, the door was opened by Signor Farinelli.

'Signorina Sinclair—'

'Can I come in?' she said. 'I have no one else to talk to.'

'Of course. What's the matter? Has something happened?' There was concern in his voice.

'I found the body,' she said.

He led her to a chair and made her comfortable, then stepped through an arch into the kitchen. 'I'll make us coffee,' he said, his back to her. 'You said you found a body—?'

Cordelia looked around the room. It was the first time she had been there, and she wondered at her temerity in imposing herself thus unannounced. The room was furnished with an old-fashioned taste, the furniture heavy and dated. Prints of pastoral scenes hung in ornate gilt frames, the lampshades bore string fringes, and there was an ancient Motorola phonograph under the window. Fra Angelico, the orange cat, was curled in a ball at one end of a chintz sofa. It was homey and comfortable and somehow also very reassuring, very normal. 'At the theatre,' she said, leaning back and closing her eyes. 'Maestro Marchesi gave me a ticket to the concert. I was invited to a party at his villa afterwards. He asked me to meet him at his office after the performance. I was the one who found him.'

The simple sounds of Farinelli running water for the kettle and reaching the coffee canister down from a shelf made her feel secure. She wasn't alone any more with her ghosts.

'I didn't know you were there,' he said, pouring dark grains into the filter.

'There was a security guard at the door, and when he let me

in, we found him in his chair. It was horrible, Signor Farinelli. I haven't been able to sleep for three nights. I can't bear to think about it, but I can't put it out of my mind either. Every time I close my eyes I see his face and the baton sticking out of his throat.'

'You must try to forget. You have to force yourself to think of something else.'

'Then the police questioned me. The chief inspector came again today and asked me more questions.'

'I heard feet on the stairs,' Farinelli said, lighting the gas ring under the pot. 'I wondered who it was.'

He emerged from the kitchen, wiping his hands, and took the seat opposite her, next to the phonograph.

'Why would anyone do such a dreadful thing?' she asked.

His large, luminous eyes settled on her like moonlight. 'It's best not to think about it,' he said. 'There's no doubt a reason—perhaps even a good one. Marchesi, as I told you once, was not a nice man. I expect he had many enemies.'

'But to kill a man, to butcher—'

'Try to forget,' he said softly.

The pot on the gas ring began to gurgle and burp and soon the warm, comfortable smell of brewing coffee filled the room. Cordelia leaned back and let the aroma enfold her. She felt better having released her anguish and having told somebody. It was a kind of absolution. Farinelli rose and poured two cups and they sat for a while in silence, each sipping, each inhabiting his own world.

'I'm so confused by it all,' Cordelia said eventually, breaking the silence. 'I thought I knew who I was, where I was going, what was important in my life. But now I don't know anything any more. I'm confused by the murder—by myself—by everything.' She turned the cup in her palms, letting its warmth flow into her, then said: 'I don't know if I can believe in anything any more.'

'Everybody believes in something,' Farinelli said. 'In themselves. In their word. In some cause or other they've taken up. In God. We have to believe in something or we can't go on, because there's no reason to go on.'

'What do you believe in?' Cordelia asked impulsively, hoping for an answer that could become hers as well.

Farinelli shrugged. 'In myself, I suppose. In God. In justice being done eventually.'

'You believe in God? That surprises me.'

He smiled. 'Why? Nothing is more natural.'

'Oh, I don't know—it just seems so irrational, I guess. Like believing in ghosts or trolls.'

Farinelli gave a wry grin and quoted: 'There are more things in heaven and earth, Horatio, than are dreamed of in your philosophy.'

'Hamlet.'

'Yes,' Farinelli nodded, 'and he spoke the truth. We live in a world where the wise man's deepest wisdom is the knowledge that he knows nothing for certain. Everything around us, even though we take most of it for granted, is utterly unknown, utterly mysterious. Light, for example, and electricity, and why we're all superstitious when we try so hard to be rationalists. Every time we think we've found an answer, our solution turns to water and runs through our hands. If the history of ideas shows us anything, it's that today's truth always ends up becoming tomorrow's fiction. In Shakespeare's day, you know, everyone believed the universe was a finite sphere, like a cosmic orange. Then Galileo came along with his telescope and declared that it was infinite. They can't both be right.'

'I prefer Galileo's answer,' Cordelia said reasonably.

Farinelli smiled. 'Preference isn't knowledge; it's merely a choice made by instinct between alternatives. Perhaps the universe is infinite, perhaps not; but it doesn't follow that, because even the most powerful telescopes can't find a boundary, there isn't one. It only means we haven't found a boundary—and never will, of course, if there isn't one to be found. But there might be one another light year, another million light years further out—and perhaps beyond that there's another universe, or ten, or a million. All we know for certain is that we don't know anything for certain. The universe is a mystery—like almost everything in it.'

'If you had been Hamlet, then,' Cordelia said, 'you would have believed the Ghost and killed Claudius?'

'Of course. The Ghost was Hamlet's own father.'

The bluntness of the response took Cordelia, who was being glib, by surprise.

'Then you believe in ghosts?' she asked.

'No,' Farinelli replied impishly. 'I believe in fathers.' He rose and returned with the coffee pot. 'A refill?'

Cordelia extended her cup.

'So,' she said, 'is this God of yours like the Ghost of Hamlet's father? Are we expected to believe in him, without doubt or question, just because he's supposed to have turned up once out of the blue and given a few orders—and then disappeared into the blue again? That strikes me as really quite irrational.'

Farinelli took his seat and sipped at his coffee. 'On the contrary,' he said, 'it's perfectly rational. The statement "There is no God" is based on no evidence at all—it's simply a guess, a shot in the dark: like looking into a black room and deciding it's empty because, without light, you can't see anything, although it might well be full of furniture, or people—or even ghosts, for that matter. It seems to me, in fact, that all the evidence points the other way. No matter how mixed with myth and legend, we have written records about a divine being and his dealings with the primitive Hebrews—and those records are perfectly consistent with what history and archaeology have to tell us, in those areas where history and science are competent to tell us things. We also have the New Testament; and if you claim its credit is impaired because the books were written by believers with a particular axe to grind, the same is true for Arrian and Thucydides and Tacitus. Nobody is impartial. Everyone who tells a story has a story to tell. And finally, we have the testimony of our own hearts—if we're not afraid to listen to them. So it strikes me as irrational to reject the only evidence we *do* have, in order to maintain a position for which there is no evidence whatsoever. The atheist, in my opinion, swallows a thousand absurdities and gags on a gnat.'

He fell silent, and Cordelia, unable to think of a reply, sipped thoughtfully at her coffee. The answer was more than she'd bargained for, and the calm vehemence of his conviction surprised and, in a way, almost frightened her; but it was something to think about.

After a few minutes, Farinelli said:

'Well, now you know all about *me*. What about you? What do you believe in?'

Cordelia thought for a moment, wondering how much to reveal, then said:

'I thought I believed in my work—in the work I'm doing for my thesis. I thought I'd found a purpose there. But now it all seems, somehow, insignificant—and so do I. Maestro Marchesi spent his life building a reputation, but what does it matter to him now? The world has gone on for several million years. He was alive for just over fifty of them—half a century—and he'll live on for maybe another fifty on the backs of record jackets. It doesn't seem like much, does it, in the grand scheme of things?'

'Too much in his case,' Farinelli said.

Cordelia gave him a cold stare. 'I thought your Bible preached charity,' she said.

Farinelli shrugged. 'It does,' he said, 'but I knew more about him than you do. Sometimes it's hard to forget.'

'Even when he's dead?'

'Even then,' Farinelli said.

The depth of his personal animus was something Cordelia had no wish to plumb. She said:

'I came to Florence to find myself—to escape from the past and work out my own identity. I thought I was succeeding, too, until all this happened. Now I seem to be right back where I started.'

The cat on the sofa unwound and stretched himself to full length, yawning, claws fanned out, then sat and stared at them through inscrutable yellow eyes. The sound of his contentment filled the room like the growl of a distant engine.

Cordelia went on:

'I needed to get away from Evanston, to start over and find my own way in a new place that had no associations with Father or with Charles.'

'Charlies is a boyfriend?'

Cordelia gave a wry smile. 'Worse,' she said. 'A husband—once. It didn't work out.'

'I'm sorry.'

Cordelia shrugged. 'It wasn't all his fault, though most of it was. I tried, but Charles was a man who loved himself too much to have any love left over for anyone else. He exploited love, even friendship: ultimately, they were the basis of his power and he affected to hold them in contempt, although there was, I suppose, something like fear at the bottom of his scorn, because he realized by a kind of instinct how potent and destructive they

could be if they ever got loose. Control and domination were what
interested him. A wife was just another piece—a pawn, in fact—
on the chess board of the futures market where he was playing
out an enormously successful career against cut-throat opposition.
He didn't have time for children, of course, and he never wanted
them—especially not a son. The thought of breeding his own
competition appalled him.'

'And your father?'

'Oh, Father?—Father is quite different. Quiet, amiable, kind—
even thoughtful, when he can spare a minute from his latest
project. But that isn't often. There's always a book to be read, a
book half-way written, a book almost finished, a book just being
started. He connects only fitfully with the world the rest of us
live in. I overheard him once tell a visitor that his best friends—
meaning Chaucer and Shakespeare and Milton—were all dead.
As you can imagine, we didn't have a lot of visitors when I was
growing up. I couldn't have school friends over, of course, because they made noise. The house was a kind of book-lined mausoleum and, as much in self-defence as out of interest, I spent
most of my time reading. We didn't even own a television set.
In the summers, because it was too hot for Father to work in
Evanston, we took a trunk-load of books and went to a cottage
in Wisconsin. It was on the lake and very beautiful, but also very
lonely. There was no one around for miles and I used to long for
September when school started again.'

Fra Angelico jumped off the sofa and crossed the carpet, tail
erect, and jumped onto her lap. He stared at her with sphinx-like
eyes, and when she ran her hand down his orange-barred back,
he stretched up and licked her chin with a sandpaper tongue. It
wasn't gratitude exactly, but it was a sign of recognition—a gesture saying that she belonged, that she was welcome. Or perhaps
he was just suggesting that it was time for his saucer of milk.

'It must have been difficult for you and your mother,' Farinelli
said.

Cordelia suddenly realized, at the mention of the mother whom
she had never known, how much she had revealed about her life
to a man who was almost a total stranger. Oddly, however, she
didn't mind. Signor Farinelli was kind and understanding. He had
invited her in when she was lost and vulnerable; he had listened

to her and drawn her out, like a priest in the confessional—and she found, as a result, that a burden had been lifted from her.

'I never knew my mother. She died when I was very young,' she said. 'No, I grew up in a man's world—and my luck with men, as you've just heard, hasn't been all that good. But then,' she added, thinking of Professor Ecco at the university as well as of Farinelli, 'maybe my luck is beginning to change.'

Farinelli smiled. 'My door is always open, you'll find,' he said, 'any time you need a friend to talk to.' He stood up and walked into the kitchen. 'Now, as it happens, I'm just on the point of attacking a quarter round of brie that I've been keeping in the icebox for a special occasion. You look as though you haven't eaten for a while. Perhaps you'd care to join me?'

'That's very kind,' she said. 'Yes, I think I will.'

She rose and followed him into the kitchen to offer her help, and for the first time in three days the grisly image of Marchesi in his chair released its iron grip on her exhausted mind.

FOUR

NICÒLO STROZZI snapped the platinum hasps on his contraband alligator-skin bag. The fact that environmentalists had made it impossible to buy such a fine suitcase legally made him seethe with fury. His blood pressure shot up to two hundred just thinking about it. What right did a pack of snotty-nosed radicals, who hadn't worked a day in their scruffy lives, have to dictate what he could or could not buy? It was intolerable. The world was going to hell in a hand basket. The damn cheek of it all made him choke with anger.

He looked around the room with a sour eye. He shouldn't, he knew, have let himself think about the damned enviro-freaks. They always set him off. He pushed them out of his mind and turned back to the matter at hand. Now—was there anything he'd forgotten to pack? No, not that he could see. So good, he was ready to check out. He walked to the window and gazed out, killing time, at the expensive villas that tumbled down a precipitous slope of lush hillside to the blue-green waters of Monaco Bay spread below his suite on the twelfth floor of the Hyatt-Regency. He had never understood why tourists took such delight in gawping at scenery. He was completely impervious to its elusive charms. Of course, if one actually owned the things one was admiring, that was a different matter entirely. But to ooh and ahh over *other* people's property was, to Nicòlo Strozzi, a monstrous and incomprehensible absurdity.

He was tired of Monte Carlo and it was time to leave. The roulette and blackjack tables had not been kind to him this time around, and the call from Franco, his chauffeur, with the news that Marchesi had been murdered had come, in a way, almost as a relief. In nine days he had lost nearly two million francs in the casino—his worst showing ever. It wasn't that he couldn't afford the money; it was a matter of face.

He mopped his brow with the linen handkerchief that was a permanent fixture in his right hand. In spite of the fact that the hotel's air-conditioning system was working admirably, he was sweating like an overworked horse. Fastidiously hygienic but also grotesquely obese, he showered at six-hour intervals and doused himself with pungent colognes in an attempt to achieve something like presentability. But nothing worked for long. Perhaps it was too much to expect, at two hundred and ninety pounds, that anything would.

As was his custom, he wore a light-weight tropical suit, hand tailored and flawlessly pressed, a red carnation in the lapel. A white felt fedora, to protect his face and balding pate from the ravages of ultraviolet radiation, lay on the bed beside his set of alligator cases. Fully attired, he looked like Sydney Greenstreet embarking for a movie-set in Indo-China.

He stared out at the waters of Monaco Bay.

So, Marchesi was dead—his throat cut like a dog. Just like the others. Strozzi shivered. Well, it was Marchesi's own damned fault. He was an arrogant bastard and he'd paid the price for it. He should have taken better care of himself.

Strozzi of course, didn't care about Marchesi—he cared only because Marchesi's death meant that he, Strozzi, had become—by a process of elimination—Pistocchi's next target. In fact, his only remaining target—the last of the five Camerati. Strozzi had no intention, however, of becoming his next victim. But Pistocchi had proven more resourceful than anyone expected, had managed to get to Marchesi in spite of his security precautions—and now, Strozzi judged, it was time to bring in the cavalry. The best defence was an aggressive offence. Barberini, the private detective, had turned up nothing—not a single lead. Either Barberini was an incompetent fool or Pistocchi was a genius at deception—and Strozzi suspected the latter. The man had disappeared without a trace. It was as if he had never existed. Yet somehow he still managed to go around cutting people's throats. From the beginning, they had all underestimated Pistocchi—badly. It was time now to call in the resources of the state. It was time to call in the police.

Apparently the police already knew something anyway. But how much, Strozzi, wondered? They had, it seemed, been poking around at the bank trying to contact him, pressing to know when he was expected back, and twice they had been out to the villa to talk to Franco. Yes, the police knew—or thought they knew—

something. But Strozzi had no intention whatever of opening up the past an iota more than was absolutely necessary. The police were paid to prevent murders in the present, not to rake through the buried entrails of ancient history. What the Camerati dell'arte had done more than thirty years ago was none of their bloody business.

There was a tap at the door.

'Entrez!' Strozzi called without turning.

A uniformed bellhop wheeling a brass trolley entered and began loading Strozzi's luggage onto the cart. He worked swiftly, unobtrusively, professionally. On his way out the door he said: 'Your car is waiting downstairs, sir. Whenever you're ready.'

'I'll come now,' Strozzi said, turning from the panorama of the yacht-bobbing harbour. He was, he knew, as ready as he'd ever be.

They descended together, without speaking, in the oak-panelled elevator. Strozzi's mind was occupied with what lay ahead in Florence. At the marble reception desk, he settled the bill prepared in advance and waiting for him. Including meals and the bar bill, it amounted to a hefty sum. The stork-faced clerk, whose veneered grin and grave features gave him the supercilious look of an optimistic mortician, glanced at the signature on the credit-card, then bowed a little too deeply from the waist.

'Merci, bien, Monsieur Strozzi. I hope you will return to visit us again soon. As you know, you are a most valued guest here at the Hyatt-Regency.'

No doubt I am, Strozzi reflected sourly, recalling his casino losses. At two million francs a week he'd be welcome wherever he went. He said without enthusiasm:

'Perhaps in the fall.'

'Very good, monsieur. May I reserve a suite for you for a particular date?'

Vulture, Strozzi thought. 'No,' he said, 'I'll ring through when I know. No doubt you'll find me a room. You've always been very accommodating.' The pun was intentional but not very good.

A sly grin cracked the clerk's servile features. 'Of course, monsieur. We always do our best for valued clients. I hope your trip is a pleasant one.'

A white limousine—Strozzi insisted on white—was waiting at the palm-fringed entrance to the hotel. His luggage was already loaded in the trunk and he handed the bellhop a fifty franc note, receiving in return a peremptory nod implying that, from the bell- hop's point of view, their business had concluded satisfactorily.

The drive to the airport was short and two hours later Strozzi's Alitalia Dash-8 commuter touched down at Leonardo da Vinci airport, thirty kilometres outside Rome. Franco, in his usual blue serge suit and peaked cap, was waiting when Strozzi emerged, puffing and perspiring, through the sliding glass panels of the arrivals gate. The muscular presence and taciturn efficiency of his chauffeur put Strozzi immediately at ease. Franco had been in his service for twenty years and had, more than once, delivered him from imminent mutilation at the hands of an irate husband or cheated business client. The bulge under his left arm might have been a particularly well-developed pectoral muscle but it was, in fact, the butt of a .9 mm Beretta pistol. Pistocchi would get a surprise if he turned up at a gunfight armed with nothing more than a knife.

Strozzi's limousine was parked in the VIP lane outside the terminal. He clambered into the walnut-and-leather rear compart- ment while Franco loaded the suitcases, then they drove north up the A1 under a copper sky toward Arezzo. The day was cloudless and oppressive, a sirocco stirring together dry desert air from North Africa with the muggy miasma that hung over southern Europe like a damp blanket. Even before they were under way, Strozzi was awash in sweat from the heady exertion of trans- porting himself through the terminal. He could have wrung a cup of water from the thick linen handkerchief he used to mop con- tinuously at his neck and forehead. As they drove, the limousine's air conditioner, set perpetually at maximum, gradually triumphed over the humidity, and the climate inside the car finally reached a level where Strozzi's brain could begin to function. Looking without interest at the passing scenery of olive groves and well- tended vineyards, he said:

'Who will I be seeing?'

Franco's ursine lips parted fractionally. 'Inspector Arbati. Two- thirty. His office.' The tone was gruff with disapproval. Franco could not condone an act of collaborating with the police—it was a genetic aversion programmed into his genes over a dozen gen- erations. Being a man of few words, he refused to allow civility to obscure his feelings on the subject.

'Arbati—' Strozzi mused. 'Isn't he the one you said was snooping around the villa while I was away?'

'The same,' Franco grunted.

They drove in silence. Strozzi's villa was in the rolling hills south-west of Florence. The place was an armed camp—and it would remain so until Pistocchi was apprehended. The perimeter of the grounds was patrolled by guards with Dobermans on chain leads. At the iron entrance-gates, a figure armed with an Uzi machine gun stepped into their path and raised his arm for them to stop, then, recognizing the car, stood aside and gave a sharp salute, as if acknowledging the return of the base commander. The limousine eased through the gates and rolled up the cobbled drive between waist-high hedges of clipped yew to a pillared porch that dated from the mid-eighteenth century. The mansion behind it, slightly earlier in date and less baroque in style, commanded the hilltop and an imposing view of the surrounding countrywide.

It was not yet noon. Strozzi showered and changed into a fresh suit, then lingered over a lunch of pepper paté au gras and chianti on the patio where orange and lemon trees fruited in sunken pots. At one-thirty, with Franco scowling at the wheel, the big car pulled through the gates and began its descent toward the domes and towers of Florence in the middle distance.

In spite of the mid-day heat the arteries of the city were clogged with buses and camera-laden tourists swarming the pavement in search of culture. It took Franco the better part of half an hour to navigate the teeming shoals and reach the Questura. By pure chance, he located a free parking spot in Piazza della Libertà opposite the austere stone façade of the police headquarters. He shut off the ignition, stepped from the car and looked carefully around, then satisfied the area was safe, opened the rear door of the limousine for Strozzi. It was a ritual repeated at every disembarkation. Strozzi went nowhere without Franco, and Franco was never more than six inches from his employer's side. If Pistocchi, intent on murder, materialized from the sea of faces in the piazza, Franco would dispatch him with a lightning blow to some tender part of his unsuspecting anatomy. The .9 mm Beretta that he packed under his armpit was only for really desperate occasions. His hands alone were lethal weapons, trained in the oriental arts of instant death, and his presence gave Strozzi (who admired the aesthetics of power) a sense of satisfaction as well as a comforting sense of security. Franco could kill, if called upon, with amazing grace.

CARLO ARBATI stood at the window of his office on the second floor of the Questura looking down over Piazza della Libertà. It was two twenty-five. He recognized the white limousine the instant it turned the corner into Via Zara. Until that moment, he hadn't been absolutely sure that Strozzi would show up. There was no reason to suppose he would, and Arbati wondered what had changed his mind, what his motive was in finally deciding to come to the police. The police, after all, had been trying to contact *him* for a week. But Arbati hadn't really been surprised when Franco, breaking his vow of surly silence with a brief moment of surly speech, had called that morning on Strozzi's behalf to set up a meeting. No doubt the change of heart—the sudden willingness to talk—was connected with Marchesi's death. Strozzi must be a very worried man. The question was, how much would he be willing to reveal (or how much could Arbati coax him into revealing) about Lo Squartatore and the secret club whose members, all except Strozzi, had become his victims?

With a critical eye, Arbati assessed the quality of the man who crossed Via Zara to the main entrance of the Questura below his window. He was grotesque and shambling, a leviathan; something close to three hundred pounds, Arbati estimated. But it was not Strozzi's size that attracted his attention. What caught his eye was the air of exhaustion—the aura of defeat and resignation—that clung to him as palpably as a second skin. It revealed itself in the droop of the shoulders, the downcast glance, the shuffling gait. Strozzi was a man who had admitted to himself that he had run out of options. He had come to the police reluctantly, as a last resort, because he had no choice. He would, of course—because his sort always did—make a show of defiance and bravado when they met. But he was a beaten man before he even stepped through the door. He reminded Arbati of one of those herbaceous trees in the Brazilian rain forest: huge and pliant—all spongy marrow with no hard, fibrous pith. The advantage in the impending interview, Arbati knew, lay entirely with the home team.

The door behind him opened and Giorgio Bruni entered.

'Good timing,' Arbati said, turning. 'He's just arrived.'

Bruni nodded. 'I know. I was watching. How do we play it?'

'By ear,' Arbati said, pouring himself a coffee. 'What's your impression?'

'He's running scared. I say we put the gears to him right off the bat.'

Arbati smiled. It was just like Giorgio to go directly for the jugular.

'In due course,' he said. 'But let's not be in a hurry. We'll give him a chance first to break under his own weight.'

'Very funny.'

Through the panes of the glass-fronted office they watched as Strozzi and his dark shadow appeared at the top of the stairs on the far side of the squad room and were given directions by the pointing finger of the duty sergeant on the desk. The climb had taken its toll. Strozzi's face was beet red and he was gasping for air and wincing as if he'd ruptured something. It took him almost two minutes, blowing like a porpoise, to catch his breath. In Arbati's office the two policemen, ostensibly busy with other work, missed nothing. At length restored sufficiently in wind to proceed, Strozzi resumed his ponderous way toward them, the scowling figure of Franco drawn warily in his wake. It was obvious that being surrounded by uniformed officers was not Franco's idea of a fun way to spend his afternoon: he was as skittish as a Bedouin at a bar mitzvah. Outside Arbati's office Strozzi paused, glanced briefly at the nameplate on the door, then pushed his way in without bothering to knock.

'I'm Nicòlo Strozzi,' he announced.

Arbati looked up from the papers he was perusing and said superfluously: 'Come in, Signor Strozzi. I've been expecting you.' He motioned toward two plain wooden chairs that stood in front of the desk. 'I'm Inspector Arbati. This is my associate, Detective Bruni.'

He did not rise or offer to shake hands. The gestures seemed neither necessary or appropriate. He wanted Strozzi at a disadvantage. There was no point in putting him at ease by pretending to be polite.

Strozzi said: 'You know Franco, of course, my chauffeur.'

'We've met,' Arbati said.

The office was intentionally bare and functional. It contained little furniture, what there was of it ill-matched and unredeemably utilitarian. There were no plants or family photographs on the

desk, no pictures on the walls. It was Arbati's theory that a bare
room facilitated truth and saved time by discouraging prevarica-
tion. The only missing cliché was a goose-necked lamp to twist
into the eyes of suspects.

Strozzi lowered himself onto one of the slat-backed chairs and
mopped at his brow. Franco, declining a seat, took up his post at
his employer's back.

'Coffee?' Arbati offered, appearing to thaw a little.

Strozzi contemplated the viscous liquid in the glass pot and
raised a heavy hand. 'Thank you,' he said, 'but no. I've just eaten
my lunch.'

Bruni, who had perched himself on a corner of the desk, gave
Franco a hard stare. 'Does he have a permit to carry that thing?'
he asked, indicating the bulge of the Beretta under Franco's arm.

Strozzi gave him a wintry smile. 'Of course he does. But presumably we're not here to discuss firearms permits.'

Arbati leaned forward and said in a quiet voice:

'You asked to see me, Signor Strozzi. I'm listening.'

Strozzi gave a tired smile. 'The shoe, I think, is on the other
foot, inspector,' he said. 'For the past week you've been snooping
around asking questions about me. Trying to track me down, in
fact, while I was away enjoying a little well-earned vacation. I'd
like to know why you were looking for me.'

'We both already know the answer to that,' Arbati said evenly.

'Let's say, then,' Strozzi said smoothly, 'I'd like to hear it from
your lips first.'

Arbati removed a case from his pocket and took out a cigarette.
'Do you mind if I smoke?'

'Not at all, inspector. It's your life.'

The Zippo's flint-wheel grated in the silence between them.
Arbati blew a plume of smoke at the ceiling, then said:

'A number of your friends have died violently in the past few
months.'

'Acquaintances, inspector,' Strozzi corrected. 'I would hardly
call them friends.'

'They were friends once—when you were at school together.'

Strozzi smiled. 'You've done your homework,' he said. 'I assume, then, that you've talked to the good fathers at Collègio San
Stefano.'

Arbati nodded. 'The current rector—Father Monticelli—was

very helpful. He provided us with detailed records of the boys enrolled at the school in the mid-1950s, yourself included. As a student, Signore Strozzi, your long suit was mathematics, your short suit was languages. Did you know they have an archive full of old pictures, by the way, all carefully labelled and dated? It was really quite instructive.'

Strozzi's grin broadened. 'I found mathematics easy,' he said. 'Perhaps that's why I've made a successful banker. In fact, I won the mathematics prize in both of my last two years at the school, but since you have the records, I suppose you know that already. I was also thin then and even reasonably athletic. It was kind of you, inspector, having seen photographs, not to have mentioned the fact.' He creased his brow. 'I take it Father Monticelli is a new man on the scene. I recall no one of that name. Monsignor Aprile was the headmaster in my day.'

It was Bruni who replied:

'Monsignor Aprile died of cancer in 1972. The other priests who taught at San Stefano when you were there are dead too, all except Father Ucello. He's over ninety now, living at a Basilian retreat in Rapallo.'

'Ah, Father Ucello...' Strozzi said, his smile suffused with the sad joy of memory. 'Truly, gentlemen, a demanding taskmaster. He taught us Latin—and God help the lad who misconstrued an ablative absolute or a passive periphrastic! Ucello was a merciless pedant, a stickler for detail and lightning quick with the cane. Tell me, did he still remember me after all these years?'

'No,' Bruni said. 'He hardly knows his own name. He's quite senile.'

'A great pity,' Strozzi said without pity.

'We have, however,' Arbati cut in, 'been able to piece together from various sources the fact that five of you formed a very close-knit group—an exclusive club, one might say—during your time at the school. You were, according to all accounts, inseparable.' He scraped the ash from his cigarette with careful deliberation. 'As it happens, four of the five members of that little band have recently met quite violent ends.'

'And you suspect me?' Strozzi asked disingenuously.

Arbati gave him a pained smile. 'No, I think you're the next one in line—and so do you, Signor Strozzi. That's why you came to see me, isn't it? The reason you've come out of hiding? You want my help.'

Strozzi folded his hands in his lap and narrowed his gaze. 'As a tax-paying citizen, I expect police protection when my life is in danger,' he said.

'Then we need each other, Signor Strozzi. We have no choice but to work together. If you refuse, I can't guarantee your safety.'

'And if I do help...?'

'Your chances improve.'

'But still no guarantee,' Strozzi said.

Arbati ground out his cigarette. 'Still no guarantee.'

'What do you want from me?'

'Information,' Arbati said. He rose and, standing with his back to Strozzi, gazed out at the gridlock below in Piazza dell Libertà. 'I need to know everything,' he said softly. 'Particularly, I need to know who you think is responsible for these murders, assuming you have someone in mind—and I imagine you do—and I need to know precisely why it is that you suspect this particular individual.'

Strozzi made his decision swiftly. He said:

'His name is Francesco Pistocchi, inspector. I hired a private detective to find him, but he's come up dry. Pistocchi must have changed his name. I expect the police, with their resources, to have better luck in running him to ground.'

'I see,' Arbati said without turning from the window. It was interesting that Strozzi should think of a police investigation in imagery drawn from a blood sport. He said: 'Perhaps you'd care to tell me why this Francesco Pistocchi should want to kill you and the others?'

'It was a long time ago, inspector,' Strozzi shrugged. 'It's ancient history now. What happened then doesn't matter any more, as far as I can see. I don't think it's any of your business.'

Arbati wheeled. 'On the contrary, Signor Strozzi, it matters a great deal. This isn't the middle ages. I can't go around arresting people on a whim. You'll have to provide me with damn good *reasons* for hunting a man down and charging him with murder.' He leaned back against the sill and crossed his arms. 'I assume the story begins at Collègio San Stefano?'

Strozzi shifted his bulk uncomfortably on the hard chair.

'No,' he said quietly, 'it began rather later, after we left the school. The five of us met there, it's true, and we were, as you said, inseparable—but the Camerati dell'arte and Pistocchi came later, after we had moved on to the university.'

'The Camerati dell'arte?' Bruni interjected.

Strozzi nodded. 'It was Marchesi's idea: a secret society devoted to restoring Renaissance music to its classical roots, dedicated to doing things the way the original Camerata intended. Marchesi wanted to bring back all the old instruments—the viola da gamba, the chitarrone. That sort of thing. He had a vision: he wanted to make a name for himself as the man who restored opera to its original form and manner. He was persuasive, Detective Bruni, very persuasive. The rest of us were young and idealistic—we went along for the ride.'

'How many members made up this Camerati dell'arte?'

'Only the five of us.'

Bruni ticked off the names on his fingers. 'Alberto Mora, Roberto Rosso, Cardinal Cafferelli, Marchesi, and yourself. All from Collègio San Stefano.'

Strozzi nodded. 'Yes, that's right. No one else knew.'

Arbati said:

'And where does Francesco Pistocchi come in?'

Strozzi studied the web-veined back of his hand. 'The original opera scores call for castrati,' he said. 'Marchesi convinced us we needed a castrato.'

Bruni glanced at Arbati and raised an incredulous eyebrow. Arbati said:

'Tell us about it.'

Strozzi shrugged his heavy shoulders. 'There isn't much to tell,' he said without visible emotion. 'Marchesi found the boy in a village in the hills—I forget which one—and we drove out one Sunday to hear him sing. He was ten or eleven at the time. He sang like an angel and Marchesi persuaded the parents it was God's will that their son should serve Him with music. We paid them a few hundred lire to bring the lad back to Florence with us. I don't think they really had any idea what we had in mind. They were simple folk and I suppose they thought Marchesi was a singing coach or something of the sort. A couple of days later, there was a little ceremony in the chapel of Santa Maria Novella.'

Arbati concealed his interest. He'd had a hunch right from the very beginning that Santa Maria Novella was somehow an important clue.

'What kind of ceremony, exactly?' he prodded.

'It was at night,' Strozzi went on, 'just before midnight. Cafferelli was a seminarian and managed to get a key to the place. We lit the chapel with candles because we didn't want to attract attention by using the electric lights. Marchesi arranged everything. He insisted on doing things the old-fashioned way, of course, the way they were originally done in the seventeenth century. He'd done a great deal of reading, you see, and knew what was required. We gave Pistocchi a posset spiked with laudanum—the opium was Rosso's contribution; he had friends who knew where to get the stuff—and the boy became quite docile. There was a big galvanized tub we'd brought in earlier in the day and left in the chancel. We filled it with hot water. Then we stripped the boy and sat him in it. I remember we had an electric kettle boiling in the vestry and kept running back and forth with water to keep the tub hot enough. The idea was to have the scrotum fully distended so that we could find the right tubes. Anyway, after half an hour we took him out and Cafferelli muttered a few words in Latin over him, then we stretched him out on the altar and snipped his *vas deferens*.' He added, as if to justify the act: 'It was quite painless and we employed sterile procedures. The lad was never in any danger.'

'Not physical, perhaps,' Arbati said. Among the stories he had heard over the course of his police career, this was perhaps the most bizarre and depraved. And Strozzi, it was evident, felt no remorse. He regarded the business as something on the order of an undergraduate prank.

For Arbati, the castration of Francesco Pistocchi brought the separate parts of the puzzle together. It explained why Lo Squartatore had selected his five victims in the first place and why Cardinal Cafferelli, murdered in his office, had been carted halfway across the city to a chapel in the distant basilica of Santa Maria Novella. The Lady Chapel, in effect, where they had discovered Cafferelli's body had been the scene of the original crime. It explained, too, the killer's deliberate attempt in each case to cut the vocal cords of his victims, no doubt as a symbolic revenge for what had been done to him. And it explained something else too. It explained something about the crimes that had disturbed Arbati from the beginning and for which he had been unable to offer any rational solution. For suddenly he understood, recalling a seemingly insignificant detail in Strozzi's dossier, what the reason was for the *order* of the murders and for their escalating theatricality and brutality. Mora and Rosso had played only bit parts—perhaps they were the ones who ferried hot water in from the vestry—but it had been enough to cost them their lives. The other three had been the major players. Cafferelli, hung over a cross, had arranged the venue in the chapel and served as acolyte in the castration ceremony. Marchesi, mutilated with his own baton, was the ringleader and had been responsible in the first place for the boy's abduction. And Strozzi—? What macabre fate, Arbati wondered, awaited Strozzi for his part in the scheme? What twisted image of vengeance, corroding in the hidden depths for the past thirty years, had Pistocchi planned as a special gesture to commemorate the murder of his final—and most hated—victim?

Arbati lit another cigarette and surveyed the mountain of flesh seated primly opposite in its tailored white suit, a red carnation in the lapel. After a moment, he said:

'You said *we*, Signore Strozzi: "*we* snipped his *vas deferens.*" I think you mean *I*. It was you who performed the operation, wasn't it?'

Strozzi's face went suddenly red. 'What if I did?' he blustered. 'I'm not on trial here.'

'In a way you are,' Arbati said reasonably. 'Human castration is a felony under Italian law. And I could throw in charges of kidnapping and unlawful confinement to boot.'

'You can't prove anything,' Strozzi muttered truculently. 'I haven't signed a confession. And I won't sign one. You've walked yourself out onto a limb, inspector.'

'You weren't always a banker, Signore Strozzi,' Arbati went on, ignoring him. 'As you said, I've done my homework. No— you started your career at the university in the medical faculty. It was only when you failed out at the end of your third year that you transferred to the faculty of business administration. A judge would find that a most interesting piece of circumstantial evidence. You were the only one of the five Camerati who possessed the necessary medical skills and knowledge to perform the actual operation. I think, Signor Strozzi, it was you who held the knife.

And I think that's why Pistocchi has saved you until the last. The others were all minor characters in the plot as far as Pistocchi is concerned. You're the one he really hates, Signor Strozzi, because on that night in the candle-lit chapel it was you who held the scalpel.'

'It was me, as it happens,' Strozzi growled, 'but so what? Whatever I did, I didn't *kill* anybody. Pistocchi is a murderer and he's out there planning to kill again. To kill me, in fact—and it's your job to make damn well certain he doesn't succeed.'

'It's my job,' Arbati said evenly, 'to catch a murderer in time, if I can, to prevent him from killing again—which means, as it happens, doing what I can to protect you. But you, Signor Strozzi, are not my primary responsibility; Pistocchi is.' Arbati's voice took on a flinty edge. 'Now, when was the last time you saw him?'

Strozzi shrugged. The fight had gone out of him. He said:

'About thirty-five years ago, sometime in the late '50s. As I told you, he was a boy of ten or eleven at the time.'

'Can you describe him, what he looked like then?'

'Yes, I think so.'

'Then our first task,' Arbati said, 'is to put you together with a police artist. I want a composite drawing of what you remember.'

'This isn't a goddamn game!' Strozzi shouted, suddenly angry. 'Who looks the same at forty-five as he did before puberty? Stop wasting my time, inspector. We're dealing with *my life* here. You've got a job to do—now, get on with it!'

Arbati steepled his hands in front of him and said calmly:

'This is the age of electronic wizardry, Signor Strozzi. All we need is a reasonable likeness that we can have computer-aged. If you can give us something good, something close to what he looked like when you last saw him, we can get close—very close indeed. It's up to you.'

'All right,' Strozzi said, mollified. 'I'll do what I can.' He made a motion to rise. 'Now, if that's all for the moment—'

'One more thing,' Arbati said. 'You made yourselves a castrato, but you didn't let him sing. Why?'

Strozzi gave a crooked smile. 'As you pointed out yourself, inspector, castration is against the law in Italy. We did our best to interest the impresarios, but prospective employers were always frightened off when they suspected the truth. We told them the lad had been injured in a farming accident, but they wouldn't buy it. We tried every angle we could think of. We even had a private recording cut of him singing something from Monteverdi to use as an advertising gimmick—that was Marchesi's idea—but nothing worked. The lad was simply not a marketable commodity.'

'So you abandoned him?'

'A crude way of putting it, inspector, but I suppose we did. We had our own careers to look out for, after all. Our plans for Pistocchi ultimately gave way to the law of diminishing returns and we had no option but to cut our losses. I don't know what became of him after we went our separate ways. I never saw him again.' He stood as abruptly as his bulk allowed. 'I've said all I'm going to say, inspector. More than I'd intended. Now, get out there and find the bastard. That's what the taxpayer is paying you to do. Good day to you, sir.'

And then, suddenly, he was gone. The expanse of his white suit, followed by the blue serge back of his taciturn companion, disappeared through the door, leaving the office to the two policemen.

After a long minute, Bruni said:

'I'd half like to turn a blind eye and give Pistocchi a go at him. The pig deserves whatever's coming to him.'

Arbati crushed the butt of his half-smoked cigarette in the overflowing astray. Whatever he was thinking about Strozzi, he wasn't ready to let sentiment compromise it. He said softly:

'Set up a meeting with an artist as soon as you can, Giorgio. I want an Identikit composite of Pistocchi out on the street as fast as we can get our hands on one. We have a murderer to catch.'

FIVE

ARBATI LEFT THE Questura at six o'clock. It had been a long but fruitful day. The meeting with Strozzi had gone extremely well—much better, indeed, than he'd had any reason to expect. With a little luck an arrest in the Slasher case was only a week or ten days away.

Pistocchi had escaped detection so far because he was nameless and faceless and because his motive for murder had been a secret buried in the memories of his victims and nowhere else. Now, all that had changed. Strozzi had given the killer a name, a face, a motive. The rest was a matter of time and patience. The moment his picture was put into circulation, Pistocchi—or whatever he now called himself—lost his anonymity, his freedom to move in the shadows and murder with impunity. A known face never remains invisible for long. Invariably, someone remembers seeing it some place...in a shop, in a restaurant, in a museum, in a piazza—and the hunt narrows and intensifies. Arbati allowed himself a smile of satisfaction. Most of the mysteries in the case had already, or would shortly be, cleared up. Yet one nagging question continued to trouble him. Why had Francesco Pistocchi waited almost thirty-five years to seek his revenge on the five members of the Camerati dell'arte for what they had done to him? It was an important question—but one to which, he knew, he might never have the answer.

He made his way toward the river through the old city, where the medieval buildings lining either side of the narrow streets seemed almost to meet in the air as their shuttered faces arched above him. In twenty minutes he would be home. The working day was over. It was time to forget Pistocchi for a few hours and think about other things. As he neared the river, the policeman in him faded and the poet began to emerge. He stopped briefly at a tobacconist's in Lungarno Corsini to buy cigarettes, then crossed Ponte Santa Trinità into the Oltrarno. His apartment was in a cul-de-sac between the river and the unfinished façade of Santa Spirito. He had chosen the location because it was central and because it was, mercifully, off the beaten track of tourist itineraries.

As he turned into the familiar street, where geraniums bloomed in wooden planters and saplings in wrought-iron cages sprouted at intervals along the cobbles like leafy balloons, he began to feel, as he did every evening when he returned home, the glow of a cautious hope that tonight, perhaps, the images of the new poem stirring in his subconscious would rise and fashion themselves into articulate phrases. The enigma of language and poetry never ceased to fascinate him. By what mysterious process was it he wondered, that ideas were converted into words and feelings into phrases? How was it possible for lifeless marks scribbled on paper to preserve the intensity of memory and desire, to replicate the power of feelings known in the blood and felt along the margins of the heart? How could mere words breathe life into the thoughts and passions that welled up from the depths of the human spirit? There *were* no answers, he knew; there were questions but never any answers. Every image he conceived was a thing mysteriously given—a something found rather than a something made—and every poem he had ever written was as miraculous in its gestation as a human birth.

His apartment was on the ground floor in the middle of a row of refurbished nineteenth-century town houses, a comfortable two-bedroom flat furnished with a warm but firmly masculine taste. The sitting-room overlooked the street and the two bed-rooms—one converted into a book-lined study—looked out behind into a walled garden bright with bougainvillaea and oleander. The kitchen was a small and windowless alcove off the sitting-room, its counter top crowded with appliances and various culinary gadgets—egg whisks, garlic presses, citrus peelers—that Arbati had seen advertised in magazines or had stumbled over in speciality shops. On a shelf beside the refrigerator was a row of well-thumbed cookbooks and, mounted on the wall next to the expensive Smeg gas range, was a comprehensive spicerack. Arbati was a dedicated and creative cook and, like many long-time bachelors, he prided himself on his culinary skill.

He changed into casual slacks and shirt and, since it was too early to think about eating, sat down at the teak desk in the study overlooking the garden. Late sunlight filtered through the leaves of a holm oak near the garden wall, casting dappled patterns around the room. Would the Muse—his fickle mistress—speak to him tonight? On the desk sat a dictionary, a thesaurus, a mug of pens and sharpened pencils—the meagre tools of his poetic trade. Under the desk an old Olivetti portable typewriter slept in its black case. Arbati composed and made his revisions in longhand, using the machine only to type up final drafts. The poems he had completed for the new volume lay in a buff folder, typed and ready for the printer—only the last poem, unfinished except for its title, remained to be written. From the pad in the centre of the desk a single word—*Androgyne*—stared up at him with a vaguely menacing air, and the wastepaper basket at his feet was full of crumpled, half-written sheets. Maybe things would go better tonight. He unscrewed the cap of the Parker fountain-pen that had been his companion through the first volume and had become, over time, something of a good-luck charm. He was ready to begin. Composing his mind, he struck a meditative pose—and waited for something to happen.

The minutes passed.

He heard the clock ticking in the hall, the sound of a distant horn, a bird whistle in the branches of the oak. The scent of bougainvillaea blossoms drifted in through the open window.

His mind began to drift. For some reason, it settled on the bearded novelist he had met a month or two earlier at the only writers' conference he ever attended. The occasion was an award presented by the Florentine Guild in recognition of Arbati's first book, *Fòglia di luce*, and praising him for the fluid lyricism of his verse. The young novelist—whose face, but not name, Arbati recalled—had cornered him after the speeches and insisted on confiding how *he* pursued the craft of writing. The words were engraved on Arbati's brain: 'Practice is the secret,' he said, 'the only thing that really matters. Anybody can write, you know. I just sit down at my typewriter and pound out ten or twelve feet a day—seven days a week, rain or shine. You wait and see, Signor Arbati; you'll be hearing about me. One day I'll be famous.' Arbati wondered if the lad was still hammering away somewhere in a garret, practising to be famous. He supposed he was. He found himself wishing that writing really was as easy as pounding out ten or twelve feet a day. It never had been that way for him. He could sit for days and get nothing. Then, somewhere in the chasms of his brain, an idea would stir, a germ of thought. He would strain after it—but it was like trying to capture mist in a jar. If he persisted, hazy images would sometimes—but not always—loom up into consciousness and he would scramble to get them down in words. Fragments, approximations, the shards of vision. Once he had a draft on paper, he became a jeweller—cutting, grinding, polishing the rough stone of his inspiration into facets that refracted a light that always, finally, remained beyond his power to grasp. He could work for weeks, even for months, on a single poem. At the end of it all what he had, even in his best poems, was never more than a ragged fragment of the vision he wanted to convey. Oh, yes—how he wished that writing was just a matter of sitting down and pounding out ten or twelve feet a day—

He wondered again if *Androgyne* was one of those projects doomed, no matter what he did, to end up in the basket at his feet. For weeks he had wrestled with it and made no progress. All he had to show for the effort were a mental outline and—the only thing actually down on paper—a title. He stared out the window and his eye settled on a pair of grey doves perched side by side, like pottery figurines, on the overhead wires. They seemed somehow a symbol of his yearning, though he didn't know how. Perhaps it was their sense of peace—the aura of contentment they gave off, like two old lovers at peace with themselves and the world. The poem was beginning to irritate him. Why was the damned things so *bloody* intractable? The subject and the way he wanted to treat it were both clear in his mind. It was to be an exploration of the mysterious harmony of masculine and feminine attributes reconciled at the root of human personality; a study of the polarities of power and grace, hardness and softness, strength and beauty that coalesce in every human identity into a seamless unity. The inspiration for the idea was Botticelli's painting of *Venus and Mars* in the Uffizi. On a dozen visits to the gallery, he had studied the painting like a lover. He knew every line and tint by heart, the detail of every plane and sensuous curve. And yet, in spite of all this, *Androgyne* remained unwritten, unbegun—an elusive phantom, a fruitless and frustrating craving...

He gave up trying to write. It was useless. Nothing would come tonight.

Leaving the desk, he wandered into the sitting-room. He was

restless and fidgety, he didn't know why. The evening edition of *La Nazione* lay on the coffee table where he had dropped it when he came in. He picked it up and tried to read. The front-page story was the report of another case of political corruption, this time in Milan, that was once again spreading its dark tentacles out to embrace the federal government. But he couldn't concentrate on the story and tossed the paper impatiently aside.

In a reflex act, done before he even realized what he was doing, he picked up the telephone and dialled her number. There was no need to check the directory or ring the operator for assistance; he knew the number by heart, although he had only dialled it once before. She had been on his mind for days. A hundred times he had been on the point of calling, but the moment had never been right. He was always nervous about these things. But now suddenly, without having planned it, he found himself holding the receiver and listening to the distant bell ringing in her apartment in Via della Scala. There was no time even to clear his throat before it was answered. She must have been sitting almost beside it.

'Signorina Sinclair?' he said.

'*Sì.*'

'It's Carlo Arbati, from the Carabinieri. I'm not disturbing your dinner, I hope.'

'No, inspector. As a matter of fact, I just walked in the door as the bell rang. I was tied up at the university.' If she was surprised to hear from him there was no trace of it in her voice. 'Have you been trying to reach me?'

He hardly knew what to say. 'No,' he managed. 'I was wondering if you were busy this evening?' He tried to sound casual but the blood was pounding in his ears and his voice sounded as if it were coming from under water.

'I thought I'd answered all your questions, inspector.'

He grasped at the straw. 'You did, yes—well, there are perhaps one or two details that still need clearing up.' *Why on earth had he said that?* Nothing—at least nothing she could provide him with—remained to be asked about the Marchesi murder. Oh God, he thought, I've done it again. I've boxed myself into a corner. Why didn't I just come out and say what's on my mind—that I'm phoning to ask for a date? Trying to salvage what he could, he said quickly, almost desperately: 'Since you haven't eaten, perhaps you'd let me treat you. I know a pleasant place quite close by. We could talk over dinner.'

There was a pause and he felt the embarrassment rising in his cheeks. He'd been a fool to call in the first place—a double fool for having used such a flimsy pretext. She was bound to see through it, bound to refuse. He felt like a prisoner in the dock awaiting the judge's verdict. He swallowed hard, anticipating defeat.

Finally, she said:

'I can manage that, I think—yes, why not? I look forward to it. What time?'

'Oh—' he said, taken aback. The possibility that she might actually accept hadn't crossed his mind and he was unprepared for it. His mind whirled and his tongue froze. He cleared his throat and composed himself with an effort, then said: 'Shall we say eight-thirty? I'll ring through for a reservation. I could pick you up, say, at eight?'

'Eight is fine. I'll be ready, inspector,' she said, and the telephone went dead.

For a long moment he stood with the humming instrument pressed to his ear, expecting her to return and say that it was all a ghastly mistake and that she'd have to cancel.

Eventually, as if it might explode, he set the receiver gently back in its cradle.

God, he thought, I'm such a silly klutz with women!

CORDELIA BATHED and changed into a navy frock with puff sleeves and Rouen lace at the neck. As she stood at the mirror doing her hair into a French roll, she wondered what had induced her to accept his invitation. She had surprised herself by agreeing—and she suspected that she'd surprised him as well. She heard it in his voice. But why had he called? Not to question her further about the murder investigation, that much she knew. They'd covered that ground twice already and established beyond a reasonable doubt that she had nothing useful to contribute. Perhaps he was lonely...or perhaps he thought that *she* must be lonely so far from home and alone in a strange land...or perhaps—well, there were a thousand possibilities. Everything would be just fine, she thought, as long as he didn't have any *intentions*. Dinner and an evening's chat were perfectly acceptable, but she wasn't ready to let a man back into her life on a regular basis—not yet; not so soon after her experience with Charles Passmore. She needed time to get her bearings; she needed time to work out certain fundamental things about who she was and what she wanted out of her life.

So why, then, had she agreed to go out with him? She pondered her face in the mirror. Partly, no doubt, it was because he'd caught her at the right moment. It had been a long day and she had jumped at the chance to have a night out, a night away from her books and the leftover lasagna in the icebox. But partly, too, she knew, it was because Inspector Arbati intrigued her, because she wanted to know what made him tick. At first, she hadn't liked him at all. He'd struck her as a cold and unfeeling fish—a typical cop. That night at the theatre when she'd found Marchesi's body, he'd come on like Inspector Japp, treating the death of a great conductor as if it were just another homicide—and she had despised him as a Philistine for it. But a few days later, when he'd come to her apartment and questioned her again, he had seemed a different person. She'd had a fierce migraine all that morning, she remembered, and had felt (and probably looked) like death warmed over—and he'd sat her down and fixed a cup of tea and talked with sympathy and real understanding about Marchesi and the shock she'd had in finding him like that, with the baton stuck in his slashed throat. It was as if, somehow, he harboured two separate beings in one body. The strange case of Arbati and Hyde. What piqued her interest was to know which of them was the root personality and how Arbati—or anyone else in his position—managed to balance, without falling into total cynicism, the contradictions between human feeling and clinical detachment that police work must necessarily involve. He was a kind of psychological curiosity and she wanted to put him under the microscope. And besides, she thought, he *is* very good looking—as a specimen for an evening's analysis.

'There,' she said aloud, surveying her hair with a critical eye. 'I'm ready. Let the evening begin.'

When she emerged from the bathroom, Fra Angelico was waiting on the balcony, licking a patient paw. She let him in and poured his saucer of milk.

'You can't stay long tonight, my friend,' she warned, crouching to stroke his back. 'Ten minutes and out you go on your furry butt. I'm expecting a gentleman visitor in a few minutes.' The quaint phrase—she hadn't the faintest idea why it had popped into her head—was something Signora Ghilberti might have said 'A *gentle*man visitor to you, Miss Sinclair,' she mimicked into the mirror—and gave a grimace. If she didn't manage to sneak the inspector past her landlady's door, the mumblenews for the next week would be unbearable. Signora Ghilberti was well-intentioned enough, but she had a fatal eye for interpreting everything in terms of confetti and wedding-bells. It probably, Cordelia thought, came of swallowing paperback romance novels in bulk. They had a way, in large doses, of working their way into the bloodstream, like lead or mercury, and poisoning the whole system.

While Fra Angelico lapped contentedly at his meal, Cordelia wandered onto the balcony. The sinking sun cast brown, elongated shadows over the lower rooftops and, from above, gave the scene around her the dappled appearance of the floor of a terracotta forest. The air was growing cool. She went back inside and hunted out a sweater to take with her, then transferred lipstick, Kleenex, and her apartment key to a sequined evening bag. She had just finished when Arbati knocked at the door.

'I'm a few minutes early,' he apologized. 'My timing is usually better.'

'That's fine, inspector. I'm ready and my furry friend here is just finishing his supper. He'll only be a minute. I told him he couldn't stay long tonight.'

As if he'd understood her words and decided to go peacefully on his own, Fra Angelico stretched and gave a languorous yawn, then stalked to the French windows in a measured, regal gait. Cordelia let him out and hooked the latch behind him.

'Did you bring him with you from the States?' Arbati asked.

'Oh, no—no, he's not mine. He belongs to the man downstairs. I just feed him. His name, by the way, is Fra Angelico.'

'Really?' Arbati grinned. 'Rather an odd name for a cat. Does he paint?'

Cordelia laughed. That had been her first question, too, when she'd heard the name. She remembered Signor Farinelli's clever retort, and replied: 'He *wants* to paint. He has the soul of a great painter. You can see it in his eyes.'

'I'll remember to look next time,' Arbati said with a straight face.

Cordelia gathered up her bag and sweater from the end of the bed. As she turned, she noticed for the first time how striking Arbati looked in his fawn suit, blue shirt, and co-ordinated paisley tie. He was, in fact, a quite remarkably handsome man.

'You're not in your official suit,' she said, 'so I guess you're not planning to really grill me.'

He gave her, she thought, an embarrassed smile and said, 'No, not tonight.'

They descended the stairs and escaped from the building without being spotted by Signora Ghilberti, then turned east along Via della Scala.

Arbati said: 'Shall we walk—or would you prefer a cab? It's not far.'

The restaurant he'd chosen was Al Lume di Candela, an upscale establishment house in a refurbished medieval tower near the river between Ponte Vecchio and Ponte Santa Trinità. The air was still pleasant and warm with the memory of afternoon sun.

'Let's walk,' Cordelia suggested. 'I never get tired of the sights.'

At Via Tornabuoni, they turned right, past the fashionable houses of Ferragamo, Gucci, and Settepassi-Faraone. A hundred yards ahead, the gothic façade of Santa Trinità rose like a stone vesper into the early evening sky.

'Were you born in Florence, inspector,' Cordelia asked, making conversation, 'or are you an import like me?'

'I was born in Tuscany,' Arbati said, 'but not Florence. I grew up in Prato, about twenty kilometres up the road. When I finished high school, I came to the Police Academy here. One thing led to another and I ended up staying. It's been almost fifteen years now.'

'Had you always planned to be a policeman?'

'No—quite the contrary,' Arbati said with a slightly selfconscious grin. 'What I really wanted to be as a boy was an astronaut. Like Captain Kirk. The Italian Space Programme didn't have any openings, so I was driven into law enforcement.'

'Seriously,' Cordelia said. 'I'm interested. I'd like to know.'

'Seriously then—no, it's not a career I planned. It just happened. Like most eighteen-year-olds, I didn't have any idea what

I wanted to do. But going off to university didn't appeal to me—it was too sedentary. I suppose I thought police work would somehow be more exciting. Close to that dream of being an astronaut, you know. In a way, of course, it has been—but if I'd known about the amount of paper-pushing that goes along with the high-speed chases,' he added with a grin, 'I might have stayed in school and settled for becoming a chemistry teacher.'

'In spite of the irony, though,' Cordelia said, 'you're glad you made the decision you did, aren't you? I have the feeling that you enjoy being a policeman.'

'Actually, yes, I do.' He gave her an appraising look and his tone grew serious. 'There's a lot of job satisfaction in keeping the streets safe for people like us to wander along. You have to remember things weren't always this way. In the old days, all these fortified buildings around us were the only islands of safety there were in a sea of robber barons and armed thugs. They were originally built to keep people *out*. The police have had a good deal to do with the fact that we've been able to turn most of them into art museums and restaurants. Too often, people forget that.'

Cordelia felt a tinge of embarrassment redden her cheek. It was as though he had sensed her attitude to policemen and was, with a gentle prescience, heading her prejudices off at the pass.

'But the real truth of the matter,' Arbati went on, 'is that police work helps ensure that justice is served. At the risk of sounding old-fashioned, I mean Justice with a capital "J"—and it's important that those of us who are in the business never lose sight of that end. In the final analysis, law enforcement and even the law itself are merely the blunt instruments of Justice. We don't always succeed, of course, and we occasionally make terrible mistakes, but the purpose of our work is to ensure—as far as it's humanly possible to ensure anything—that good in the end actually *does* win out over evil.'

'Why, inspector,' Cordelia said with a grin, 'I believe that you're secretly an idealist.'

'No,' Arbati smiled, 'that's not how I see it. An idealist is someone who is unrealistic. My dreams are realizable because truth and justice aren't just abstractions. They're real and they're worth fighting for. If I didn't believe that, I couldn't do what I do.'

At the end of the block they turned left into Via della Terme.

Al Lume di Candela, their destination, was a medieval tower on the south side. As they walked toward it, Cordelia began to sense that Arbati was a more complex—a more intriguing—man than she'd given him credit for being. He had passed already in her mind beyond the stage of being a specimen for psychological analysis: he had become a real human being. It was, she thought suddenly, probably going to be an enjoyable as well as an interesting evening.

Their table was in an alcove, almost a private room, connected by an archway to the main dining-room. The glassware and silver cutlery sparkled on starched table linen in the flickering light of wall-mounted candles. It was a setting that was intimate and yet also sociable. She wondered if he had requested it especially.

'It has character,' she said, glancing around appreciatively.

'One of my favourites,' Arbati said, pleased with her pleasure. 'It's a family operation and the food is authentic Florentine. Their acquacotta is superb and I can recommend the osso bucco.' He consulted the wine-list briefly. 'Shall we go with one of our local chiantis?'

He was on familiar ground—a fact she noticed when the *maître d'hôtel* had spoken to him by name. At her apartment he had seemed stiff and a little awkward, but he had begun to relax and open up as they walked. She wondered again what had prompted him to ask her out. Something in his voice on the phone had told her it was a spur-of-the-moment decision. Her acceptance had been equally impetuous. A coincidence of impulses—something meant to be.

'Chianti is fine,' she said.

The waiter arrived and took their order. When he had gone, she said:

'So, tell me about your investigation. What kind of progress are you making there? I don't suppose, by the way, that you really *do* have more questions to ask me about the maestro's murder, do you?'

He gave a little wry, helpless grin. 'No,' he said, 'no—I don't know what made me say that on the phone. Nerves, I guess.' He sipped at his wine, as if debating how much he could reveal, then said: 'As a matter of fact, we had an important break in the case this afternoon. For some time we've suspected that a multiple murderer, very selective in his choice of targets, was taking revenge for something that happened a long time ago. The man had killed before—three times, in fact—and, frankly, we expected him to kill again. So, Marchesi's death wasn't really a surprise. But until today, we didn't have any idea what the killer's motive was. Now we do.'

Cordelia's face darkened. 'Are you saying that you *expected* Marchesi to be murdered?'

'Not at all, no. We expected *someone* to be murdered. We had no idea that that someone would be Antonio Marchesi.' He paused for a moment, then explained. 'Over the past two and a half months, three prominent figures—Marchesi makes it four—have died violently in the same manner. All of them had their throats slashed. Two of the murders occurred before you arrived. The third you probably know about—he was a Roman Catholic cardinal. Umberto Cafferelli. His body was left hanging on a cross in Santa Maria Novella basilica.'

Cordelia nodded. 'It happened the day I arrived. At least, that's when the body was discovered. I walked right past the murder scene on my way from the train station to find my apartment.'

'Then you walked right past me,' Arbati said, adding with a smile, 'without speaking.'

'A terrible oversight, inspector. Can you ever forgive me?'

'Only if you call me Carlo.'

'Okay, Carlo. So—am I forgiven?'

'Yes, but don't let it happen again.'

'No, inspector.'

Their soup arrived. On silent feet their waiter materialized bearing a steaming tureen, ladled out a serving to each, replenished their wine, then disappeared. The soup was acquacotta, a speciality of the house—literally 'cooked water,' but actually a vegetable purée in a meat broth. It was magnificent.

'*Very* nice indeed,' Cordelia said, savouring the spiced, ambrosial afterglow.

'If there's one thing we Florentines do well,' Arbati agreed, 'it's cook water.'

'You were saying,' Cordelia said, her curiosity still unsatisfied, 'that you'd had an important break in the investigation. Can you tell me something more about it—or is it a police secret?'

Arbati pursed his lips. 'The names are confidential,' he said, 'but the gist of it is that we now know both the killer's identity

and his motive. After the Cafferelli murder, we noticed that the
victims up to that point had all been students at the same school
in the mid-1950s. What we didn't have, however, was anything
concrete to connect them, apart from their having once been in
the same place at the same time. And we didn't have anything
that pointed to a single motive for killing them. When it became
clear that the school was important, however, we began the job
of tracking down every boy who was there in the relevant years
and started asking questions. It turned out that a couple of them
remembered that a group—including the three murder victims to
that point—had formed a kind of secret club called the Camerati
dell'arte.'

'And Marchesi was one of them?'

Arbati nodded. 'By all accounts, he was their guiding spirit.'

'And what were these Companions of Art so secretive about?'

'They had the idea they'd get rich and famous by restoring
Renaissance opera to its roots.'

'It doesn't exactly sound like a recipe for murder,' Cordelia
said, taking her last spoonful of acquacotta.

'It needn't have been,' Arbati said, 'except that they decided
they needed a castrato. They abducted a young peasant boy and
emasculated him.'

'Good God!' Cordelia exclaimed, stunned. 'That's grotesque!'

She set the spoon slowly back on her plate and was silent for
a long moment, then said:

'Did you talk to Marchesi about this?'

Arbati shook his head. 'I didn't get the chance. He wasn't the
kind of man who was willing to accommodate himself to other
people's schedules. I tried to arrange a meeting, but he insisted
he was too busy to talk and put off meeting until after the opening
of the Monteverdi festival. By then, of course, it was too late. At
the time, I had no reason to insist, to press the issue. There was
no evidence to suggest that Marchesi was in any danger, and I
didn't know, then, what the Camerati had allegedly done. I only
found that out today when a witness came forward and filled in
the missing pieces.'

Cordelia's head was spinning. For years, she had admired Mar-
~si, had looked on him as a kind of idol. She couldn't accept,
~ickly and with so little preparation, that he was involved in
~tting such an inhuman crime. It was as if her own father,

in addition to his known faults, were out of the blue accused of being a cocaine baron or a clandestine axe-murderer.

'I can't believe it,' she said, shaking her head. 'I can't believe he'd do such a horrible thing. What about this witness? Can you trust he's telling you the truth?'

'Oh, yes, I think so.'

'How can you be so sure?'

'Because he's the last of the Camerati,' Arbati said softly. 'He's Lo Squartatore's next target.'

They were silent for a time.

'I wish you hadn't told me,' she said finally.

'Then I wish you hadn't asked,' he replied.

Their waiter returned bearing plates, sauces, a tall pepper-mill, more wine. The soup course was cleared away, the table crumbed, the main course laid, the glasses recharged.

'Your health,' Arbati proposed, raising his glass. 'Now,' he said, steering for less troubled waters, 'you told me once that you were in Florence to write a thesis. About music if I remember. Tell me something about it.'

They talked as they ate. Cordelia gradually put Marchesi out of her mind and warmed to her subject. She was surprised how knowledgeable Carlo was about music and she found herself, before long, even forgetting that he was a policeman. The more they talked, the more she found in him to admire. In fact, she realized, she was beginning to quite like him. He was intelligent, sensitive, witty, well-read. She found herself comparing him with Charles, her ex-husband. Both were boyishly good-looking, even handsome—but there the similarity ended. Charles Passmore was a loud and shallow egotist who inflated himself by deflating others and whose only real topic of conversation, apart from himself, was the Nikkei and NASDAQ exchanges. Carlo Arbati, in contrast, was quiet and (she realized) almost shy, cultured and considerate, as good a listener as he was a talker—and someone, too, who was genuinely interested, for a change, in what *she* had to say.

Charles—Carlo: the same name in two different languages a world apart. It was certainly an odd coincidence.

She said finally, tired of talking about herself:

'What about you, Carlo? What do you do when you're not

hunting down the enemies of society? You must have something that gets you away from your grisly vocation now and again.'

'I do, yes,' he said with a small, self-deprecating grin. 'Something quite improbable. You wouldn't guess it, I imagine, in a dozen lifetimes.'

'All right then,' she said, taking up the challenge, 'since you put it that way I'll have a go. But—wait a minute! What's in it for me? What do I get if I'm right?'

'Dessert,' he offered.

'You're on, mister.' She narrowed her eyes and studied his face. 'Okay—' she said, 'you look like the daring, devil-may-care type who, I'd say…yes, who drives racing cars for Ferrari on the weekend.'

He shook his head. 'Sorry. Not even close.'

'Hmmm,' she said. 'Something less audacious, then. Let's see. Let me think. Okay, I know—you breed piranha in your bathtub for use as game-fish.'

'Wrong.'

'Drat! I thought I had it. All right, then—one more guess.' She gave him a long and searching stare. 'I've got it this time,' she said intrepidly. 'Italy *does* have a secret space programme and you spend your weekends floating around in an anti-gravity chamber in a laboratory somewhere in the Apennines, training to be the first human being to blast off for Saturn.'

Arbati laughed. 'Close,' he said, 'but no cigar. It's outer space, but not that far out.'

'All right. I give up then.'

Arbati folded his arms. 'I write poetry.'

'No—! Really?'

'Yes, really. I told you you'd be surprised.'

'More like stunned, stupefied, flabbergasted.'

'Why? Did you think all cops were Philistines?'

Cordelia toyed with her fork, avoiding his eyes. 'Until tonight,' she said, 'I confess I probably did. But you're changing my mind in a big hurry.' She looked up and said: 'Tell me about your poetry. Have you published any?'

'I have a new book coming out in the fall.'

' new book. So, you're an old hand at it! What kind of poetry write?'

shrugged. 'Oh—ordinary poetry, I suppose. I ask myself

what makes me tick, why I think and feel the way I do about life, about the things I see and hear and smell around me—and then I try to find words to recreate those experiences. Poetry is about seeing old things, everyday things, in new ways—as if you were seeing them for the first time. Even more, I suppose, it's about seeing yourself in the things you experience. Little things, mostly; things we take for granted. I know that a rainbow in the sky or a sparrow pecking about in the gravel—even a falling leaf—can set me suddenly to rights. When I'm writing about them, I always have the sense that somehow I'm trying to find a symbolic language for something inside me rather than describing anything that's external to myself. How can I put it? Well, what I mean is that I have the obscure feeling when I look at nature that what I'm seeing is in some mysterious way the dim awakening of a forgotten truth of my own inner nature. I know what Plato meant when he said that all our knowing is, at bottom, a kind of remembering.' He stopped and gave a sheepish grin. 'Does any of that make sense, or am I talking Greek?'

'German, maybe—but not Greek,' Cordelia laughed. 'I have a *hazy* sense of what it is you're driving at—but that's about as far, I'm afraid, as my puny command of German will carry me. I've occasionally read poems that made me feel what you describe, but it's not the way my brain usually works. I suppose I'm too much of an Aristotelian at heart ever to wander that far away from the security of cold, hard facts.'

'I have a friend like that,' Arbati said, thinking of Giorgio Bruni. 'He feels the same way but is less charitable in the way he puts it. He thinks I'm just plain crazy.'

'We Aristotelians can be rather cruel,' Cordelia nodded. She went on: 'But tell me, when did you first know you wanted to write poetry? Was it an instinct you were born with?'

'Perhaps it was,' Arbati nodded, 'but I didn't start young. I wrote my first poems when my parents were killed in a car accident a little over ten years ago. I was looking for answers, I suppose, and began putting ideas down on paper, trying to make them reproduce what I felt. Anyway, once I got started, I just kept going, until now it's become a sort of consuming passion. I spend most evenings and weekends working on some poem or other. It's hard to explain what happens to me when I write: there's no higher high than when it flows, and no lower low than when it doesn't. Heaven or hell—and nothing in between. But I don't have any choice in the matter any more. I'm hooked. When it comes, I write; when it doesn't, I sit and fret in my chains until it does.'

'Are you working on something at the moment?'

'I was afraid you were going to ask me that,' he said with a grimace. 'It's a poem called *Androgyne,* about the paradox of masculine and feminine attributes in human personality. I've been wrestling with it for weeks and, to tell the truth, I don't know any more which of us will end up winning—the heroic poet or the poem that's fighting tooth-and-nail not to be born.'

'It sounds fascinating,' she said. 'Tell me about it. What's it about?'

'Well,' he said, 'it started with a painting I saw in the Uffizi, a Botticelli—'

The gelato came and went, then the coffee and Cointreau. Arbati talked with animation and Cordelia listened, interjecting a thought here, helping to round out an idea there. It was like the give-and-take of a graduate seminar. The idea of the poem was exciting; the man describing it to her more fascinating still. She wondered how she could ever have thought he was a Philistine. She was surprised when she looked up and saw they were the only customers left in the empty restaurant. The waiters were sweeping the floor and clearing the linen from the tables.

Arbati paid their bill and they walked under a starry sky along the banks of the Arno, taking the long way home. The evening was cool and Cordelia pulled her sweater around her shoulders. Arbati took out a silver case and lit a cigarette.

'A bad habit, I know,' he said, giving her a crooked, boyish grin. 'Like my poetry, it's an addiction, I'm afraid.'

'You could have smoked in the restaurant,' she said. 'It doesn't bother me.'

'It bothers some,' he said.

She folded her arms and felt a warmth that wasn't entirely physical spread through her. It was the kind of simple courtesy that would never have occurred to Charles Passmore in a million years.

...erhead, a new moon rode at anchor among an armada of ... heir tiny rush-lights spangling the watery heights. On the ... the roof-lines of the city melted imperceptibly into an indigo sky. The streets of Florence, apart from the clip-clop of the odd horse-drawn *calèche*, were silent and deserted. The world belonged to darkness and to them.

At the foot of Via Prospero, they paused and leaned on the coping of the stone retaining-wall, looking down at the dark ribbon of river, its surface silver with reflected stars, and Arbati said:

> *'Sull' Arno d'argento si spiega il firmaménto—d'*

'Yours?' she asked.

He smiled in the darkness. 'No, I wish it were.'

They turned up Via de Fossi, walking slowly, reluctant to reach their destination too quickly. At the entrance of Pensione Ghilberti, he opened the door and held it for her.

'Thanks for agreeing to go out with me,' he said.

'I almost didn't,' she confessed. 'I'm glad now I did though.'

He saw her framed like a vision in the soft light of the open door and said:

'We could do it again sometime, if you'd like.'

'Yes, I'd like that, Carlo,' she said. 'I really would like that.'

SIX

WHEN SIGNOR Vittorio di Banco left the bank for lunch at one-thirty, there was a spring in his step. He smiled broadly at the tellers in their bronze cages and tipped his hat at Signora Foscari from the Accounts Department (whom he was known to detest) as he passed her on the steps. It was most uncharacteristic behaviour. The younger tellers giggled behind his back, the older ones cynically supposed he was off to meet a woman. No one had ever before seen the pinched and sour chief teller in so carefree and cheerful a mood. In the twelve years that his gaunt form had patrolled the hushed sanctum of the Banco di Firenze, scarcely anyone had ever seen him smile.

His buoyant mood was not, however, caused by the prospect of meeting a woman. There would be time for that later. His expansiveness was the result of the fact that, finally, it was the first of June. In his darker hours, he had thought it would never come, that some unforeseen catastrophe—a giant asteroid, a nuclear holocaust—would consume the world before the promised day arrived; but the sun had risen that morning as on other days before it, and the passage of six uneventful hours since he left the house had dispelled the niggling residue of his fears.

He made his way along the street with glee in his pumping heart. The sights and noises of the city, normally intolerable to him, did nothing to disturb the equanimity of his spirit. He hardly noticed the diesel-spewing buses and honking taxis; he was not outraged by the gaggle of package-tour Japanese, gawping and gabbling, who momentarily obstructed his path. If he had been musical, he would have whistled a tune. Not being gifted in this way, he contented himself with a slight, rhythmic swinging of his arms.

At the café near the Bargello, his usual lunch-time stop, he did not go in for his customary bowl of minestra di fagioli. He could eat later. There was something that had to be done first. Continuing north, he turned right into Borgo degli Albizi and a short walk brought him to a glass-fronted shop displaying posters of skiers on snowy slopes and bathers on golden beaches. He had selected the Ventura Travel Agency for the simple reason that their window had first introduced him to the face of paradise. He slowed and let his eye drink in the glossy image one more time. The brightly coloured poster showed a sickle of beach lapped by translucent green water. In the foreground, stretched under an umbrella and surrounded by bikini-clad nymphs, was a middle-aged man, thin and ordinary, who bore a vague resemblance to himself. The man was grinning toothily at the camera—as well he might—and giving a thumbs-up sign. In the background, hidden among palms and hibiscus, were the balconies of an elegantly refurbished French colonial hotel. The caption read: 'Auberge de la Vieille Tour, Guadeloupe.'

In three weeks he would be on that beach. The tan and the nymphs would follow.

A silvery bell tinkled over the door as he entered and he stood in a drab office where three metal desks, separated by moveable partitions, waited to serve clients. At the moment he was the only client in sight. A rack of sheeny, dog-eared brochures leaned drunkenly near the door and a line of filing-cabinets ran along one side of the room. The remaining wall space was covered with curling posters of exotic places. It was a dingy and uninviting establishment, but they were selling dreams not décor.

Only one of the three desks was occupied and the woman who sat behind it looked up from a paperback novel when the bell over the door sounded. She was in her fifties with dyed platinum hair, heavy lipstick and enough jewellery to give her the illusion of being armour-plated. Arching, pencilled eyebrows engraved high on her forehead gave her otherwise wooden face an expression of perpetual surprise.

'May I help you?' she enquired, not standing.

Di Banco sat in the vinyl-covered chair opposite. He said:

'I'd like to buy an airline ticket. To New York.'

He would not fly to Guadeloupe directly. That would make his movements too easy to trace. His plan was to fly to New York, stay in a hotel for a day or two, then buy an Amtrak ticket to Miami. From there, Air France offered direct flights several times a week to the island.

She sat forward, flashing a synthetic smile. 'For what date?'

'The fifteenth,' he said. 'Two weeks from today.'

'You have to leave from Leonardo da Vinci,' she cautioned. 'There are no flights to North America from Peretola.'

Di Banco knew that. 'No problem,' he said.

She checked the schedule on her computer screen. 'I have a flight departing at 16:50, via London Heathrow, arriving at Kennedy Airport in New York at 8:20 on the sixteenth.'

'That will be fine,' he said.

In a locker at Santa Maria Novella station an expensive new set of luggage, filled with everything he would need, was ready and waiting. Alitalia operated an airport train twice-daily from Florence and he could check his bags directly through to New York when he bought the ticket. It had all been carefully thought out. On the morning of June the fifteenth, he would leave for work at eight-thirty, after his usual breakfast of a lightly-salted poached egg on toast, and walk without a farewell or a moment of regret into his new life as Vittorio Moroni, retired banker and man of leisure.

She took his name and passport number and punched the information in on her keyboard. While awaiting confirmation, she said to make conversation:

'A business trip or are you travelling for pleasure?'

'A little of both,' he said, offering no more.

They sat in silence, eyeing each other like adversaries. When at last the printer gave a startled whine and spewed out a length of track-paper, she turned to it with evident relief. 'There,' she said, tearing the holed margins away and restoring her professional smile, 'this is your flight confirmation. The ticket will take a day or two. Is there an address where I can send it to you?'

'I'll drop by for it,' he said, folding the sheet carefully into his wallet. He had no desire to explain to Lydia why he was receiving a single ticket to New York in the mail. He added: 'It's more convenient. I work in the neighbourhood.'

Back in the street, he felt like leaping for joy. The deed was done, the Rubicon crossed. There were other arrangements to make, but the decisive step had been taken; and somehow, for the first time, it all felt *real*. From now until the fifteenth, he would be living on pins and needles.

He felt suddenly like doing something different, like kicking over the traces of routine and doing something new, something daring, something out-of-character. He walked along by the river, looking, without knowing what he was looking for. And then he saw it: Harry's Bar. It was dark and crowded. He took a table near the window and listened with thrilling ears to the hum of Italian and American English around him. It was a taste of the future. When the waiter appeared, he ordered a club sandwich and a martini. American food. Just like the movies.

He returned to the bank at three o'clock, light in head and heart. The martini was more potent than he'd expected. At his computer screen, he had difficulty keeping the lines of green numbers in focus. And then he found he wanted nothing more than to lie down and sleep. The afternoon dragged its weary length around the four faces of the mahogany tower-clock in the central foyer. Finally, eternity having passed in the interim, the deep chime sounded closing time and the doors were locked. The effects of the martini had long worn off.

Di Banco shut down his terminal. The tellers were gone and he checked that their cash-drawers were open and empty, then crossed the echoing hall to the entrance where the main door was opened for him by the security guard. What would be the point nowadays, he thought wryly, of trying to smuggle money out in your underwear? It was the age of computers, and there were easier—and much safer—ways of doing it.

'Good night, Angelo,' he said.

'Good night, Signor di Banco.'

The late afternoon sun was warm. Di Banco took off his suit jacket and started for home carrying it over his arm. Home, he thought irritably. What was waiting for him there? He patted the bulge where his wallet lay and consoled himself with the thought that it was only for two more weeks. He could stick it out.

He walked west, into the sun, and found that he needed to get out his sunglasses. The closer he came to Via dell Scala, the more his mood seemed to sour. Enduring those last two weeks, he began to sense, would be harder than he thought. Now that he had actually bought his ticket, the idea of waiting—of treading water with the image of the Auberge de la Vieille Tour dangling so tantalizingly in front of him, tempting but just out of reach—was suddenly an intolerable prospect.

By the time he reached the entrance of the building where he had endured the indignities of plebian insignificance for the last twelve years, he was in a thoroughly testy frame of mind. He pulled open the door—and the Sinclair woman stepped out, as if she had been lying in wait, and brushed past, her nose in the air, her eyes fixing him with a cold, fish-like glare.

'Bitch,' he thought.

Grumbling under his breath about pinko Yanks sticking their goddamn noses in where they had no goddamn business, he mounted the stairs heavily to the pensione on the first floor. Lydia was in the tiny kitchen. It was not really a separate room—or even a real kitchen—but the end of a walled-off corridor running off the sitting-room that had been equipped with an electric hot-plate and antique icebox. He hung his suit-jacket in the closet and took up *La Nazione* from the table, then slumped into an easy chair. Lydia was arranging flowers in a glass bowl. He could see her fiddling and fussing with them in the alcove-kitchen, her back toward him.

'I'm sorry, darling,' she said over her shoulder. 'I thought I'd have these ready before you got home, but that nice Sinclair girl—you remember, the American we met a couple of weeks ago at Olivia Ghilberti's—dropped around and we got talking. I'll have these flowers finished in no time. How was your day, darling?'

'Boring,' he said, retreating behind the paper.

'I always think flowers add such a lovely touch to a home,' she said, stepping back to survey her handiwork.

He wondered if she talked when there was no one else around. She was incapable of silence. She had to fill the air with the sound of her own voice, just to prove to herself that she was still alive.

He lowered the paper. 'What and when are we eating?'

The other tenants would be gathered at the communal board downstairs, feasting on pasta and wine. Di Banco, who detested their rough conviviality and poor taste in everything, chose not to honour them with his presence. Instead, the di Bancos ate the evening meal in the isolated splendour of their two cramped rooms, Lydia doing what she could to cook for them on the primitive hotplate. They had a special arrangement with the landlord at a slightly reduced rent.

Lydia turned, smiling. 'Dinner's a surprise tonight,' she said. 'I was afraid you might have smelled it when you came in. I found the recipe in a magazine.'

Christ, he thought, another experiment. He said:

'I hope it's edible. I've had a hard day.'

'Do you want me to rub your temples?'

'No, just get the food ready and leave me to my paper.' His voice was harsher, perhaps, then he intended, but she took no offence. She never did.

He watched her move with quick, precise steps—setting the table, folding their napkins into little tuxedos, stirring a pot of something simmering on the hotplate, opening the wine to let it breathe. Meals were her domain, a woman's world. He never interfered as long as it was something he could choke down.

He couldn't help noticing how dowdy she was beginning to look. Wisps of dark hair escaped from the barrettes that had anchored them and her blue cotton dress, long out of fashion, fell to mid-calf in an unflattering way. She had put on weight. There was a time when he had loved her but it was so long ago he could hardly remember it. Now everything she said, everything she did, seemed to get on his nerves.

He disappeared behind the paper. What he saw, however, was not the day's news but a stretch of beach and a grinning figure giving him a thumbs-up. In the distance he could hear the rhythmic tumble of Caribbean breakers and the harsh cry of macaws from the waving palms...and there came to his nostrils, when he strained and closed his eyes, the perfume of tropical blossoms and the silky, freshly-washed scent of waist-length golden hair—

Lydia's mindless babble cut across the dream:

'—and then, if you can believe it, she tried to get the stain out with lemon juice because somebody had told her lemons contained an acid that—'

The jabber shattered the fragile amphora of his reverie into a thousand fragmented shards.

'Oh, *shut up*, Lydia,' he snapped. 'For God's sake, give the air a rest.'

He felt the breeze stir as she ran past, and then he heard her sobbing in the bedroom. Santa Madre di Dio, he thought sourly. There'd be no peace for the rest of the night if he didn't try to make things right. He folded the paper and forced himself upright.

She sat on the edge of the bed, her face buried in her hands, her narrow shoulders heaving convulsively.

'I'm sorry,' he forced himself to say, nearly choking on the words.

'I only want to make you happy,' she sobbed. 'It's all I've ever wanted. But everything I do makes you angry. What can I do to make you happy, Vittorio?'

There was no answer to the question.

'Come on,' he said. 'Let's not let dinner spoil.'

SEVEN

FRANCESCO PISTOCCHI backed the stolen Volvo into the deepest shadows of a clump of bushes beside the cart track that ran off the main road. He wanted to be ready for a quick getaway. He couldn't see the villa from here. It was beyond the brow of the hill. But then, the watchers at the villa couldn't see him either. He would make the last two hundred yards on foot, moving stealthily—like an Apache. He liked the idea (learned from American westerns) of the feathered underdog, his knife clenched in his teeth, making a surreptitious attack on the well-guarded fort and then melting without a sound, undetected, into the embalming cover of darkness. Only in the cruel light of morning did the stunned and marvelling cavalry-troopers find the scalpless corpse of their colonel in his blood-soaked bed, where he had died without a peep or whisper. A feral smile curled at the corners of Pistocchi's lips. The image appealed to his quixotic sense of the proper romance of revenge. He liked to have a little fiction woven into the weft of his reality.

It was past midnight and the night was dark, lit by a cuticle of moon. A fitful breeze moved among the branches of a copse of dreaming pines. Somewhere in the distance an owl hooted. A good omen. In the grass and trees around him the insects of night scraped out a tuneless nocturne on their tibial fiddles.

He stayed away from the road. They would be watching the road. Instead, he climbed toward the villa through a sloping vineyard, its tended rows conducting him, like a line of ineluctable corridors, toward the fatal object of his desire. Of all the Camerati it was Nicòlo Strozzi he most relished the prospect of killing. It was Strozzi, the one who held the knife, that he had waited for, had dreamed about—and saved purposely until the last. Saved until this moment. The others had been no more than insipid stages on the way to the fulfilment of the vengeful blood-lust that gnawed like an acid in the corroded crucible of his disordered soul. It was Strozzi he wanted. It was Strozzi—and Strozzi alone—that he had always and only wanted.

The vineyard ended and the ground rose steeply. Using hands and feet, he scaled the small escarpment with a feline grace, noiselessly, his movements fluid and instinctive. Reaching the top, he crouched, surveying the scene. The grounds of the estate unrolled before him, climbing a gentle incline set with cypress and sculpted yew to the black silhouette of the mansion etched almost invisibly on the sable background of the sky. There were no lights burning in the house. There was no sound except the tremulous chorus of night insects.

Pistocchi had studied the layout for more than two months. Before the time when the armed guards and Dobermans had come—and that hadn't been until after the death of Rosso, his second victim—he had explored the grounds and probed the interior of the villa until he knew the placing of every shrub, the location of every lamp and chair, the position of every infra-red detector. He could move about the villa and its grounds as easily as if he were in the familiar surroundings of his own home. On a dozen occasions he could have killed the unsuspecting Strozzi—but that would have been too easy, too kind. He wanted Strozzi to see the others die first; he wanted him to know that death was out there stalking him, circling ever closer, closing in on him slowly, surely, inevitably. He wanted him to sweat blood, to wake up screaming in the night, his heart racing, his fat body clammy with fear. And to ensure that result, he had even sent Strozzi a note—short and graphic, something to help him visualize his own end, to help him anticipate the character of his impending demise. After receiving it, Strozzi had disappeared for a time; but after a week he had returned—as Pistocchi knew he would. Strozzi could no more live away from Florence than a man could forsake the land and choose to live like a fish in the sea.

Crouched downwind, Pistocchi squatted on his haunches and waited—a shadow in a world of shadows. His dark eyes were fixed on a point where the perimeter wall made a sharp turn before continuing across the southern boundary of the estate. He did not have long to wait. He heard them well before his eyes managed to pick them out of the gloom: a telltale rustle of feet, a clink of metal, a muffled cough carried to him on the moving air.

The pair of uniformed guards, armed, each with a Doberman on a chain lead, made their way toward him under the shadow of the wall. Instinctively, Pistocchi hunched lower to the ground, seeking the anonymity of earth, his eyes never leaving them. They passed—as they passed every thirty minutes around the clock—and he watched as their disappearing backs were swallowed once more by the shadows. Their punctuality was their Achilles' heel, the flaw in their method. The regularity of their patrols made them easy to plan around. By the time they returned, Pistocchi would have finished his work and melted, undetected, into the night—a silent Apache.

He gave them five minutes. When he was sure they were beyond earshot, he broke cover and, running low, crossed the ribbon of open ground to the perimeter wall. He took a plastic bag from his pocket and, where the dogs had passed, liberally sprinkled a handful of the strong black pepper he'd bought that afternoon and ground to a fine, insidious powder in a mortar. The next time the Dobermans passed the spot, sniffing and snuffling, there would be no scent of human presence. There would be only sudden, blinding pain—and the dogs would smell nothing for at least a week. It was a nice touch, Pistocchi thought. He'd remembered the trick from an old Paul Newman movie he'd once seen. *Cool Hand Luke*, he remembered, it was called.

With a cat-like agility, he sprang onto the wall and dropped, almost inaudibly, his flexed knees absorbing the shock, into the grounds of the sleeping villa. There was no time to waste. In twenty-five minutes the patrolling guards would be back with their unsuspecting dogs and there'd be a hell of a ruckus. He took his bearings, then sprinted, keeping low, holding to the shadows, toward the louring mass of the house. Strozzi's room was on the second floor at the front, to the right of the main entrance. The servants and Strozzi's chauffeur—a surly-looking Cro-Magnon whom it seemed best to avoid—had rooms on the ground floor at the back near the kitchens. There were three or four guards scattered throughout the grounds, but they had no dogs. Pistocchi knew their stations and could, if necessary, deal with them easily. The thing he had learned about guards from watching them over the past week was that, trained to expect trouble, they w ways unprepared. They operated on the assumption th training made vigilance unnecessary. If Pistocchi inadvertently encountered one of them, that assumption would prove fatal.

He reached the house without incident. The first three windows he tried were securely locked; the fourth, a small casement whose sill was at chest height, was locked, but he was able to jemmy it without difficulty. Eighteenth-century houses had not been designed with cat-burglars in mind. He swung the window open and vaulted up, listened for a moment, then leapt without a sound into the coal-black interior. It was, as he knew from earlier explorations, an anteroom off the library—and the library, he knew, was one of the rooms to be avoided. Like the two rococo salons and the dining rooms, the pilastered front entrance and the main staircase of white marble, the library was equipped with sophisticated motion detectors connected to a central alarm system. But Pistocchi had discovered a back way, an alternate route that led, through a series of negligible rooms and passageways, to a back staircase seldom used and apparently forgotten when the electronic deterrents were installed.

A leopard on familiar terrain, he moved on silent feet through still rooms and along airless corridors. Not once did he have to pause, uncertain, and feel his way forward in the darkness; the route was one he had played out in his imagination a thousand times. His eyes burned like coals in their sockets, and a maniacal grin distorted the curve of his jaw into a twisted, demonic parody of joy. Already, in his mind's eye, he could see Strozzi's startled eyes springing open, wide in terror, as the sudden hand clamped over his mouth and, a second later, the honed blade sliced through the cords and living sinews of his neck. And then, as he had promised, he intended, before he left, to cut the testicles from Strozzi's fat carcase and cram them into the yawning rictus of his breathless mouth. It was to be the sweetest moment of his revenge.

He reached the junction where he had to cross the hallway that was the main east-west axis of the house. It was the only point where, for a few seconds, he would be exposed. An ineffectual night-light in a skirting board socket threw long shadows and a little gloaming light along the walls. He paused and listened intently. Beside him, an enormous mirror reflected his image back at him. He neither heard nor saw anything, and stepped into the hall. The figure in the mirror moved cautiously beside him, step for step—and then, remarkably, erupted in a violent explosion of falling, flying shards. Out of the corner of his eye, Pistocchi had seen the muzzle-flash further along the corridor. The man had turned the corner into the hall at the same instant Pistocchi had started to cross it. In the half-light, mistaking reflection for substance, he had fired at a phantom. He must have been awake in the house and heard Pistocchi jemmy the window, then set out to investigate.

Instinct took over. When the mirror shattered, Pistocchi had thrown himself back, scrambling for the cover of the dark passage he had just left. He had, he figured, no more than ten seconds before the man realized his mistake and raised the alarm. The shot would not have carried outside the house, and, inside, startled out of sleep, the occupants would be awaiting some second sign to tell them they hadn't been wakened by a dream. Circling around through a parallel passage, he emerged into the hall at a point ten feet behind his assailant. The man was edging cautiously forward, pistol extended, still uncertain whether he had downed his target. Silently, stealthily, Pistocchi stepped up behind him and, closing one hand over the man's mouth, drew the razor with the other in a firm arm across the yielding flesh of his throat. The man jerked convulsively and the gun fired a second time, the wayward shot embedding itself harmlessly in the plaster ceiling. For a long moment Pistocchi held the man in an iron grip, letting his life pulse out, then, when he went limp, dropped him to the floor.

The body fell heavily on its back, its sightless eyes starting in death, its open mouth parted in a voiceless scream. Pistocchi recognized the man. He had seen him many times before. It was Strozzi's chauffeur.

Sounds of commotion echoed through the house. Thumps, voices, banging doors. Someone shouted *'Franco! are you there?'* Then other voices, lights, footsteps—

Driven like a hunted beast, Pistocchi retraced his steps to the anteroom next to the library. He sprang through the window, landing in a crouch on the grass below, ready for anything. The arteries in his temples beat like drums. Above him, lights appeared in several windows. From their stations around the ground, guards began converging on the house, hesitantly at first, gathering speed as they realized something was seriou each loping figure preceded by the wavering pencil of a flashlight beam.

Picking his moment, keeping to the shadows, zigzagging like a broken-field runner, Pistocchi split the seams between them and, once free, made a headlong dash for the stone wall encircling the estate. From his left, outside the wall, came the frenzied yapping of the Dobermans, alerted to the activity within. Behind him, flood lamps suddenly lit the villa as if it were a public building on a holiday—and a siren began to wail. But it was too late. Pistocchi had reached the top of the wall, where he stood for a moment looking back, silhouetted against the starry sky like a wolf on a promontory, and then jumped into the darkness and disappeared.

He scrambled down the embankment and burst into the vineyard, slapping wildly at tendrils stretching out to resist his passage. His carbuncular eyes burned into the night with the rage of a thwarted vengeance: Strozzi still lived. He wanted to throw back his head and howl out his fury like an animal.

At the far edge of the vineyard he slowed his pace. He was beyond capture. Behind him suddenly, like the voice of the infernal damned, a blood-curdling ululation split the air, drowning even the siren's wail. The dogs had found the pepper.

EIGHT

'NEXT, PLEASE!'

The ruddy-faced butcher slapped the package neatly tied in brown paper down on the counter and turned away to serve another customer. There was a line waiting behind Cordelia. Stepping back, she counted her change and dropped the kilo of expensive fillet into her bag. She hated shopping for food. It was time-consuming and always a hassle. She would never understand, not in a million years, why some people positively enjoyed it—but then some people, she thought, are like Indian fakirs. They find beds of roses in every spiky couch that life forces them to lie down on. The image of Lydia di Banco flashed through her mind before she could head it off.

Now—was there anything else? She checked the list in her purse: fillet, broccoli, carrots, bananas, kiwi fruit. There was plenty of cheese in the icebox at home—a block of cheddar and, she thought, still some camembert—and there was plenty of wine. Well then, that was everything—thank goodness!

She started for the exit.

As always, Mercato San Lorenzo teemed with colour and life. The glass-domed market building, where exotic importers and local farmers competed for the consumer's lire, opened early and sold every comestible known to man. It was only eight-thirty in the morning but already the place was filled to overflowing. Over crates of oranges and under bunches of bananas, arms gestured and voices haggled. Cordelia felt suddenly overwhelmed by it all. The world seemed to close in on her and she felt trapped in a realm where nothing was familiar, where she could hardly breathe, where everything was inexplicably threatening. Plastic trays holding strips of tripe soaking in brine struck her eye like knots of twisting, squirming eels and, from a refrigerated case, a row of decapitated sheep's heads leered menacingly out at her. She turned away in sudden panic. The market had become a cornucopia of carrion and spilled viscera: a house of death. Even the tomatoes were corpses. At a fishmonger's stall, rows of squid and red snapper eyed her leeringly from their beds of crushed ice. The gastronomic world pressed in around her like the jaws of a vice.

The exit loomed ahead and she dove through it, drawing a deep, relieved breath. In the piazza outside, the air was fresh and the sun warm. Gradually, her breathing slowed to normal. It was silly of course, but she felt as if she'd had a brush with the Grim Reaper. A premonition almost, a presage of unspecified disaster.

She turned to happier thoughts. The fillet was for the beef Wellington she'd promised Signor Farinelli. She had planned the dinner for more than a week. It was, in a way, a special thank-you to him for having been there when she'd needed someone to talk to after finding Marchesi's body. She wanted to show her gratitude—and she was also curious to find out more about Farinelli. He was a fascinating but at the same time, somehow, an elusive man: kind, understanding, cultured, a brilliant mind; yet also reserved and even secretive. She remembered how, that afternoon in his apartment, he had talked openly about things like God and faith but avoided saying anything personal about himself. She'd try, this time, to get him to open up more. She wanted to know him better. She hoped, in fact, they might become friends as well as neighbours. A man who had named his cat Fra Angelico was a man worth knowing more about.

She cut at a diagonal across Piazza San Lorenzo, where the canvas-covered stalls of the outdoor clothing-market, that sold everything from practical underwear to exquisite mohair sweaters, spread its gaudy pavilions under the austere brick façade of a cathedral that looked much the same as it had in Michelangelo's day. Florence was a city of such contrasts: the sublime and the mundane side by side, saints and merchants, art and finance, the sacred and the profane. Yet there was never a hint of conflict, of strain, of inappropriateness in the converging opposites. Florence was a city that dissolved contradictions, that reconciled opposites, that somehow, miraculously, made living sense of the paradox of time and eternity in a city where God and men were equally at home.

She hoped Signor Farinelli liked beef Wellington. She'd put it on the menu because it was an elegant yet simple dish—cooking simply wasn't her long suit—and because it was the one thing that her ex-husband Charles, so fussily critical about everything, had repeatedly praised. It was something she felt confident about offering to a special guest. It was odd though, wasn't it, she reflected, that she'd come to Florence to get away from men—Charles and her father—and had ended up having men as her closest friends? But Signor Farinelli and Carlo Arbati were as different as day and night from the men who'd been part of her life back home. It wasn't simply that they were more thoughtful and cultivated; it was that they were willing to take her on her own terms, to respect *her* opinions and ideas, were willing, in fact, to treat her as a human being, an equal, instead of dismissing her as just another woman. She'd have to bring the two of them together sometime, she thought suddenly—maybe for a meal. They'd like each other, she was sure of that. They were alike in so many ways.

At the corner of Via Randinelli, a flower-seller caught her eye. Florence: the idea of flowers was in her very name—*Florentia*, the place of flowers. She stopped and bought a bouquet of long-stemmed carnations in a green paper sleeve and carried them home before her like a trophy. They would brighten up the table, would give the evening life.

THE TELEPHONE SHATTERED the silence and his concentration.

'Damn!' Arbati muttered.

The new poem—the elusive *Androgyne*—had at last started to come. Word-draped images had begun floating up like silver bubbles—transparent, insubstantial, ephemeral—from the subconscious depths, and he had been scrambling to capture them, to fix them in inky strokes before they fell away and were lost again in the fathomless abyss—until the raucous shrill of the telephone had catapulted him, suddenly and unceremoniously, back into the arms of reality.

He put down his pen and silenced the insistent instrument. The voice at the other end was Giorgio Bruni's.

'Sorry to bother you at home, boss,' he said, 'and on the weekend, too. I'm out at Strozzi's villa. Somebody broke into the place last night.'

'Was Strozzi hurt?'

'No, he's fine. Shook up and sweating a little harder than usual, but he's okay. I can't say the same for his man Franco, though. Slashed from ear to ear, he was, like a gutted mullet. Doc Mangiello just left with the body. He'll have a full autopsy ready sometime this afternoon.'

'Pistocchi?' Arbati asked.

'No doubt about it. Same m.o. as the other killings, severed carotid artery. The weapon was probably a straight razor. Our boy Franco got off a couple of shots at the intruder but there's nothing to suggest he even winged him. One round smashed up an antique mirror, the other went into the ceiling. Not exactly what you'd call crack marksmanship.' Bruni's voice paused, then went on: 'This Pistocchi is good, Carlo. Very, very good. Somehow, in the dark, he managed to get around behind Franco on his home turf. He must have known the layout of the villa like the back of his hand. My guess is that Franco fired and missed, hitting the mirror, then Pistocchi circled around and caught him from behind. Franco's second shot was probably a reflex, an involuntary jerk when his throat was cut. It was slick, Carlo, very slick.'

'What about the security people? What were the rest of the troops doing while all this was going on?'

'Until now, Strozzi didn't let them inside the house. He's a man who likes his privacy. He made the rent-a-cops stay outside. They apparently didn't realize anything was wrong until the lights started going on like Christmas all over the house and, by then, it was too late. Pistocchi slipped through them like a dose of salts. Like I said, Carlo, he's bloody good.'

'Keep me posted then,' Arbati said.

'There *is* one more thing,' Bruni said. 'It's the reason I called actually. Strozzi wants police protection. He's a taxpayer, he says. He's entitled.' He paused, then added, distancing himself, 'I told him I'd ask.'

'What exactly does he expect from us—as a taxpayer?'

'He wants you to post men at the bank and he wants a police driver. He says his rent-a-cops can't be everywhere.'

Arbati's face darkened. The problem with people like Strozzi was that they thought the police existed for the sole purpose of safeguarding their personal assets and interests. Wealth, they believed, conferred on them rights and privileges denied to ordinary citizens and lesser taxpayers. After a long moment, Arbati said:

'I'll put two men at the bank, starting first thing Monday morning. Tell Strozzi he can find his own chauffeur. We're not a bloody delivery service.'

'Can I use those words?'

'If you want. Just make sure he gets the message.'

Arbati rang off.

There was no point in trying to go back to the poem: the mood was broken.

He stood at the window for a time, looking out, thinking.

The Slasher murders were, in many ways, the most disturbing case he'd ever handled. They revealed too much about human callousness and greed, and it was difficult to know, when push came to shove, who the real victims were—or was. Pistocchi's actions, of course, could hardly be condoned; but it was easy (almost too easy) to sympathize with the desire for revenge that drove him. The men who had castrated and then abandoned him had done so for gain and with an eye only to their own profit. He had been an object to them—a thing—never a human being. They had mutilated and cheated him out of manhood, had inspired his trust and then betrayed it—all without a qualm or a quiver of conscience. Their interest in him, as Strozzi had made plain that day in Arbati's office, was as a marketable commodity. And now, years later, they were reaping the wages of their sin. But why had Pistocchi waited so long to strike back—almost thirty-five years? Had the poison of his hatred, held in check but always lurking under the surface, festered until it had become a malignancy raging out of control? Had he perhaps tried to see the men who had marred him, tried first to talk with them, and been spurned—perhaps laughed at? What was it that had finally tipped the scales of his sanity—for he *was* insane, Arbati was certain—and launched him on the murderous spree that had taken five lives in the space of less than three months? His crimes were not excusable but they were understandable. He would be caught and held to account for them. But the guilt for his deeds would have to be shared, before the bar of eternal justice, by the five Camerati who three decades earlier had mutilated him into the avenging angel of their own destruction. They had made a monster, a nemesis, and it had returned to destroy them. And if, somehow, Strozzi managed to survive Pistocchi's fury—Arbati vowed—he would still pay with prison for the part he had played. Justice demanded that much at least.

His stomach growled. With a start, Arbati realized he still hadn't eaten. He'd risen at six and started working on *Androgyne* and had lost track of the time. It had been a case of *carpe musam*, seizing the Muse while she was willing to be seized. For weeks she had been coy and elusive but this morning, for some reason, had wakened singing like a thrush. He had learned over the years not to question her sudden moods: he took gratefully what she offered when she chose to give it. Poetry was above all else a matter of timing—and the times were never of *his* choosing.

He made himself a mushroom omelette, seasoned lightly with tarragon and garlic, and ate it at the desk in his study. Before him, on a scribbled sheet, lay the results of his morning's labour. Not much perhaps—a novelist wouldn't have been impressed by the meagre word-count—but it was a beginning. Arbati's births, mysterious and painful in their contractions, were never easy— but then, too, they were seldom prosaic either. He read the lines over and liked what he saw. It had been a good morning.

His sudden success with *Androgyne* had something—though he didn't know exactly what—to do with Cordelia Sinclair. She was always in his thoughts. Even when he wasn't actually thinking about her, she was still there, hovering in the side-aisles and transepts of his mind. He was attracted to her in many ways. Physically, of course. She was a strikingly beautiful woman. Her beauty, indeed, struck a familiar chord in him—as if, somehow, he had known her always, as if she were in some mysterious way a permanent attribute of his conception of the ideal. But the attraction was not simply physical. He admired her attitude to life and to herself. She was determined to make something of herself. She had things to prove—but only to herself. Unlike other liberated women he'd met, hers was not an ego always looking anxiously over its own shoulder—one of those brittle spirits spurred by envy to prove themselves against the odds in a man's world. She kept the idea of her career in perspective: as an aspect of life and not a substitute for it. She struck him, indeed, as one of those rare people who took the parable of the talents seriously. She considered it a sacred trust to develop the potential of those abilities she had been given at birth and sent into the world to trade with. There was nothing selfish in her wish to succeed. She was motivated by a desire to repay the gifts she had received— tenfold, a hundredfold if possible—to the master of the vineyard when he returned for an accounting. But she probably, he thought with a smile, wouldn't approve of hearing it put in those religious terms. She was too much of an Aristotelian—or thought she was—to see it in quite that way.

From somewhere in the secret chambers of his soul, he felt the first faint stirrings of a renewed inspiration. His Muse was about to reopen the gates of her song. He unscrewed the top of his Parker fountain pen, took out a fresh sheet of paper, and waited for the music to begin—

THE BEEF WELLINGTON was a great success. Cordelia cleared the table and poured their coffee.

'A wonderful meal,' Farinelli said, leaning back, as contented as Fra Angelico after a saucer of milk. 'You needn't have gone to so much trouble—but I'm glad you did. I haven't eaten that well in months.'

'You were saying,' Cordelia said, 'that your first job was at Teatro Comunale—'

'Ah, yes. Well, it was hardly a glamorous position,' Farinelli said, gazing out through the French windows. The view was better, he noticed, than the one from his flat on the floor below. 'I was only a janitor, as I think I told you once. My duties were vacuuming the auditorium after performances and cleaning the toilets. Hardly noble pursuits.'

'We all start somewhere,' Cordelia offered.

Farinelli laughed. 'But seldom so far down the ladder,' he said. 'Well, I didn't have much choice about where I started, I suppose. I lost my parents when I was quite young and spent my adolescence on the streets. I had very little in the way of formal education. Basically, I had to be satisfied with whatever came along.'

'My own start was a lot easier,' Cordelia said, a little guiltily.

Farinelli gave her an old-fashioned look. 'Don't apologize for something you had no part in choosing,' he said. 'Besides, I wasn't unhappy. I had plenty of time to read—to make up for the schooling I'd missed—and I got to see all the performances for free.' He added, 'From the wings, of course, not from the paying seats.'

'Is that when you started writing?'

Farinelli shook his head. 'No, that came later. There was an opening for an apprentice reporter at *La Nazione* and I applied. I'd read more than anyone else who was interviewed and I g͞ the job, but it wasn't what I expected. I was young a͟ visions of myself writing headline stories under immense pressure and being lionized at gala receptions for my fearless honesty and ability to get at the truth hidden under the froth and lies. But my editor had other plans. He sent me out to cover fires and purse-snatchings, occasionally a minor human interest story. It wasn't much fun, but it did teach me one thing. It taught me how to write.'

'So you threw over the newspaper job, turned to freelancing, and never looked back?'

Farinelli laughed—a sweet, musical sound like a chiming of bells. 'Good heavens, no! You really are a romantic at heart, aren't you? It wasn't that easy and it certainly wasn't that fast. Yes, I quit my job at the paper after about a year, but it wasn't a smart move. I ended up back on the streets without a lira, scrambling to find odd jobs just to keep body and soul together. I wouldn't go through that period of my life again for all the tea in China. Anyway, I spent a lot of time reading, mostly about music, and one day it hit me that what I ought to be doing was trying to put that knowledge to some kind of use. I don't know why I hadn't thought of it before. Well, the long and short of it is, there was a production of *La Bohème* in rehearsal at Teatro della Pergola. I started attending the rehearsals, just sitting quietly in the back row where nobody noticed me. At the end of a week, I was as much inside the maestro's head as the musicians in the pit were. I knew the effects he wanted, how he saw the pieces fitting together, and what he was trying for in the whole performance. I could have directed the thing myself, I think. Well, since I couldn't actually be there on opening night—much too pricey for my budget—I went home instead and wrote a long review of what I knew would be happening. It was pretty florid, as I recall, but it also contained a lot of insight. Then, bright and early the next morning I hand-delivered a copy to every newspaper and arts journal in the city. One of the smaller magazines bought it—and from there, as you said, I never looked back.'

'It ~~was a~~ clever idea, using the rehearsals like that.'

~~He~~ grinned. 'Well, it was a *sensible* idea, which is prob-~~ably more than most~~ of the established critics had thought of it. They ~~go to the perf~~ormances already knowing what they want and ~~knowing wha~~t they already know. God preserve them from ~~ever having to exp~~erience anything fresh! Their reviews never do any more than reaffirm the *status quo*. It's odd, isn't it, that theatre critics should be such closet conservatives? Anyway, my review was centred on what the maestro's vision of the opera was. It was a new way of reviewing—measuring a performance by what it was trying to do instead of judging it by preconceived standards—and it attracted attention in the right quarters. From that day, in fact, I've always written my reviews with what I've learned from the rehearsals in mind. Over the years it's proven itself a very workable strategy.'

Cordelia nodded. 'And that's why you were at the rehearsal of *Orfeo* in Teatro Comunale the day I had my interview with Maestro Marchesi. You were watching to see how he wanted the musicians to interpret the work.'

'Exactly. I was watching every move he made.'

'I assume you were there on opening night as well.'

Farinelli grinned. 'Oh yes. I can afford the price of admission now.'

Cordelia noticed his cup was empty. 'More coffee?' she asked. 'I should have been paying more attention. You'll think I'm a terrible hostess.'

'I doubt that, Signorina Sinclair, after the way you've spoiled me tonight. Perhaps just half a cup, yes, thanks.'

'I've often wondered,' she said, pouring, 'how it is that people find the careers they end up choosing. I was just thinking about a police inspector I've been out with a couple of times. He's the one in charge of investigating Marchesi's murder. Carlo Arbati. Well, it turns out he's a poet as well as a policeman.'

Farinelli nodded. 'I know his work. It's very good indeed. I didn't know he was a policeman though.'

'It's odd, isn't it? I mean, the two things don't seem to have anything in common. In fact, in a way, they're almost antagonistic: the one devoted to brute facts, most of them about ugly matters like murder, the other devoted to exploring our finer feelings.'

'Oh, I don't know,' Farinelli said with a grin. 'They seem similar enough to me. For one thing, they both involve a good deal of detective work—at least deciphering a modern poem strikes me as being a lot like solving the Saturday crossword. I exclude your friend Arbati's work, of course. As I said, he's very good—which is to say, he's hardly modern at all, mercifully.' He sipped at his coffee, then said, 'What's he like as a human being?'

Cordelia checked herself before blurting out that he was a quite wonderful man. 'Oh,' she said, 'I'd describe him as thoughtful, caring, intelligent. Old-fashioned, too, in a good sense—a gentleman.'

'I told you you were a romantic.'

'What's romantic about being good?' Cordelia said, perhaps a little defensively.

'Nothing, I'm sure,' Farinelli said with a knowing smile, then changed the subject: 'What's he working on at the moment? Something new, I imagine?'

Cordelia nodded. 'A poem called *Androgyne*. It's about the reconciliation of male and female characteristics in human personality. His argument is that we all have both—masculine and feminine traits, that is—and that they're balanced, though in different proportions, in each individual. Personality is the subtle tension of the two held in a creative equilibrium and working together in unison.'

A shadow seemed to pass over Farinelli's face. It happened so quickly that, if she'd blinked, she would have missed it. He was silent for a moment, then said:

'I wonder, though, if it's really that simple. It strikes me that something as complex as human personality, with all its contradictions and inconclusiveness, won't really bear reduction to a simple formula. What is it the English Jesuit, Hopkins, says?

O the mind, mind has mountains; cliffs of fall
Frightful, sheer, no-man-fathomed. Hold them cheap
May who ne'er hung there.

Of course, Hopkins was describing the state of religious despair—but I wonder, still, if his sense of the essential ambiguity and dark mysteriousness of personality isn't closer to the reality of things than the optimism of your friend Arbati's dualistic paradox?'

Cordelia cradled her chin on her hands and watched him with fasci... He had a way of expanding and deepening every idea ... is path. She'd seen it before at Signora Ghilberti's ... he time she'd talked to him in his apartment after ...

... to say,' Farinelli went on, 'is that in the final ... don't seem to know very much about this thing we call the self. If I ask myself who and what I am, I find I can't answer the question. I can describe my external appearance and I can describe the things (or at least some of them) that I think and feel, but I can't see or describe or even begin to understand the enigmatic "I" that makes my body move and makes me think and feel the things I do. Now, because the central "I" that makes me me is unknown to me, except insofar as it reveals itself in what it makes me think and do, I'm a complete mystery to myself. And yet I never doubt for a moment that this unknown inner self actually exists—because, you see, if it didn't exist, then the thing I call *me* would be nothing more than the sum of its cells plus the sum of its mental acts, all of them either predetermined or randomly capricious. I simply can't envision the self behind the self I know in such mechanistic terms. I'm a creature of will, of desires, of fears and terrors. I love, I hate, I laugh, I cry—and I do all of them because, in some mysterious way, I *choose* to do them—' He stopped suddenly, his face reddened. 'Oh, dear,' he said, 'I've done it again, haven't I? I've turned a pleasant after-dinner chat into a seminar. I'm sorry. One thing you really do have to learn about me, my dear girl, is never to let me get the bit between my teeth.'

'On the contrary,' Cordelia said, 'I intend to encourage it at every opportunity. In fact, what I'd like to do sometime is get you and Carlo together. I know you'd like him—and the fireworks would be terrific to watch.'

'At the time and place of your choosing,' Farinelli said, rising to go. 'But I've trespassed on your hospitality long enough for one night. Again, my thanks for a wonderful dinner—and my apologies for the lecture.'

She walked him to the door.

'One question,' she said. 'If we can't know even ourselves, what *can* we know?'

Farinelli shrugged. 'Nothing,' he said. 'We only know *about* things. That's the sad wisdom of the human condition—all we can, in fact, know.'

'It isn't much, is it?'

'Perhaps not,' he said. 'And yet it strikes me as being, sometimes, more than enough.'

NINE

VITTORIO DI BANCO knew the instant he arrived at the bank bright and early on Monday morning that something was seriously amiss. The tellers were whispering among themselves and casting furtive glances at a man in a dark suit hovering near the marble island where customers filled out deposit and withdrawal slips. He'd been waiting at the door when the bank opened and he was trying now, not very successfully, to make himself look occupied with a loan-application form.

'Who is he?' one asked *sotto voce*.

'I don't know,' another teller replied.

'I overheard Signora Fogari say there's another one upstairs outside the director's office.'

'Really? Something big's going on. I wonder what?'

But di Banco *knew*—knew who the men were and what was going on. It was the police. He knew the look—plain suit, short hair, careful eyes—and he knew they had come for him. A cold shiver ran down his spine. They wanted to catch him in the act, red-handed. But how on earth, he wondered, had they found out—? He'd left no careless clues, no paper trail to follow. There were only the electronic transactions, and it would take trained auditors, even with their fine-toothed combs, at least three or four days of tough slog to uncover any of those.

Di Banco's heart raced; his mind was numb. With a supreme effort of will, he made himself be calm; he forced himself to be rational, to consider the problem logically. Maybe they hadn't come for him—maybe they were after somebody else—maybe they *didn't* know about the missing money, about Guadeloupe, about the secret account at the Royal Bank of Canada in Grand Cayman. He tried to believe it, but it was no good: they knew—yes, he could feel it—*they knew*.

He stumbled to his desk, his mind reeling. But who had betrayed him? And then he knew: *Lydia!* She must have found the brochures behind the loose board at the back of the closet and then phoned the police. Damn it all! Or else she'd gone through his wallet and discovered the airline ticket to New York. *How could she do this to him?* After twenty years of marriage, how could she turn in her own husband? He wanted to howl at the injustice of her infidelity. She hadn't even given him a chance to explain—

'Are you feeling all right, Signor di Banco?'

The assistant chief teller, stout and iron-corseted, stood above him like a spectre from Wagner's *Die Walküre*, staring down at him through dark-rimmed spectacles.

'I'm fine.'

'You look sick,' she insisted. 'Why don't you take some aspirin and lie down for a bit?'

'I said I'm fine,' di Banco snarled.

'Well,' she sniffed, stalking off, 'excuse me for caring!'

He collected himself and switched on his computer. The familiar green screen calmed him, acting like a narcotic. He thought: I mustn't panic. I must act normally. At lunch-time I'll go back to the agency and book an earlier flight, one that's leaving tonight. Everything I need is packed and waiting in the locker at the station (he blessed his foresight here) and there's no reason to come back to the bank after lunch. I can just disappear now, today—a few days early.

He talked himself into composure, the rational lobe of his brain counselling the emotional half like a therapist talking a jumper off a bridge. By ten-thirty he was an image of self-control and sangfroid. Calm, cool, collected—icily ataraxic. In short, his usual self.

And then, at noon, suddenly and quite unexpectedly, the auditors arrived to study the bank's books. They were three weeks ahead of schedule—or at least, the schedule that di Banco had expected them to follow. Panic gripped his bowels.

The auditors unpacked their leather attaché-cases in the conference room and laid out spread-sheets on the long mahogany table. Portable computers connected to the mainframe were rolled in on trollies for them. Di Banco knew that he was doomed. It was all over for him. They must know *everything*.

His skin went cold and clammy and his eyes glazed o heart pounded under his ribs like a muffled drum at a fu felt nauseous.

At twelve-thirty—half an hour before his usual time—he left for lunch. The strain was unbearable; he could stand it no longer. Every instant he expected one of the auditors, gaunt and grim-faced, to emerge from the conference room and whisper something into the ear of the hovering policeman—then there would be sirens, handcuffs, humiliation as they frog-marched him out through the marble foyer to the waiting paddy-wagon. And so, before it could happen, di Banco carefully shut down his computer, tidied the papers on his desk and, without a word to anyone, did something he had never done in the whole of the twelve years he had worked at the bank: he left early. The look on his lined, haggard face was that of a man leaving the doctor's office after having learned he had terminal cancer.

Although it had never happened before, no one at the bank was surprised to see him go early. The chief teller looked truly awful. He should, they told one another, take the afternoon off and go home to bed.

Once in the street, di Banco headed north, walking quickly, giving no thought to food, his mind fixed only on his destination—on salvation. It took him fifteen minutes to reach it. He didn't pause to dream over the poster of the Auberge de la Vieille Tour in the window. He didn't even notice it. He shoved through the door of the Ventura Travel Agency and advanced, like a marathon runner approaching the tape, on the desk occupied by the same woman—platinum-dyed and top heavy with jewellery and makeup—who had originally sold him his ticket. She was filing her purple nails with a lethal-looking object the size of a dirk. Di Banco heaved a sigh of relief. He was sure she'd remember him.

'I need to change my ticket,' he announced.

She raised a pencilled eyebrow, and the file, still poised, ceased filing.

He passed across the precious ticket. 'I need to leave today,' he said. 'This afternoon. It's urgent.'

'Have a seat,' she said, laying the weapon grudgingly aside. 'I'll see if there's anything I can do.' Then, with a hint of disapproval, 'You've left it rather late, you know.'

'I'll stand,' he said shortly—adding, 'Not my fault. Circumstances beyond my control. Just do what you can.'

She glanced at him coldly, then at his ticket, then studied the computer screen in front of her. After due and careful consideration of the electronic data, she said, 'Sorry—it can't be done. Nothing available today. Everything's full—tight as a nun's knickers. Nothing at all today.' Was the repetition, he wondered, intended to rub the salt of frustration into his wound? She added with a bloodless smile: 'If you want, I can get you on a flight just after noon tomorrow, at 12:20. It's the first available flight.'

'Too late,' di Banco mumbled. 'Must be today.'

She shrugged. 'You can try stand-by.'

He shot her a poisoned look, snatched back his ticket, and groped for the door. Stand-by was risky. He was a banker. He could only be happy with a sure thing in his hand.

Outside, he stumbled along the street, not knowing where he was going, his mind in a fog. He had the air of a swimmer being pulled down by an undertow. His breathing was laboured. His heart fluttered in his chest. His eyes wouldn't focus. There was no escape—he was cut off...trapped...doomed.

Without knowing how, without knowing why, he found himself inside a shop, staring into a case displaying a large selection of knives behind locked panes.

A clerk approached.

'I'll have that one,' di Banco said, pointing.

The clerk removed a sturdy butcher's knife, sharp-pointed, triangular, with an eight-inch blade. He slipped it into a cardboard sleeve.

'Will there by anything else today, sir?'

'Nothing else.'

In the street, di Banco ducked into an alley, discarded the bag bearing the shop's logo, and stuffed the weapon in its cardboard sheath into his belt under his suit-jacket. He didn't know why he had bought a knife; he knew only that he needed it. The rational half of his brain had stopped functioning. He was in the grip of irrational passion.

AT THE SAME TIME di Banco left the knife-shop, Cordelia Sinclair and Carlo Arbati were just starting down the sloping path lined with neo-classical statuary that led, under a canopy of oak and huge box trees, to Piazzale dell'Isolotto. They had eaten lunch together at a quaint trattoria overlooking the river, then crossed Ponte Vecchio to saunter for an hour in the sanctuary of the Boboli gardens. It was becoming a noon-time ritual.

'It came in a rush,' Arbati said, speaking of *Androgyne*. 'It often happens like that. The first draft spills out in a white-hot burst, then there's a long period of grinding and polishing to get the poem into final shape.'

'So, when do I get to see it?' Cordelia asked.

'When it's finished.'

'Not till then?'

'No.'

'Not even a sneak preview?' she pressed. 'Just a peek—'

Arbati laughed. 'Most people have to wait until it's published. You only have to wait until it's written. You're already privileged.'

'I know that,' she said, feigning a pout, 'but I'm also curious. In a way, I feel like I have something of an investment in the thing, you know, since we talked so much about it over dinner the other night. You can't blame me for being interested when you made me that way. And besides, insatiable curiosity runs in the Sinclair genes. It's a hereditary cross—quite a heavy one, in fact—that we've always had to bear; and I should warn you that we've never managed to do it with much grace.'

Arbati shook his head. 'A family cross, eh? This genetic curiosity of yours, is it ever fatal?'

'Sometimes—yes. As a matter of fact, I had an uncle who—'

'Never mind your uncle,' he winced. 'Anyway, these things invariably skip a generation. You're no doubt quite safe.'

'You're willing to take that chance?'

'Yes.'

'Damn!'

They had the gardens almost to themselves. Overhead, stratospheric winds tugged rags of cloud over the face of the sun and little shadows raced up the hill to greet them. At the bottom of the hill lay an enormous fountain with a grove of orange and lemon trees planted on an island in the centre. When they reached the fountain's edge, Arbati stopped.

'I *do*, as it happens, have a little present for you,' he said. 'Maybe it'll take that curious mind of yours off *Androgyne*.'

He took a slender volume from his pocket, its brown cover embossed with a gilt oak leaf, and handed it to her.

The cover read: Carlo Arbati, *Fòglia di luce*.

Tears of surprise came to her eyes and words deserted her.

'It's my first book,' Arbati said, filling the void. 'I've inscribed it for you inside.'

She opened the cover and, on the flyleaf, in Arbati's calligraphic hand, she read: *To Cordelia Sinclair—an inspiration. Carlo Arbati. 6/7/'93.*

'I don't know what to say,' she stammered. 'It's wonderful.'

'I'd be more convinced if you tell me that *after* you've read it,' he said with a grin.

She stared at the inscription with glistening eyes. '*An inspiration—?* I don't understand.'

His grin broadened. 'That's my second surprise,' he said, taking her hand. 'There's something I want to show you.'

'What?'

'Be patient. You'll see.'

They left the Boboli gardens and recrossed the Arno.

'Give me a hint,' she begged. 'Just a tiny one.'

He shook his head. 'Not a chance.'

At the north end of Ponte Vecchio they turned right under a covered walk that brought them to the entrance of the Uffizi Gallery. Cordelia was dying of curiosity. He bought two passes to the gallery and led her down the long, vaulted hall to the Botticelli exhibition at the far end. They stopped in front of the *Venus and Mars.*

'There,' he said. 'Does that remind you of anything?'

Tilting her head to one side, Cordelia considered the image of the two gods reclining on the grass, their bodies facing different directions—close and intimate, but not touching. Mars, the figure behind, was languid and disarmed, his head drooped back in sleep. In front of him was Venus, her auburn hair falling in ringlets to frame an oval face, her watchful eyes open, her rich sensuality refined and deepened by the aura of spiritual aspiration she radiated. They were separate individuals, yet they gave the impression of being one figure, a single being, the mysterious embodiment of an indivisible ideal from which neither part could be withdrawn without imbalance or distortion.

'*Androgyne?*' Cordelia asked.

Arbati nodded. 'They complete each other. Strength and grace in equilibrium. But you'll notice that Venus wakes while Mars sleeps. In the ideal personality, masculinity is held in check by femininity. It can't be the other way round: if Mars were the one awake while Venus slept, the painting would be saying something entirely different. Then, in fact, it would be an image of benevolent tyranny. The point is that masculinity is a centripetal force—egocentric and exclusive; femininity, on the other hand, is all-embracing and centrifugal. The feminine attributes of human personality—grace, beauty, love—aren't self-contained, self-limiting; they always aspire outward and upward, seeking points of contact with physical, but especially with spiritual realities, that exist outside themselves. That's what Botticelli is saying: masculine and feminine traits are both necessary attributes of personality, but Venus—the feminine principle, the one who's awake— is the only one that can bridge the gap between the self and other selves, between the real and the ideal, between heaven and earth.'

'And that's what your poem is about?'

'Pretty much, yes.'

They stood silent for a moment contemplating the old canvas. Then Cordelia said:

'It's very powerful. I can certainly understand why it inspired you.'

'Yes, but it needed a catalyst,' Arbati said.

'A catalyst—?'

'Take a close look at Venus.'

Cordelia focused hard on the goddess clothed in white samite, on her auburn hair and composed, ethereal features. Finally, she said:

'She's very beautiful, but I don't see—'

Arbati turned and met her eyes.

'Isn't it a little bit like looking in the mirror?'

WHEN DI BANCO passed through the revolving doors and stepped into the marble-tiled foyer of the Banco di Firenze, it was just turning three-thirty, the big clock over the main entrance bonging the half-hour. For the first time in twelve years Vittorio di Banco was late—indeed very late—returning from lunch. Yet, he had not eaten. He couldn't face the prospect of food. For two hours he had wandered the streets without ever once thinking of his stomach.

Outwardly, he seemed calm, rational—normal. He walked to his desk, nodding to the tellers as he passed, and began sorting through a pile of computer printouts. The only indication that something was amiss was his granite face. The narrow features, normally pinched and sour, were without expression: the eyes were dull and vacant, the face blank—a mask.

For close to half an hour he worked through the pages in front of him like an automaton, making occasional notes. Then, as if prompted by some inner signal, he rose and, speaking to no one, crossed under the domed vault to the elevators. He pressed the Up button—the doors before him parted—he stepped inside and pushed the button for the fifth floor. The brass-and-oak doors closed and the elevator began its oiled ascent.

At the top the doors opened and he stepped into a carpeted room, well-lit, opulently furnished, decorated with potted ferns. From a chair opposite the elevator a man looked up, studied di Banco's face, then returned to his magazine. Another policeman: the same suit, the same hair, the same eyes. The woman at the teak desk swivelled from her computer as the chief teller approached. She was petite and dark and attractive, in her mid-twenties.

'Ah, Signor di Banco, we don't often see you up here.'

'I must see the director at once,' he said hoarsely, without further preamble.

'Do you have an appointment?'

'No. It's urgent.'

She sensed that something was wrong. She said:

'May I ask what it's about?'

'It's confidential—and personal.'

She nodded sympathetically. 'I'll see what I can do.'

She disappeared through a door bearing a plaque marked *Chairman*. Di Banco looked around the office. It was richly appointed in leather, brass, and polished hardwood. The anteroom of power and privilege. He had never, in twelve years, been inside the director's office. He looked across at the policeman but the man did not raise his eyes from the magazine. It never occurred to di Banco to ask why he seemed to show no interest in him.

The secretary returned. She said:

'You can go in. He has an appointment at four-thirty. You have about twenty minutes.'

Her voice was soft with concern. Perhaps the chief teller was ill, or his wife—possibly diagnosed as dying of cancer. The chairman's secretary had a lively imagination.

Di Banco entered the sanctum. It was a large room containing expensive furniture, expensive artwork. One wall was floor-to-ceiling glass overlooking the city. The director sat in a high-backed armchair behind a huge cherry wood desk. He wore a white suit, a carnation in the lapel, and was mopping at his neck with a handkerchief. A look of benign indifference was spread over the features of his pig-like face.

Di Banco closed the door and crossed the oriental carpet. Before Strozzi could utter a word, di Banco had leaned forward on the desk, resting his weight on both palms, and was growling in a low voice curiously devoid of emotion:

'You want to destroy me, you bastard. Well, it won't work.'

Strozzi flinched as if he'd been backhanded. 'What the—!'

'Shut up and listen,' di Banco ordered in a voice of unnatural calm. 'For years I've watched you cheat and steal your way up to this office. I know all about you. I know the kind of scum you are. Yes, I've been watching you, Signor Director—and, what's more, I've got the records to prove it.'

'I don't know what you're talking about,' Strozzi blustered.

'Don't play games with me,' di Banco hissed. 'I've tracked your career on the computer. I know about the shady deals, the laundered money, the extortion. I'm very good on the computer. For twelve years I've watched you—oh no, you didn't know I was watching. You didn't even know I was alive, did you? How many times have you passed me in the hall without knowing who I was? I was nothing to you, Signor Director, a nobody, merely a cipher—but I was watching.'

'What is it you want,' Strozzi said impatiently. 'Where is all of this going?'

'I'll tell you where it's going,' di Banco said. 'You made a fortune and now you want to ruin me for taking a few million lire. Well, it won't do, Signor Director. I'm not going to jail alone. If I go down, you're going down with me. I know what you've done. I've got proof.' His voice dropped ominously. 'And now,' he went on, 'I want some answers. I want to know how you found out about me, how you know about New York, the Cayman Islands, Guadeloupe. Was it my wife? Is Lydia in this with you?'

'You're insane,' Strozzi breathed. 'I haven't the faintest idea what you're talking about.'

Suddenly, di Banco was leaning far over the desk, his face purple with rage, his eyes on fire. *'Was it Lydia?'* he screamed. *'Did Lydia turn me in?'*

It was then that Strozzi realized his chief teller *was* insane. Strozzi knew nothing about New York or the Cayman Islands. He knew no one named Lydia.

'Get out!' he boomed—and at the same instant stamped down on the button under his foot.

The shrill of the alarm brought di Banco temporarily to his senses. Fear filled his face, then panic. His eyes darted from side to side. He looked for a hole to scuttle into but there was none. When he realized he was trapped, his face hardened, his eyes burned with a cold flame. By the time the policeman in the outer office had flung open the door and rushed in, di Banco was behind the chairman, holding a knife at his throat. The secretary stood in the doorway, her eyes wide, her mouth opening and closing wordlessly like a beached mackerel.

'Get back!' di Banco ordered.

The policeman froze. 'Drop the knife,' he said quietly. 'This will get you nowhere.'

'Get back or I'll slit his throat.'

Sweat poured from Strozzi. His eyes bulged in terror and an inarticulate gurgling rose from his throat. Di Banco yanked Strozzi's head back, gripping a fistful of the fringe of yellow-white hair in his fist, and flourished the knife menacingly.

'This isn't the way,' the policeman said.

'For God's sake, he means it,' Strozzi whimpered. 'Do as he says.'

Slowly, the policeman began to retreat.

'Close the door,' di Banco ordered. 'If you come back, I'll kill him.'

The door closed and they were alone.

Di Banco relaxed his grip. 'Don't move,' he said.

He crossed to the door and locked it, tossing the key onto the floor, then took up his position again behind the chairman.

Neither spoke.

Immobile, like a statuary grouping, they fixed their eyes on the silent door and waited for something to happen.

TWENTY MINUTES LATER the elevator doors opened. Arbati and Giorgio Bruni, accompanied by three uniformed officers, entered the outer office. The two officers Arbati had assigned to watch at the bank in case Pistocchi made an appearance were waiting for them. The chairman's secretary, gibbering and incoherent, had been led away into the safe-keeping of the matronly director of Accounts, who was attempting to calm her with a cup of hot cocoa.

'What's the situation?' Arbati asked, looking around.

'He's in there with a knife,' one of the plainclothes men said. 'Di Banco. Vittorio di Banco. Age forty-two. Been with the bank twelve years. Worked himself up to chief teller. Small, wiry guy—Caucasian—middle height—brown hair. A bit mousey, I'd say. Always been very quiet, according to folks here. Did his work, then went home; never caused trouble. Nobody can figure what happened, though he was acting strange earlier in the day— like something had upset him.'

Arbati nodded. 'A knife,' he said. 'You said a knife, not a razor.'

'That's right, sir. Heavy gauge, sharp point, about eight inches. Looks like a meat knife.'

'You're sure the man in there isn't Pistocchi—the man in the Identikit composite?'

'Absolutely, sir. No resemblance.'

Arbati surveyed the office. It was exactly what he expected Strozzi's lair would look like. Conspicuously yet austerely elegant. Look but don't touch. Sit but don't get comfortable. My money, not yours. He said:

'Has anybody talked to him?'

'No, sir. We were waiting for you.'

Arbati sat in the secretary's swivel chair and flipped on the intercom.

'This is Inspector Arbati of the Carabinieri. Can you hear me, Vittorio?'

'If you come in, I'll kill him.'

There was fear in that voice. Arbati said:

'I won't come in unless you want me to. I just want to talk— okay? Is Signor Strozzi there? Is he okay?'

'I'm here,' said a quavering voice. 'I'm okay.'

So far, so good. The hostage was alive and, it appeared, unharmed. Arbati pictured the porcine features dripping with sweat, the flawlessly pressed white suit drenched and sagging.

'We need to solve this thing, Vittorio,' Arbati said smoothly, placatingly. 'We need to find a solution without anybody getting hurt. Tell me what you want. I'll see what I can do.'

There was no response. The intercom emitted only a mechanical buzzing.

'Can you hear me, Vittorio? Tell me what it is you want. Maybe I can help.'

It was essential to get him talking. After a long minute, a distant voice said:

'How do I know I can trust you?'

'We have to trust each other, Vittorio. I'll trust you and you trust me. It's the only way we can end this thing. So, let's agree to trust each other—okay?'

There was no response.

Arbati said: 'Do you want something to eat? Some coffee?'

'No.'

'Tell me what you want, Vittorio. Let me help you.'

'I don't want anything. I don't know what I want.'

Arbati's shoulders relaxed. Now the situation was clear. Di Banco was dangerous only because he was terrified. He'd made no demands because he had no demands to make: he didn't want money or a getaway car or safe-passage out of the country. He had no plan at all. Something—Arbati had no idea what—had suddenly snapped in the man's brain and a normally placid man had turned all his rage, in frustration, on the nearest authority figure. Already (Arbati knew) di Banco regretted his actions, but had no idea how to get out of the mess he was in. He was frightened and confused. If Arbati was patient, if he was calm and sympathetic, he could talk him out.

There was a sudden clamour in the stairwell behind him and Arbati wheeled round in the chair. The fire-door burst suddenly open, spilling half a dozen commandos in camouflage fatigues carrying assault rifles into the room. One of them wore earphones and carried a radio transmitter on his back, the antenna slashing the air above him like a sabre. At the same instant the elevator doors parted and a rugged, pock-faced individual, also in battle-fatigues, issued forth and surveyed the scene. He lowered his weapon.

'Major Broschi. Army Rapid Deployment Force,' he announced. 'Who's in charge?'

Arbati stepped forward. 'Inspector Carlo Arbati. Carabinieri.'

Broschi signalled his men to secure various corners of the room, then turned back to Arbati.

'What's the scoop, inspector?' he said.

'The director of the bank—Nicòlo Strozzi—has been taken hostage by the chief teller, a man named di Banco. Di Banco has a knife.'

'Through here?'

'Yes.'

'Is this di Banco character alone?'

'Yes.'

'Right,' Broschi said. 'I've got men on the roof. We're going in. Move your boys back out of the way.'

Arbati stepped in front of him. 'There's no need,' he said. 'Di Banco will come out on his own. He's terrified. I'm talking him out.'

'Step aside, inspector.'

'This is my case, major,' Arbati said, unmoved.

Broschi gave him a glacial stare. 'You've just been relieved, mister,' he said with a low growl. 'Now get your shiny cop's ass out of my face.'

He signalled the man with the radio, who muttered something into a throat mike, then the commandos gathered before the chairman's oak door, weapons at the ready. On a signal from the radioman, Broschi put the heel of his heavy boot with everything he had into the polished wood above the handle and the door blasted inward. At the same instant there was a crash of glass and two commandos, lowered by rope from the roof, exploded in through the wall of windows. Two shots were fired.

Behind the cherry wood desk, Nicòlo Strozzi lay in the high-backed chair, his head thrown back and his mouth open. In the centre of his forehead was a neat round hole and the rear half of his head was splattered on the wall behind. Beneath him, cowering unharmed on the floor where he had thrown himself at the first sound of trouble, Vittorio di Banco whimpered audibly in inarticulate terror—and gouts of blood dripped from above onto the back of his shirt like the first heavy drops of a summer storm.

Broschi stalked to the scene and stared down in disgust.

'Jesus Christ,' he spat at his commandos, 'you assholes shot the wrong goddamn guy!'

ONE

PART FOUR

Pistocchi

LYDIA DI BANCO twisted her hands disconsolately in her lap. She had been crying again.

'What will happen to him?' she sobbed for the hundredth time. 'He's not a bad man. Why are they keeping him in jail? Why won't they let him come home where I can look after him? Oh, what will happen to him?'

Cordelia ran a hand over Lydia's dark hair and tried to comfort her.

'Everything will turn out all right,' she whispered. 'Everything will be fine.'

But of course everything would not be fine. Signor di Banco had held a man captive at knife-point. And who knew what else he might have done besides? He must, after all, have had a reason for taking a knife into the bank and holding the director hostage. No, he would be in jail for a long time. Everything would definitely *not* be all right.

They sat on the frayed sofa in the di Bancos' tiny sitting-room. It was a shabby place, the furniture old and worn, the curtains cheap and sun-rotted around the edges. The di Bancos lived a marginal existence with barely money for necessities. There were no luxuries that Cordelia could see except the colour television set and an antique *étagère*, probably inherited, which held a collection of Doulton figurines, also doubtless inherited. It was a dismal and oppressive place in which to be incarcerated alone, waiting, probably for years, for her husband to be released.

When Cordelia had returned from the library, there were police cars in front of the di Bancos' building down the street. Signora

Ghilberti, who never missed a thing that happened on the block, had filled her in on the details. The police had been with Lydia for over an hour, she said, and her husband was in custody. The director of the bank was dead. It had been on the radio news. It was all *too* terrible. Signora Ghilberti had been in a particular flap because of the publicity. She didn't want to have sightseers coming around, staring and pointing and giving the neighbourhood a bad name. It seemed an oddly minor and selfish concern at such a time, but perhaps, Cordelia thought charitably, it was just Signora Ghilberti's way of dealing with an unwelcome shock.

Poor Lydia, she thought. Poor sad, luckless Lydia—

The police were just leaving when Cordelia arrived to see if there was anything she could do. Lydia came to the door, her tearstained face dazed and broken. It was obvious she needed company, needed a friendly face close at hand, someone to help her come to terms with the sudden cataclysm that had shattered her life. Cordelia hadn't wanted to stay long. She was tired and hungry, but she hadn't had the heart to refuse Lydia's mute plea— so she'd gone in and made tea and listened to the rambling, sob-punctuated account of the wife's lament.

'I never loved anyone else,' Lydia said through her tears. 'I never wanted to love anyone else. He can be a difficult man, I know, and sometimes his temper makes him do things he regrets, but I know he loves me too. We met when we were still in school, you know, and got married as soon as we could. That was over twenty years ago. I don't know what I'll do without him—' Her voice cracked and tears streamed in renewed rivulets down her cheeks. 'I'll have to learn to be strong,' she said bravely, wiping her eyes. 'He needs me now. He needs to know that I'm here for him—that I'll always be here for him. I have to be strong now for both of us.'

Cordelia listened and tried to sympathize, tried to understand— but it wasn't easy. Her heart was torn in two directions. On the one hand, from the first instant they'd met that day in Signora Ghilberti's flat, she had disliked Vittorio di Banco—if for nothing else, she thought, he deserved what's coming to him for the way he treats his wife—but, on the other hand, her heart ached for Lydia with the primal ache of universal femininity for a suffering fellow creature. Poor, blind Lydia...who loved the husband who beat her and humiliated her because she had nobody else and nowhere else to turn. And *that,* of course, Cordelia thought sourly, was because a male-dominated society had, for countless centuries, conditioned its women to be eunuchs. But, no—no, it wasn't that simple, was it? At least not in this case. No doubt it was true that society had trained Lydia to suppress her own personality, her own needs and desires, and to live life as an extension of her husband. No doubt, in having done so, society was unjust, pernicious, myopic and perverse. But as Cordelia listened to the halting, broken story of all her husband meant to her, of how her universe revolved around his sun, she began to realize, in spite of her own ideology, that what was most real in the whole affair was the love of one human being for another. In the final analysis, what was real—and perhaps it was the only thing in the whole sordid affair that *was* real—was Lydia di Banco's love. It was neither conditioned by society's expectations, nor would (or could) it be destroyed by society's condemnation. Her love was, and had always been, a gift in her power and she had given it freely. In other circumstances she might, perhaps, have bestowed it differently, but it had always been in her power to bestow it where she would—and she had chosen to bestow it on Vittorio di Banco. His unworthiness merely magnified the value of the gift.

As she listened, Cordelia began to be aware of something she had not understood before. The first faint glimmerings of a new insight broke like the rays of an unexpected dawn over the dark, encircling palisade of her preconceptions. Much to her own surprise, she began to find that the patronizing pity she had at first felt for Lydia was being transformed, as time passed, into something akin to admiration. Lydia's love was loyal and generous and brave and free. The path she had chosen was not one that *she,* Cordelia Sinclair, could—or would—have trod with such a man; but that was only *because she would have chosen not to do so.* Lydia's choice was right for Lydia because it was Lydia's own choice, made freely and willingly. For Cordelia or anyone else to insist that she should choose differently than she had would be to insist, in effect, that Lydia should stop choosing for herself at all. It was a difficult—even a humbling—thought for Cordelia, who wanted other women to be strong like her, to be assertive and independent, to break free of domineering husbands as she had done and make new lives for themselves. But was her truth the only truth? Or was it only the truth for her...?

There was a knock at the door. Cordelia rose and opened it. On the other side stood Signora Ghilberti, holding a steaming casserole between quilted oven-mitts.

'I don't suppose either of you has even *thought* of eating,' she said, sweeping in. 'Signorina Sinclair, help me set the table. Lydia, dear, you put the water on for tea.'

When the table was set and the water boiled, the three of them sat around a folding card-table in the cramped sitting-room. In her brisk, efficient manner Signora Ghilberti soon transformed the gloom and tears into talk of knitting-yarns and cooking and, eventually, the new gentleman—a rather enigmatic Welshman—who had taken over the greengrocer's shop on the corner.

'He's from Aberystwyth, you know,' Signora Ghilberti said, pronouncing the name with relish, triumphantly. She had spent her honeymoon on the Welsh coast, cooing and spooning on the windswept rocks with her Guido and staring dreamily, in love with love, over the grey waters of the Irish Sea. After all the years she still retained a proprietary feeling about Wales. 'So at last,' she said with a categorical air of closure, 'we'll finally be able to buy decent leeks, in season.'

Cordelia was unaware that this was holy ground. She ventured onto it without trepidation.

'I've never understood the Welsh passion for leeks,' she said. 'As far as I can see, they're just over-sized green onions.'

'That,' Signora Ghilberti said shortly, 'is like dismissing Brussels sprouts as being nothing more than miniature cabbages.'

Not a bad analogy, Cordelia thought. Green onions and nasty little cabbages.

'He has a past,' Signora Ghilberti confided in an intimate tone, speaking again of the Welsh greengrocer. 'Something strange and deeply romantic. I can hear it in his voice. Ah, those Welsh voices! Well, we'll find, I predict, that he's served in the French Foreign Legion or been a fur-trapper in the desolate, barren wilds of northern Canada. Driven perforce from home, from his beloved Aberystwyth'—the word rolled like honey from her tongue—'by blighted love is my guess. I'm seldom wrong about these things, you know. I have an eye for them.'

Cordelia suppressed a smile and thought, as she often d⋮

Signora Ghilberti's company, of Virginia Woolf. A latter-day romantic of the school of Ossian.

Lydia said: 'I find his Italian very difficult to follow. I have to listen so carefully to understand what he says.'

'It's the lilt,' Signora Ghilberti said definitively. 'The Welsh are all terribly musical. The Negroes of the North, one might say. Think of all those coal-miners' choirs.'

Cordelia winced. But Signora Ghilberti, blissfully ignorant of the solecism, pressed forward with a dissertation on the lyrical quality of Welsh speech, drawing in Dylan Thomas and Richard Burton and anybody else she could think of who spoke as if they were singing to illustrate her thesis.

By the time they had cleared away the dishes and folded down the table, it was almost nine o'clock. A drowsy numbness stole along Cordelia's veins. Perhaps the long day was catching up on her; perhaps it was just the soporific weight of Signora Ghilberti's tuna-and-maccaroni casserole lying on her stomach. Whatever the cause, she longed to make her excuse and cross the street, alone, to the privacy of her own quiet sanctuary.

She was searching for the right words to say when Signora Ghilberti, steering Lydia firmly by the elbow, announced with her customary authority:

'You can't possibly stay here alone, dear. Not tonight. We'll pack a few things and you can come and stay with me for a day or two. I have a pullout couch in the spare room you can use for as long as you want. You'll be quite comfortable there.'

Over her shoulder, Lydia threw Cordelia a wan smile of gratitude and resignation and allowed herself to be led away.

'I'll check in on you tomorrow,' Cordelia said. 'Everything will turn out fine.'

On the stairs, the burden of Lydia's troubles seemed to melt away and her thoughts turned to the thin brown-covered volume waiting for her on the bedside table. *Fòglia di luce,* poems by Carlo Arbati. *Leaves of Light.* Fancy that, she thought—a policeman's poems. No, no. Poems by Carlo Arbati who just happens, coinci‑   to be a policeman. And a rather special policeman,

the street and walked the half-block to the door the ostrich-plumed entry hall of Pensione Ghil‑   er, as it always did, as being the entrance to an entirely different world—a through-the-looking-glass world of vicarage teas in lace-curtained drawing rooms and whiskered gentlemen with monocles reliving the twilight chiaroscuro of lost empires. On the first-floor landing, as she passed Signor Farinelli's door, the melodious *sostenuto* of a counter-tenor—was it Alfred Deller?—scented the air like an alien perfume. She'd heard him playing the recording before. It must be a favourite. She recognized this time what it was: Orpheus's lament, *'Tu se' morta, mia vita, ed io respiro,'* from Monteverdi's *Orfeo*. She remembered how, at the rehearsal in Teatro Comunale, it had brought tears to his eyes. What special meaning did it hold for him? Was it somehow connected with the pain of losing his parents so young, or growing up on the streets alone?—or was there some other pain in his past of which she knew nothing? Perhaps he'd once been married and his wife had died, or perhaps…well, perhaps, one day, she'd work up the courage to ask him.

On the next floor up, she unlocked her door and flipped on the overhead light. Fra Angelico was waiting at the French windows. She unlatched them and let him in.

'I've kept you waiting tonight, my friend,' she said.

He gave a curt meow, as if to acknowledge his long-suffering, and stalked to the refrigerator, tail erect. Patience anticipating its reward.

She poured milk and watched him lap it up, crouched, his eyes closed, contented. It was hard to understand why some people disliked cats. Those who did misread satisfaction and composure as arrogance. The anthropomorphic fallacy. Cats with human personalities: catastrophic. I'm getting silly, she thought. The day is catching up with me.

While Fra Angelica lapped his libation, she washed her face and changed into a cotton-print nightgown. It was too early for bed but not for comfort. Fra Angelico stretched and ambled to the door.

'Where do you go at night, my friend?' she asked, letting him out. 'I suppose your lady friends are out there waiting for you, are they?'

He crossed the balcony, jumped onto the coping between two potted geraniums and looked back at her—and winked. A deliberate wink, she could have sworn.

Good Lord, she thought, I'll have to be careful what I say around him. Who knows how much he's taking in?

The idea of an implicit understanding between them amused her. A conspiracy of species.

It was just past nine-thirty. She crawled into bed, adjusted the gooseneck lamp on the nightstand and fluffed the pillows behind her neck, then opened the volume of Carlo's poems and began to read. A breeze curled in at the open casement, stirring the hair against her cheek. The poems were beautiful, lyrical, mellifluous—the verses running like little silver rills over the palate of her imagination.

But she found she could not concentrate. The brave, wistful face of Lydia di Banco kept interposing itself between her attention and the printed page. Poor Lydia. And yet it was not Lydia who was lost and confused, Cordelia sensed; it was she herself. She felt an emptiness she couldn't explain, a longing she couldn't express.

She laid the book aside and sat on the edge of the bed. She got up and wandered to the window. She looked out over the tiled roofs and star-studded sky. The soft light in the room behind her reflected her image back to her from the polished pane: the window was also a mirror. She looked at herself looking out and wondered:

Am I afraid to love?

Did marriage to Charles Passmore destroy forever the possibility of my falling in love again—the possibility of ever again giving myself fully to another without the crippling fear of losing what I give and having a mockery made of it?

Lydia's face, superimposed on her own, hovered in the shadowy glass. In the background, the lantern of the Duomo, heavenward-pointing, etched itself on the backdrop of the fathomless sky. Lydia had found herself by losing herself. She was not annihilated or mocked by love; she was, rather, defined and given purpose by it. Love was her identity. It was the centre and circumference of her circle, reconciling irreconcilable opposites, giving meaning and substance to her life. It wasn't much perhaps, in Lydia's case, but it was something—and it was enough.

A troubling thought arose.

Had she herself, Cordelia wondered, ever really known love?

She had known passion, certainly, and desire—but had she ever in her life known love?

Or was love something she feared only because it was unknown?

TWO

THE MORNING WAS warm and sunny, the air luminous and transparent. Cordelia cleared away the few breakfast dishes and checked her hair in the mirror. From the bathroom window, the hills outside the city seemed closer, as if they had made a stealthy advance during the night on the sleeping suburbs—an illusion of light in the clear, still-unpolluted morning air. By noon, the exhaust of cars and buses would drive the hills back to their accustomed distance, but for the moment there was a pristine freshness and beauty about everything. It felt—the way some mornings unaccountably do—like a new beginning: as if life were somehow being experienced for the first time.

Her shoulder bag and a vinyl file-case containing pad and ballpoints were on the bed. She snatched them up on the way past, locked the apartment door, and descended the stairs with eager steps. It was going to be a very busy day. At the bottom of the stairs she paused in the anachronistic Edwardian foyer and tapped on the door. It was opened by Signora Ghilberti.

'I'm just on my way out,' Cordelia said. 'How is she this morning?'

'Still sleeping,' Signora Ghilberti said. 'She had a restless night, poor thing. But don't you worry, dear, I'll take care of her. I'll look after everything.'

'Thanks,' Cordelia said. 'I know you will.' She added, excusing herself in advance: 'I won't be home for dinner, by the way. I've been invited out.'

Signora Ghilberti's face cracked into a knowing smile. 'Your policeman friend again, is it?'

'Yes, it's my policeman friend again.'

Outside, the street was full of faces, bright with purpose, each scurrying to its appointed task. The image of Signor di Banco locked up alone in a grey concrete cell flashed briefly across her mind's eye. How many years would it be, she wondered, before he'd be able to enjoy again a simple pleasure like walking down a crowded sidewalk? She closed the street door behind her, stepped briskly onto the pavement, and joined the streaming throng, walking eastward into the rising sun along Via della Scala toward the centre of town.

She spent the morning at one of the long tables in the Registri di Stato Civile, where rotary fans churned slowly overhead, redistributing the heat without alleviating it. She had written yesterday to Julian Wain, her thesis supervisor at Northwestern, promising a draft of the opening chapter of her dissertation in two weeks. But before she could begin writing, she needed to do some last-minute research on the birth, marriage, and death records of the various members of the Camerata. It was dog-work and she had put it off until last, but she felt exhilarated nonetheless. Tomorrow she would begin the actual writing. *Tomorrow*—! The word sent a tremor through her body. The beginning of the end of four long years of courses and exams and deadlines and incredible slog was finally in sight—that glorious moment when, after months of preparation and countless revisions of her abstract, she would put the first words of the thesis itself down on paper. Then, words would grow into paragraphs, paragraphs into pages, pages into chapters, chapters into a book—and finally, after an oral defence (the last hurdle), she would be Cordelia Sinclair, Ph.D. *Doctor* Cordelia Erin Sinclair. It was almost a reality—close enough that she could almost taste it.

She worked through the leatherbound folios one at a time, noting down in her precise script each laconic entry in the civil record of the lives of men who had been alive at the same time and in the same place as Machiavelli and Michelangelo. It made her blood tingle in her veins to think that such men had once passed each other in the street, had once stood chatting and laughing, perhaps in the piazza outside that very room! The record of the living past trembled in her hands—and she couldn't help wondering, as she turned the thick, age-spotted leaves of handmade paper, whether the bureaucratic hands that had penned those neat, bloodless statistics had any conception of the importance, for future generations and future centuries, of the men whose lives they were recording. But she'd met enough civil functionaries in the course of her life to know (she was quite certain) the answer to that question in advance—

At one o'clock, her stomach growling, she slipped out for a

bowl of ribollita at a nearby trattoria, but was back at the long oak desk before two. Carlo expected her at six and she wanted everything finished up before she left. She didn't want to have to come back to the Registry Office tomorrow—because tomorrow was the day she began the writing.

The afternoon passed quickly. She looked at her watch at three-fifteen, and again as she returned the last of the heavy, leather-bound registers to the archives desk. It was twenty minutes to five. Perfect timing, she thought happily. Yes, everything was running exactly according to schedule.

She packed up her things and left the Registry Office, walking home along Via Condotta, then cutting through Piazza della Repubblica past the austere Façade of Palazzo Strozzi. Via Torna-buoni was crowded with tourists in loud shirts and loose dresses, hunting out bargains in the exclusive salons of Ugolini and Fer-ragamo. There was a festive atmosphere in the air as if people were expecting the arrival of a carnival. She kept up a brisk pace down Via del Sole and reached the front entrance of Pensione Ghilberti just as a hundred campaniles across the city began to chime the hour. Should she check in on Lydia? Not now, no, there wasn't time. Anyway, Lydia was in capable—perhaps too capable—hands. She'd have little time to feel sorry for herself under the aggressively maternal wing of Signora Ghilberti.

She closed the door softly and tiptoed through the ostrich-plumed foyer and up the stairs. On the second-floor landing, as she passed Signor Farinelli's door, she heard music—the same aria from Monteverdi's *Orfeo* she'd heard for the past two days—playing on the phonograph. She furrowed her brow. Why was he listening to the same piece over and over? For a fleeting moment she wondered if something was wrong, but dismissed the idea as foolish. Probably he was writing an article for some journal and steeping himself in Monteverdi for inspiration. She could ask him about it later. Right now, there wasn't time.

She bathed and changed into a chambray blazer and pleated skirt with button front. Simple and elegant, without being se-vere—a perfect outfit in which to celebrate the end of the research phase of her work. She combed her hair out, curling the bangs, and pulled the sides back into a barrette. For jewellery, she de-cided on the string of pearls with matching earrings she'd bought at Gheradi's on Ponte Vecchio for the opening performance of the Monteverdi festival at Teatro Comunale. She wondered whether Signor Farinelli playing the music from the *Orfeo* downstairs was in some subliminal way responsible for the choice. For an instant, Maestro Marchesi's face flitted through her memory. She was surprised how seldom she'd thought of him since that terrible night—but then in truth, she rationalized, he'd been almost a stranger. She'd talked to him only once in her life and then only for an hour. Yet a tremor of guilt tugged at her heart to think that someone who had once, however briefly, been so important a figure in her life should now mean so little. He had passed like a meteor through the sky above her—bright, flaming, evanescent—and been swallowed without a trace in the surrounding darkness.

At 5.38, coiffed and dressed, she was back in the street, headed for Via Zara. It must be something of a record, she thought, pleased with herself. Bathed, dressed, hair and nails done in under three-quarters of an hour. Who was it who'd said women dawdled over dressing—?

She had never been to Carlo's office. It would be an interesting, even perhaps a slightly unnerving, experience. La Questura: Police Headquarters. The phrase had an ominous ring and a little *frisson* of apprehension tingled along her spine. She couldn't help thinking again of poor Signor di Banco. What on earth, she wondered, had possessed him to act the way he had? What fear or repressed fury had made a sorry little man like Vittorio di Banco so angry that he'd found the courage to hold a man hostage and threaten his life with a knife? Well, whatever it was, his aggression hadn't come out of the blue. She was sure of that. There was much more to the story than she—and no doubt more than even Lydia—knew. Still, no matter what lay behind it or however much he deserved his fate, it was sad to think of him cooped up in a grey concrete cell. It must be awful for him.

An orange ATAF bus lumbered past, shifting gears, and enveloped her in a rancid blast of diesel fumes. Civilization could carry a heavy price-tag and there were times, she thought, when you had to wonder if it was even heading in the right direction.

The Questura was a functional, featureless building near Piazza della Libertà. She asked for Carlo at the front desk and was directed to the second floor. His office was a glass-fronted cubicle on the far side of a large, open room crowded with desks. He was on the telephone and there was someone in the office with him. She tapped on the glass—he looked up, smiled broadly, and waved her in.

'I'll just be a minute,' he said, cupping his hand over the receiver. 'This is Giorgio Bruni. Giorgio—Cordelia Sinclair. Yes,' he said into the mouthpiece, 'yes, I'm still here.'

Bruni and Cordelia shook hands. 'I'm off then,' Bruni mouthed at Arbati. 'See you tomorrow.' He turned to Cordelia: 'You two are off to dinner, I hear. You should try La Maremmana. Positively the best spaghetti scoglio in town. You won't regret it.'

'I'll mention it,' Cordelia said. What a funny little man, she thought. Baggy clothes, one eye turned out: a Florentine version of Columbo.

On his way out, Bruni turned and said with an elfish grin: 'He's a good catch, signorina. Marry him before he gets so old that nobody wants him.'

Arbati shot him a poisoned look—but it was too late. Bruni was already gone.

While Carlo finished on the phone, Cordelia looked around the office. There wasn't much to see. A battered desk, three wooden chairs, a row of metal filing-cabinets, a peeling table with a hot-plate and obviously well-used glass-globe coffee pot. There were no photographs, no pictures on the wall, nothing to give the place a personal touch or to suggest, even in a subtle way, that its occupant was a man of cultivated sensibility and a published poet. She found that this disappointed her. It was a room without warmth, without grace, without style. A sterile, faceless room. It was hard to believe it had anything at all to do with the Carlo she knew.

Near the door was a corkboard with a composite sketch—like ones she'd seen in television murder mysteries—pinned on to it with bright red thumbtacks. The drawing caught her eye and held it briefly: there was something familiar about the face, but she couldn't place it.

Arbati rang off. 'Sorry about that,' he said. 'And about Giorgio too. His idea of what constitutes humour isn't everyone's cup of tea.'

'I thought he was cute.'

Arbati laughed. 'Cute—? It's not the word I'd have chosen.

But, anyway—as long as you weren't offended. Now, where shall we eat?'

'Your friend Giorgio recommends La Maremmana, for the spaghetti scoglio.'

Arbati rolled his eyes. 'He does, does he? It's a nice enough place in its way, but this is an extra special celebration—the end of all that nasty, boring research. You *did* finish, didn't you?'

Cordelia nodded, unable to keep a silly grin off her face.

'All right, then,' Arbati said with authority, 'such a momentous event in the life of a future Doctor of Music clearly calls for something more—' he searched for the right word '—well, something more elevated than La Maremmana. More intimate and less crowded. Let's walk for a while and think it over,' he suggested. 'There's no rush. It's early yet. We can work up an appetite while we think about where to go.'

They started for the door. The composite drawing on the corkboard drew Cordelia's eye to it like a magnet. It seemed to follow her as she moved.

'Who's that?' she asked, moving up for a closer look.

And then suddenly, almost before the words were out, it hit her: *Signor Farinelli*. The mouth was wrong and the cheekbones a fraction too high, but there was no mistaking those large, luminous eyes that seemed, even in a rude sketch, to hold the spectator spellbound. It was the eyes that had first attracted her attention.

Arbati stood behind her, looking over her shoulder. 'Pistocchi,' he said. 'It's a computer-aged image of Francesco Pistocchi. The one we're looking for in the Marchesi case—as well as several others. We're pretty sure he's Lo Squartatore.'

'Really—?' The blood froze in her veins. Her eyes stared ahead without seeing.

'Why do you ask?' Arbati said. 'Have you seen him someplace? In the theatre the night Marchesi was killed, perhaps?'

Cordelia forced calm into her face and voice. She shook her head slowly, deliberately:

'I thought for a moment there was something familiar about him—but, no...no, I've never seen him before.'

Arbati switched off the overhead fluorescents and opened the door.

Cordelia said, merely in order to say *something*, to fill the air with the familiar comfort of sound: 'You should brighten this place up, you know. Bring in some flowers or something.'

Arbati gave a sly smile. 'Now, why would I do a thing like that? I don't want my visitors—at least not my usual visitors—to feel too cosy in here,' he said. 'That would entirely defeat the purpose. People who feel too much at home have a tendency to say whatever comes into their heads, to make things up. I want them to tell me the truth. No, I don't think flowers would do at all.'

'I see,' she said, suppressing a fresh wave of guilt.

They walked along the banks of the Arno, down Lungarno Vespucci, toward the setting sun. Banks of cloud lay low on the distant hills, gathering strength although the sky overhead was clear and blue. There would be rain, Arbati knew.

Cordelia's mind tossed in a turmoil. She couldn't believe it—it was impossible—and yet something at the back of her brain told her that it must be true. Her heart and head were locked in a mortal combat. The Signor Farinelli she knew—the man who had talked to her about God and calmed her down after she'd found Marchesi's body, who'd eaten her beef Wellington and told her how he got started in journalism—was generous and compassionate and gentle. There was no murder in him. He couldn't be a killer: it was completely, utterly and completely *impossible*. And yet, the face in the drawing—the face of a killer—was mysteriously and inexplicably *his* face. There was no doubt about it. It was impossible; yet it was true. What did it mean? How could she possibly resolve such an irreconcilable contradiction? But there had to be an explanation. What then—? Were these two people in the same body, a split personality?—or was there someone else, a vicious killer who merely looked like Signore Farinelli on the loose out there waiting to kill again—?

'You've being very quiet,' Arbati said. 'Is anything wrong?'

She forced a smile. 'I was just thinking.'

'About what?'

'The drawing in your office.'

'Pistocchi? What about him?'

'I was wondering what made him commit those terrible crimes. Do you think he's insane?'

'Probably,' Arbati said, thrusting his hands into his pockets. 'Probably he is.' He was silent for a moment, then said: 'It's been almost thirty-five years since the Camerati dell'arte—that's what they called themselves—mutilated him in the chapel of Santa Maria Novella cathedral. For more than three decades Pistocchi lived with the daily reality of what they'd done to him, and yet, so far as we know, never attempted to do anything about it until three months ago. And then suddenly—beginning with Alberto Mora, the textile magnate—he started murdering them. The only explanation I can think of is that something finally must have snapped in his brain. The hatred he'd suppressed over all those years must have built up like magma at the core of a volcano until something—we don't know what, and it was probably something quite insignificant anyway—triggered an explosion.'

Cordelia was only half-listening. Her mind was filled with the image of Farinelli's face she'd seen on that afternoon, two weeks earlier, during the rehearsal of Monteverdi's *Orfeo*. She had turned to say something to him and seen the silent tears welling in his eyes. And then she remembered the music she'd heard every time in the past two days that she'd crossed the landing outside his apartment—it was the same aria: Orpheus's lament from Monteverdi's opera—and she realized with a sudden, blinding clarity what it all meant...and *whose* voice it must be singing on that recording—

They paused in their walk and Arbati leaned on the coping of the retaining wall, looking back along the silver ribbon of the Arno. 'There's something else,' he said. 'Pistocchi's last victim was supposed to have been Strozzi, the bank director who was killed in that foul-up at the Banco di Firenze. Pistocchi had saved him on purpose until last; he wanted Strozzi to be the crowning glory, the pinnacle, of his revenge. He'd already tried to kill him once, and failed, at his villa out near San Gimignano. If I'm right and Pistocchi *is* in fact mad, then losing forever the chance to kill the man he blamed more for his mutilation than any of the other Camerati is likely to have unhinged him completely.' He turned and looked Cordelia hard in the eye as if he somehow suspected that she wasn't telling all she knew. 'What you have to realize is that he's a very dangerous man—unpredictable and highly volatile. I want you to promise me that, if you *do* see him, you'll let me know immediately. Pistocchi is a walking time-bomb. He could go off any place, any time.'

Cordelia's head swam. In her roiled brain, thought tumbled

over thought like waves crashing and boiling along a storm-battered beach. Oh, how right she'd been about the dark, secret pain she'd sensed in Farinelli's past! No wonder he'd killed them, no wonder he wanted revenge—and yet, how could *he* have killed them, how could *he* be a cold-blooded murderer? It made no sense. The Farinelli she knew was kind and gentle and forgiving and sensitive and entirely placid. Farinelli—Pistocchi, the same person?—no, no, no, it just wasn't possible...

'I want you to promise me,' Arbati said again.

She looked at him as if he were a stranger. What had he been saying? She hadn't taken in a word of it.

'Of course,' she said, managing a smile, not having the faintest idea what she was agreeing to.

His shoulders relaxed. 'Well now, what about food?' he said. 'Are you starting to feel those pangs of hunger yet?'

'If you are,' she said.

'Well, frankly, I'm starved. Let's see—why don't we try Il Cestello?' he proposed. 'It's a proper setting to celebrate the birth of a thesis. We can look down over the whole city while we eat. Like a couple of gods surveying their estate.'

'It sounds exciting,' she said, wondering how she could possibly manage now to force down even a single mouthful.

THREE

FARINELLI SAT bolt up-right, unmoving, in an old chintz armchair encircled by the pool of yellow light that fell from a shaded floor lamp. The rest of the apartment was buried in stygian darkness. As if he had fallen into a trance, his eyes were fixed ahead, unblinking, unseeing. From the speaker of the old-fashioned Motorola Hi-Fi at his side flowed, like a rich perfume, the sweet, exquisitely delicate voice of a male soprano *mai più non tornare, ed io rimango—*

He had learned about Strozzi's death in the newspaper. From every newsstand he passed, the headline had screamed out at him, making a mockery of Pistocchi's wild, untameable craving for revenge: BANKER SLAIN IN BOTCHED RESCUE ATTEMPT. He knew how Pistocchi would react; he knew that the black paranoia burning in his brain would make him lash out—blindly, rashly—at the first object in his path when he learned the news. The only way to stop him was to stay alert, to keep control away from Pistocchi, to keep him in the dark. For more than a day since seeing the headline, Farinelli had sat in the chintz-covered armchair, not daring to move except to relieve himself, except once to take a glass of milk, except often to reset the stylus on the turning disk. For more than a day he had guarded the gates of consciousness against the return of Pistocchi, that leering Apollyon of the clanking chains who sought to drag his immortal soul down in iron trammels—screaming, bound, despairing—into the infernal pit of deepest hell. He had fought his return with an inhuman vigilance, with the Olympian wakefulness of a supernatural will, and he had held him at bay for more than a day, for more than a day, for more than a day, for more than a day...

Wearily, his heavy head nodded forward, overcome, seeking the sweet oblivion of sleep.

But no rest came. Instead, there was a voice—

So art thou to revenge, when thou shalt hear! The words of Hamlet's father, spoken from the craggy lip of the sulphurous tormenting pit: goading words spoken also to *him,* to Farinelli, in the dead of night in dreams that made his seated heart knock at his ribs in terror—and heard, too, even in broad and waking day, whenever the insinuating voice intrigued to howl him into fury from the blood-dimmed fields of ancient, never-to-be-forgotten wrongs. The hate-driven, asomatous cry of Francesco Pistocchi.

So art thou to revenge—

His eyes closed, then reopened abruptly. No longer were they wistful and sad; they shone now with a hard, bright, unnatural light—a demonic luminosity.

Strozzi had been the last. Strozzi, the one who, in the candle-flickering chapel, had held the knife and done the deed. From tartarean depths, the spear-sharp images returned, drawn link by link up the iron chain of unpardoning memory. Never would he forget, never would he forgive what they had done.

In the hushed and darkened chapel they gave him something to drink. A drug. They immersed him naked in a tub and ferried water to keep it hot. As if standing outside himself, Pistocchi watched; he saw it all. 'He has an angel's voice,' the maestro said. 'It is the will of God,' the cardinal replied. Piously, they chanted a psalm over him in unison, their voices like the rolling of a far-off tide, and took him from the water; and by the altar waited Strozzi with the knife. They stretched him, yielding, drugged, on the cold marble. He scarcely felt the wound. 'Clean up the blood,' said one. They took him down and dressed him in a plain, white gown. When it was done, the cardinal, bending, dipped up water from the tub and crossed Pistocchi's forehead, saying: 'This is a new beginning. From this day I christen you Farinelli, the last and best of the castrati—in the name of the father, the son and the holy ghost.'

Now, they were all dead: Mora, Rosso, Cafferelli, Marchesi, Strozzi. He had killed them all—all except Strozzi, the one he wanted most of all.

Strozzi had died too soon, too easily, too painlessly.

He had been cheated out of Strozzi. He had tried, once, to cut h   ke the others, but there had been guards and dogs.
           was too late.

          rose in Pistocchi's gorge, nearly choking him. He
          arkness through a haze of blood. His breathing
          w, the rasping of a hunted boar. He wanted to

tip back his head and howl like a mad dog, like a damned soul in the lowest circle of Dante's Hell—

The record-changer lifted the stylus and there was silence.

Pistocchi's hard, carbuncular eyes closed, then reopened. The anger in them had dissipated.

Farinelli rose and set the armature back on the turning record. He had relaxed his vigilance; he had nearly lost control. A cold sweat bathed his forehead. Pistocchi had escaped for a moment, had broken out—but then the record had stopped, diverting him, and Farinelli had been able to regain control.

An organ prelude swelled from the crackling speakers and then the sad and solitary solo voice began again: *Tu se' morta, mia vita, ed io respiro?* Farinelli listened, staring into oblivion. Uncomforted. Afraid.

Just after eleven he heard the girl come in. He heard her climb the stairs and pause on the landing outside his door as if undecided, as if debating with herself whether to knock, and then she continued her climb. Cordelia. The only one who loved him. The others—tigers, hyaenas. What! have his daughters brought him to this pass? He liked the girl. She was sincere and open and sensitive—and she had suffered, too, in her way. She had endured the tyranny of a husband who had consumed her and spat her out. She knew about betrayal and disempowerment. In a way, she understood what he had suffered—his castration, his loss of selfhood. But she had broken free and started again. For him, there could be no new beginning. Because Pistocchi was always there, lurking below the surface, there could never be the promise of a new dawn for Farinelli in this nether world. He carried hell within him like a gnawing cancer, metastasizing its corruption into every limb and organ. He was a walking grave.

Oh! who, cried his beleaguered soul in anguish, will deliver me from the body of this death?

In the darkest hour before the dawn, the rain started. At first, big drops only, single, isolated; then a heavy drumming downpour, draining the inexhaustible aquifers of the starless sky. It drove against the windows and battered the metal table on the balcony. It cleansed and purified, washing the dirt from roofs, and ran in purgative runnels down the streetlamp-shining midnight streets.

Farinelli closed his eyes—and for the first time in more than a day, for the first time since he had learned of Strozzi's death, he slept.

FOUR

AFTER A NIGHT of fitful tossing and turning, Cordelia still had made no decision about what she was going to do. She made herself get up and try to eat but she wasn't hungry. Even the idea of food made her feel slightly queasy. She tried to think, brooding over a cup of coffee at the kitchen table and staring out at the silent dome of Santa Maria del Fiore, but her mind was blank and uncooperative. The picture-postcard view of quaint roof-lines beyond her window was grey and depressing. The rain that had poured in torrents in the middle of the night had stopped now, and only a mist-like drizzle oozed from the sombre sky. It was a miserable day with no prospect of the sun in sight.

She dressed without knowing what she intended. Should she go and see Farinelli—confront him—offer to help? But what could she say to him? how help? No, no—there was nothing she could do— Then what option was there? None...none. She picked up the telephone. She would call Carlo and tell him what she knew. It wasn't too late. Pistocchi was volatile, he'd said, a ticking timebomb that could go off at any moment. Then why, if she was going to end up telling Carlo about Farinelli anyway, hadn't she told him last night? Their dinner at Il Cestello and the special evening he'd planned to celebrate the end of her research had been ruined by her moody silence. She hadn't told him then because Farinelli was her friend. And had that changed? Was Signor Farinelli no longer her friend? No—she admired and respected him and, in a way, she even loved him. The man she knew as Farinelli was kind and gentle and self-deprecatingly witty. He had opened up his life to her, had told her about his orphaned childhood and how he'd finally found his feet and started his career writing reviews. He was also a brilliant man, a wise man—a philosopher. He had talked to her about God and the reasonableness of faith, about the mystery that surrounds us everywhere in the universe, about the dark enigma that lies at the heart of human personality—and oh! if she had known then about him what she knew now, she would have folded him in her arms and let him cry out the pain that was in his heart! She set the telephone softly back in its cradle. No—she couldn't phone Carlo and tell him about Farinelli. Carlo knew only Pistocchi, a killer. *But she knew Farinelli.* She trusted him and she wanted with all her heart, desperately, somehow to help him. Farinelli wasn't Pistocchi. They were two separate beings, unrelated, unconnected. The man who had named his cat Fra Angelico was simply incapable of committing the crimes Pistocchi was accused of. And she had no business with Pistocchi; she had no desire to disturb him. Let him sleep. The only one she wanted to see—to comfort and help, if she could—was Signor Farinelli.

But she needed time to think.

She put on a jacket to keep the weather off and left the apartment. In the rain-soaked street, she turned her collar up and walked quickly, staring straight ahead, not knowing where she was going, not knowing what she expected to find. Her eyes were dull, her face an empty shell. Passing faces turned, offering mute sympathy, silently questioning. She didn't notice them. On she walked.

Her mind was in a turmoil. She didn't know where to go, who to talk to. And she *needed* to talk to someone. She needed to get her feelings out where she could examine them, where she could deal with them. But there was no one she could turn to. Not Carlo, obviously. Not Lydia. Not Signora Ghilberti—because she needed someone who would *listen.* Oh, how alone she felt! Professor Ecco, of course, would have helped, but he was away for the week at a conference in Venice. There was no one else. The words from Coleridge's poem that had once before, after Marchesi's death, popped into her mind, returned and drummed in her brain like the tolling of a bell:

Alone, alone, all, all alone,
Alone on a wide wide sea!
And never a saint took pity on
My soul in agony.

She knew the agony of the old mariner's aloneness. She understood his fear of the mysterious unknown. She felt, like him, alone in an empty universe.

As she walked, the city around her struck her eye as old and ramshackle, the buildings seedy and dilapidated—shabby rather then venerable with age. She had never imagined Florence could look like this. After an hour she found herself, without having planned it, in front of the black and white face of the basilica of Santa Maria Novella. She remembered that first day, the day she had arrived in Florence: she had stepped from the train station and seen this same church. Its façade of alternating marble had seemed to her, she remembered, an allegory of good and evil intertwined. There had been police cars in the street and, although she hadn't known it at the time, a body inside. A body hanging on a cross: Cardinal Cafferelli. And Signor Farinelli—no, no, no, *Pistocchi*—had killed him, had cut his throat like a dog and left him hanging there. It was appalling, unspeakable. And then, later on the same day, they had sat together in Signora Ghilberti's drawing room, drinking tea and chatting as if nothing had happened. *The same day!* Horrible—!

She shuddered.

The drizzle had worked through the thin jacket and reached her skin. Her hair was soaked and hung in matted strands. Her teeth were close to chattering.

It started to rain again. A sudden shower, warning of worse to come. She took shelter in the stone portico of the church. She stood for a time looking out at the falling drops dancing on the puddles in the piazza and then something—curiosity perhaps, or maybe because she felt chilled—made her try the heavy oak door of the basilica. It was unlocked—and she opened it and slipped inside. The interior was dusky and as silent as a tomb. The arching roof overhead and rows of supporting columns down either side led her eye down a vista of carved marble to the high altar and the figure of the crucified Christ at the front. There was no one else in sight. She was alone in the huge, empty building. To the right of the altar a rack of blue votive lamps flickered at the base of the Virgin's statue. She advanced slowly, tentatively—not certain why she was doing so, not certain why she was even there. She had not been inside a church for many years. A stranger in a strange land. Her feet echoed hollowly on the paving underfoot.

The house of God. Vast, silent, empty.

AT HIS DESK on the second floor of the Questura, Carlo Arbati was on his fifth cigarette and third coffee of the morning and the working day had only barely begun. He couldn't keep his mind on the work in front of him. He was worried about Cordelia. Worried sick. He had thought about her all night and hardly slept a wink.

She knew something about Lo Squartatore that she was keeping back from him—something that, for some reason, she was *refusing* to tell him. When she had picked him up last night at his office, she had recognized something about Pistocchi's picture. Arbati had seen it in her eyes, her voice, her manner. She protested that she'd never seen the man before, but Arbati had been a cop for too long not to recognize the body language of deceit. Either she had seen Pistocchi someplace or—much worse—she actually knew him.

And for some reason she had decided to protect him from justice and the law.

He swirled the coffee in his mug, staring into it as if the dark grounds at the bottom would afford him an insight, a sudden revelation.

The dinner at El Cestello to celebrate the end of her thesis research had been a disaster. She had hardly spoken two words all evening and every attempt to coax the truth out of her had been met with dark looks and truculent silence. She had complained of a migraine and, after a monkish repast where neither spoke, he had taken her home early and left her at the door. He couldn't force the truth out of her unless he brought her in formally for questioning. And he had no intention of doing that if there was any way of avoiding it. She meant too much to him— far too much, he now knew—for him to treat her as a hostile witness and risk losing her.

There was a perfunctory tap on the door and Giorgio Bruni bounded in with a simpering ear-to-ear grin splitting his elf-like face. He looked like the cat who ate the mouse who ate the cheese.

'Well,' he said with a lascivious grin, 'so how was the big date last night, eh? Tell me all. Like, for starters, did you take up my hot tip about the spaghetti scoglio at La Maremmana?' Then he saw the look on Arbati's face and froze in his tracks. 'Oh dear,' he said, suddenly sober, 'I think I've just put my foot in the doo-

doo, haven't I? I take it things didn't go well. If you want to be alone, Carlo, I can come back later.'

Arbati shook his head. 'No—no, stay. I need to talk.'

Bruni poured himself a coffee, then sat in one of the slat-backed chairs in front of the desk. 'So, tell me what happened,' he said softly.

Arbati ground out his cigarette and lit another. He said:

'She knows who Lo Squartatore is. She probably even knows him personally.'

Bruni's eyebrows arched. 'She told you that?'

'No, it's what she refused to tell me.'

'Meaning what, exactly?'

'Meaning I read it in her face when she saw the Identikit composite,' Arbati said. 'She knows Pistocchi. But when I asked her if she knew him, or had seen him someplace, she denied it.'

'I see. And you're sure you *did* see it? In her face, I mean.'

The look Arbati shot him said there was no doubt.

Bruni nodded. After a moment, he said: 'What are you going to do?'

Arbati knocked the ash off his cigarette and used the burning end to scrape the loose ashes into a little pile like a burial mound. 'That's the problem,' he said. 'I haven't the faintest idea what I'm going to do.'

They were silent for a time and then Bruni cleared his throat and said:

'You may have to bring her in for questioning.'

Arbati nodded. 'I know,' he said. 'It may come to that.'

From the look in Arbati's eye, Bruni knew how much that admission had cost. And he knew something else too: he knew that Arbati was in love with Cordelia Sinclair. He said softly:

'And then again, of course, it may not. There are options to exhaust, Carlo, before we come to that one'—though, in truth, he couldn't think of many. Changing the topic, he asked: 'Does she have any idea how much danger she's in?'

'I did my best to impress it on her.'

'That wasn't my question,' Bruni said bluntly. 'My question was: Did you get through to her? We've seen what this man can do, Carlo; we know what he's capable of. We've cleaned up after him, remember? He's a psychopath—and since he was deprived of the pleasure of killing Strozzi, he's not likely to be in a very good humour. In fact, he's going to be completely erratic, completely unpredictable. She's playing with a kilo of gelignite, Carlo. Almost any bloody thing—a bump, an unexpected little jar—could trigger a cataclysmic explosion. If you really do love her, my friend, you'll tell her that—straight out. Whatever the consequences.'

It was not often that Giorgio Bruni talked like that to his boss. In fact, he could never remember having done it before. But there was a first time for everything.

For a long moment, Arbati sat like a man in a trance. Then, finally, he leaned slowly forward and reached for the telephone.

'Not on the phone,' Bruni said with a pained grin. 'Go to her, man. *Go to her.*'

AT THE FRONT OF the church, under the gaze of the Crucified One, were a few rows of ornamented pews. For a time Cordelia stood, her hand resting on the back of the last row, looking up at the pierced hands and feet, the wounded side, the mocking crown of thorns. It seemed presumptuous—even sacrilegious—to press further into the sanctuary, to pass forward among the seats of the faithful, to transgress the barrier she had set up in her mind between aesthetics and religious belief. Looking down from the high frescoed ceiling and recognizing no such division, the figures in Masaccio's *Holy Trinity*, wonderful in their simplicity, surveyed and embraced the universe below them with a benevolent regard.

Cordelia moved forward and slipped surreptitiously into the last pew. The oak seat was hard and unyielding, not contoured to the curves of her human form. No sound reached her ear except the calm, regular intake and exhalation of her own breath. A single candle burned on the altar. She caught the faint scent of what might have been furniture polish. She pulled the thin fabric of her jacket closer around her shoulders, seeking its warmth. She felt glad to be inside, out of the rain. A certain tranquillity crept over her. For a time she simply sat there, in solitude, nurtured by the profound peace around her—that seemed somehow to mirror something that lay inside her too, beyond the confusions and tribulations of life, at the unruffled centre of her own being.

At length, since it was his house—his peace and serenity—she had invaded, she raised her eyes to the figure hanging above the altar.

Oh God, she thought, why must you be a hidden god? If you would show yourself, many would believe. If you would raise your head, there where you hang, nailed and bloody, and speak to me, I would believe. But that's the point, I suppose, isn't it? If you did raise your head and speak, then I'd have no option but to believe; there'd be no room for faith. Your speaking would take away my will no doubt, my freedom to trust. Thomas doubted until he saw; but when he saw, then he could doubt no more: Doubtless Thomas. It would have been better for him to have struggled with his fears. So I understand, Lord, why it is that you don't raise your head and speak to me. But what of us latter-day Thomases who, through weakness, still need something in the way of vision in order to believe? What are we to do, Lord? Are the restraints that truss us to the world and make us the slaves of sense mere ropes of sand that we have twisted into binding cable? Must we be wise in blindness? Oh, Lord, I would love you, but I am afraid. Afraid of faith, afraid to trust and let myself go in order to embrace you. Afraid of being made a fool—

She started like a guilty thing surprised. She realized, suddenly, that she was praying—at least it sounded very like a prayer. In spite of everything she knew about her convictions concerning religion, she had come into the house of a God she didn't believe in and had caught herself speaking unawares to him as if it were the most natural thing in the world. And yet, for some reason that she couldn't explain, she didn't feel silly about it. She only started to feel foolish when her head began to question the unpremeditated actions of her heart.

She rose and retreated, abashed, down the aisle toward the exit.

Outside, the rain had modulated into a thin drizzle, like the last oozings from a wine-press. She felt a calm she did not understand, a peace beyond her power of understanding. When she had first gone into the church, she had been restless and confused, uncertain what to do about Farinelli. Yet now—although she had herself decided nothing consciously—she had the sense that everything had nevertheless been decided. It was strange. She still had no idea what she was going to do, but she was no longer anxious or concerned about it. She was calm because she was prepared to trust, without knowing their intent, the rousing emotions that she felt stirring silently in the secret places of her heart.

She turned up the collar of her jacket and stepped from the

marble portico into the misting day, walking quickly across the puddled pavement of Piazza Santa Maria Novella in the direction of Pensione Ghilberti.

ARBATI PARKED IN the street outside and took the four flights of stairs up to her apartment on the top floor two steps at a time. His chest was heaving and his heart pounding by the time he reached the door. He knocked loudly, then stepped back and waited.

There was no response. He tried again, this time calling her name, but with the same result.

He stood for a moment, wondering what to do, then took a card from his wallet and wrote in large letters on the back: CALL ME IMMEDIATELY. IT'S IMPORTANT. CARLO. He stuck the card in the crack between door and jamb, immediately above the lock, where she couldn't miss it.

There was nothing more he could do.

He descended the stairs and was reaching for the handle of the street-door when the apartment door on the ground floor opened. A woman in her sixties in a flower-print dress stepped into the hall and gave him a haughty, appraising look, before asking in an imperious tone:

'Is there something I can help you with, signore?'

It was obvious from the accent, although her Italian was very good, that she was English.

'I'm looking for Signorina Sinclair,' Arbati said, turning back toward her, his hand still on the brass doorknob. 'Apparently she's out. I don't suppose you can tell me where she is?'

Signora Ghilberti bridled at his directness. She said stiffly: 'And may I inquire who wishes to know?'

Arbati released the doorknob and adopted a conciliatory tone. 'Excuse me,' he said. 'I didn't mean to be abrupt, but the matter is quite urgent.' He produced his identification card and held it out for her. 'I'm Detective Inspector Arbati, of the Carabinieri.'

The scowl on Signora Ghilberti's face lifted like a dark cloud pulling away from the face of the sun. 'Oh—' she trilled. 'Inspector Arbati—yes. Signorina Sinclair will be sorry to have missed your visit, I'm sure. She went out about an hour ago.'

'Did she happen to mention where she was going?'

'Gracious, inspector, no. I wasn't actually *speaking* with her, you understand. I only happened to see her through the window as she was going out. I was watering the begonias, you see, at the time.'

Signora Ghilberti, Arbati thought, was the sort who wouldn't miss much that passed in front of her window. Her begonias must see a lot of water in a year. He said:

'If you should happen to notice when she returns, I'd be grateful if you'd ask her to contact me at once at the Questura. As I said, the matter is quite urgent.'

'Of course, inspector. But I shouldn't think she'd be back until supper time. She spends most days working in the library at the university, often until after six.' She added, slyly, giving him a knowing look, 'But then I imagine you knew that already, didn't you?'

'Perhaps I'll try there on the way back to headquarters,' he said, anxious to be away. 'Thank you for your help, signora.'

'Not at all, inspector,' she fluted after him, 'anytime at all.'

In the car, Arbati considered his options. Perhaps a visit to the university was a worthwhile gamble, but he wasn't hopeful. The research was finished. Today she was to have begun the writing. There was no reason for her to return to the library. On the other hand, it was the only lead he had to follow up. She could be any place. Oh God, he prayed, let her be safe! Don't let her do anything foolish.

He checked the rear-view mirror and pulled out into traffic. If she wasn't at the university, he would go back to his office and wait for her call. There was, in fact, nothing else he could do.

IT TOOK Cordelia less than ten minutes to walk the half-mile from Santa Maria Novella to Pensione Ghilberti in Via della Scala. Arbati, who had just left, was two blocks away, mired in traffic. At the entrance to the building, Cordelia crossed her fingers and prayed that Signora Ghilberti wasn't lying in wait for her, as she often had been in recent days, watching to press her into service helping to keep Lydia's cheer up. (In fact, Signora Ghilberti was at the back with Lydia, kneading dough for currant rolls in the kitchen.) She closed the heavy entrance-door quietly behind her and crept up the stairs from the silent foyer to the second floor. Outside Farinelli's door she stopped and listened: there was no music, no sound of any kind. She wondered if he was even home.

For a moment, she debated with herself whether to carry on up the next flight to her own apartment and change out of her damp clothes, but then changed her mind and knocked.

He took a long time to answer. She almost turned away. Then the door opened.

'I need to talk to you,' she said.

He looked terrible. He was unshaven, his eyes red-rimmed, his clothes loose and rumpled as if he had slept in them. She wondered if her knock had wakened him.

'It's not a good time,' he said.

The voice was gruff and there was a wariness in the eyes she hadn't seen in them before.

'I know about Pistocchi,' she said. 'And I know about what the men he killed did to him.'

The eyes started, then relaxed into a look of resignation. He opened the door and stood aside to let her pass.

The apartment was dark and stuffy. The shutters were closed, the drapes drawn, the only light a yellow pool cast by the shaded floor lamp near the Motorola Hi-Fi. The air was close and a musty smell pervaded the room as if the house were in mourning. At one end of the chintz sofa Fra Angelico, the cat, slept curled in a ball, oblivious to all around him.

Farinelli closed the door and, standing in front of it, said:

'Who told you about Pistocchi?'

There was an edge of wariness and, she thought, even of fear in his voice.

'I saw his picture at the Questura,' she said.

The muscles in his face tensed.

'The police know about Pistocchi then—' he said.

He spoke slowly, deliberately, as if coming to terms with catastrophic news, like learning that he had an inoperable brain tumour.

Cordelia watched him carefully, remembering Carlo's words: *Pistocchi is a dangerous man, a time-bomb. He can go off any place, any time.* But she hadn't come to confront Pistocchi; she had come to comfort Farinelli, to help him if she could—and it had been Farinelli, her friend, that had met her at the door. She said:

'I didn't tell them. They don't know about you. They're looking for Francesco Pistocchi.'

It was a dangerous gamble. It left her vulnerable. She waited for the explosion—waited with bated breath for the blood to rise in his eye and a cruel smile to twist his lip; waited for him to realize that only one witness stood between him and escape—and then to lunge and take her by the throat. But there was no explosion. There was no blood-dimmed eye, no cruel smile. The tension drained from his shoulders as if he had laid aside a burden and his eyes, grey and luminous, relaxed into a question. She knew then that she'd been right to trust her instincts, right to believe in him. It was Pistocchi who was the killer—not Farinelli, not the man who'd wept in the theatre, who'd eaten her beef Wellington and talked about the mystery of self-consciousness and how none of us really knows anything about the hidden self at the centre of his own being.

'Why?' he said simply. 'Why didn't you tell them?'

She smiled. 'Because I knew you couldn't be a killer. Because I have faith in you. Because I'm your friend.'

A frown creased his forehead. He said:

'I have killed.'

Cordelia shook her head. 'No, not you,' she said. 'Pistocchi is the killer, not you.'

Farinelli left his station at the door and sank into the armchair beside the Motorola, the lamplight spilling over him like a spotlight from under its fringed shade. He folded his hands in his lap and waited, as if preparing to submit to an interrogation.

For the first time, Cordelia looked around the room and noticed how dark and airless it was. How drawn and unkempt he looked. She realized then that he must have been sitting in that chair for many hours before she arrived, that he had probably spent the night in it. She asked:

'Have you eaten?'

'No.'

There were eggs in the refrigerator. She scrambled two, made toast, and put on a pot of coffee. Before long, the rich aroma of brewing Java was percolating through the apartment, giving it an air of warmth and hominess. While she cooked, Farinelli sat in the armchair without stirring.

'How did the police get Pistocchi's picture?' he asked at last. 'There are no pictures that I know of. He doesn't like being photographed.'

'It was a drawing, actually,' Cordelia said over her shoulder. 'Carlo said it had been computer-aged. Apparently someone—I don't know who—described to an artist what Pistocchi looked like as a boy and then the artist's sketch was fed into a computer. They use the same technique for tracing missing children from old photographs. It was a surprisingly good likeness, I must say. They're terribly clever these computers, aren't they?'

'Strozzi,' Farinelli mumbled to himself. 'It must have been Strozzi.'

She brought the food on a tray and set it on the coffee table. There was an extra cup for herself.

'Do you mind if I let some light in? It's dingy in here.'

He shook his head heavily, as if nothing mattered any more. 'I don't mind,' he said.

She parted the heavy drapes and threw open the shutters. The sky was still grey, but in the east there was a brightness that suggested the sun was trying to break through. She sat in the armchair across from him, the same one she'd used the day she'd come to him so upset after finding Marchesi's body and so desperately in need of a friend to talk to. She couldn't help thinking how ironic life was—for now the roles were reversed, and she was there trying to comfort him.

He ate ravenously. She wondered how long it had been since he'd eaten his last meal. A long time, at any rate. She said, filling the silence:

'The last time I was here, you talked about religion. Do you remember what you told me? You said it was unreasonable not to believe in God, that atheists swallow a thousand absurdities and reject the one really obvious truth. Maybe what you said had some effect. Anyway, I went into a church today. I was walking around, trying to decide what to do, and I found myself standing outside a church—so I went in. I don't quite know why. It felt strange at first, as if I was trespassing, if you know what I mean. I didn't belong; I was an outsider prying around on the inside. Anyway, I sat down in the back row and looked up at the Christ over the altar—and I started talking to him. Not out loud, of course, but in my mind. It was strange. I felt, I suppose, that I ought to say *something* to him, there in his own shrine.'

Farinelli wiped his mouth on a napkin. 'Did he answer?'

Cordelia blushed. The question was so blunt, so matter-of-fact.

He was always surprising her by saying things she never expected. She thought for a moment and then said:

'Yes—in a way, I suppose he did. Not directly, of course. But there was an answer, of sorts. I was confused, I remember, when I went in; but when I came out, I felt—I don't know—not better, exactly, but somehow *clearer.* It wasn't until I left the church that I decided finally to come here and see you. Before that, I didn't know what I was going to do.'

'Your other option was going to the police?'

'Yes.'

'I'm glad you came here first,' he said. 'But, to tell you the truth, it's what I would have expected of you anyway, you know.'

She sipped at her coffee and said:

'It's strange, isn't it, how we sometimes make decisions without making them consciously? It's as if, somehow, they were being made for us. The mind is a funny thing. Where you would see the hand of God, a psychiatrist would see the operation of the subconscious.'

Farinelli smiled. 'Isn't that just another of their chimeras?' he said. 'When you dig down, the subconscious is nothing more than the rationalist's description of his own ignorance. What do they know about it? Have they seen it or weighed it or measured it? It's just another of their hypotheses. They feel better naming things they don't understand because then they can pretend they actually do know about them. The subconscious is like aether or phlogiston: putting a label on the unknown takes the mystery out of it and makes it manageable.'

She was glad to see Farinelli coming out of his torpor—talking religion seemed to do that for him—but at the same time he wasn't being quite fair.

'Surely,' she said, 'there *is* a level of activity below conscious knowing. It doesn't much matter what we call it. We all know it's there. We all experience it.'

'It matters very much what we call it,' he said. 'Why do you call it the *sub*conscious? You said "a level *below* conscious knowing." Doesn't that beg the question? Right at the start, you see, you want to demystify the unknown—or at least relegate it to a secondary importance—by incorporating it as a sub-set of the known. It's more manageable, less dangerous, that way.'

Cordelia nodded. 'Point taken,' she said. 'But that doesn't imply that this—let's call it "the *unconscious*"—is necessarily, or even probably, *above* or *outside* the individual.'

'Of course not,' Farinelli agreed. 'That's not my point at all. I'm not trying to *prove* the existence of faith or God; I'm merely trying to leave room for them. Rationalist explanations rule them out at the start by prejudicing the issue in favour of materialism. But, ironically, their argument is quite irrational. Their method deals only with empirical facts—so, whenever scientists bump into a mystery, they convert it into something they can deal with. They tell us, for example, that light is made up of particles or waves—and they can't decide which. Why? Because they don't know. In other words, it's a mystery. And the same is true of all their first principles: they're all assumptions designed to demystify the mysterious. In the final analysis, everything we know—whether we're talking about physics or about faith—has its roots in the unknown. So it's certainly arbitrary, not to say capricious, to pretend that some mysteries are acceptable and others are not. Because the concepts of faith and God are ideas beyond reason, it doesn't follow that they're *contrary* to reason—or, if you argue that they are, merely because they're mysterious first principles beyond the grasp of rational proof, then we have to throw out all first principles and end up admitting we know nothing about anything at all. On that line of reasoning, physics is as speculative and as flawed as faith. The only sensible thing to do is accept the first principles, examine the data supporting them, and then see what happens.'

It was amazing, Cordelia thought, how deeply he thought about things. And her mind kept asking: *How can this man—so intelligent, so rational, so normal—possibly be responsible for the cold-blooded murders of five human beings?* It was utterly incredible. It was inexplicable. It was a complete mystery. She said:

'You might say I made a start on accepting one of those first principles today, when I went into that church. Now, as you say, I suppose I'll just have to wait and see what happens.'

Farinelli smiled sheepishly. 'I've done it again, haven't I? I've trapped myself into taking advantage of you as a captive audience. But I did warn you once before never to let me get the bit between my teeth.'

'I don't mind at all!' Cordelia said with genuine feeling. 'I love listening to you talk. No, you've given me a great deal to think about—again. I'm really very grateful.'

'And you are very kind, my dear.'

The cream had filmed over the top of his neglected coffee. 'Let me freshen this up,' she said, feeling slightly embarrassed at the compliment. 'There's half a pot still out there. I'd hate to see it go to waste.'

In the kitchen, she took a minute to rinse his cup and plate under the tap. As she tidied the counter, she decided it was time to take the bull by the horns. She said:

'The police know you as Francesco Pistocchi. Do you want to talk about him? It might help to talk.'

She waited a few moments, but there was no reply. Had she been too blunt, too direct? Perhaps she'd offended him—

'Of course,' she added quickly, 'we don't have to talk about him if you'd rather not.'

There still was no reply.

She wiped her hands on the dishcloth and refilled their cups. The instant she walked through the arch into the living-room she knew that something was different. Very different. The man in the armchair awaiting her return was not the man she had left only moments ago. The eyes were not Farinelli's eyes, soft and thoughtful. They were bright and sardonic, glinting with a cold fire. The lines in the face were hard, impersonal; and an ironic, almost demonic, grin played at the corners of his mouth. The cat, she noticed, was suddenly awake, standing where he had slept, his back arched, his coat bristling. A shiver ran down her spine.

'Sit down,' he commanded. 'You wanted to talk about Pistocchi—so let's talk about Pistocchi. What do you want to know?'

'Where is Signor Farinelli?'

He laughed. A high, coarse, grating laugh.

'He's gone,' he said. 'I got rid of him.'

'And you're Pistocchi?'

'Correct.' He grinned broadly, dangerously; then said sharply: 'Sit down. We'll talk.'

She set the cups on the coffee table between them and took her seat. She couldn't beat him to the door. Should she scream? Lydia and Signora Ghilberti were only a floor below. No, it was pointless. Even if they heard, they'd be no use. Pistocchi was a powerful man. She looked around for something to defend herself with, in case it came to that. There wasn't much. All she had left was talk.

'You don't like Signor Farinelli, do you?'

'I hate him.'

'Why?'

The lips curled into a snarl.

'He's weak. He's soft,' he spat contemptuously. 'All he ever does is read and talk, talk, talk. Mr Smarty-pants, Mr Mouth: that's what I call him. I heard him jawing to you. I have to sit and listen, you know. I can't close my ears.'

'Does *he* know about you?'

'Of course he does. He tries to keep me locked inside, but sometimes I get out. Like now. Sometimes I can't take it any more, you know what I mean?'

She had to play for time. Pray that something would happen. Pray that Farinelli would come back. She said:

'No. Tell me.'

'Sure. Sure, I'll tell you. It's like this: For years he kept me locked up. I tried to come out, but he wouldn't let me. Then I started getting stronger, you know, smarter. I tricked him.' He said proudly, 'Now I come out pretty much when I want to. I'm pretty smart, you know. Smarter than I look. If it wasn't for *me*, those swine would all still be walking around.'

'It was you who killed them—Maestro Marchesi and the others?'

'Sure it was me. I had to, didn't I? *He* wouldn't have done it. Never in a million years. He doesn't have the guts. Like I said, he's soft. That's why I hate him.'

'I know what those men did to you,' Cordelia said. 'It's shocking.'

'Ha! What do you know about it, lady? You weren't there Oh—it was shocking, all right. And *he* let it happen. Farinelli let it happen. I wanted to take off, make a run for it, but he didn't have the balls. Ha! that's a laugh, eh? Didn't have the balls. That's rich! Anyway, I got 'em back, I guess—I got even, didn't I? Slit the bastards' throats. Bloody pigs. All except Strozzi—' His face went suddenly black. He stared at the cup in front of him, fighting for control, then snapped. 'Get me some wine. I hate coffee.' Suddenly, without warning, he snatched up the cup and hurled it against the wall, the sound of its breaking ringing like an explosion in the tense silence. Fra Angelico, arched and wary on the sofa, hissed and spat, striking out in Pistocchi's direction with an armed claw.

Pistocchi regained his composure. His voice dropped ominously, 'If you make a run for the door, lady, I'll kill you.'

'Aren't you going to kill me anyway?' Cordelia said, fighting back her terror. She had to keep him talking. It was her only hope.

He beamed. 'You're smart, lady, you know that?'

'Well?'

He shrugged. 'Probably. I can't let you walk out of here and go to your boyfriend in the police, can I? But, who knows,' he said brightly, 'maybe you can talk me out of it, eh? You're a good talker. I've heard you talk. I was inside listening, you know. You *are* going to try and talk me out of it, aren't you?'

'Do I have an option?'

'No.'

'Well then, I guess I'll try.'

'I like you, lady! You got real spunk, you know that? Now, get my wine—then we'll see how good you are, okay?'

The wine was on the sideboard in a wicker-covered container.

'Take some for yourself,' he said. 'A last supper, sort of. You can even have a crust of bread if you want.'

'I'll pass, thanks,' Cordelia said, pouring.

'Very good,' Pistocchi said approvingly, 'very clever. Let this cup pass from me, huh? I get it. Like I told you, I'm smarter than I look.'

She set the glass in front of him. As she did so, he grabbed her wrist, spilling some of the wine, and pulled her harshly toward him. There was a wicked, leering grin on his face.

'You're pretty, lady, you know that? You've got a great body. I haven't ever had a woman. I don't know what it's like. Maybe I should take you into the other room and find out, eh? What do you say, lady?'

'I thought you wanted me to talk,' Cordelia said, struggling to free her arm. She tried to control her breathing, to keep the tremor out of her voice, but it wasn't easy.

Pistocchi pushed her away roughly. 'I'm not good enough for you, am I?' he said sulkily. 'I'm not really a man. That's what you're thinking, isn't it?'

Shaking the blood back into her bruised wrist, Cordelia backed toward her chair, feeling behind her with her good hand. She sat down and stole a glance at the table beside her. There was a heavy ornament made of brass, a dolphin. She could use it if she had to as a weapon. It wasn't much but it was better than nothing. *Oh—where was Signor Farinelli? Why didn't he come back?* She sat coiled and wary, her eyes fixed on Pistocchi's face. Like Fra Angelico, she was ready to spring.

'Who is Strozzi?' she asked. 'You mentioned somebody named Strozzi.'

He narrowed his eyes, judging if she was baiting him—decided she wasn't—then said: 'The one who cut me. I was saving him till last. I was going to do something *real* nasty to him. With his genitals, you know. Cut them off and cram them down his throat—'

'The bank director?' Cordelia said, diverting him. 'He was one of them?'

Pistocchi swirled the wine and swallowed a mouthful. 'The worst of them. Rotten luck, huh? His getting knocked off like that, I mean, before I could get to him. That really pisses me off.' He swallowed another mouthful. 'That's enough about Strozzi. I don't want to talk about him any more. You got any other questions?'

She nodded toward the Motorola. 'Tell me about the record.'

He grinned from ear to ear. 'That's me singing, you know. They made that before they cut me, in case they botched the operation. Said they wanted a record of what I sounded like. Pretty cold-blooded, I thought. Anyway, we went to a private studio and they paid the guy to make a recording. I got it on the first try. I was good, you know. I had a great voice.'

'*Did* something go wrong in the operation?'

'Naw—it went good. So then they used the record to try and sell me but it didn't work, so they ended up dumping me. Mind you, *they* all went off and got rich—but me, well, they just ditched me. Debagged and dumped, that's what I was. Just a kid, too. They never gave me a red cent. That's why I killed them.'

'But you still listen to the record,' Cordelia said, steering away from the topic of death.

'No, no—that's Farinelli, the *artiste.* I'm sick of the damn thing. I was never interested in the music; I wanted the applause—

and the money.' He stopped abruptly and removed a straight razor from his pocket, snapping it open. 'That's enough talk. You didn't convince me. Sorry, lady, you lose.'

Cordelia stared at the razor, mesmerized. Her heart was in her throat. She didn't know if she was even still breathing: her breath seemed to have stopped.

'There are two ways we can do it,' Pistocchi said, testing the edge, enjoying himself. 'You can scream and carry on—in which case I'll take my time and carve you up nice and slow. Or you can go quietly, and I'll do my best to make it quick and painless. You choose, lady. What will it be?'

Cordelia stared at him dumbly, her mind and heart racing. Her throat felt as if it were choked with soot. She couldn't have spoken if she'd tried.

He stood up. 'Well then,' he said, 'we'll have to put it to the test, won't we?'

She turned and grabbed for the brass dolphin, but her hand was trembling so much that it slipped through her fingers and fell with a hollow thump to the floor. She found herself standing…backing away. Her breath was shallow, her heart pounding. Pistocchi moved slowly around the table, coming after her, his granite face cold and set—an expressionless mask. It was as if everything was happening in slow motion. She was aware of every breath he took, of every bone and line in his face, every movement of muscle, every pulse that beat in his veins; the air between them drummed with his heartbeat.

As he passed the end of the sofa, the cat arched and spat, his ears flat, his fangs bared, his eyes screwed to narrow slits. Pistocchi took a swipe with the razor—missed—and the cat raked him on the wrist with a lightning claw, drawing blood. Pistocchi cried out and struck again, but the big cat was too fast for him. It leapt onto the sofa-back, then bounded onto the sideboard and disappeared through the open window that led out to the balcony. It was all over in two seconds.

Cordelia kept backing—backing—backing…

Slowly, deliberately, he resumed his advance toward her. She felt the wall behind her. She was trapped; she could go no further.

'Be a good girl and don't make a fuss,' he purred.

There was no emotion in his eyes, no feeling. He was inhuman, a machine.

'Stop him, Signor Farinelli,' Cordelia whispered. 'Stop him—!'

Pistocchi froze in his tracks. His lips arched into the twisted parody of a smile and he gave a contemptuous snort. '*Him?*—help you? Ha! that's a laugh! "*Oh, save me, save me, Signor Farinelli. Save me from the nasty killer-man.*" Ha, ha, ha! What a joke! He hasn't got the guts to help you, lady.' His voice dropped to a snake-like sibilant hiss: 'He hasn't got the guts to try and stop me.'

Cordelia forced herself to look directly into the basilisk eyes.

'Stop him, Signor Farinelli,' she said. Her voice was surprisingly strong, surprisingly controlled. 'I could have gone to the police, you know that—but I came to you first. I came because I have faith in you, Signor Farinelli, because I know you—because I know you're stronger than Pistocchi. He's killed the guilty; now he wants to kill the innocent too. You mustn't let him destroy us, Signor Farinelli—both of us. You can't let him win. You can't let evil win out over good. You have to stop him. You don't have any choice.'

Pistocchi stepped forward, the last pace, and his eyes took on an evil glint. The hand holding the blade came up—

But then something happened. The triumphant look on Pistocchi's face turned to bafflement—then to snarling anger—and finally to writhing panic—the eyes staring wide and the cruel mouth parted in a lurid rictus of terror. Against the blind terror of Pistocchi's desperate and struggling will, the honed edge of the razor, guided by a stronger power, lifted and was drawn with slow deliberation across the side of his throat above the thyroid cartilage, severing the left jugular vein. There was a gush of blood, then a steady, pulseless stream.

With a cry of anguish, high and piercing, Pistocchi dropped the blade and grabbed at the wound, the dark blood flowing between his frantic fingers. And then he fell, life ebbing, and lay on the floor staring up at her with an immense, soul-deep loathing.

The eyes closed, then opened again—large, luminous, kind. Farinelli's eyes. His mouth moved and Cordelia knelt, taking his head in her arms, straining to make out the words but unable to catch them. All she could hear coming from his throat was a soft gurgling sound, like water oozing through a fissure in the broken earth.

'God bless you, my friend,' she whispered, the hot tears misting her sight. 'I knew you wouldn't let him hurt me. I knew it. I had faith in you.' Slowly, Farinelli's large eyes closed, never to open on the world again. Spread on his lips were the faint beginnings of a smile, arrested and frozen by the arrival of death.

For a long time, unable to move, she sat like a pietà, cradling the heavy body in her arms, and the silent tears rolled down her cheeks like drops of molten lead. At last she rose and moved, as in a dream, to the telephone.

Carlo must have been sitting at his desk and answered on the first ring.

'He's dead,' she muttered, almost inaudibly.

'Cordelia—? Cordelia, what's happened?' His voice was taut with concern.

'He killed him.'

'Are you all right?'

'Yes, I'm all right. He's dead, Carlo.'

'Who's dead? Where are you?'

'In Signor Farinelli's apartment. Farinelli killed Pistocchi. They're both dead.'

'I'll be right there,' he said—and the line went dead.

As she waited, Cordelia sat beside the body of her friend, stroking his hair. Outside, the pale sun broke for a moment through the louring cover of grey cloud and then disappeared again. She felt empty and as cold as marble. She was alone with the dead. She needed someone to hold her—now more than ever in her life.

'Oh, hurry, Carlo, hurry,' she whispered. 'Please, please, hurry—'

FIVE

'STILL,' ARBATI SAID, 'it was a crazy thing to have done, pushing your way into the lion's den like that. The man was a walking time-bomb and you very nearly got yourself killed, after all. I'm just thankful you got out in one piece.' He added, 'Very thankful, actually.'

From the couch in the sitting-room, Cordelia could see him in the kitchen, his back to her, mixing their drinks. A Campari for her, a scotch on the rocks for himself. It was over. She had spent the night in hospital under mild sedation, for observation. That morning, she had talked for an hour to a psychiatrist—a stooped man with a frizzled mane of white hair and silver-rimmed half-glasses perched at the extremity of his nose. The spectacles were apparently just for show since he never bothered to look through them. In the end, the limit of his expertise had resolved itself into a prescription for valium. 'You're a strong young woman,' he'd said in a grating, paternalistic way. 'These should take care of any residual side-effects from your ordeal. If you start having nightmares, call me.' She wouldn't need him again, she knew—or his pills.

Carlo had picked her up at the out-patients' entrance and taken her to lunch under the pergola of a pleasant trattoria near the Sant' Ambrogio market. Life was beginning to return to normal. After lunch, they spent the afternoon walking in the Boboli gardens, enjoying the sun and being together, and then had come back to Carlo's apartment. She was in good hands. She was picking up the threads of her life, moving on, leaving the dead to bury the dead. Their dinner reservation was for eight, at Il Cestello. This time she intended to enjoy the view and the company. She'd made a real hash of it the last time.

'It maybe was a crazy thing to do,' she said, 'but at the time I didn't think so. It was something I had to do. Farinelli wasn't a murderer and I had to give him a chance to tell me so himself.'

Arbati returned with the drinks. 'But you hadn't taken Pistocchi into account.'

She said: 'I didn't know Pistocchi. I didn't care about him either. I only cared about Farinelli. He was the wisest and one of the kindest men I'd ever met. I'd have felt like Judas if I'd turned him in without giving him a chance to explain. I couldn't have lived with myself.'

They sat in silence for a time, the only sound intruding on their solitude the ticking of the clock on the mantel.

'Your friend Farinelli is an interesting case,' Arbati said, breaking the silence. 'His situation reminds me in a way of that painting I took you to see in the Uffizi.'

Cordelia nodded. 'Botticelli's *Venus and Mars?* How so?'

'Well, it's as if Farinelli and Pistocchi, instead of bringing the two gods together into a single integrated personality, somehow kept them locked away in separate compartments. The two sides of his personality weren't reconciled; they were antagonistic. You remember in the painting that Venus is awake but Mars is asleep—the point being, I take it, that in a sane and balanced personality the feminine traits predominate over the masculine. Grace and compassion, I mean, predominate over aggression and raw power. In your friend's case, everything was fine as long as Farinelli, the Venus-principle, was the one awake and in control; but whenever Pistocchi, the Mars figure, woke up and took over the reins, there was mayhem.'

Cordelia remembered Farinelli's words: *In the final analysis we really don't seem to know very much about this thing we call the self. I can describe my external appearance and I can describe the things I think and feel, but I can't see or describe or even begin to understand the enigmatic 'I' that makes my body move and makes me think and feel the things I do. As soon as I start to think about what I am, I discover that I'm a complete mystery to myself.*

'I wonder,' she said, 'if it's really quite that simple. Who was it, after all, who pulled the blade across Pistocchi's throat? Mars or Venus? If we follow your division, don't we have to say that it was Mars, the principle of aggression and power? How could Venus commit such an act? But then we're left, aren't we, with no option but to say that Pistocchi, the Mars-principle, killed himself—that he committed suicide. But that's not what happened. Farinelli killed Pistocchi. I know—I was there—I saw it happen.'

She sipped her Campari and saw in her mind's eye the face of Farinelli, his sad, luminous eyes shining on her like a benediction.

It was not surprising, given what he faced in his own life, that Farinelli had seen personality as an enigma, an unknowable mystery. And accepting that mystery had made it possible for him to accept others. It had also led him to see the limits of human knowing. It was as if he had come to interpret his mutilation as the symbol of a universal truth of the human condition—as if he'd understood and been able to accept that, in a way, we're all castrati cut off from truth and absolute knowing by the impotence of our relativity. We see parts, never the whole. We know in part, never in whole. And yet, for all our unknowing, we know that our partness is part of a greater wholeness—and we have faith that, one day, we will come face to face with it. Farinelli had had such faith. He'd seen clearly into the darkness far enough to know that blindness is the prelude to sight—

'But let's not talk about the past,' she said. 'Let's talk about the future, about happy things. Tell me about your poem.'

Arbati gave her an elfish grin. 'I thought you'd never ask,' he said.

He set his drink on the table, then rose and disappeared into the study. A moment later he returned with a sheaf of pages.

'It's finished then?' Cordelia said, her eyes shining.

'Almost,' he said. 'It still needs a little polishing. But I'm almost there.'

Cordelia gave a little pout. 'This time,' she said, 'I insist on having a sneak preview even if it *isn't* actually finished. I hope you're not expecting me to beg.'

He laughed. 'No—you don't have to beg. I guess you've earned it.'

They sat at either end of the couch, facing each other. Arbati slipped off his shoes and stretched his legs out along the cushions. Cordelia did the same. To a spectator, she thought, we must look a bit like the two figures in Botticelli's painting. Clearing his throat, Arbati began, self-consciously at first, to read the words in front of him in his deep, musical baritone.

Cordelia closed her eyes and let the verse surround her. She was at peace with the world, with herself, with him. She trusted herself to the future. She knew that at last she had found herself, that today and this moment were the beginning of the rest of her life—yes, yes.

A LOVE **TO DIE** FOR

CHRISTINE T. JORGENSEN
A Stella the Stargazer Mystery

First Time In Paperback

MURDER IN THE STARS

Jane Smith quits her boring job, ditches her faithless boyfriend and employs her unique talents to become Stella the Stargazer. Now she's offering horoscope advice for the lovelorn in a Denver newspaper.

The ink is barely dry on her first column offering advice to a lost soul looking for "a love to die for" when she stumbles upon the body of the owner of her favorite lingerie shop—stabbed to death with a pair of scissors.

Add a police detective she *almost* liked before he accused her of murder, toss in her own uncanny sixth sense and an expressive pet chameleon, and her future is a bit unpredictable...especially with a killer gazing at Stella.

"Stella's quirky humor, human frailties...will endear her to many readers."
　　　　　　　　　　　　　　　　　　　—*Publishers Weekly*

Available in March at your favorite retail stores.

Take 3 books and a surprise gift FREE

SPECIAL LIMITED-TIME OFFER

Mail to: The Mystery Library™
3010 Walden Ave.
P.O. Box 1867
Buffalo, N.Y. 14240-1867

YES! Please send me 3 free books from the Mystery Library™ and my free surprise gift. Then send me 3 mystery books, first time in paperback, every month. Bill me only $4.19 per book plus 25¢ delivery and applicable sales tax, if any*. There is no minimum number of books I must purchase. I can always return a shipment at your expense and cancel my subscription. Even if I never buy another book from the Mystery Library™, the 3 free books and surprise gift are mine to keep forever.   415 BPY A3US

Name	(PLEASE PRINT)	

Address		Apt. No.

City	State	Zip

EAST BEACH
RON ELY

First Time in Paperback

A Jake Sands Mystery

KILLER SERVE

Jake Sands has given up the high-risk life to seek obscurity after the murder of his wife and child. He now lives in gorgeous and upscale Santa Barbara—spending days in heaven and learning to live life after hell. Routine is his one constant: running, breakfast at his favorite coffee shop and conversations with his favorite waitress, Julie Price.

So when Julie is murdered, Jake can't leave it alone. Outfitting himself in neon shorts and wraparound shades, he hits the volleyball scene to hunt for a killer. And he discovers a game as volatile as a missing forty-million-dollar lottery ticket—in a world where the high score wins...and losers pay a deadly price.

"A plot that packs action and logic" —*L.A. Times*

Available in February at your favorite retail stores.

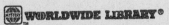 **WORLDWIDE LIBRARY ®**

EAST

A PERMANENT RETIREMENT
JOHN
MILES

First Time in Paperback

A Laura Michaels Mystery

NO CORPSE IN THE BROCHURE

Timberdale is more like a resort than a retirement village. The residents harbor more secrets and scandals than a soap opera does. Life is never dull. But in fact, it is turning deadly.

Cora Chandler, dressed in a pretty blue housedress, her hair in rollers, is the first to die of unnatural causes. But not the last.

Laura Michaels, single mother and sociology student, enjoys her work at Timberdale, despite her wildly eccentric boss or gorgeous, man-eating co-worker. And now Laura's job includes murder. She's accused of the crimes by an Agatha Christie wannabe, bashed over the head...and is unwittingly headed straight for a rendezvous with a killer.

"...an entertaining read with plenty of puzzlement."
—Booklist

Available in February at your favorite retail stores.

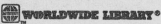

DEADLY PRACTICE
CHRISTINE GREEN
A Kate Kinsella Mystery

First Time in Paperback

NURSING A GRUDGE

Kate Kinsella has fallen on hard times when her work both as a nurse and as a private medical investigator dries up. Until she gets a break—if one can call it that—with a murder.

Friend and landlord Hubert Humberstone—also the undertaker and local busybody—practically tosses her into the investigation of Jenny Martin, a nurse whose body is found in the trunk of her burned-out car. She had been beaten to death.

Kate not only gets Jenny's old job, but she's hired by the mother of the chief suspect, and starts probing the most convoluted—and most dangerous—case of her career.

"Impressive...fine writing and skillfully drawn players abound."
—*Publishers Weekly*

Available in March at your favorite retail stores.

DEAD